BIRDS OF PASSAGE

"What is most refreshing about *Birds of Passage* is Robert Solé's complete disregard for anthropology or cultural generalisation. The Batrakani's – francophile Egyptian monarchists from Syria, and Greek Catholic Jesuits – embody a culture that is theirs alone, and at full flower for little more than a generation. It is a captured moment of history which focuses on the customs and eccentricities of a miniature civilization"

EDWARD STERN, *Times Literary Supplement*

"Robert Solé, a discreet, almost distant observer, retraces with astonishing exactness and subtlety the story of an Egypt brutally seized by the century's convulsions"

TAHAR BEN JELLOUN, *Nouvel Observateur*

"Winner of the Prix Méditerranée, this leisurely, satisfying novel breathes the nostalgia of a crowded family gathering"

Publisher's Weekly

"Delightful"   RICHARD EDER, *New York Times*

"When the library of Alexandria is completed at the end of the year, there will be a celebration to honour those who have written about the city – among them Robert Solé. Solé's novel is rich with observation and unforgettable characters"

VICTORIA THOMPSON, *Australian Review of Books*

ROBERT SOLÉ was born in Cairo in 1946. He moved to France at the age of 18. He has combined his career as a journalist with that of author, and works for *Le Monde*.

JOHN BROWNJOHN is one of Britain's foremost translators from the German and the French.

Robert Solé

BIRDS OF PASSAGE

Translated from the French by
John Brownjohn

THE HARVILL PRESS
LONDON

First published with the title *Le Tarbouche* by Editions du Seuil, Paris, in 1992
First published in Great Britain in 2000 by The Harvill Press

This paperback edition first published in 2001 by
The Harvill Press, 2 Aztec Row, Berners Road, London N1 0PW

www.harvill.com

1 3 5 7 9 8 6 4 2

© Editions du Seuil, 1992
Translation © John Brownjohn, 2000

Robert Solé asserts the moral right to be
identified as the author of this work

A CIP catalogue record for this book is available from the British Library

ISBN 1 86046 817 9

Designed and typeset in Centaur at
Libanus Press, Marlborough, Wiltshire

Printed and bound in Great Britain by Mackays of Chatham

Half title photograph courtesy of the Sabit Collection, Cairo

CONDITIONS OF SALE

To Élisabeth

Prologue

Less than two hours after my birth at the French hospital in 'Abassiya, Georges Bey Batrakani turned up there in all his glory. Close-shaven, perfumed, and more elegant than ever, he possessed the agreeably rotund figure of a sixty-six-year-old with a voracious appetite for life. A burgundy tarboosh, planted firmly on his head and tilted at a slight angle, lent him a definite touch of style.

Georges Bey reached the first floor of the maternity wing and lengthened his stride. The wax-polished corridors resounded to his masterful tread as he made for Room 14 followed by his rather breathless chauffeur, who was hugging an enormous basket of roses.

"Mabrouk, mille mabrouks!" he said brightly, on entering his daughter's room.

He slipped something into her hand as he bent down to kiss her: a little treat ordered three months earlier from Eliakim, the celebrated jeweller in Malika Farida Street.

Viviane, limply enthroned in a big white bed, was looking radiant. She had only just given birth, but already she saw the world through new eyes. I was her first child – a boy.

My grandfather cast a preoccupied glance at the swarthy baby that was held out for his inspection in its lavender-blue wrappings. He had come to see the new mother, not me, as if to make up for an appointment he'd failed to keep twenty-three years earlier. This time he had made it a point of honour to get there before every other member of the family save his son-in-law – a son-in-law who, though highly delighted, was rather bemused by the squalling object that had been thrust into his arms, firmly and authoritatively, by a nun in a starched coif.

Viviane's room, which faced east, was flooded with early morning sunlight. Through the french windows, which had been left ajar to mitigate the stifling heat, came the singsong cry of a stewed-bean vendor — *"fuul medammis, fuul medammis!"* — as he summoned housewives to bring him their breakfast pots and pans. The Cairene summer was lingering on, reluctant to depart, in that late September of 1945.

Syrian families like ours were emerging from a tolerably pleasant Second World War of which they had heard no more than distant detonations. For five years Cairo had been the playground of thousands of Allied soldiers fighting in the Western Desert. Plenty of our own people had enjoyed themselves during this khaki interlude and some had even profited from it, but the future seemed less assured. Would Egypt persist in her hectic desire to become Egyptian?

Detecting clouds on the horizon, the more pessimistic Syrians sought to melt into the background, an old, chameleon-like reflex instilled by several centuries of harassment under the Ottoman Empire. Many of our families Arabized their children in the cradle, at least formally. André, Pierre and Paul were quietly superseded by 'Adel, Nabil or Rafiq. Girls presented less of a problem: in their case, parents continued to draw on the stock of occidental saints.

"You're thinking of calling him Rafiq?" Georges Batrakani exclaimed. "The very idea! Why not Charles, like my poor dead son? It would give me so much pleasure."

One couldn't resist such an appeal, least of all when it came from Georges Bey. Viviane's dreamy smile seemed to denote approval, and my father was too taken aback to think of an immediate response, so they called me Charles.

Duty done, the man in the tarboosh departed for a business lunch at Shepheard's with the chauffeur at his heels. In the corridor of the maternity wing he bowed to Professor Martin-Bérard, who had bedazzled my mother when she first consulted him, and whom she continued to extol for four decades to come.

Monsieur Martin-Bérard, I salute you in passing. Without detracting from your merits as an obstetrician, I suspect that your French nationality had something to do with all those compliments heaped on you by a pretty young Syrian mother and her women friends. They adored France without having a drop of French blood in their veins, just as they knew Paris by heart without ever having set foot there – but that you must surely have guessed while palpating their deliciously rounded bellies.

And what of us, the occupants of those bellies, the Rafiqs or Nabils, Pauls or Pierres? You, monsieur, were our first contact with the outside world. When our noses or rumps emerged, the hands that hauled us out were French: France was there to greet us! In other words, the concept of a motherland has never been too well-defined in our minds.

They called us Syrians, an ambiguous appellation that took no account of Lebanon. More particularly, it implied that we belonged to another country – as if our families, though established in Egypt for ages, hadn't permanently severed their links with Damascus, Aleppo, or Sidon!

But didn't we ourselves maintain that ambiguity for form's sake and because we needed to be different? Egypt was inhabited by Britons, Greeks, Italians, Armenians, Jews. In default of being true-born or slightly European Egyptians, we were Syrians.

We did not, if the truth be told, know much about our ancestors. Family trees seldom grew in our soil, and few of Egypt's Syro-Lebanese troubled to consult the meagre records available.

Throughout my childhood, I heard grown-ups debate our origins with a wealth of imprecision. Facts were relatively unimportant to us. What mattered was the way they were presented and commented on. Anything was true if uttered with sufficient conviction. Sunday lunches were the favourite venue for such verbal jousts.

"We come from Lombardy," Georges Batrakani decreed. "I have in my possession a little notebook in which my great uncle Habib recorded all his wedding expenses. It's written entirely in Italian."

"That means nothing!" retorted his cousin the jeweller. "Everyone spoke Italian in those days. Batrakani comes from *batrak*, the Arabic for patriarch. One of our ancestors must have been a bishop of senior rank. I think he was elected during the siege of Antioch."

"A bishop? Hark at him! Since when have bishops had descendants?"

"You're all talking nonsense!" cried Aunt Nini from the other end of the table. "We're descended from the Crusaders, it's an established fact."

"Established by whom, pray?"

"Are you calling me a liar?"

"Neither a liar nor anything else, *ya sitti*. Everyone knows that at Damascus, in the patriarchal records — "

"Have you seen them?"

"No, but I know — besides, it's been proved — that the Batrakanis left Macedonia in the sixteenth century, or possibly the seventeenth, and settled in Syria. Batrakani is a Greek name like Sakakini or Zananiri."

"And that, no doubt, is why we're called Greek Catholics," concluded the lady of the house, blithely mingling religion with geography. "Ready with your plates, everyone, the *molokhiya* won't wait."

My uncle Michel Batrakani, who had a degree in history, was a case in point in this context. He might even have gone on to obtain a doctorate if heaven had endowed him with a less whimsical disposition and a little more ambition. I'm indebted to him nonetheless: without the aid of his papers and his diary, I could never have embarked on this account. But for him, I should have had to rely on the more or less doctored, more or less embellished recollections of other members of the family.

By the time Michel visited the maternity wing late that afternoon, my mother's room was a veritable flower garden. If the french windows hadn't been opened to their fullest extent, she would have been asphyxiated by the scent of all the bouquets that cluttered the tables, chairs, and part of the bathroom.

My uncle felt a trifle foolish with his dozen cellophane-wrapped gladioli, but Viviane gave him no time to dwell on them.

"Michel, you'll make an ideal godfather. *You* at least will have one good story to tell my son. He was born thirty years after your encounter with the sultan. It's a fact, work it out for yourself."

To his great embarrassment, Michel found himself holding a godson in his arms — he, a forty-year-old bachelor more at home with his books and his memories than with the living. He would gladly have dispensed with such an honour, but how could he deny such a young and charming sister, especially when she invoked 13 May 1916? She was right: it was nearly thirty years ago — thirty years already.

"I should point out that my son changed his name this morning. We wanted to call him Rafiq, but Papa insisted on Charles. Mind you, Professor Martin-Bérard thinks Charles is a splendid name."

"Honestly, the French! They're all Gaullists these days."

"There isn't an obstetrician to touch him."

Michel, who had no reason to doubt this, nodded vaguely. He had already reascended his own little cloud.

"So it's settled, *ya Micho*? You'll be his godfather?"

He nodded and smiled, gazing absently at the flowers. His sister's reference to the sultan had taken him back three decades. The vases of roses and gladioli scattered around the room reminded him of the floral decorations on the school steps one very special morning in May 1916, when springtime had a rendezvous with history . . .

PART ONE

The Sultan Was Fond of
La Fontaine

I

At ten thirty-five this morning the sultan visited the school. I recited "Le Laboureur et ses enfants" to him. He congratulated me.

Not an adjective, not a single embellishment. Michel Batrakani's pen had inscribed the paper with absolute economy, as if forbidding that rather runny violet ink to swoop and soar; as if all epistolary emotion were prohibited that evening; as if the importance of the occasion demanded the precision of an entomologist, the style of a justice's clerk.

The Jesuits keep careful records, fortunately, and everyone knows how wordy my godfather would later prove to be, omitting no detail of that famous day which began with a disaster.

Mademoiselle Guyomard, the French governess, claimed to have woken Michel on the stroke of six. Liar. She had been roused from her dreams by the driver of the school bus, who tooted his horn several times before giving up and continuing on his way.

Ten minutes later, with face ill-washed, hair unkempt, and satchel flying, Michel was sprinting along Shubra Street. He leapt aboard a moving tram, only to find himself in a harem car reserved for women. At the next stop he took to his heels once more, bootlaces flapping perilously as he leapt over the mounds of dung in the roadway. He ran till he was out of breath, cursing Mademoiselle Guyomard and all the saints in the calendar. Guyomard, he snarled, *homard, homara* (she-ass) . . . But his imprecations, whether French or Arabic, sounded a trifle false. No ill humour was really proof against the intoxicating sweetness of a May morning in Cairo or the sight of *labkh* acacias in bloom.

The Collège de la Sainte-Famille — the almost unchanged school which I myself would attend forty years later — was already in turmoil. Displacing the air with sweeping gestures and loud voices as they stood beside their horses at the foot of the Virgin's statue in the outer courtyard were three officers of the sultan's guard, come to inspect the final preparations for his visit. Palace musicians in blue-and-white uniforms were getting out their brass instruments or tuning their violins. The porter had removed his paunch from the little window of his lodge and was watching them open-mouthed, so Michel was able to dash past without having to give an account of himself.

To mark this historic visit, the windows had been draped with the flags of Egypt, France and the Vatican. The chill corridors were lined with carpets rented for the occasion, the steps adorned with flowers. "His Highness is very fond of flowers," the Jesuits had been informed by Zul-Fiqar Pasha, the grand chamberlain.

As ten-thirty approached, the sultan's car, preceded by several police-men on motorcycles, entered the courtyard from Bustan al-Muski Street. The Father Rector, flanked by senior members of his staff, was waiting at the foot of the steps in company with the aptly-named Albert Defrance, France's minister in Egypt. When Hussein Kamil alighted from his car the priests bent to kiss his hand in turn, a gesture he charmingly dissuaded them from completing.

The first port of call was the philosophy class, where Father Brémond was discoursing on conscience. Questioned in the sovereign's presence, one of the pupils quoted an extremely pertinent dictum of Emperor Augustus'. The members of the retinue nodded in token of their approval.

On leaving the classroom escorted by the Father Rector, the sultan evoked a response that went the rounds of the school.

"There are times," he said, "when conscience and duty conflict."

"True," replied the Jesuit, "but conscience must always have the final say."

It was a crisp, clear-cut answer typical of those soldiers of Christ, with their luminous gaze and luxuriant beards, who had come to fight the good fight in our rather easy-going part of the world.

The sultan and his retinue entered the fifth-form classroom.

The pupils sprang to their feet and stood there almost at attention, scarcely venturing to look at the slender figure in the close-fitting black *stambouline* and tall, dark red tarboosh. Sixty-seven years old, the sultan eyed them mildly over his enormous moustache.

Father Korner had left his rostrum to greet the sovereign and inform him that the French lesson that Saturday morning was devoted to the fables of La Fontaine.

"La Fontaine?" the sultan exclaimed. "Why, I was just going to mention him."

Monsieur Defrance and the grand chamberlain greeted this happy coincidence with an exchange of smiles. The teacher gave a little bow, then turned to face the class.

"Michel Batrakani," he said, punching out the words staccato, "can you recite *'Le Laboureur et ses enfants'* for His Highness?"

Michel rose like someone in a dream. Eyes glued to the blackboard, he began to declaim in a loud singsong, taking care to roll his Rs:

> *"Travaillez, prenez de la peine*
> *"C'est le fonds qui manque le moins . . . "*

The sultan mimed applause when Michel had finished.

"Bravo, my boy."

Then, followed by all the other dignitaries, he graciously withdrew.

Trembling with joy and deaf to every word of the remainder of the lesson, Michel spent the next fifteen minutes digesting his success. Deliciously transfixed by twenty-four pairs of eyes, or so it seemed, he continued to recite *"Le Laboureur"* between his teeth, rosary fashion, until the bell rang.

A handsome olivewood desk had been placed in the vice-principal's office, and on it lay a visitors' book. This parchment volume, illuminated by the nuns who undertook book restoration, bore the sultan's arms on the front, and, on the back, the French and Egyptian flags linked by the Croix de Guerre.

"I revere them both," said the sultan, as he was handed a pen with which to inscribe his name beside the seal of the Society of Jesus. He bent over the document, then stopped short.

"What is the date by your calendar?

"The thirteenth of May, Highness."

"The thirteenth! An inauspicious number — I should prefer not to write it down."

One or two embarrassed smiles made their appearance.

"We do not share your fear of it, Highness," the vice-principal felt called upon to say.

But the sultan had several good reasons for fearing strokes of fate. At that very moment, while he was endearing himself to the Collège de la Sainte-Famille, a British military court was trying the two men who had done their best to assassinate him at Alexandria the previous year. Hussein Kamil had been on his way to the Mosque of Sidi 'Abd-ar-Rahman, there to perform his Friday devotions, when a metal sphere, hurled from a balcony, struck the neck of one of his carriage horses and fell to the ground without exploding. The bomb, whose fuse was defective, had contained a charge of nitroglycerine and eighty nails.

It was the second attempt on Hussein Kamil's life since the British had installed him in December 1914. Egyptian nationalists could not forgive him for having replaced his nephew, Khedive 'Abbas, who had been deposed when war broke out because of his pro-German sentiments. Hussein had ascended this demi-throne with the title of sultan to show that Egypt, now a British protectorate, was part of the Ottoman Empire no longer.

So the sultan was superstitious. In the end, however, he applied his pen to the visitors' book and inscribed it simply: "Hussein Kamil, May 1916." Monsieur Defrance and the grand chamberlain glanced at each other in relief.

A large dais, transformed into a Damascene audience chamber with the aid of a makeshift throne and some multicoloured hangings, had been erected in the intermediates' playground. The whole school was drawn up facing this platform in neatly aligned ranks. Michel, standing on tiptoe, looked around for his two brothers as if his mere expression would apprise them of the cataclysmic event that had just occurred. As a result, he missed the whole of the Father Rector's admirably flattering preamble.

"Your Highness is endowing the dawn of your incumbency with a splendour reminiscent of the happiest reigns of the greatest caliphs of the past. How comforting it is for us Catholic, French priests, to be thus encouraged in the performance of our daily tasks! May we long continue to perform them under your aegis! To us, that would denote the consoling certainty that we were working at one and the same time for Egypt, for France, and for God."

Applause gave way to reverent silence as the sultan began to speak.

"A man's worth does not derive from education alone, but, first and foremost, from moral instruction. Just now, in one of your classrooms, I heard a rendering of La Fontaine."

Michel's heart leapt.

"I myself learnt forty of his fables," the sultan went on, "under my teacher, Monsieur Jacolet. Note how much moral instruction La Fontaine imparts! Look at '*Le Chêne et le Roseau*' – look at '*La Cigale et la Fourmi*' . . . "

There followed an astonishing, unprecedented occurrence. The sovereign of Egypt, son of Isma'il the Magnificent and great grandson of Muhammad Ali, proceeded to recite in a solemn, sententious voice:

> "*Nuit et jour à tout venant*
> "*je chantais, ne vous déplaise.*
> "*Vous chantiez? J'en suis fort aise.*
> "*Eh bien! Dansez maintenant.*"

The Father Rector gave the signal for applause. Michel clapped his hands frantically, anything but jealous of his unexpected confrère.

The sultan's concluding words were destined to overjoy his Jesuit listeners:

"What I also like about you is your respect for faith: you have pupils of every religious denomination, and you respect them. I myself am a believer, and, when all is said and done, we worship the same God. Your work is good, and you perform it with devotion. I pray that it may continue for centuries to come."

The sultan indicated two members of his retinue, then turned to the assembled teachers.

"Here are two of the fruits of your labours," he said informally. "You see? Your efforts weren't wasted."

The teachers applauded and the pupils gave a threefold cry of *"Ya'aish as-sultan!"* Then the band struck up the Egyptian anthem and the *Marseillaise*. Hussein Kamil slowly descended the steps from the dais, conferring numerous smiles and handshakes as he went.

The ranks broke up in some disorder. Michel took advantage of this to run up to his elder brother and blurt out the news.

"I recited *'Le Laboureur et ses enfants'* for the sultan!"

André eyed him with amusement.

"You might have worn matching socks."

One was black, the other dark blue. Michel turned puce.

"Never mind, it doesn't matter," André went on in his habitually kindly way. "Recite *'Le Laboureur et le sultan'* for me."

2

Many were the times I heard tell of the sultan's visit to the school. It was an event destined to illumine my entire childhood and part of my adolescence, and I still, on occasion, debate it with members of the family to this day.

For me, 1916 remains a beacon and a milestone — the chronological milestone *par excellence*. It stands for the thick of the First World War, for Verdun and Douaumont, for Michel aged eleven and André aged twelve, for the year when the tarboosh idea germinated in my grandfather's head and Édouard Dhellemmes first appeared on the scene. It was six years before my mother's birth and twenty-nine before my own.

When at last I tracked down an old collection of *Le Journal du Caire*, I pounced on the edition dated Sunday, 14 May 1916, as excitedly as the child who had recited for the sultan the previous day. A bold headline announced that another German attack at Douaumont had been repulsed. Not a word about the school visit. I scanned the other three pages and finally came across a modest article on the subject. Although there was no mention of La Fontaine, the newspaper undertook to publish a detailed account of the occasion on the morrow.

I know that Michel searched vainly for the said article in the days that followed. *Le Journal du Caire* had broken its promise but gained a reader who dashed to his father's study every evening, on returning from school, to decipher that ill-printed rag. Failing to find any reference to the school, he meditated at length on the celebrated pronouncement of Khedive Isma'il, the sultan's father, which appeared at the head of page one every day: "My country is in Africa no longer. We form part of Europe."

Egypt in Europe ... Some months later, for having included that daring postulate in his geography homework, Michel got the only zero he was ever awarded during his school career with the Jesuits.

It was Édouard Dhellemmes who would preserve the most accurate recollection of Sunday, 14 May 1916. He could still describe it in a wealth of detail after half a century, repudiating the more fanciful versions purveyed by Maggi or Henri Touta. It should, however, be pointed out that his Cartesian intellect and elephantine memory were aided by the fact that that Sunday lunch was his first contact with the family and, at the same time, with Egypt.

The Frenchman had little trouble in finding a cab when he left the Muski. Ever since the outbreak of war the cabbies of Cairo had cold-shouldered Egyptian customers and lain in wait for British or Australian soldiers, whom they blithely charged twice or three times the usual fare. Édouard had been mistaken for a Britisher, which pleased him only up to a point.

The cab turned left off Shubra Street into a street flanked by sycamores and acacias.

"Here, meestairr!" called the cabby, reining in sharply outside a house in the Italian style.

Édouard alighted from the cab and held out a note. The man promptly pocketed it, cracked his whip, and drove off without tendering any change. Faintly annoyed, Édouard shook his head before ringing the Batrakanis' bell.

The *sufragi* who came to the door was wearing his Sunday best: baggy black trousers, Turkish slippers, and a kind of bolero embroidered with gold thread. His left cheek bore a long scar. He took Édouard's panama and showed him into a handsome oval drawing room that opened on to the garden.

My grandfather had been asked to entertain Édouard Dhellemmes by the commercial councillor of the French agency in Cairo:

"Monsieur Dhellemmes is the son of a Lille industrialist. He was invalided out of the army and is interested in the Egyptian market. I'm sure you'll be able to give him some good advice. We're very keen to encourage such ventures in the present situation. To sit back and let the British and Italians take over the territory vacated by Austrian and German firms would be criminal, don't you agree?"

When Yolande Batrakani entered the room, Édouard Dhellemmes bent gracefully over her hand and kissed it. My grandmother was enchanted, telling herself yet again how utterly charming these young Frenchmen were. Her husband followed her in.

"Delighted to make your acquaintance, Monsieur Dhellemmes," he said in his powerful but mellow voice. "We always lunch *en famille* on Sundays, and our French friends are like honorary members of the family."

Of medium height, Georges Batrakani wore his thirty-six years with elegance. His dark complexion and oriental features contrasted with a pair of honey-coloured eyes inherited from elsewhere. The faint smile that hovered on his sensual lips helped to underline this appearance of oscillating between two worlds.

"He's the accredited agent for several foreign brand names, so he knows the market like the back of his hand," the commercial councillor had told Édouard. "Divide what he tells you by two, but take a leaf out of his book. These Levantines talk big but act with moderation."

In between answering the doorbell, the *sufragi* served 'araqi and sweet lemonade. Édouard, who had been expecting an intimate lunch, was rather taken aback by the successive new arrivals: a sister of Yolande's, a brother of Georges's, sundry cousins. All were quick to treat him like an old acquaintance, however. They eagerly inquired after his state of health, insisted on knowing whether he had had a good voyage, and trusted that his quarters in Cairo were satisfactory.

Édouard very soon felt at home. All the fatigue and forebodings of the journey evaporated in this congenial setting. People back home in France had painted an alarming picture of Egypt – sweltering heat, filth, polluted water, cholera – yet here he was in a handsome house quite the equal of any mansion in his own Boulevard Vauban. He was surrounded by warm-hearted people who spoke French extremely well, even if they did roll their Rs like cooing doves and employ some peculiar idioms.

Édouard gave an account of his voyage. The crew of the *Lotus* had been haunted by fears of a submarine attack ever since leaving Marseille.

Twelve days of vigilance and false alarms ensued. As soon as the ship's bell rang, every passenger made a dash for the lifeboats. Life jackets had to be worn at all times, even during meals.

The *'araqi* was going to his head in a pleasant but rather perfidious fashion. Glass in hand, Édouard found himself chatting with ladies of whom most seemed to follow the latest Paris fashions, with their jersey suits of cherry red or apple green, their long necklaces and jade cigarette holders. They spoke of prices, which had risen steadily since the outbreak of war, discussed the end-of-season sales at Orosdi-Back, and complained of the charity raffle at the Grand Continental two days hence, which the organizers had scheduled for an impossible hour.

"Three in the afternoon, in May! They're crazy, honestly! We'll simply melt, my dear! I shall say so to Biba . . . "

At table Édouard was seated between Yolande Batrakani and her sister Maggi, whose superb breasts seemed about to escape from her daring *décolletage* at any moment.

"Have you ever had *molokhiya*, Monsieur Dhellemmes?"

While it was being served, the Frenchman covertly observed Ferdinand Batrakani, my grandfather's elder brother, whose hundred kilos were situated at the far end of the table. Nando, as he was nicknamed, had evolved an entire ritual for the consumption of *molokhiya*. Napkin knotted around his neck, he began by depositing a mountain of rice on his plate, then excavated a volcanic crater in the summit and poured in a big glassful of vinegar with finely chopped onion floating in it. Using his podgy fingers, Nando added some gobbets of meat, chicken and dried bread. Finally, he inundated the whole edifice with two big ladlefuls of dark green soup strongly flavoured with garlic – only to repeat the whole operation when the dish came round again.

"Your *molokhiya* is a great success," Maggi told her sister. "Remind me to congratulate Usta Sami before I go. You've an absolute treasure there, you know."

Conversation flowed briskly. Édouard found it a trifle difficult to follow such a spate of words sprinkled with Arabic, but the other guests regularly remembered his presence and supplied him with translations and explanations. They even, on occasion, anticipated his questions.

Talk turned to Patriarch Cyril VIII, whose funeral had just been held in Cairo with great pomp and ceremony.

"Faggaala Cathedral was draped in black," Maggi whispered to Édouard, who found her voice disturbingly erotic. "Our patriarch's embalmed body was illuminated by candles and seated on a gilded throne. He was wearing his tiara and holding his crosier. People who went up to him thought he was alive — one woman even spoke to him, I promise you! Everyone was there: the governor of Alexandria, the French minister, consuls, senior magistrates, the whole of the upper crust . . . "

"Tell me," Édouard asked, "why do you, being Orthodox — "

"We aren't!" everyone exclaimed.

"But I thought that a patriarch . . . "

Georges Batrakani sighed, telling himself that it would take a hundred years to explain the subtleties of oriental Christianity to this likeable Frenchman.

"No, my dear sir, we're Greek Catholics: Greek, but not Orthodox; Catholic, but not Roman."

"And you're Egyptians as well?" asked Édouard, already getting lost.

"Of course," said Yolande.

Her husband was surprised by this response.

"Egyptians? Really? How and in what way?"

Édouard turned a bewildered gaze on each of them in turn.

"It's rather hard to explain," Georges said at length. "Our families originally came from Syria. Up to now, as you know, Syria and Egypt have both formed part of the Ottoman Empire. There exists a universally applicable Ottoman nationality, but to that has been added, over the years, an Egyptian nationality. We are Ottomans, 'local subjects', as they say here. But are we truly Egyptian? Legal authorities differ on that point. Besides, what has it meant to be an Ottoman since 1914, when Egypt became a British protectorate? The situation may resolve itself after the war."

"I'm sure it will," Édouard said politely. Engrossed in the sight of Maggi's slender brown hands, he had just lost the thread.

With a twitch of her eyebrows, Yolande Batrakani signalled to the *sufragi* to serve the pudding.

"What about this war, Monsieur Dhellemmes?" she demanded. "When are you going to end it for us?"

"It's only a matter of months, madame. We're giving the Boches a terrible hiding at Douaumont."

"Just don't end it too soon," Ferdinand Batrakani called from the other end of the table, and he broke into a long peal of coarse laughter.

Everyone knew how well Georges's elder brother was doing out of the present situation. Fat Nando exercised his talents as a speculator and moneylender in the Delta. On the outbreak of war he had bought land there dirt cheap from smallholders alarmed by the abrupt closure of Egypt's foreign markets. Since then the war had been a regular boon to farmers. The Allies needed vast quantities of cotton to clothe their soldiers and reinforce their tyres. Not only had the whole of the 1914 harvest been sold, but prices had recovered from their big fall and were starting to exceed pre-war levels. Nando's bank account and his fleshy face were swelling simultaneously.

My grandfather had also been shrewd enough to stockpile merchandise and exploit shortages.

"You see, my dear sir," he explained to Édouard Dhellemmes, "all these foreign soldiers are a stimulus to trade. Last year, in order to maintain their army, the British increased their expenditure in this country by something in the region of five million pounds. Very nice, eh?"

It was too hot to serve coffee on the terrace. The lady of the house merely had the french windows opened wide to present her lunch guests with a better view of some magnificent Youssef Effendi mandarin trees.

The Batrakani children and their cousins trooped in to pay their respects to the French visitor.

"Well, Micho," said Maggi, "did you really recite a poem for the sultan?"

By general request, Michel gave another recitation of *"Le Laboureur et ses enfants"*. Applause rang out and fragrant, resounding kisses were bestowed on him. My godfather was questioned about the circumstances of his exploit, the sultan's attire, the Jesuits' comments. Then the children ran off to reimmerse themselves in their favourite game, the genealogy of the kings of France.

"We're going to see Max Linder's *La Très Moutarde* at the American Cosmograph tomorrow night. Would you care to join us?" Yolande asked Édouard Dhellemmes.

Édouard accepted with alacrity, the more so since sexy Maggi would be there too.

"Before the film," Georges said, "you might like to look in at my office in Opera Square. We can have a chat about your plans."

At four that afternoon, when the heat was intense and fat Nando had fallen asleep in his armchair, snoring loudly, Édouard was driven back to Shepheard's by the Batrakanis' coachman.

3

It was the most charming hotel in the Middle East. Founded by an Englishman in 1841 and rebuilt half a century later, when the premises were extended and equipped with electric lighting, Shepheard's incorporated the ancient palace in which Napoleon Bonaparte had once installed his headquarters. The management had carefully preserved the sycamore behind which General Kléber's assassin had hidden, and the splendid grounds, with their palms and banana trees, were home to a score of frisking antelope.

The hotel's famous terrace was guarded on the street side by two small stone sphinxes purloined from a temple at Memphis. It made an exceptional observation post. Édouard Dhellemmes spent the whole of Monday morning there, sipping chilled beer and watching Cairo parade past before his eyes.

A small crowd was permanently encamped at the foot of the steps: cabbies, guides, monkey showmen, beggars of every description. Water-carriers trudged along the street bent double beneath the weight of their bulging goatskins. They were quickly overtaken by effendis in Turkish jackets, erect and ultra-dignified figures mounted on donkeys. From time to time a shiny limousine came gliding up to the kerb, and the Shepheard's bellboys, with a deferential air, would hurriedly open the door for some pasha or other.

The hotel's English lady guests missed no detail of this spectacle. They would rise and crane their necks to watch coffins being borne along in the midst of hired mourners in black veils. Two minutes later they would be back on their feet, all of a flutter, to observe the arrival of a luxurious landau preceded by barefoot grooms who ran out into the roadway brandishing canes and yelling at pedestrians to stand aside.

A cannon fired from the Citadel announced that it was noon. Édouard Dhellemmes ordered one last beer before going in to have lunch and a siesta. The never-ending spectacle had left him exhausted.

At five that afternoon, refreshed and restored, he left the hotel for his business appointment.

A few minutes' walk from Shepheard's, Georges Batrakani's office was situated on the third floor of a handsome building overlooking Opera Square. Two clerks in shiny oversleeves were lethargically at work beneath an enormous ceiling fan. My grandfather occupied an adjoining room redolent of cigar smoke and eau de Cologne.

He burst out laughing when the Frenchman wondered why so many European women should be sitting, apparently at a loose end, on the terrace at Shepheard's.

"Ah no, my dear sir, it isn't what you might think. Those ladies are British officers' wives. They were authorized to come to Egypt to spend a few days with their spouses, but many of the latter are detained in the Suez Canal or out in the Western Desert. So the ladies are enjoying a solitary, enforced holiday – the hotels are crammed with them. The British authorities have been obliged to prohibit any further landings of women not resident in Egypt. I note that *you* were granted an entry visa, incidentally."

"Yes," Édouard said with a smile, "thanks to a little wire-pulling."

The Dhellemmes cotton mill at Lille had been in a state of suspended animation since the outbreak of war. Édouard, who had inherited some shares from his father, occupied a marginal position in the firm. Called up in 1915, admitted to hospital with a bad bout of pneumonia after only a few weeks, and finally demobilized, he had travelled to Cairo to explore the Egyptian market on the advice, and with the assistance, of a cousin in the diplomatic corps.

"If I were you," Georges Batrakani said slowly, puffing at his cigar, "I'd take an interest in the tarboosh."

Édouard looked mystified.

"That's right, the tarboosh – the fez, if you prefer. Until war broke out that sector was dominated by some fifteen Austrian firms with an annual turnover of more than thirty thousand pounds. Not bad, eh? Well, the Austrians aren't entitled to sell anything here, not now, and the representative of their consortium, Brüder Stross, has just been asked to sell up. That leaves a gap to be filled — even outside Egypt, perhaps, because Morocco, Tunisia and Tripolitania also import Turkish headgear, albeit of a different shape."

Georges asked the Frenchman to excuse him for a moment. Going next door, he opened a cupboard and took out four capacious cardboard boxes. One of the clerks jumped up and helped him to carry them in.

Georges opened one of the boxes and removed a big, cup-shaped cap of red felt with a black tassel hanging down the back. "This is the *Watani*, the standard product," he explained. "It's worth the equivalent of two francs twenty-five. Then there's the '*Abbasi* at three francs fifty. Next we have — note the difference! — the *Excelsior*, priced at five francs. But the king of Austrian tarbooshes and the most elegant, beyond a doubt, is the *Eagle* here. Feel the material, feel how soft and silky it is. You see? The *Eagle* is well worth its thirteen francs!"

For the next few minutes, Édouard Dhellemmes felt like the target of an experienced huckster. A salesman to the marrow, the Levantine seemed capable of selling anything, even other people's wares. His velvety voice might almost have persuaded one to devour those silky tarbooshes like so many luscious fruit.

"You see, Monsieur Dhellemmes, prices have soared since imports ceased. Today, tarbooshes cost two or three times as much as I indicated just now. The result is that certain Jews and Syrians in Cairo have given up wearing them. They've adopted western headgear, which is considerably less expensive."

"So the tarboosh is threatened with extinction."

"You must be joking! The present situation is clearly temporary. The Egyptians have worn the tarboosh for more than a hundred years. They'll never be able to dispense with it. This form of headgear has become a national attribute."

Georges Batrakani reverted to the Austrians, whose business methods he had observed closely and with undisguised admiration.

"Commercial travellers used to come from Vienna every year. They came to see their customers and note their special requirements. They not only studied changing fashions; sometimes they actually initiated them. There are fashions in tarbooshes, you see, and different ways of wearing them."

My grandfather proceeded to launch into a brilliant account of the evolution of the tarboosh in Egypt. Returning to his cupboard, he removed a number of engravings and spread them out on his desk side by side.

"Here's Muhammad Ali, the founder of the reigning dynasty. Look at his strange headgear: you could scarcely call it a tarboosh. Under 'Abbas and Sa'id — there they are — the fez began to acquire shape and height, but it still had no lining. Now look at Sultan Hussein, the present sovereign: it was the British who introduced the tall, rigid tarboosh lined with straw, which has the merit of retaining its shape. No need to press it every day like the old-fashioned tarboosh: once a week is enough."

"So tarbooshes need pressing?"

"Of course. There are *tarbouchiers* all over town who will brush and press them for you."

More and more interested, Édouard Dhellemmes plied my grandfather with questions. "But you know the Egyptian market so well, Monsieur Batrakani," he said at length. "What's to prevent you from manufacturing tarbooshes yourself?"

Georges stared at him in amazement.

"Manufacture tarbooshes of this quality *here*? Out of the question! One needs excellent cloth, one needs machinery and qualified personnel. Above all, one needs method and organization. Where would you find all those things in Cairo? Ask anyone: Egypt has neither the resources nor the vocation to be an industrialized country. You manufacture the tarbooshes in France, and I'll sell them for you here."

After talking for another good hour, they arranged to meet a little while later at the entrance to the American Cosmograph, where Yolande and Maggi would join them.

Opera Square had been sluiced with bucketfuls of cooling water, and a gentle breeze was dispersing the last of the noontide heat. In a thoroughly exuberant mood, Édouard went off to buy some Turkish cigarettes on the other side of the square. He was feeling more and more at home in this charming, teeming city. At the risk of poisoning himself, he proffered a coin to an itinerant vendor who, with a big glass pitcher propped on his hip, sang the praises of his carob- and tamarind-flavoured drinks while clicking some little copper cups between his fingers.

Having drained his cup at a gulp, Édouard made his way down a neighbouring side street. The *tarbouchier*'s establishment Georges had mentioned was a diminutive shop whose counter was arrayed with copper moulds of various sizes. Customers entered, removed their tarbooshes, and handed them over without a word. The shopkeeper picked up one of the moulds, sandwiched the headgear between the two halves, and turned a handle. A cloud of steam went up. A few minutes later the tarboosh was removed, stiff as a board and still steaming.

Delightedly, Édouard headed for the Ezbekiyah Gardens, of whose giant banana trees he had heard great things. A strange sight awaited him outside the entrance. The balconies of several nearby houses were occupied by half-naked women calling, singing and making obscene gestures manifestly designed to entice foreign soldiers.

Édouard walked on. For want of anything better, he would have preferred the forlorn Englishwomen on the terrace at Shepheard's. His spirits rose still higher at the thought of his imminent reunion with lovely Maggi of the slim brown hands.

4

"So you're staying at Shepheard's . . . "

Édouard Dhellemmes thought he detected a mixture of approval and envy in my grandfather's expression.

"We used to go there on Sundays when I was a child," Georges said pensively.

His father, Élias Batrakani, had then been employed by a Syrian merchant in the Muski district. No businessman himself, he watched others growing rich around him. Élias was not mercenary. He simply liked to observe money at close quarters, to toy with and talk about it.

That was why, every Sunday afternoon after his *molokhiya* with onions, my great grandfather would walk his family past Shepheard's and down Shubra Street. It was a way of rubbing shoulders with affluence, a free show that would help to cultivate his children's tastes.

Stationed outside the hotel in the shade of a mimosa tree, the Batrakanis would scan the terrace with the two little sphinxes, hoping to spot some Austrian prince in transit or some Italian diva on tour. They pictured all the marvels concealed behind those apricot-coloured walls: the arabesques, the Persian carpets, the gilded bathtubs in which wealthy Englishwomen wallowed while listening to the call of the muezzin.

"The sun will be setting soon," Linda Batrakani would say after a while. "If we want to go to Shubra . . . "

Having hailed a cab and negotiated a fare, Élias would hoist fat Nando on to the seat beside the driver, and they would trot the length of the famous thoroughfare in which all Cairo's most luxurious carriages assembled at the close of day.

Shubra Street was a broad avenue that ran along the Nile, flanked by ancient sycamore trees whose branches joined hands to form a vault overhead. To be seen there were princes out riding on horseback, their white silk *kufiyas* embroidered with gold thread, or teams of thoroughbred mares drawing carriages in which black, frock-coated eunuchs watched over coveys of harem women, their doe-eyed faces screened from view by transparent veils.

All along the avenue, Élias Batrakani would tell stories in Franco-Arabic, laced with Italian exclamations, in his fine baritone voice. They were wondrous tales replete with gold and tears, exciting anecdotes in which the protagonists — princes, princesses, or slaves — fulfilled their destiny aboard majestic feluccas or behind impenetrable *mashrabiyas*. Élias did not have the dispassionate approach of the ordinary storyteller. His stories were still fresh, having unfolded on his doorstep some years earlier; he himself trembled with pleasure or dismay as he recounted them. And if he sometimes exaggerated, it may simply have been for the sake of veracity, of fidelity to his own awakened dreams.

Georges never tired of hearing about 'Ain al-Hayat, the young orphan girl who was given a home by Khedive Isma'il and destined to marry his son Hussein, the future sultan. He knew the story of their wedding in every little detail.

"The khedive wanted to marry four of his children at the same time," Élias would say. "He decreed that the wedding celebrations should go on for a whole month. Throughout the weeks preceding the signature of the marriage contracts, countless trunks and chests filled with crockery, silver and precious objects — necklaces, bracelets, tiaras, chibouks, censers — could be seen arriving at the four palaces. These marvels were displayed on silk cushions and protected against theft with steel mesh. Then, for four days, they were paraded through the streets of Cairo under escort, to enable us to feast our eyes on them. I've no need to tell you how sumptuous they looked!"

We, too, were treated to these stories several decades later. They had been enriched in the interim with a number of episodes that rendered them still more coherent, still more true . . .

* * *

During the 1860s, after their arrival in Egypt, Élias and Linda Batrakani had seen the modern city take shape before their eyes. Of course, Cairo had already ceased to be the big, chaotic medieval village whose sole horse-drawn carriage caused panic in the streets whenever it emerged from Shubra Palace. Muhammad Ali and his successors had removed the mountains of garbage that used to rot away in the middle of the city. They had installed road-sweeping, watering and lighting systems, drained the Ezbekiyah marshes, built a number of palaces beside the Nile, and enclosed them with plantations of palm trees and carobs, mulberries and acacias.

Generally speaking, however, Cairo had retained its ancient structure intact. The capital's outward appearance, if not its character, did not really change until the time of Khedive Isma'il. "My country is in Africa no longer. We form part of Europe . . ."

"In 1867," Élias told his children, "the khedive returned from Paris thrilled by what he had seen there at the World Exhibition. I say the khedive and not the viceroy because, in the meantime, Isma'il had purchased that title from the Sultan of Turkey. Everything in the world is for sale, my dears . . .

"Isma'il was firmly resolved to apply Haussmann's principles to Cairo. He had to act quickly, very quickly, if he was to present the image of a prosperous modern city to the foreigners who would attend the opening of the Suez Canal in two years' time. The capital became an immense construction site. Avenues were driven through it and squares laid out. Isma'il even sent for Barillet-Deschamps, the creator of the Bois de Boulogne, to transform the Ezbekiyah Gardens into a park in the English manner, complete with grottoes, bridges, and miniature lakes. Two years later, the city was strewn with elaborate, stylistically hybrid façades that camouflaged half-finished buildings, foul alleyways, and sprawling slums.

"For history wouldn't wait, my dears. The world's maps had just been declared obsolete, now that Ferdinand de Lesseps had managed to draw a blue line between the Red Sea and the Mediterranean."

For the hundredth time, Élias described the lavish inauguration of the canal in the presence of Empress Eugénie, Emperor Franz Joseph, and nine hundred other distinguished guests. Balls, concerts, firework displays, circuses, dromedary races, the aerostat, illuminated buildings, women singing on balconies.

"Wasn't Verdi there?" Georges put in, to relaunch the storyteller.

"Certainly not! *Aïda*, with which it had been intended to inaugurate Cairo's new opera house, was still unfinished. That masterpiece wasn't premièred until December 1871, but what a première it was! On the black market, seats were rented for their weight in gold. The women of the court were hidden from view in boxes covered with grilles through which their sparkling jewels were all that could be seen. Isma'il sat right through the performance, which lasted, mark you, from seven in the evening till half-past three in the morning! When the curtain fell at last, the entire audience rose and broke into cries of 'Long live the khedive! Long live the khedive!'"

"What about Verdi?"

"Verdi never crossed the Mediterranean. He hated travelling by sea. When the applause subsided, they hurried to the telegraph office to inform him that his work had been a triumphant success."

Élias knew whole passages from *Aïda* by heart. When guests were present, he took little persuading to sing them after the Sunday *molokhiya*.

It has to be said that the canal turned his head a little. Having christened his first-born Ferdinand and his next child Eugénie, he proposed to call the third one Francis Joseph. His wife complained to the parish priest of Darb al-Geneina, who sent for Élias and drew attention to his dangerous departure from tradition.

"Francis and Joseph might have been all right for twins, *habibi*, but this won't do. Besides, you should have christened your eldest son after your poor father. His name was Girgis, wasn't it?"

So Francis Joseph became Girgis, or Georges. After all, wasn't Egypt "part of Europe" now?

"Believe it or not," Élias Batrakani would tell anyone who cared to listen, "I nearly made a fortune out of the Canal!"

The fortune went to Habib Sakakini, member of a humble Greek Catholic family from Damascus which had settled in Egypt. Like Élias, Habib possessed neither money nor qualifications. One day, when he was twenty, he spotted an SOS from Ferdinand de Lesseps in the newspaper: enormous rats were devouring the canal workers' food, destroying equipment, and spreading disease. Every means of eliminating these obstacles to peaceful excavation had been tried, but to no avail. A substantial reward awaited the person who solved this problem.

Young Sakakini answered the advertisement. Why not import some cats, he suggested: they would be only too happy to devour the rats. The construction bosses looked sceptical, but they had nothing to lose. Several hundred cats were transported to the site in cages. First starved and then released at strategic points, they denuded the Canal Zone of rats in short order.

Not long afterwards the inventor of this deratification technique was appointed to drain the Cairo marshes. Once again he worked wonders, and a year later the authorities enlisted him to meet yet another challenge: Cairo's opera house had to be completed within six months.

The khedive lavished gifts on Habib Sakakini. Elevated to the rank of pasha, he now enjoyed a reputation that extended to Constantinople. Sultan 'Abdel-Hamid presented him with a palace at Faggaala in a district that still bears his name.

"I thought of cats too," Élias would explain, "but I was too busy to answer the advertisement that day."

"What a shame!" was the unfailing response of his listeners, who wondered why the luckless man hadn't put a bullet in his head.

As for young Georges, he listened to the grown-ups and pondered in silence, trying to fathom the real reasons for Habib Sakakini's success. How did you work your way up from cats to pashadom? How did you carve out a place in the sun?

5

The first of Michel's eleven diaries isn't my favourite. One senses that
the writer was a reserved, industrious boy incapable of giving his pen free
rein. The sensitive, temperamental adolescent of later years had yet to
pierce the pages, which still read like a piece of evening homework. Was it
that the Jesuits had taught Michel to suppress his emotions, or should his
reticence be attributed to a fear that his secret diary, concealed beneath the
mattress, would some day come into the prying hands of Mademoiselle
Guyomard?

15 May 1916

Yesterday the Father Rector and the masters went to the palace to pay their respects.
The sultan couldn't see them because he was in conference with the minister of
finance. But the fathers were kindly received by Zul-Fiqar Pasha, who told them:
"His Highness was very pleased with his visit to the school. At dinner last night
he kept saying that anyone who wants to have well-educated children should send
them to Saint-Famille and nowhere else."

The Jesuits had learnt to operate the Arab telephone. They had no
difficulty in acquainting the bourgeoisie of Cairo, by way of their pupils,
with the sultan's appreciative remarks about the school.

Georges Batrakani feigned annoyance when Michel transmitted them
to him. "That's a bit hard on the Brothers at the Christian schools that
educated *me*."

To my grandfather, sending his children to a Jesuit school was a mark
of social advancement. All the youngsters in his wife's family attended

Saint-Famille, which was the most expensive school in Cairo, the hardest to get into, and – the sultan was right – the one that offered the best education.

The Jesuits had returned to Egypt in 1879, after a century's absence, charged by Pope Leo XIII with recapturing the schismatic Copts who dared to call themselves Orthodox. Provided for this purpose was a free seminary in Cairo and a mission in Upper Egypt. Saint-Famille did not appear on the agenda. The Jesuits established the school on their own initiative, thereby infuriating the Brothers at the Christian schools that had hitherto enjoyed an educational monopoly. In the end, however, all the Lord's workers found places of their own on the banks of the Nile. A tacit division of labour evolved: the Brothers taught the rank and file while the Jesuits, being more elitist, were the sole purveyors of Greek and Latin.

18 May 1916

Victor Lévy hates me. He hasn't said a word to me since the sultan's visit. He tells everyone I'm "Korner's pet". I'm sure it was him that threw away my silkworm.

"*Le Laboureur et ses enfants*" still rankled with the only Jew in the class. Being top in recitation, he felt cheated. *He* was the one who should have recited in front of the sultan.

Rather discomfited, Michel secretly acknowledged that his last term's 17 out of 20 was less meritorious than the 19 awarded to Victor Lévy. This troubled him so much that he debated whether to accuse himself in the confessional. But what exactly was the offence in question? It didn't appear in the catalogue of standard horrors, with their fixed penalties. If offence there had been, it was at least shared by Father Korner. And, since it was Father Korner who usually heard fifth-formers' confessions . . . In short, everything argued against giving the affair a pious sequel.

The summer holidays were approaching. All that remained was to organize the Father Rector's annual festival, with its gifts in kind for the poor. Michel and his brother André brought rice and lentils, but some of the boys made a conspicuous entrance that day, followed by servants bearing live geese or leading sheep.

In the middle of June the whole of Cairene society, with the sultan at its head, departed for Alexandria to cool off for two or three months. Michel was already dreaming of bathing from the Casino San Stefano beach with his brothers and cousins as he had done the year before. The youngest wore large gourds attached to their waists to help them keep afloat. Michel recalled the wealthy Muslim family who used to turn up in the mornings, their carriage overflowing with children. Seated beside the coachman was a black, exceedingly ugly eunuch with a weird voice. They used to eye him covertly with a touch of uneasiness . . .

The holidays provided the occasion for grand family reunions in the villa belonging to the Alexandria cousins.

Maggi shocked everyone with her daring summer outfits, while fat Nando, seated before mountains of prawns, sea bream and grilled sardines, devoted hours to cramming his maw. But the real star of these extended meals was my great grandfather, old Élias Batrakani. Indefatigably, in a voice wellnigh proof against fatigue, he would transport his listeners back thirty-odd years to the start of the British occupation.

"When 'Arabi Pasha – devil take him! – rose in revolt in 1882, the European residents flew into a panic and fled *en masse* by train or sea. As for us, *ya haram*, we didn't even have French-protected status, which would have enabled us to join a special convoy bound for Palestine.

"The Batrakanis lay low in mortal fear throughout the events of 1882. The British bombardment of Alexandria gave rise to the most ridiculous rumours. 'The British fleet has been destroyed,' claimed our idiot of an Armenian neighbour. 'Admiral Seymour has been taken prisoner.' Every day an overexcited crowd awaited the admiral's arrival at Bab al-Hadid station, and every day a false Seymour was arrested outside the station and paraded through the streets amid jeers from the bystanders.

"The British had, in fact, made short work of 'Arabi's army, but we didn't breathe easy until the fourteenth of September. That was when General Drury Lowe's cavalrymen rode down Shubra Street at dusk, after racing across the desert for a hundred kilometres.

"We were on the balcony," Élias recalled. "The Bengal Lancers, who were galloping along at their head, reined in abruptly on catching sight of a minaret and broke into cries of *Allahu-Akbar!* To our horror, they were Muslims! Fortunately, our fears were soon dispelled. A few days later I took Nando with me to Opera Square to watch the occupying power's first ceremonial parade. Remember, Nando?"

The fish eater nodded with his mouth full. He preserved a very vivid memory of that day. Standing beside his father in dust-coated boots, he had inhaled the scent of the horses and filled his ears with the clatter of their hoofs.

"What a spectacle it was, my dears!" Élias went on. "The parade of the victors of Tell el-Kebir was preceded by two flags riddled with bullet-holes. Following them came twenty thousand men. Not a drum or bugle broke the silence, which rendered their march-past more impressive still. It was a feast of uniforms and colours. What with the scarlet tunics of the artillery, the pearl-grey trousers of the infantry, the pleated kilts of the Scottish regiments, and the indigo blue uniforms and turbans of the Indian cavalry, it seemed that five or six foreign armies had invaded Egypt simultaneously!"

On that historic day in September 1882, Élias Batrakani got there well in advance to set up his photographic equipment. He transported it all to the site on donkeyback with Nando's assistance: tripod, screens, lenses, camera, and a score of photographic plates in wooden cases. As ever on such occasions, the photographer was very soon surrounded by a throng of curious onlookers. He disappeared beneath his black cloth – covered with white cotton sheeting to reflect the heat – and spent an age getting ready. Then, without warning, he manufactured a flash that drew cheers from his audience.

Nando was then still too young to realize that his father was not, in fact, a fanatical photographer. Élias was as fond of being looked at as he was of looking through the lens. Too poor to afford a villa, a horse and trap, or even a liveried *sufragi*, this fake roving photographer strutted around with his black box as a means of impressing other people. His apartment in Faggaala was filled with uninspired, ill-composed photographs yellowed by negligence, not to mention stacks of plates that had never been developed and reposed in hatboxes.

"You remember the Jesuit, Nando?"

A Jesuit on the opposite pavement, accompanied by some young Coptic Catholic seminarists, was trying to talk a British soldier into letting him cross the road. Having finally succeeded, he set off into the gap between two squadrons of cavalry. The seminarists, in their black cassocks, little overcoats and dark red tarbooshes, followed at his heels. Children from poor families, they were enjoying their first outing since the end of 'Arabi's rebellion. They had come to see the parade, but it was Élias's camera that intrigued them most of all.

The French Jesuit stationed himself beside the photographer with an air of authority, compelling Nando to step aside.

"Poor France!" exclaimed the Jesuit in an undertone. "To think that our ships, which had also been lying off Alexandria, were ordered to refrain from going into action and to head for the open sea! Poor France! It was she that should have planted the cross here. By entrusting that task to others, God doubtless meant to punish her for her crimes."

Turning to Élias, the priest added gravely: "I don't know if Egypt will become more Christian, monsieur, but I fear she may well become English."

6

Édouard Dhellemmes had to return to France on 15 June 1916. A few days before he sailed for Marseille my grandparents and Maggi took him to the French hospital in 'Abassiya to attend a musical matinée given by the Syrians of Cairo for wounded soldiers from the Dardanelles.

Édouard was waiting for them at the foot of the terrace outside Shepheard's. Today he had exchanged his boater for a magnificent tarboosh.

Georges Batrakani congratulated him on this innovation with a cordial *"Mabrouk!"*

Instinctively, Édouard made to raise his hat to Yolande and Maggi, who were sitting in the barouche. The tarboosh fell to the ground and was swiftly retrieved by a one-legged beggar.

"My dear fellow," Georges said with a smile, "you don't raise your tarboosh to a lady, nor even to the sultan himself. Besides, you went at it the wrong way. A tarboosh isn't a hat: you take it in both hands."

So saying, Georges took the tarboosh from the beggar and, using both hands, gently replaced it on the Frenchman's head.

"There. It suits you very well. You should wear it at a slight angle, though, it looks more stylish. But in your place I would have gone for something a little paler. With your colouring . . . "

Édouard blushed to the roots of his hair. Yolande thought him charming and Maggi could have gobbled him up.

The survivors of the Dardanelles had been seated in the hospital's largest ward, which was adorned with flowers and tricolour flags. The Levantines facing them in their Sunday best stood grouped around the French minister, who thanked them for their welcome initiative.

A Syrian lawyer belted out the *Marseillaise* with choral accompaniment. Maggi bent and whispered in Édouard's ear.

"He presides over one of the mixed courts. Nice voice, don't you agree? I think he's going to sing *La Madelon* as well. In a minute you'll be hearing one of my young cousins, Zouzou, a perfect sweetheart. She recites poems of her own composition . . . "

Maggi's bracelets tinkled as she gestured with her lovely brown hands. Her heady perfume intoxicated Édouard, who was sweating under his tarboosh. He even forgot to applaud when young Zouzou made her entrance in a red-white-and-blue gown and a Phrygian cap.

Riding back in the barouche, Édouard confessed to being surprised. "I didn't know France was so popular here," he said.

Georges smiled, sniffing his cigar.

"What do you expect, my friend? Some people are French by blood, others because they live in France. We are French in our hearts."

Édouard probably wasn't the first person my grandfather had treated to this aphorism, but it sounded right and was well received.

"I'd never have believed it," Édouard persisted, "not in a country under British occupation for thirty-five years."

"So? The British wield political and economic power. We respect them, but we've no love for them."

"If your father could hear you, Georges!" Yolande broke in.

Georges's cigar had gone out. He chewed it with a pensive air. "Yes," he said, "it's true, my father always had a soft spot for the British . . . "

7

I believe that my great grandfather's anglophilia stemmed, in essence, from his civil servant's temperament. Élias Batrakani was made that way: he liked his superiors on principle. If Egypt had been occupied by Russia he would have been a Russophile; if she had been invaded by the Chinese, he would have been pro-Chinese.

His sons Nando and Georges, who liked to claim that commerce was in their blood, were not cut from the same cloth.

That blood type must have skipped a generation. Unlike his commercially gifted sons and his own father, who had done well out of taffeta in the old days at Aleppo, Élias Batrakani had no head for business. In 1883 he abandoned his counter in the Muski and happily donned a pair of shiny oversleeves.

The British were recruiting personnel. Anxious to take the local administration in hand and reform it, they were looking for reliable intermediaries with a knowledge of Arabic and other languages and a modicum of general education. Few Muslims and Copts fitted this job description.

"From Britain's point of view," Élias used to say at this period, "we Syrians are manna from heaven. Well, why not? We have the education."

All that my great grandfather possessed, in fact, was a certificate of primary education, but he knew Arabic and French, could get by in Italian, and spoke a smattering of English. He looked good, too, being adept at dressing above his means. The ministry of public works offered him a job as a grade-four *wakil idara*, or deputy departmental manager.

From now on, Élias swore by Captain Simpson, his immediate superior. It was Simpson this, Simpson that. Whatever the subject under discussion, whether political or economic, religious or botanical, the *wakil idara* would gravely cite his pink-cheeked, fair-haired oracle with the toothbrush moustache, a former Indian Army officer.

"We've occupied Egypt to protect the Europeans living there and consolidate the khedive's authority," Captain Simpson explained. "We're only here on a temporary basis. We shall leave the day this country has been stabilized and reformed and is capable of governing itself. Some plants are frail: they need staking if they're to grow straight."

But the years went by and the stake took root. Leave Egypt? There was no more talk of that from Captain Simpson, who played polo three times a week at the Khedivial Sporting Club. The British came increasingly to regard their frail plant as an indispensable strategic position on the route to India. Having poured scorn on the Suez Canal at the time of its conception, they were now its principal users and beneficiaries.

"The British have become Canal-lovers," Élias Batrakani proclaimed in 1890, as triumphantly as if he himself were the author of their conversion.

But the ministry of public works would henceforth administer another epic operation connected with water: the taming of the Nile by British engineers. Captain Simpson gave vent to some definitive pronouncements on the subject which Élias, with the earnest demeanour of an evangelist, used to pass on at Sunday lunch, convinced that he was impressing his cousin Rizqallah, a journalist.

"If it weren't for the Nile, Captain Simpson says, Egypt would be merely arid desert. But the Nile has always played tricks on the Egyptians, supplying them with too much water in winter and not enough in summer. We must make good use of that water, sharing it out equitably and systematically. That, he says, is as much a question of morality as technology, and both were sorely lacking before the British arrived in 1882."

Élias rapped out the words, half surprised that his journalist cousin wasn't taking notes. Young Georges was all ears. At school they learned about the Rhône and the Saône, the Pyrenees and the Massif Central, the cities and departments of France. Egypt was not in the curriculum.

"As Simpson says, the course, gradient and capacity of irrigation canals were worked out in former times with no regard for common sense. Thousands of peasants had to be mobilized to dredge them under the helpless gaze of French engineers. Irrigation and drainage were combined as if the veins and arteries of an organism served the same purpose. Some canals were filled to the brim for irrigation purposes when they ought to have been used for drainage. Saturated with salt, their water overflowed on to the land, with catastrophic results."

Linda, my great grandmother, would interrupt the orator to serve *molokhiya* or *kubeiba labniya*, and Cousin Rizqallah, whose newspaper, *Al-Ahram*, was subsidized by France, seized the opportunity to have a go at the British. But Élias, his rich baritone slightly muffled by mouthfuls of meat, regained the floor. In deferential tones he enumerated the names of the new heroes of the Nile: Mr Read, Major Brown, Colonel Ross . . . Those champions had not only reorganized the drainage and irrigation systems but initiated the construction of a dam at the head of the Delta.

"Ever since that dam has been in operation," Rizqallah objected, "the two branches of the Nile have dried up completely in May and June."

"I know," Élias conceded irritably. "It works too well, that's the only trouble. Our Anglo-Indian engineers are going to arrange it so that the water can flow down to the sea. But if there's one thing I can't endure" – and here he gave Rizqallah a withering glance – "it's the sniggers of the French. They're obviously praying to heaven that something nasty happens to the dam!"

Then, in a confidential tone, as if he regretted having to say this in the presence of the press:

"Our engineers are well advanced with their plans for a reservoir capable of holding – wait for it! – four billion cubic metres! Where to construct this gigantic reservoir? At Aswan, Wadi Halfa, or in the Fayoum? Simpson favours the latter . . . "

Young Georges itched to see the reality of this all-powerful person of whom he had heard so often. He was finally granted an opportunity to do so in March 1891.

"No outing to Shubra tomorrow afternoon," Élias told his family proudly. "Captain Simpson has invited us to attend a military display at Gezira."

The lone cold-water tap on the Batrakanis' floor was in constant use that Sunday morning as they soaped and titivated themselves. Linda, who had positively insisted on trimming her lilac gown with frills, implored her Armenian neighbour to help her, and the two women stitched away by candlelight the whole of Saturday evening. Élias himself, for all his grand airs, was suffering from a bad case of nerves.

Mrs Simpson was a kind of parade horse with flaring, disdainful nostrils. She barely glanced at the Levantines in their Sunday best and went on chatting with some English ladies of her acquaintance. The captain was looking very dapper in a white linen jacket, black trousers, and a red tarboosh. He kissed hands in the French fashion, and the touch of his ginger moustache, which was stiff as a besom, made Linda shiver all over.

The elegant stands would not have disgraced Ascot. Khedive Tewfiq was playing a walk-on part beside the British consul general, Sir Evelyn Baring. Poor Tewfiq, neither his glittering attire nor his black beard was enough to lend him even a semblance of personality. He was utterly eclipsed by the future Lord Cromer's massive frame, his vitality and intelligence, sophistication and power.

Two military bands played in turn. Contingents of infantry, cavalry and artillery paraded past, one by one, but the *pièce de résistance* was a reconstruction of an attack on a British encampment in the Sudan. After all, hadn't troops commanded by Sirdar Grenfell and Colonel Kitchener just ended a years-long series of setbacks in this Egyptian colony by inflicting a severe defeat on the Mahdist devils?

In front of the stands, coal-black Sudanese charged the British camp with spears and savage cries, then celebrated their victory with a rather laughable fantasia. All at once, however, rifle and artillery fire was heard. With cavalry in support, British infantrymen converged from all sides, cut the Sudanese to pieces in a trice, and raised the Union Jack once more. The spectators rose and broke into deafening applause while the two bands struck up "God Save the Queen".

"An immaculate performance," Élias commented on the homeward journey. "Not a gaiter button missing."

"All that was missing were the Egyptian soldiers sent into action in the Sudan by British officers," retorted Linda, with a political conscience of which no one would have suspected her.

So proud of her scalloped lilac gown, Linda had felt terribly humiliated by Mrs Simpson's supercilious gaze.

8

Every last detail of the sultan's visit to the Collège de la Saint-Famille had been prearranged by the Jesuits with the aid of Grand Chamberlain Zul-Fiqar Pasha, an erstwhile pupil of theirs. Michel did not discover this until seven months later, when Father Korner let it slip.

> *20 December 1916*
>
> *I realized today why Victor Lévy didn't recite in front of the sultan! He got his 19 out of 20 for Lamartine's "Le Lac", but that day, to please the sultan, the lesson HAD to be on La Fontaine. Father Korner chose the person who'd got the best mark for "Le Laboureur".*
>
> *I tried to explain this to Victor Lévy, but he turned his back on me. He doesn't speak to me any more, and he still calls me "Korner's pet". I hate him.*

Victor Lévy was mistaken. If the Jesuits could be said to have a pet Batrakani it was André, Michel's elder brother, not Michel himself. A high-minded youngster, he was one of the pupils that gave them "the greatest consolation".

André and five other senior boys had been selected to make a week-long visit to Upper Egypt during the Christmas 1916 holidays. Its purpose was to show them the mission at al-Minya, one of the Jesuits' proudest achievements.

My uncle set off feeling like an explorer. Until then, no member of the family had ever been hare-brained enough to venture south of Cairo. Those barbarous regions were all right for European tourists – still few and far between at the time – but not for Levantines like us, with our natural predilection for the north, the Mediterranean, and modernity.

The six boys had arranged to meet at Bab al-Hadid station. Even at that early morning hour the concourse was filled with a vociferous, chaotic throng. Semi-licensed porters in filthy *galabiyas* plucked at passengers' sleeves and fought over their baggage. A locomotive standing alongside the platform spat intermittent jets of steam in their faces.

This being André's first trip without the family, he was titillated by the prospect. Although she had insisted on packing his bag herself, Mademoiselle Guyomard would not be there to nag him unmercifully.

The concourse rang with the voices of itinerant vendors tirelessly crying their wares. A showman tossed his monkey at the audience, causing a startled peasant to fall over backwards. Everyone roared with laughter. The clamorous crowd gave off a powerful aroma of sweat and caraway seeds.

From time to time the station noises were overlaid by the braying of a stray donkey near the ticket office. No one seemed to care, with the possible exception of a British policeman who, riding crop in hand, was supervising man and beast amid the pall of steam and smoke.

André was jostled by a black, sinister-looking eunuch who was clearing a path for some veiled ladies bound for Alexandria. They made their way to Platform 1, silently entered the compartment reserved for them, and were locked in.

Where were they going, the mysterious creatures? Just to Alexandria, or on to Europe? Rumour had it that these Turkish society women were escorted to the ship in due form, but that, once aboard, they hurried to their cabins and donned gowns in the latest Paris fashion.

Half an hour later, lulled by the swaying of the train to al-Minya, André was daydreaming about that locked compartment. He imagined himself in the midst of those women, coaxing a laugh here, a whisper there. He pictured the milk-white faces under their dark veils, the cigarettes flavoured with rose water, the slender, gentle, audacious hands . . . Abruptly, he drove such reprehensible thoughts from his mind and concentrated on the fields of berseem and cotton gliding past the window.

Absolutely flat, the immense plain was traversed by a multitude of little silver irrigation ditches. All that relieved the monotony of the landscape were one or two grey, cuboid houses nestling in clumps of palm trees, or an occasional peasant, naked as the day he was born, urinating beside the track with his swarthy penis glistening in the sun.

The six boys and the Jesuit accompanying them were met at al-Minya station by Father Choquet, a member of the mission. At his bidding, they boarded an open cart pulled by a scrawny nag that had to stop after a hundred metres to let a noisy procession pass.

"It's those confounded Protestants again," the missionary grumbled, "trying to lure children with their big drum and tambourines. The sects have great recourse to publicity when opening their schools."

When the first French Jesuit had installed himself at al-Minya in 1887, in company with a Syrian friar, the town numbered only a handful of Catholic Copts. He had had to struggle hard to develop that meagre flock. The best way to convert Orthodox Copts was to open free schools, but the Protestants had since adopted the same tactic.

The next day, André and his friends were to be taken by Father Choquet on an "apostolic reconnaissance". Roused from their slumbers at dawn, they mounted some little grey donkeys that were awaiting them in front of the nuns' quarters and jogtrotted to the mouth of the village, leaning well back with their feet almost brushing the ground.

Reaching a canal bank, the donkeys instinctively slowed as if attuning themselves to the millennial torpor of the surrounding countryside. They passed haughty-looking camels, laden with sugar cane, whose heavy tread sent up little puffs of dust. Black-clad women, walking erect with earthenware pitchers on their heads, drew their veils over their faces and held them in place with their teeth as the boys approached. Others, squatting at the water's edge, gossiped as they washed clothes and cooking utensils while hordes of ragged, barefoot children swarmed everywhere, their faces covered in flies.

Towards eight o'clock Father Choquet halted outside the home of a Coptic family recently converted to Catholicism. The mud-encrusted peasant who came running from the fields to welcome "Abuna Shawki" was thin as a rake, but his wife's rounded belly gave promise of an impending baptism. It would be their twelfth child.

The house, built of unbaked bricks coated with alluvial mud from the Nile, was thatched with straw, and stacked on the flimsy roof were the cakes of sun-dried dung that served as fuel. Hens picked their way among the visitors. The furniture was limited to a big cupboard bereft of doors and some mattresses lying on the mud floor itself.

"Many schismatic peasants don't even know how to cross themselves," the Jesuit said in French. "When you ask them about their religion, they simply show you the crosses tattooed on their wrists. It's not surprising: schismatic priests visit these peasant farmers only once a year at harvest time, and then only to claim their tithe. They themselves are scandalously uneducated. When I asked one the precise moment during Holy Mass at which Our Lord descends upon the altar, he had the effrontery to reply: 'Our Lord is omnipotent; he descends whenever it suits him!'"

André and his friends got a nasty fright as they were leaving the village. The party was suddenly bombarded with stones by some Muslim children lying in wait behind a wall of dried mud. Struck on the flank, the donkey just ahead of André's brayed with pain and reared, almost unseating its rider. Another beast received a kick from its immediate neighbour and bolted. Miraculously, although stones continued to fly, the party reformed in Indian file some fifty metres further on, as though nothing had happened. Father Choquet turned to address the group in spirited tones:

"Missionaries have to be ready for anything!"

André was captivated by this whiff of adventure.

Not long before midday they paused to nibble some sesame-seed bread in the shade of a eucalyptus tree.

"In this country," the Jesuit told them, "one's work is never done. It's not enough to reap after sowing. One sometimes sees whole families of converts relapse into schism – whole villages, even. Steadfastness isn't the oriental's pre-eminent quality!"

Sow and reap . . . Such were the ideas that milled around in André's head a little while later, when the little party was heading for a dispensary run by nuns. There, a Syrian sister was welcoming an endless succession of sick people, many of them suffering from eye infections. The numerous babies that hung from their mothers' breasts seemed half-asleep.

"It's very interesting work," the Jesuit explained. "The nuns don't confine themselves to tending the body; the soul benefits as well. This dispensary enables them to pluck many a flower for Our Lord. Last year, the nun you see here presented a hundred and twenty-three children with their passports to heaven!"

9

André gave an enthusiastic account of his visit to al-Minya. He described the mission, detailed the number of conversions, cited the Jesuits' remarks word for word.

Georges Batrakani listened to his eldest son with a trace of surprise. He himself had never kept company with priests at such close quarters — nor, to be frank, had he felt any the worse for it. His contacts with religion since completing his education with the Brothers had been limited to Sunday Mass, which was looked upon as an extended family reunion, a kind of obligatory aperitif preceding the sacrosanct *molokhiya*, but one that could sometimes have unpredictable consequences.

It happened in February 1902, during the eleven o'clock service at the church of Darb al-Geneina. My grandfather, then twenty-two, was bored stiff. These Greek Catholic Masses seemed interminable. The officiating priest, attired in his finest vestments and followed by altar boys bearing enormous candles, made numerous entrances and exits through one of the three doors of the iconostasis. He censed the altar and the faithful while the precentor, standing to one side in his Sunday best, warbled in a nasal voice:

"Aghios O Theos, Aghios Athanatos . . . "

In the pews reserved for them on the left of the aisle, ladies fanned themselves in time to the languid rhythm of the litany. Every now and then they would look up at the painted heaven on the domed ceiling overhead, a pale blue heaven populated by doves and cherubs. At the back of the nave, portly gentlemen exchanged devout comments on the latest cotton prices at Minet al-Bassal.

Just before Communion, Georges caught the eye of a very young girl in a black veil who had turned, ever so slightly, in his direction. He was instantly captivated by her mischievous face. When the time came for Communion she went up to the priest to receive her consecrated bread dipped in wine. The spuriously contemplative expression with which she returned to her place was quite irresistible.

The sequel to Sunday Mass at Darb al-Geneina richly repaid an hour-and-a-half of liturgical drudgery. It was a veritable open-air salon enlivened by laughter, exclamations, and banter.

The unknown girl was standing beside a middle-aged man whom Georges recognized at once. He was Alexandre Touta, timber merchant and member of the prestigious board of the Greek Catholic Benevolent Society.

After many salutations and embraces and much noisy chit-chat, the Touta family boarded a carriage drawn by two white horses. Georges watched them drive off towards Shubra with a tightening of the heart.

The little Georges knew about women at this time consisted mainly of tittle-tattle overheard at the Café Shisha, near the opera house, where he and his friends were served by pert waitresses to the strains of a Viennese band. At the next table, young bloods would regularly recount their erotic exploits with female tourists picked up on the terraces of the big hotels. If they were to be believed, those European birds of passage were insatiable — in fact, the sexual athletes had formed a *"terrassiers'"* club that threatened to founder at any moment for reasons of sheer exhaustion. Georges and his friends rather envied them, though they only half believed them.

The *terrassiers* told how, one afternoon at the Gezira Hotel, some English girls deprived of snow had invented a novel sport: Egyptian tobogganing. Having seated themselves on big silver trays at the top of the main staircase, the delightful creatures would then, under the lustful gaze of the hotel's *sufragis*, glissade to the bottom uttering little shrieks.

The *terrassiers* also told of a nightclub in the Muski where scantily clad Nubian girls danced in close proximity to the tables. Pretending to be stung by bees, they called out *"Nahla, nahla!"* and proceeded to feel themselves all over in search of the insidious insects. Driven to despair, they removed one garment after another. Then, brushing against each other and panting ever harder, the dancers struck a multitude of lascivious, provocative poses. Finally they went and perched on the laps of the male customers, who stuck coins to their moist breasts.

Georges was sexually aroused by these stories. One day, when he was twenty, some friends persuaded him to visit Cairo's red-light district. Entrusted to an exceedingly fat and dirty Greek prostitute with a nasty-looking sore on her leg, he felt like a victim of rape. This experience left him with an alarming mental picture of the female body which haunted him for months.

Alexandre Touta's daughter reappeared in the same place at eleven o'clock Mass the following Sunday. Georges, who had taken care to sit across the aisle from her, vainly tried to catch her eye. It was not until the *kyrie* that she favoured him with a sidelong glance. She persisted in staring at the cherubs on the cupola throughout the rest of Mass.

That same evening Georges went to see the parish priest of Darb al-Geneina and inform him of his marriage plans. The *curé* burst out laughing.

"One of the Touta girls? Forget it, *habibi*! They're too grand – they'll have their sights set on a better match than you. I could suggest someone else . . . "

"No, Abuna, she's the one I want."

Although annoyed by Georges's insistence, the priest remembered that Linda Batrakani had been one of his most faithful parishioners.

"On your own head be it," he growled at length. "I'll fix you an appointment with Alexandre Touta. He'll explain to you, in his own way, what you refuse to understand."

The appointment was, in fact, fixed for the following Saturday. Meantime, Georges disclosed his plans to his father, who was staggered.

"You want to marry a Touta girl – you, a justice's clerk on four pounds a month! Are you crazy? They'll show you the door – they'll humiliate you. Ah, if only your poor mother were here . . . "

The Toutas' prestige stemmed less from their money, which was divided among too many heirs, than from their name and background. In company with the Kahils, the Bahris and a few others, they were regarded as one of the most long-established Greek Catholic families in Egypt – far superior to all the *nouveaux riches* who had converged on Cairo during Isma'il's reign and made their millions overnight.

"You, a justice's clerk on four pounds a month . . . " Yes, but who had prodded him into becoming a justice's clerk? After gaining his *baccalauréat*, Georges had dreamt of becoming a mixed court barrister and enrolling at Cairo's recently opened French law school. That, however, would have entailed financing his further education and covering the cost of a trip to Paris for the final examinations.

"My name isn't Simpson or Rothschild," Élias had told him. "You're the family's first *bachelier*, what more do you want? If the mixed courts interest you so much, try the clerks' office. I hear they're taking people on."

On Saturday afternoon Georges was shown into the Toutas' drawing room by a barefoot *sufragi*. The timber merchant shook hands with Georges but remained standing, as if his proposal of marriage were unworthy even of discussion.

"What are your present circumstances?" he asked, point-blank.

"I intend to make a fortune," Georges replied calmly.

A brief silence ensued. Clearly taken aback, Alexandre Touta invited him to sit down.

Moments later, with his chest well out and his hands firmly grasping the arms of a Louis Seize *bergère*, Georges was holding forth with plenty of conviction.

"At present I'm a justice's clerk at the mixed courts, but I plan to go into business. I've already made a modest start . . . "

Some weeks earlier, while glancing through *Le Bosphore égyptien*, he had been struck by the number of advertisements for pharmaceutical products. The one that had particularly attracted his attention related to Dr McBride's orange-blossom seeds: "This remedy, acknowledged in Egypt and Syria to be remarkably effective against sterility, may be purchased from Madame Habib Salhani, Abdel-Malek Sayegh Building,

Faggaala Street, for 80 piastres a box of six seeds. Any box that does not bear Madame Salhani's seal must be considered counterfeit."

Georges had gone to Faggaala Street with the intention of asking this seemingly astute woman for her advice. There was no shop at the address mentioned. Madame Salhani, who operated from home, received him in her dressing gown and a strong smell of fried aubergines. A woman of fifty or so, she had a flabby figure but a lively eye. Flattered that a young man should have come to consult her, she gave him coffee and told him her life story. Finally, after an hour, she confided her intention of retiring in the near future and put him on the track of Brown's Emulsion, a panacea that enabled babies to cut their teeth without discomfort and adults to retain the youthful sparkle in their eyes.

"For one pound a month I've rented a room in a building overlooking Opera Square," Georges told Alexandre Touta. "The premises are minute, but it's a good address. I've also written to fifteen French, German and Austro-Hungarian laboratories offering to become their agent in Egypt. Ten of them have failed to reply and the other five have turned me down, but I'm not disheartened. In any case, Brown's Emulsion is selling quite well. Some of my customers have found it possesses anti-tubercular properties."

An experienced businessman, Alexandre Touta regarded Georges in some perplexity, pensively fiddling with his ring.

"Marguerite is my younger daughter," he said at length. "First I must marry off Yolande, her elder sister, a gentle, charming girl. You might care to meet her."

Georges, thoroughly disconcerted, found it hard to conceal his mental turmoil.

"This doesn't commit you to anything," Alexandre Touta went on. "We're giving a little party next Sunday. Do come."

Georges left the house feeling hurt and angry. A prey to conflicting emotions, he walked the streets of Shubra for a long time without any real idea of where he was going.

He had triumphed, in a sense. "You might care to meet her . . . " It was an invitation, a form of encouragement, almost a solicitation, but what a slap in the face as well! If he now asked for the hand of Yolande when he wanted her sister, Marguerite, wouldn't it indicate that their family was his sole interest?

Besides, what was she like, this girl Yolande? As attractive as her younger sister? Even more so, perhaps . . . Plain curiosity prompted Georges to attend the party. He had been too bent on marrying a Touta for three whole weeks to throw in his hand just like that. What would he have looked like to his father, his brother Nando, his friends at the Café Shisha? How delightful, on the other hand, to be able to broadcast the tidings of such a match!

Georges rang the Toutas' bell at six the following Sunday evening. This time the *sufragi* was wearing a waistcoat and gilded slippers. The three reception rooms were brilliantly illuminated.

Marguerite, no longer veiled, looked stunning in a green gown. Yolande, less pretty and more reserved, advanced on Georges as instructed, bearing a tray of *petits fours*. Attracted by his honey-coloured eyes and lively manner, she fell for him at once. They exchanged a few banalities under the watchful gaze of Yolande's elegant mother.

A jeweller's daughter, Madame Touta was reported to take regular sand baths near the Great Pyramid. Her servants would bury her up to the neck and leave her like that for hours on end, her head shielded from the sun by a skullcap set with precious stones. One day, having walked off, they heard their mistress screaming for help. She was bareheaded: her skullcap had been stolen by some Bedouin children, never to be seen again.

Alexandre Touta came over to Georges flanked by two young men, one the height of sartorial elegance, the other rather odd-looking. "Allow me to introduce my sons," he said, "Henri and Edmond."

"Papa tells me you're in pharmaceuticals," said Henri, very man of the world.

"Pharmaceuticals?" Edmond broke in eagerly. "In that case, you must know. I've heard tell of a preparation that enables one to endure crowds."

"Brown's Emulsion, no doubt," said Georges with a hint of a smile.

"Really? You think so?"

* * *

Georges Batrakani and Yolande Touta were married at Darb al-Geneina church on 8 January 1903. The young bride had chosen her sister Maggi as a witness. The parvis was strewn with flowers. Ex-Captain Simpson, now a colonel, had sent a very fine basket of flowers, together with his excuses: he was detained by a vulture shoot in the Muqattam quarries in honour of a visiting Hohenzollern prince.

"What good form!" Élias Batrakani kept remarking to the members of the Touta family, none of whom had ever heard of Simpson. "The colonel remembered to send flowers in spite of all his preoccupations. No doubt about it: the English are true gentlemen."

In the course of the grand wedding dinner held at Antoun Yousef de Shubra Hotel, my great grandfather regaled his table companions with an account of the draining of Cairo's sewers, an operation that had mobilized the whole of Colonel Simpson's department.

"The streets have no drains," he explained. "In the cobbled or macadamized sections, the water collects at low points, so the only way to cross them is by car or on an Arab's back. And where there are no cobbles or macadam, soil and debris combine to raise the ground-level more than a metre above the local inhabitants' floor-level . . . "

During the sweet course Élias felt in his waistcoat pocket and produced some of the little slips of paper that accompanied him everywhere. They were covered with figures.

"Cairo has at least four hundred thousand inhabitants," he declared. "Allowing for 1.25 litres of excrement per person per day, I arrive at a figure of five hundred thousand cubic metres a year. Yet the volume of sewage conveyed to the municipal sewage works amounts, believe it or not, to less than thirty thousand cubic metres . . . "

Élias went on to give a detailed description of the historic occasion on which he accompanied Colonel Simpson to Port Saïd for the unveiling of Ferdinand de Lesseps' statue.

"Talking of the Canal," he continued, launching into his party piece, "did you know that I nearly made a fortune in the 1860s? It was all to do with rats . . . "

10

Yolande did not, in fact, bring much in the way of a dowry. Alexandre Touta felt that giving away his elder daughter to a young man without a position constituted a handsome enough wedding present in itself. Georges was treated to some words of encouragement and a hundred Egyptian pounds, neither more nor less. He spent the bulk of that sum on installing himself and his wife in a sparsely furnished apartment in Shubra. Their domestic staff consisted of a short-sighted Sai'idi maidservant who persisted in confusing spoons with forks.

It was not until three years later, after the birth of André and Michel, that the young couple were able to employ a *sufragi* in the person of Rashid Abu-l-Fath, who entered their service one night in November 1906, under rather unusual and definitely unforeseen circumstances.

The carriage lamp of the cab taking my grandfather home to Shubra had gone out halfway there. The cabby, being as improvident as all Cairo cabbies, had no spare candles in his box, so he hailed a young, *galabiya*-clad vendor who was crying *"Shama'a, shama'a!"* at a crossroads and brandishing his sticks of wax.

Tossed from the cab, the coin went rolling along the ground and vanished into the darkness.

"Where is it?" asked the youth.

"Go look for it," the cabby growled.

"Why should I?"

"I said go look for it, son of a dog!"

The candle seller seized the horse's bridle as if to prevent it from moving on. A whip cracked, bloodying his face and making him cry out.

Dabbing the wound with the hem of his *galabiya*, he walked up to the cab to enlist Georges as a witness.

"What's your name?" asked my grandfather, after telling the cabby to wait.

"Rashid."

Georges liked the sound of his voice. He asked him a couple of questions, then: "If you want a regular job, Rashid, I may have something for you."

The unknown youth darted forward and kissed his hands.

Early the next morning he presented himself at the Batrakanis' apartment in Shubra. He was very dark-skinned, almost black, and his left cheek bore a purplish gash. He was engaged at twenty piastres a month, all found.

So Georges now had a *sufragi*, which lent him a little more standing in the eyes of his in-laws. He took another step up the ladder some years later, when he engaged a French governess. The rather vague way in which he spoke of this acquisition led people to believe that Henriette Guyomard had been specially imported from Paris to look after his offspring. In reality, she had already spent some time in Shubra with the Dames du Bon Pasteur. Although there was talk of an unhappy love affair, no one knew exactly why this inhibited spinster had landed up in Cairo in 1905 and remained there ever since.

But that was not enough to equal the Toutas. Yolande's brother Henri had hardly got married before he treated himself to a butler and a coachman. As for Edmond, he enjoyed the services of a manservant.

"I've got two brothers-in-law," Georges Batrakani used to say. "A good-for-nothing and a crackpot."

The crackpot didn't embarrass him unduly. Edmond Touta was, in fact, a rather likeable part of the scenery. A slightly deranged young man who sported a floppy mauve bow tie all year round, he amused everyone with his forays into Egyptian demography – a positive obsession with him. Edmond's eccentric whims enlivened the childhood of my uncles, my mother, and my own generation in turn.

Henri Touta, the good-for-nothing, dabbled in the stock market and nursed his private income. Married to a distant cousin of Sakakini Pasha, he lived in a fine house in Qasr ad-Dubaara, Cairo's smartest residential district. Henri had been educated by the Jesuits at a time when the Collège de la Sainte-Famille still numbered very few Syrians among its pupils, as he never failed to recall. His Latin tags, slipped in at the drop of a hat, had the merit of annoying Georges Batrakani, to whom they were incomprehensible gibberish.

Henri made himself still more unpopular from 1910 onwards by acquiring the title "count" from the Principality of Liechtenstein, which had appointed him its consular representative. Count Henri Touta's diplomatic duties did not seem overly onerous, the consulate's address being identical with that of his home in Qasr ad-Dubaara.

"Count my backside!" grumbled Georges.

But his brother-in-law was not the only Syrian in Cairo to boast a title. Count Zogheb, for example, represented Denmark and had acquired that country's nationality. There was even a Prince Lutfallah. Some of the Eïds were Belgian and some of the Zananiris British. Our families had always included Greek Catholics who contrived to offer their services to foreign countries and thus obtain a title, a protected person's status, or a genuine nationality.

II

"It's absurd," Mademoiselle Guyomard kept saying, "quite absurd. That child can't be left in the midst of a filthy, hysterical mob. He'll get lost. He'll hurt himself or catch the Lord knows what disease!"

Michel let the pestilential creature run on. Now that his father had agreed, her opinion didn't count.

"If Micho wants to go out in the streets," Georges Batrakani had said, "let him. Zaki need only go too."

The coachman jumped for joy when he was asked to get ready. Attending the sultan's funeral was certainly no hardship! His enthusiasm ended by alarming Yolande, who saw to it that Rashid, a more level-headed character, went along as well. And so, flanked by a coachman and a scar-faced *sufragi*, my excited godfather made his way to Opera Square to watch the mortal remains of Hussein Kamil pass by.

"If you can't see properly," his father had told him, "you can always join us at the office."

Georges's office was in an exceptional position. Several friends and relations had been invited there for the occasion, because the funeral cortège, after leaving 'Abdin Palace at three p.m., would pass through Opera Square before heading for Ar-Rifa'i Mosque. It was rumoured that some balconies with a good view of the palace had been rented out for twelve pounds the afternoon.

Hussein Kamil had died on 9 October 1917, less than three years after acceding to the sultanate. So ill-received on his arrival, the lover of fables and flowers had gradually endeared himself to the Egyptians.

He even managed to pardon the two men who had thrown a bomb at him in Alexandria.

Michel had memorized, like a poem, the heartfelt message from Rushdi Pasha, the prime minister, announcing "the disappearance of a beloved sovereign" and evoking "the tears" that would be sure to flow "both in palaces and in the humblest cottages". One person who wouldn't be shedding any tears, Michel told himself, was envious Victor Lévy! The Jewish boy still hated him as much, but the rest of the class, who had forgotten about the affair, did not follow his lead.

A huge crowd was massed along the route of the procession. Michel and his two escorts failed to get into the front row and couldn't try their luck on the other side of the square because the British soldiers lining the pavements would not allow anyone to cross. One or two crafty individuals had scaled the equestrian statue of Ibrahim Pasha; others were clinging in clusters to the street lights.

A gunshot made the crowd jump, then another, and another. The firing came from 'Abdin Barracks. Michel counted twenty-one seconds between each report, but the Citadel's guns were also firing. The detonations sounded further away and came at longer intervals.

"A hundred and one!" Michel said to Zaki, who could only just count on the fingers of one hand.

He made another attempt to insinuate himself into the front row, but was roughly repulsed. With a heavy heart, he decided to retreat to his father's office, having first informed his bodyguards. The *sufragi* cleared a path to the building with his elbows.

At least twenty people were assembled on the office balcony. Others had stationed themselves at the windows or were waiting inside nursing glasses of beer and discussing the rumours that were circulating in town. Nando's two hundred pounds were ensconced in a big leather armchair. From time to time his laugh rang out with the explosive force of a cistern being flushed. He had every reason to feel cheerful: the war, which showed no signs of ending, was making him more and more money.

Old Élias Batrakani was determined not to miss the funeral in spite of his semi-paralysed legs. The porter, assisted by two other *bawabs*, had carried him up to the third floor in an armchair. Seated in the middle of the balcony, Élias commented on events with all the self-assurance of a retired civil servant from the ministry of public works.

"The sultan suffered from stomach trouble. He regularly took the waters at Châtel-Guyon before the war."

"His first wife's name was 'Ain al-Hayat, wasn't it?"

"Ah, thereby hangs a tale! Imagine, 'Ain al-Hayat was a young orphan girl when Khedive Isma'il took her in . . . "

A mixed court barrister was leaning on the balustrade. "What a crush," he said, gazing down at the crowd with a pensive expression. "Who would have guessed, at the beginning of Hussein Kamil's reign, that all Cairo would mourn his passing?"

"What a crush indeed!" exclaimed Edmond Touta, mopping his brow with his floppy mauve bow tie. "There must be several tens of thousands of people down there. Alarming, isn't it?"

The attention of the balcony's occupants was attracted by an incipient scuffle at the foot of the building. A spectator attempting to cross the square was being detained by a British soldier and several of his comrades, who had come to his aid. The man resisted violently and was struck several times before reappearing with his face covered in blood.

"But it's Zaki!" Georges Batrakani exclaimed.

He turned instinctively to satisfy himself that Michel was safely on the balcony, then inveighed against his roughneck of a coachman and resolved to fire him on the spot. No more coachman, no more carriage: he would better himself in the eyes of his customers and competitors by buying a motor car – a dark blue one, perhaps, since red was reserved for the sultan's vehicles . . .

The band drew nearer. Everyone was eager to catch a glimpse of Fouad, the dead man's half-brother, who had been chosen to succeed him.

"Why Fouad? Why not Kemal ed-Din, the crown prince?" asked Maggi, looking very elegant in a black satin gown.

"The English don't want Kemal ed-Din," the mixed court barrister explained. "Think of it: a man reputed to be pro-Turkish and anti-British! Besides, he refused to succeed his father. 'I've no wish to be an operetta sultan' – that's what he said."

The barrister fell silent as a swelling murmur went up from the crowd: the cortège was approaching. First to be seen were the sultan's mounted lifeguards in their glittering uniforms. Then, carried by marine pallbearers, came the coffin.

"*Sic transit gloria mundi,*" Count Henri Touta said gravely.

Behind the coffin, walking very erect with his paunch well corseted, came Fouad. The contrast between him and gaunt Hussein Kamil could not have been more striking.

Georges Batrakani, chewing a cigar as he leant on the stone balustrade, said jokingly, "Some change of regime – or should I say regimen!"

"To think that Fouad applied for the throne of Albania only three years ago . . . "

"He's up to his eyes in debt. For him, the sultanate is a gift from the gods."

Hussein Kamil's successor, who sported a curly moustache, was surrounded by princes and ulemas. Bringing up the rear, as if to demonstrate the diametrical difference between protocol and the reality of power, came the British high commissioner and commander-in-chief.

"Hussein was loyal to the British," said someone on the balcony. "He did his utmost to keep the country calm."

"Yes," said the mixed court barrister, "I think he genuinely hoped for an Allied victory. All the more credit to him, considering how attached to Turkey some members of his family remained."

"They say his own daughter fainted on hearing that the Russians had captured Erzerum."

"Hussein was loyal, but he wasn't repaid in kind. The high commissioner left him completely in the dark. This summer, when he was received in audience at Ras at-Tin, all he spoke of was yachting, of the wind that had filled or failed to fill his sails. The sultan almost burst a blood vessel."

"There are some who saw Hussein on the verge of tears these last few months. He swore he had absolutely no idea what the British intended to do with Egypt after the war."

"He even threatened to abdicate if they humiliated him too publicly . . . "

Michel listened, his eyes glued to the cortège as it slowly disappeared from view down Busta Street.

That night he wondered if it wasn't his duty to hate the British.

PART TWO

Post-War Arrivals

I

In her latter years I used to visit Maggi Touta at her hotel in Helwan, near Cairo. Life in that peaceful spa, with its lush vegetation, still adhered to the leisurely pace maintained by its gardeners, carpenters, chair-menders and horse-drawn carriages.

Night was falling, but she made no move to turn on the lights. The song of the cicadas drifted in from the grounds.

Still beautiful despite her wrinkles, my great aunt told me of her youthful love affairs in a strangely disturbing voice, quite heedless of propriety. My adolescent self drank in her forbidden words, trying as best I could to conceal my emotions.

I suspect that she derived a certain sensual pleasure from this. After all, her reminiscences enthralled and held me at her mercy like the recipient of a caress. With half-closed eyes, the retired seductress used me as a pretext for reliving the supreme experiences of a lifetime. Occasionally she would pause in mid sentence and slowly raise a long black cigarette-holder to her lips. At such times the room seemed filled with the cicadas' song.

"In 1919," Maggi told me, "I was a strict follower of Paris fashions, thanks to the women's pages in *Le Journal du Caire*. After the war I wore *décolletés de la Victoire*, dresses cut very low at the back. Whenever we were alone together, Georges would instinctively slip his hand into that low-cut 'V'. His touch made me shiver all over . . . "

Maggi brought her lips close to her brother-in-law's face. "But you've got nothing on underneath," he murmured in surprise and delight. The dress slipped off one shoulder, then the other, to reveal a pair of breasts fit to spell the damnation of every monk in Syria.

Georges ran his fingers over those twin marvels, caressed them and buried his face in them. Then, abruptly, he carried Maggi, now half-naked, to the four-poster bed. Their embraces had all the violence of long pent-up desire. Panting and moaning, the young woman was crushed beneath her lover's body. She wrapped her legs around him, sank her teeth in his shoulder, raked his back with her nails. All at once, she emitted a long groan that robbed Georges of his last defences.

"A little while later," said Maggi, "I was walking round the bedroom, naked except for my necklaces, in search of my gown. Georges told me I was as beautiful as a naiad. You know what a naiad is, *habibi*? When I passed close to the bed, he put out his hand and drew me towards him once more . . . "

Maggi fell silent, and the cicadas sang on. Her cigarette glowed in the darkness, striking a spark from one of her rings. I held my breath, heart pounding, cheeks on fire.

We got on well together.

Maggi Touta was only sixteen when Georges married Yolande in 1903, but she was such a handful that her parents, being rather worried about her, had already started to look around for a husband. Although she attracted suitors in plenty, none of them took her fancy. She always contrived to spoil the interviews conducted at home, going so far as to spill glasses of cordial over the dresses of her potential mothers-in-law.

Maggi was eighteen when a Scotsman from the ministry of health, one John McBurroughs, fell in love with her at a dance and proposed. Unable to endure any more family pressure, she accepted without think-ing and was married off within the year.

The Scot didn't know a word of French or Arabic, and his accent in English was of the broadest. The Toutas found him quite unintelligible.

"What did your husband say?" Alexandre once asked his daughter when the couple were dining *en famille*.

"How should I know?" Maggi replied, and – to her parents' consterna-tion – roared with laughter.

John McBurroughs used to ride out to the Pyramids every week. One Sunday in February 1906, for some unexplained reason, his mare threw him. He landed on stony ground, inflicting multiple injuries on his massive frame, and was close to death by the time they found him.

Maggi mourned his demise without undue sorrow but declined to return to the parental home, claiming to be too attached to the memory of her short-lived spouse to leave the apartment in Qasr al-Nil Street where they had moved in eighteen months before. It was in that chic, three-roomed abode in the very centre of town that Maggi would later try out so many lovers of varying height, build, and nationality.

In 1903, shortly after his marriage, my grandfather landed the agency for two small European pharmaceutical companies. This he owed to his perseverance and the excellent address of his office in Opera Square, a diminutive room with an equally diminutive window overlooking an inner courtyard. On emerging from the courthouse in the evenings, Georges would take a large suitcase and deliver medicines to private customers in person. He also sold to pharmacies. This reminded him a little of his childhood. Haggling was still a universal practice in the 1890s. Whenever someone in the family fell ill, Élias Batrakani would send his son to Medawar, the chemist, two or three times a day, saying, "Go and ask that thief what his best price is."

Georges believed in the power of advertising. Against the advice of Yolande, who thought him wildly improvident, he borrowed twenty Egyptian pounds from his brother Nando and bought space in *Les Pyramides*, the French-language daily. There he placed seductive little advertisements extolling the merits of Brown's Pills, which had "effected innumerable cures at every level of society", or of Dr Machard's Dragées, which "restore virility without detriment to any other part of the body".

Sales took off slowly. Georges borrowed another twenty pounds from Nando in order to extend his publicity campaign to two more newspapers and sing the praises of Francis-Joseph's Laxative Water, "which dislodges any obstruction". In the autumn of 1904, by which time he estimated that his income would permit him to live in reasonable comfort, he abandoned his position as a clerk to the mixed courts and doubled the floor space of his office by renting the small room next door. But his desire to succeed was already leading him into other ventures.

The recent Anglo-French agreement had entirely dispelled any worries European financiers may have entertained about the future of Egypt. Capital flowed in, hundreds of millions of shares were issued in Cairo, and property prices boomed. This money-hunt was not confined to the wealthy. People gambled on everything, even the Egyptian Land Bank's premium bonds, which were hawked in the street by the sellers of lottery tickets.

Georges hadn't saved a single piastre, but that didn't prevent him from buying, on credit, a small plot of land on the outskirts of Bulaq. Four months later he sold this for a profit of thirty per cent and promptly acquired another plot twice the size on the same terms. Early the following year he pushed his luck still further by purchasing some land in the morning and selling it the same evening.

It started to dawn on his in-laws that Georges was making money. Henri Touta, Yolande's elder brother, who was living on his private income at the age of twenty-four, came to consult him. He did not regret it: six months later his investments were earning him a hundred per cent interest.

Alexandre Touta himself paid an unheralded visit to his son-in-law's office in Opera Square, ostensibly to impart some advice.

"Take care, *habibi*, don't do anything rash. I want to know where you're putting your money — my daughter's money."

Father Touta departed with several useful tips and tried to make the most of them, but, not possessing Georges' know-how, he often came unstuck. It was one thing to shine as a timber merchant, another to do so as a property speculator.

The financial crisis of 1907 hit Cairo like a bolt from the blue. Within days the banks were refusing all credit and share prices plummeted. Even the price of urban building-land started to fall.

Panic-stricken, Alexandre Touta hurried off to see his son-in-law.

"Take care, *habibi*, don't do anything rash."

But not even Georges knew how to extricate himself. He was encumbered with numerous titles and plots of land purchased with the aid of bank loans obtained at enormous rates of interest. From his point of view, the latest development was an utter disaster.

It took him three long years to clear his debts. Concentrating his efforts once more on pharmaceutical products, he worked very late at the office, which was lit by a single bare bulb.

One night in November 1908, there was a knock at the door. Georges's visitor was a young woman in a black veil: Maggi! She had come, she said, to ask his advice about investing a small sum of money.

They had been covertly eyeing and mentally undressing each other at family gatherings for the previous five years, conversing with the spurious familiarity of a brother- and sister-in-law.

Maggi had scarcely deposited her handbag on a packing case when their lips met. She had nothing on under her dress.

They made love with a ferocity and rapidity that left them both dazed. Then Maggi resumed her veil and departed without a word.

They never spoke of that lightning encounter and avoided each other's eye at family lunches. Georges was haunted by the thought of his infidelity to Yolande, and Maggi herself, who was devoted to her elder sister, felt terribly guilty. As if to obliterate her fall from grace, she took the first lover that came along.

In 1912, having managed to repay his creditors and double his income from pharmaceutical products, Georges bought a handsome house in Shubra. By then Yolande had given him four sons, but he continued to be haunted by the memory of Maggi naked beneath her dress. At lunch on Sundays, he and his sister-in-law exchanged glances of growing intensity.

A few days after the outbreak of war, he rang the bell of her Qasr al-Nil Street apartment.

"I was passing, so I thought I'd look in . . . "

This time their affair went on for several weeks. Then Maggi took another lover – while waiting to resume relations with Georges.

Meantime, each of them was doubly attentive towards Yolande. My grandfather had a great deal of affection and respect for his exemplary wife, who fulfilled her conjugal duties without demur, eyes closed. He took infinite pains to ensure that she knew nothing of his intermittent affair with Maggi.

Life was an odd business, he told himself. Twelve years earlier he had wanted one of the Touta daughters, and heaven had given him both!

2

"It's strange," Georges told Maggi. "It's been blissfully peaceful here all through the war, and as soon as the guns stop firing in Europe the rifles start popping in Egypt."

Overtaken by the curfew one night in March 1919, he had failed to return home to Shubra. No cabby was prepared to drive via Bab al-Hadid, where groups of demonstrators armed with cudgels had broken some shop windows. The police had provoked a veritable massacre by firing into their midst.

Georges did not get home until gone midnight, after a long and hazardous detour via Bulaq. By then Yolande was terrified and in tears. She had already sent Rashid, the *sufragi*, to reconnoitre the deserted streets three times, and three times he had returned with nothing to report.

Rashid, who had encountered his brother Sabri twice since the beginning of the disturbances, knew that he was taking an active part in the popular insurrection. He tried in vain to fathom Sabri's motives, but the two men were worlds apart. Years later, after collecting a number of eye-witness accounts, Sabri's son would write in his book, *An Officer's Career*: "Nothing predestined my father to become a revolutionary — nothing save the poverty and injustice that prevailed in our country and the arrogance of the British."

Ever since the start of the riots Sabri Abu-l-Fath had been hurrying all over Cairo, from Bulaq to 'Ataba, rather than miss a single skirmish or demonstration. One day he would be at Giza, helping to paralyse the tram depot, the next at Bab al-Khalq, bringing the omnibuses to a standstill and unhitching their horses. At night, exhausted and overexcited, he would return to his den in Sayida Zeinab and flop down on a tattered mattress.

Sabri had no time to think of his wife, nor of the six children who had remained in the village. He had hardly set eyes on his youngest, Hassan, whose birth three months ago had added to his debts. Debts? It was better not to think of them. Would his lifetime suffice to pay them off? An *ukka* of beef now cost sixteen piastres as against eight before the war. Mutton, too, had doubled in price, and so had alcohol for spirit stoves. Sabri's meagre wage was far from having kept pace with this alarming rise in prices, and, anyway, he would not be paid because of the strike. But he and his comrades lived on nothing during these tempestuous days, or on what people cared to give them: a few beans for breakfast and at midday more *fuul* and a tomato in a hunk of bread.

Sabri had quit his village in the Delta when war broke out, to work at the Alma cigarette factory. It was a premonitory move. Some weeks later the district was sealed off by British soldiers and the bulk of the fellahin present were declared volunteers and marched away by force, like prisoners, to be enrolled in the Labour Corps. Many of them ended up in loathsome hospitals where they died of typhus.

The village 'umda, or mayor, had actively participated in their recruitment. He began by recommending the wealthiest villagers – the ones who would pay him good money to avoid conscription. The rest he simply listed as a matter of course. It was he whom the British called on in the middle of the war to requisition livestock and organize compulsory collections for the British Red Cross. The cross in the land of the crescent . . . The mayor owned a big house painted pink and had already acquired three wives. Several of the conscripted peasants swore to have his blood, and one morning he was found at the bottom of the canal with his skull stove in.

Sabri and his comrades saw the world in a different light from 23 November 1919 onwards. That was the day on which a delegation or *wafd* led by Sa'ad Zaghloul Pasha had called on the British high commissioner and demanded independence. National independence!

The workers saw this as the remedy for their misfortunes: the British had to be kicked out.

Being an ex-minister, Sa'ad Zaghloul did not put it to Sir Reginald Wingate as discourteously as that. He and his associates were not savages, after all. "Britain is the strongest of the great powers, and the most liberal," the Wafdists explained diplomatically. "In the name of the libertarian principles that guide her, we ask to be her friends." But everyone got the point.

His Majesty's Government responded in March of the following year: Sa'ad Zaghloul and three of his associates were deported to Malta. The next day, Egypt rose in revolt.

Sabri took to the streets in company with several thousand students who had come to demonstrate in his part of town – a surprising encounter between vociferous intellectuals and an illiterate peasant struck dumb with emotion. Five of the students were felled by a burst of machine-gun fire in Sayida Zeinab Square. Sabri bore one off in his arms, severely wounded in the stomach, and laid him down in the lee of a shop with a broken window. Before he died the young man took a handkerchief and moistened it in his blood.

"Here," he muttered, "take this to Sa'ad Zaghloul."

"Stiff with dried blood," recounts the author of *An Officer's Career*, "that handkerchief remained at the bottom of my father's pocket."

A week later Sabri went with several comrades to Opera Square, where they tried to persuade the cabbies to go on strike. They were out of luck. The cabbies, who had no wish to lose the custom they derived from the Sunday races at Gezira, responded with a volley of oaths. The two groups were on the point of coming to blows when an extraordinary procession of carriages and motor cars entered the square: some Egyptian women, the majority veiled and several of them pashas' wives, were parading through the streets in support of independence. The workers gave them an ovation.

But events in Cairo paled beside what happened in the provinces. At Beni Soueif a mob invaded the court and seized the British judge before proceeding to wreck the government offices. At Madinet al-Fayoum, Bedouin attacked the British garrison and inflicted many casualties – four hundred, according to some reports.

On 18 March, when the cabbies and carters of Cairo finally struck, Sabri went to Shubra with a sizeable delegation to encourage other workers to follow their example. They went first to the Alma cigarette factory, then to the Sednaoui furniture factory, and finally to the Batrakani tarboosh factory. At the last port of call, Sabri climbed on a chair and harangued the labour force with particular vehemence: "I know these Batrakanis. My brother Rashid has worked for them for years. Can't you see how they're exploiting you and sucking your blood?"

Batrakani tarbooshes had at last seen the light early in 1919. Initially hampered by the war, Édouard Dhellemmes and my grandfather had found their plans thwarted by the prohibitive rise in manufacturing costs at Lille. This compelled them to fall back on Cairo. Premises of adequate size were available on the outskirts of Shubra, but they had had to equip them, obtain the raw materials, and recruit men capable of adapting themselves to industrial production.

The manufacture of tarbooshes did not seem especially complicated. The woollen material was felted by being churned in a cauldron containing hot water and soap powder. It then went into a mould, had its nap raised with teasels, and was shaved. All that remained was to dye it and give it the requisite appearance. Preliminary experiments indicated, however, that it was difficult to achieve an even finish when shaving and dyeing the felt. As for the product's durability, that could only be ascertained by use.

"We're behindhand enough as it is," Georges told his French partner. "The Italians and Czechs are busy moving into the places left vacant by the Austro-Hungarians, and we must be wary of that little local factory at Kaha. It's improving its products and charging rock-bottom prices at the same time."

So Batrakani tarbooshes were launched on the market without more ado. My grandfather, who was more of a salesman than an industrialist, felt confident that he could combine the advantages of his various competitors. He would produce a tarboosh that was cheap thanks to local labour costs, but lend it an exotic touch with the aid of an equivocal form of words: *"Fabrication à la française"*.

The *Versailles* sold for 400 piastres a dozen, with a discount of up to twenty per cent; the *Marseille* cost 350 piastres, the *Clemenceau* 320.

The Shubra factory had only just gone into full production when the Cairo riots broke out and some ringleaders invaded the premises. Production ceased and the workers walked out, not to return that day. On the morrow they claimed to have been stopped *en route* to the factory. Georges was furious, and he wasn't the only one.

"I'll put this fire out with a blob of spittle!" declared a British official in Cairo.

But the fire continued to spread, and His Majesty's Government grew impatient. Finally, on 24 March 1919, the war hero General Allenby was appointed high commissioner for Egypt and the Sudan, with instructions to restore order. Two weeks later he announced the release of Sa'ad Zaghloul.

Sabri was apprised of the news by a great hubbub that shook the whole of Sayida Zeinab. He raced down the dilapidated stairs of his tenement building, four at a time, and ran out into the street, where he hugged passers-by in a state of euphoria and high excitement. The *fuul* vendor was already capering around his little cart. Taxis sped past filled with uniformed Egyptian soldiers waving flags. Sa'ad Zaghloul's name was shouted, chanted and sung *ad infinitum*.

Next day a vast procession left Bab al-Hadid headed by cadets from the military academy and the chief of police. All Egypt paraded past, from judges of the native courts to Muslim theologians, from Coptic priests to stage actors and employees of the street-watering company. The demonstrators cheered Sultan Fouad as they passed 'Abdin Palace, but did he really deserve their plaudits? That same morning he had swathed himself in the caftan of his ancestor Muhammad Ali – which was too big for him – and solemnly declared, "Whenever I feel the blood of that genius flowing in my veins, I feel myself burn with love for our beloved country." The inhabitants of his beloved country were promptly requested to "desist from demonstrations which have, in certain places, provoked regrettable consequences."

A huge crowd awaited Sa'ad Zaghloul's arrival at Bab al-Hadid station, singing, shouting and fainting in a frenzy of anticipation. Sabri and his comrades waited for several hours. At last, after numerous false alarms, they had to face up to it: their hero would not be coming that night. Sorely disappointed, the demonstrators broke up into groups and dispersed into the neighbouring streets.

Rashid's brother was not far from the Ezbekiyah Gardens when the people around him broke into a run. Instinctively, he followed suit, then heard two shots ring out.

Sprawling on the ground with his cheek against the warm asphalt, Sabri saw the pool of blood beside him steadily expand. He hadn't felt himself fall; now he was watching himself die. A spate of images traversed his mind's eye during the long minute that followed, and among them was that of his son Hassan, three months old, whose face he scarcely knew.

3

"Of course you back them, the beggars!" said Georges Batrakani. "You think it's perfectly in order for them to create havoc, smash shop windows and prevent us from working."

The office staff had gone home a good hour ago. Georges and Makram were sitting there on their own without the lights on. As ever, they would argue in the gloom, by the light of Georges's cigar, while Makram would roll a cigarette and never smoke it. It had been this way ever since they first met at school: in daylight they had nothing to say to each other; once darkness fell, they bickered.

"You think it's all right for them to stop us working and paralyse the national economy."

The Copt did not reply at once. He knew from experience that my grandfather needed to vent his bile. Anything he himself said at this stage would have no effect – indeed, it wouldn't even gain a hearing.

As the firm's accountant, Makram visited the office once a week, which meant on average four arguments a month. He had worn black ties and suits ever since the establishment of the British protectorate in 1914, having sworn to wear mourning until the last British soldier left Egypt. Georges, who attributed this gesture to a fit of ill temper, had found it amusing at first, but time went by and Makram continued to wear black all year round. His former schoolmate had long ceased to notice this sartorial quirk.

"You Syrians can't understand," Makram murmured after two or three minutes' silence, his nose buried in a tin of Matossian tobacco.

"I see, whereas you Copts — "

"Who said anything about Copts? We're Egyptians. No one could be more Egyptian than us."

"Yes, don't tell me. You go back to the pharaohs."

"History is important, Georges."

"Less important than geography, Makram Effendi! You're an island in a Muslim sea."

The Copt shook his head. "There are neither Muslims nor Christians in the nationalist movement, just Egyptians. Haven't you seen all those flags in the streets in the last few weeks — flags bearing the cross and the crescent? A priest from my district actually went and preached in a mosque last Friday."

This year, 1919, Easter had fallen on the same day for Catholic and Orthodox alike, a coincidence that had lent still more impact to the fraternization tours on which Muslim delegations had embarked in the various patriarchates. Makram was delighted by this.

"The Armenian vicar only knew Turkish, so his speech had to be translated, but Monsignor Meletios of the Greek Orthodox spoke excellent Arabic. You Greek Catholics emerged with even greater credit. It seems that Khalil Mutran aroused the visitors' enthusiasm by reciting a poem of his."

"Childish nonsense, the whole business!" Georges exclaimed between two puffs at his cigar. "Dangerous, too!"

The Shubra factory had almost resumed normal production by the beginning of April, and tarbooshes were once more arrayed on the shelves awaiting delivery to big stores or wholesalers. But a whiff of insurrection still hung in the air, and Georges didn't like it. He felt more at ease with ambiguity than disorder. Although he had little liking for the prevailing regime, he thoroughly distrusted those who sought to over-throw it. Being a second-class citizen, he felt personally threatened by change and violence.

"Woe betide those who don't join the nationalist movement," Makram said earnestly. "They risk being left behind."

Georges shrugged. "You must be joking. You really think I'm going to run after the rabble? What for, anyway? Higher wages? No, thank you! Or to 'kick out the British', as you put it? Egypt would be incapable of governing herself! In any case, it's all hot air, all *kalam*. Things are already returning to normal. Playtime is over, Makram Effendi!"

Georges's first encounter with Makram — their first collision — had taken place twenty-nine years before, early one morning in October 1890. The alleyways of Khurunfish had no street lighting at that period, and every pupil went to school carrying his own lantern.

Georges was zigzagging through the gloom, taking care where he put his feet. The satchel propped on his hip weighed at least three tons, and the strap kept slipping. From time to time he hitched it fiercely back into place.

Not a glimmer of moonlight. He could only just make out, fifty yards away, the imposing façade of the school that represented the final and compulsory stage in this blind man's assault course.

"Mind where you're going, you idiot!"

Georges halted abruptly. He had almost bumped into a dim figure of his own height. Concealing his alarm, he answered in the same vein.

"Idiot yourself, *ya fellah!*"

The two boys were standing nose to nose. Each had instinctively raised his lantern for a look at the other's face.

"Out of my way, or I'll squash you the way the British squashed 'Arabi!" said Georges, who had regained his courage.

"I spit on the British!" the unknown boy retorted in Arabic, and aimed a jet of saliva at Georges's feet.

They were on the verge of coming to blows, but flickering lights and muffled voices indicated that other pupils were approaching. They couldn't fight in front of witnesses.

Adjusting their satchels, Georges and Makram walked on in silence, this time side by side. They would settle accounts later on, once more in the dark, because the school opened its doors at six in the morning and did not close them again until seven-thirty at night.

So his name was Makram.

"You're a Copt?" asked Georges, when they met again that night, lanterns in hand.

"Is there a law against it?"

"A schismatic Copt?" Georges persisted.

"You're the schismatics. We're orthodox."

"Would you have the guts to say that in front of Brother Onésime or Brother Philotée-Jean?" Georges said sarcastically.

He had no real wish to pursue this theological duel. Converting Copts was the Brothers' job, not his. One occasionally heard at school that a schismatic had abjured and swelled the ranks of the small Coptic Catholic Church, which was kept at arm's length by the European religious. But, Catholic or not, the convert in question remained a Copt — an ineradicable blemish in the eyes of our Greek Catholic families.

Together, the two boys set off down the dim alleyways of Khurunfish. They had embarked on a dialogue that was destined to continue for sixty-six years.

4

Egypt slowly recovered from the riots of 1919. Being a good civil servant, my great grandfather Élias Batrakani waited until order had been fully restored before departing this world. He gave up the ghost on the very day Sultan Fouad was finally blessed with the male heir for whom he had so long besought heaven. Michel did not fail to juxtapose those two events in his diary.

> *12 February 1920*
>
> *Nonno Élias died yesterday, only a few hours after the birth of Prince Farouq. "One generation ousts another," said Mlle Guyomard, not that anyone had asked her.*
>
> *We went to the cemetery by car. Although the chauffeur's driving has improved a little, Maman kept her eyes shut throughout the trip.*
>
> *Last year Nonno had a very large tombstone of Italian marble erected. The vault is much finer than the Toutas'. It bears only two inscriptions: "Linda Batrakani 1847–1894" and "Élias Batrakani 1841–1920".*
>
> *Sultan Fouad is so happy to have a son at last that he's going to have meat distributed to the poor in the mosques. He has named him Farouq, having called his daughter Fawqiya because the letter "F" brings him good luck.*
>
> *It seems that Farouq has blue eyes. This is not surprising, says Papa, because Sultana Nazli is the great granddaughter of Suleiman Pasha, who was none other than Colonel Joseph Sève, a Frenchman.*
>
> *Guyomard won't admit that Farouq has blue eyes.*

Michel gives the impression of having been less affected by his grandfather's death than by that of Sultan Hussein three years earlier. It is true that Élias Batrakani had been going downhill for some time, and that he was even beginning to lose his wits.

At Alexandria in the summer the former ministry of public works official used to spend whole mornings in one of the Casino San Stefano's reclining chairs, gazing at the horizon.

"When the sea has gone," he would say, "our engineers will construct a railway line linking Egypt with Europe. Will many stations be needed? Simpson favours a non-stop express route . . ."

My great grandfather left behind the memory of a gentle, conciliatory man. The only time he ever really flew off the handle was in 1890, when the prime minster of the day, Riyaz Pasha, proposed to reserve government posts for "genuine Egyptians". This measure was directly aimed at us, the Syrians, and Lord Cromer was compelled to intervene to have it revoked.

"To think that Riyaz himself is a Turk," thundered Élias Batrakani, "and that he succeeded Nubar, an Armenian! Any day now, they'll appoint a Persian or Austro-Hungarian premier who'll come and give us lessons in being Egyptian!"

The fact remains that when he died in 1920, fifty-nine years after settling on the banks of the Nile, Élias was still unable to claim formal Egyptian nationality. We were only "local subjects", even then. The great powers – or "the Impotents", as he used to call them in his rare fits of anger – were still tinkering with the Treaty of Sèvres, one purpose of which was to settle the fate of demi-citizens of our kind.

It was on a Saturday in October 1920 that Georges Batrakani, in a celebrated tirade, appealed to France to shoulder her responsibilities. The Treaty of Sèvres, already signed but not yet ratified, was a source of great anxiety to Syrians newly arrived in Cairo. This did not apply to my grandfather, who, having been born in Egypt, felt only half involved in the debate. Because of his natural tendency to wear several hats at once and exploit every opportunity, however, he wondered whether Egyptianized Syrians like himself could not obtain foreign status under the international regulations then in being.

That night, the French agency was ablaze with light in honour of a

Parisian company playing *Andromaque* at the Cairo Opera. The *kawaases* set the tone at the entrance with their blue uniforms and gold stripes. The heavy windows had been half opened to admit the cool night air. Chandeliers quivered above the heads of the guests, who circulated amid a pleasant clutter of marble mosaics, carved doors, display cabinets, and *mashrabiyas*. Originally done up for the Comte de Saint-Maurice, one of Khedive Isma'il's equerries, this mansion had preserved an air of chaotic opulence rather unsuited to an embassy, but the general atmosphere was charming.

When my grandfather was shown into the first reception room, several actors were clustered around Georges Abyad, considered to be the father of the new Egyptian theatre. A distant cousin of the Toutas and formerly stationmaster at Alexandria, Abyad had trodden the boards with an amateur company before being spotted by Khedive 'Abbas.

"Is it true, monsieur, that you have performed *Othello* in Arabic?" asked a young blond actress.

"Not just *Othello*, mademoiselle! We have also adapted *Oedipus* by Sophocles and Casimir Delavigne's *Louis XI.*"

Henri Gaillard, the new French minister, caught sight of my grandfather standing beside a window. He went over to him, doubtless telling himself that a few minutes with this shrewd Syrian were never wasted. Being a good businessman, Georges Batrakani always had something to impart: inside information, an original remark, a suggestion, a warning — even one of those local *nokat*, or jokes, that were more enlightening than a consular report and fun to come out with oneself at the dinner table.

Previously in Morocco, Henri Gaillard had succeeded Albert Defrance. He knew Egypt through and through, thanks to his knowledge of the Orient and of the Arabic language. He was credited with some rather unorthodox intelligence-gathering methods. My grandfather had once sighted him on the terrace of a café in the Muski, wearing a tarboosh, smoking a hookah, and deep in conversation with some other customers. Short, tubby and rather unprepossessing, the diplomat must have been taken for a Greek or Tunisian shopkeeper. Georges had pretended not to see him. He could not, however, swear that the other man had not caught his eye.

After voicing a few oriental courtesies and some technical observations on the solidity of the window, Georges adroitly steered conversation towards the Treaty of Sèvres.

"I cannot bring myself to believe, *monsieur le ministre*, that France will ratify such a dangerous document."

"R-really?" said Henri Gaillard, who was suspected of stammering to gain time for thought.

He knew perfectly well what Georges was driving at. The Syrians of Egypt were on the spot. They had to choose between two nationalities: that of their country of origin, Syria, which was now a French mandated territory, or that of their adopted country, which had become a British protectorate. They were currently unsure of possessing either. The British occupation and the dismemberment of the Ottoman Empire had rendered their status more indeterminate than ever.

"Under the Treaty of Sèvres," Georges emphasized, "all Syrians resident in Egypt before December 1914 will be considered Egyptians unless they opt for Syrian nationality within twelve months. In that case, however, they will have to return to their country of origin and transfer all their assets there."

"P-precisely."

"But don't you see, *monsieur le ministre*? We're being officially designated Egyptians for the simple reason that we live in Egypt. Those who elect to be Syrians will be granted an absurdly short space of time in which to settle their affairs. The alternatives are clear as daylight: we can leave and ruin ourselves or stay and disavow ourselves."

"Disavow yourselves? Why?" protested Henri Gaillard, who had suddenly lost his stutter. "Until now you were Ottoman subjects more or less assimilated with the Egyptians. You're being offered the chance to become Egyptians proper. What's the problem?"

"The problem, *monsieur le ministre*, is that we have preserved our traditions and our religion – a character in keeping with our education and our history. We're now being asked to burden ourselves with the nationality of a race that isn't our own. Who can guarantee that the future constitution of an independent Egypt will conform to our customs and ideas?"

"In short, you want Syrian or Lebanese nationality."

"Yes, coupled with the right to continue to reside in Egypt."

"But Monsieur Batrakani, why should you be interested in living in Egypt with Syrian or Lebanese nationality?"

My grandfather didn't beat about the bush. Plenty of Syrians wanted to benefit, like the Europeans in Egypt, from the so-called Capitulations, a system that granted them separate courts of justice and exemption from taxes.

"That's impossible, Monsieur Batrakani. The Egyptian authorities would never consent to it. There are several tens of thousands of Syrians in Egypt. Besides, as you know full well, the Capitulations are being more and more strongly contested in principle. The Palestinians and Mesopotamians are in the same position as you, but the British don't claim a similar system for them."

"The British are asses, *monsieur le ministre* — if you'll pardon the expression. Before the war, to preserve their influence, they may have had an interest in preventing the Syrians of Egypt from placing themselves under French protection. It's different today, because they're responsible for protecting all foreign nationals. On the contrary, isn't Great Britain interested in seeing the numbers of foreign residents increase as a pretext for interfering more often in the Egyptian administration?"

The diplomat had to admit, in his heart of hearts, that this argument was valid. At the same time, he could well imagine Batrakani going off to the British high commissioner and assuring him, hand on heart, that Britain could always count on the loyalty of the Syrians of Egypt. They might be naturally drawn to France, but weren't they anglophile from self-interest and necessity?

"If by some mischance the terms of this Sèvres treaty had to be applied as they stand," my grandfather pursued with a great show of indignation, "the consequences would be disastrous. France is the Syrians' natural protector, but they would never forgive her . . . "

Henri Gaillard assumed the mournful expression of a man bereft of speech by some grave malady. Some of Georges Batrakani's arguments had impressed him. With a final stammer, he undertook to convey his remarks to the Quai d'Orsay.

It was not an empty promise. In the archives of the Quai dated 1 November 1920 I found a dispatch from Henri Gaillard to his minister of foreign affairs. He quoted several of my grandfather's arguments and wound up as follows: "The Syrians are our best supporters in Egypt."

The Treaty of Sèvres was never applied, though for reasons that transcended our humble selves, and the controversy over Egyptian nationality dragged on for years to come.

5

Georges was fond of invoking his ancestors, but what exactly did he know about them? The history of the Batrakanis has always been extremely hazy. None of us has ever delved into the archives at Aleppo or Damascus, where traces of our long sojourn in Syria must survive.

I would not say the same of the Toutas, whose roots in Egypt go back to the eighteenth century, and about whom we have learnt a great deal thanks to Michel's research. My godfather contributed three invaluable pieces on them to *Les Cahiers d'histoire égyptienne*. The first, entitled "Antoun Touta, customs officer at Rosetta", was published in 1948. The other two, "Hanna Touta, Napoleon's mameluke" and "Boutros Touta, a physician in the reign of Muhammad Ali", appeared in a single issue the following year, and many copies of them were reprinted separately. We children read and reread them with as much pleasure as we derived from the novels of the Comtesse de Ségur, even though the meaning of certain words completely escaped us.

Resident in Aleppo during the seventeenth century, the Toutas were big merchants who imported silk from Persia for sale to European dealers. The hazards of history – and zealous proselytism on the part of Jesuits or Franciscans – had swung these Greek Orthodox Christians towards Rome. Their knowledge of French, and sometimes of another foreign language, put them in the position of privileged intermediaries. Although France offered them a certain measure of protection, the local potentates, who had nothing to fear from such second-class citizens, happily entrusted them with important posts.

In 1690 or thereabouts, some of the Touta clan packed their bags and went off to Sidon in the north of Palestine — a strange move, or so it seemed, on the part of such prosperous, long-established Aleppans. In fact, they were only responding to a shift in the commercial fulcrum: from now on, silk and cotton would be produced and traded in on the coast. This new Eldorado attracted not only Aleppans but Damascenes and farmers from Mount Lebanon.

Did our ancestor Antoun Touta live in Sidon, or did he belong to the branch of the family that remained in Aleppo? Impossible to tell. The only certainty is that this club-footed merchant was the first of the Toutas to leave Syria in 1740 and settle at Damietta, in Egypt.

He was not an expatriate in the true sense, Michel explains, since Egypt and Syria both formed part of the Ottoman Empire. Damietta was readily accessible from Sidon or Beirut, Tyre or Acre, because it then maintained the closest commercial links with the Syrian coast.

It was also, at the time, a thriving seaport — the foremost in Egypt. Hundreds of Greek Catholics had gone there in quest of fame and fortune — and, no doubt, of peace, because life in Syria had become intolerable. The Greek Orthodox hierarchy had been persecuting them in the most abominable way since their Church had officially sided with the Pope.

Damietta was a paradise in comparison. A small Maronite community had been resident there for a considerable time, as had some Franciscans, who carried on their missionary work under the aegis of the European powers. The Greek Catholics from Syria arrived without any clergy of their own, so they shared Damietta's only church with the Maronites and employed the Franciscans to keep their registers of baptisms, marriages and deaths.

Antoun Touta had certain contacts among the French sea captains who came to purchase rice in Egypt. Their vessels put in to Damietta with their holds filled with bolts of cloth and ready-made garments, which they endeavoured to dispose of secretly on their own behalf. Antoun and other Greek Catholics acquired this merchandise duty-free and sold it at a good profit on the Egyptian market, having skilfully contrived to rid Damietta of its licensed French dealers. They also traded with Jedda, via the Red Sea, and with Leghorn, where they had a number of cousins.

When Antoun the Lame arrived in Damietta, Egypt's principal customs houses were still run by Jews. Thirty years later all such posts were held by Greek Catholics. This was the outcome of a struggle for influence on a grand scale – one in which Jews, Greek Catholics and Greek Orthodox had engaged throughout the region.

The key post in Egypt was that of chief customs officer. Its incumbent controlled not only the port of Old Cairo but, through it, all the customs houses in the country. This coveted appointment, which could bring in as much as three hundred thousand gold francs a year, was secured in 1771 by the Greek Catholic Yousef Bitar.

It would seen that our forebear Antoun was on good terms with the new boss of Egypt's customs houses. Although he was never given charge of Damietta, he did obtain the more modest but still lucrative post at Rosetta. Thirty thousand gold francs, not to mention any fringe benefits, were well worth another change of abode.

6

Strangely enough, Michel's diary contains no hint of the cataclysm that overtook the family late in January 1921. He makes no mention of it until some weeks later, when the whole affair was settled. It seems that no one apart from my grandparents got wind of it right away.

At ten o'clock one morning André entered his mother's bedroom, which was hung with pink silk and overlooked the garden.

"Maman," he announced with an air of elation, "I've something very important to tell you!"

Yolande Batrakani, seated at her dressing table, murmured a vague reply as she gazed into the mirror. She was alarmed by the bags that had recently appeared beneath her eyes and was busy masking them with a new Patou face powder.

"I've decided to become a Jesuit."

She didn't flinch.

André smiled. He'd been euphoric ever since his interview with the vice-provincial.

Then he saw her slowly turn, stiff as a Cicurel mannequin pivoting on its turntable. Big tears trickled down her cheeks, moistening the orange-tinted powder she had just applied.

"But why, my darling?" she asked in a breathless, tearful voice. "Why? Don't you love us any more?"

He was dumbfounded.

"Quick, go and tell your father," Yolande went on, fighting back her tears. "Hurry, he'll be leaving for Alexandria any minute."

André descended the stairs like an automaton. He didn't even have to knock on the study door, which was wide open. Georges Batrakani was stowing some files in an overnight case, whistling as he did so.

"Come in, *ya ibni*. You look awful. What's wrong?"

Having begun on that note, the interview promised to end in disaster. André was tempted to invent some excuse and turn tail, but the thought of his mother dissuaded him.

"On the contrary," he said firmly, "everything's fine. I've decided to enter the Society of Jesus."

Georges looked up.

"Is this a joke?"

"No, Papa. It's all been arranged with Father — "

"*I* arrange things around here!" Georges broke in angrily. "You don't think I'm going to let my son — my eldest son! — dress up in a cassock, do you?"

"It's a question of dedicating my life to God, Papa."

"Leave that to other people! Families like ours don't exist to supply the Church with priests, they exist to *run* it. One day, if you succeed in life, you'll join the board of the Greek Catholic Benevolent Society. Meantime, you'll study law."

"But Papa — "

"That's enough. Forget this ridiculous idea — and tell Suleiman to get the car out. My train leaves at eleven thirty-five."

Having informed the chauffeur, André went back upstairs to see the mother whose reaction had dismayed him so much. Yolande was still at her dressing table, repairing the ravages wrought by her recent fit of crying. Not wanting to distress her further, André gave her a little wave in the mirror and walked out again.

He had always been afraid of his father. For some days now, however, he had felt capable of standing up to anyone. It was all settled: he was going to be a Jesuit. All that remained was to win his mother over and obtain the paternal consent for which the vice-provincial hoped.

He needed the backing of a third party, but which one? Nando? Maggi? Henri Touta? All would find their nephew's arguments incomprehensible. The parish priest? Georges Batrakani cherished a lofty disdain for Greek Catholic priests, whom he accused of being ignorant and idle, if not downright dishonest. Sponsorship of that kind might well prove disastrous.

Why not the patriarch himself? He was a friend of the Touta family and, in Georges Batrakani's eyes, an embodiment of power.

André bent to kiss the patriarchal ring.

"A pleasure to see you, *habibi*. How are papa and maman?"

It was common practice among oriental clerics to baby-talk the young. My uncle detested the habit, but he didn't show it. Monsignor Cadi waved him into a gilded armchair. Muttering a polite form of words, André sat down. A fat bluebottle came and landed on his knee.

"I've decided to enter the priesthood, Beatitude."

"What wonderful news! *Mille mabrouks!* How happy papa and maman must be!"

Carried away by the patriarch's melodious voice, André mistakenly failed to strike while the iron was hot.

"I shall write this very day to the superior of the seminary at Jerusalem," the patriarch went on. "They'll welcome you there with open arms."

"But Beatitude, the thing is . . . I want to become a Jesuit."

"A Jesuit? You're mad! Who put such a preposterous idea into your head? Come now, you mustn't desert your Church!"

André had given no thought to this aspect of the matter.

"But I've no intention of leaving our Church," he replied mechanically. "I want to be a Jesuit *and* a Greek Catholic priest."

"There's no such animal! They'll make a Roman out of you."

André stammered a little, then stressed that the Society of Jesus no longer wished to seem a foreign body in the East. He would ask and be granted permission to remain within his rite — or return to it after ordination.

The patriarch, looking profoundly sceptical, shook his head.

"Our Church is in mortal danger of latinization, don't you realize that? In Syria at the beginning of the last century we were sorely persecuted by the Greek Orthodox, may God forgive them! Then we were massacred by the Muslims. Today, it's the western Catholics who are making every effort to reduce our numbers. You youngsters enter French religious colleges. They're good establishments, I don't deny, but the seminarists are made to attend Latin Masses only. They become unused to our splendid liturgy — they become strangers within their own Church."

André didn't dare to interrupt the patriarch, who was steadily working himself up.

"The European missionaries despise us, don't you see? They criticize our liturgy and poke fun at our vestments. We're treated like second-raters. The schismatics notice this, what's more. 'That's what we can expect if we amalgamate with Rome!' — that's what they tell themselves."

The bluebottle was buzzing around Monsignor Cadi's pectoral cross. He shooed it away with a curt gesture before continuing his monologue.

"The Catholic Church possessed a great pope at the turn of the century: Leo XIII, God rest his soul. He, at least, understood us. Unfortunately, his successor Pius X permitted the Orientals to communicate in the Latin rite. What a mistake! What a triumph for the European missionaries! And now you, a Batrakani, one of our very own, propose to go over to the other side and become a Jesuit!"

André's throat was dry. "Beatitude," he said with an effort, "I understand your concern, but I feel sure I shall be able to serve our Church as a Jesuit. You'll see, I promise you . . . "

The bluebottle had landed on the patriarch's sleeve. He shut his eyes for a moment or two. Then he said, in a weary voice, "Act as your conscience dictates, *ya ibni*. May God bless you."

André emerged from the patriarchate with a lighter heart, but he had taken only a few steps when he realized that the purpose of his visit had not even been broached.

21 February 1921

We're not allowed to utter André's name at table. Papa flies off the handle at the very mention of his eldest son. "He's not my son any more; I've written him off," he said the other day, in a deliberately provocative manner. Maman started crying.

The atmosphere at home is becoming unbearable. The Father Rector's phone call achieved nothing: Papa accused him of corrupting a minor. At school I've sensed several boys looking at me oddly.

26 February 1921

Guyomard has done at least one smart thing in her life: yesterday she took André's letter from the postman and gave it straight to Maman, knowing that Papa would have tossed it into the wastepaper basket without even opening it. My brother asks our parents to forgive him for the distress he has caused them, but he isn't going back on his decision.

15 March 1921

The mystery surrounding André's mode of departure from Egypt has been more or less dispelled. It appears that the Fathers provided him with a cassock and a passport. He was on board ship within four hours of leaving Cairo. Even if they'd been notified, the police couldn't have stopped him in time.

Michel was too sensitive not to feel the full impact of the dramatic event that had just disrupted his home. What with his mother's tears and his father's mute fury, he didn't know which way to turn. His nights were haunted by absurd dreams in which André appeared as traitor and victim alternately.

He dreamt that Sultan Hussein was feebly calling for André on his deathbed:

"Ask the Jesuits – ask anyone you like, but find that youngster for me. No one has ever recited La Fontaine to me so beautifully, not even my teacher, Monsieur Jacolet, who taught me forty of his fables."

Zul-Fiqar Pasha, the grand chamberlain, went to the school in person to inquire the name and address of the young prodigy, then came and hammered on the Batrakanis' door. He bumped into André while Mademoiselle Guyomard uttered a series of hysterical cries . . .

7

Early in the autumn of 1922, almost two years after André's clandestine departure, Édouard Dhellemmes visited Cairo with his wife Françoise. A pale-skinned, frozen-faced Flemish woman, Françoise had never before set foot in Africa. She found the air too balmy, the streets too crowded, the Nile too wide, and the food — even at Shepheard's — too spicy.

"Édouard positively insisted on taking me to the Muski this morning," she told my grandmother, who had laid on a spread in her honour. "The stench was utterly unendurable."

Mademoiselle Guyomard gave an approving nod. She herself would never have been rash enough to mingle with the Arabs of the Muski.

Françoise Dhellemmes might have been burlesquing herself the whole time. She voiced persistent disenchantment and strove to contradict everything her husband said.

As for Édouard, whose third visit to Cairo this was, he continued to see Egypt through rose-tinted spectacles. The first time, in May 1916, he had come to reconnoitre; the second time, in January 1919, to set up the tarboosh factory. This third trip had been intended primarily as a sightseeing tour, but his wife's presence largely spoilt it. There was no question of their leaving Cairo; it was all Édouard could do to get Françoise as far as the Great Pyramid, which she barely glanced at, nor would she even consider a trip to my grandfather's estate in the Delta along roads unsuited to motor vehicles.

"We'll go next time, when you're alone," Georges muttered to Édouard. "Try to come during the cotton harvest."

To make matters worse, Cairo had been afflicted with gusts of *khamsin* since the previous day. The hot, dry desert wind was laden with fine grains of sand that found their way through the smallest crevice, blotting out the sky and making breathing difficult.

"*Khamsin* means fifty in Arabic," Yolande said knowledgeably, in an attempt to strike up a conversation with Françoise.

"Why fifty?"

"Because it lasts for fifty days," hazarded my grandmother, who had never asked herself that question.

"No, no," Georges cut in. "It never lasts for longer than three or four days at a time. It's called *khamsin* because it blows at fifty kilometres an hour."

"Not a bit of it!" protested Henri Touta. "*Errare humanum est!* The *khamsin* owes its name to the fact that fifty per cent of it is sand."

"Fifty per cent? But that's an exorbitant rate of interest, *ya Comte*," remarked Nando, breaking into an interminable peal of laughter.

Startled, Françoise Dhellemmes watched his monstrous two hundredweight of flesh out of the corner of her eye as he brayed with mirth, making the glasses ring.

Two more explanations of the origin of the *khamsin* were advanced with similar assurance. Conversation became livelier and voices rose in pitch. Édouard Dhellemmes wondered how people so precise in matters of business could be so vague about their everyday surroundings. He himself had read a definition of the *khamsin* in Baedeker's Guide, his bible. This stated that it often occurred during the fifty days that spanned the equinox, and wasn't the autumnal equinox only three weeks away? He cursed himself for not having timed his visit differently.

Rashid the *sufragi* was waiting patiently behind Françoise Dhellemmes with the tureen in his hands.

"Won't you have some more *kubeiba*?" asked Yolande.

"No, thank you," the Frenchwoman replied stiffly. It infuriated her to see that her husband had already helped himself to another plateful of unidentifiable meatballs floating in rather sour white sauce and was avidly inhaling their aroma.

Three of my uncles — Michel, Paul, and Alex — were seated with their cousins at one end of the huge table. Little Lola, aged four, had already gone off for a rest with her two dolls, Alsace and Lorraine. As for Viviane, who was only twelve days old, she would make an appearance when lunch was over.

Georges, frowning, uttered periodic injunctions to Alex to sit up straight, whereupon Yolande would whisper something in the ear of her fourth and, reputedly, favourite eleven-year-old son, whom she had placed on her left. But a minute later Alex would be fidgeting again as if nothing had been said. Not even the Jesuits could make him behave, every form of punishment notwithstanding.

Françoise Dhellemmes, who was seated opposite Edmond Touta, cast an occasional glance at his unkempt hair and floppy mauve bow tie. He chewed his meat in silence, looking thoroughly abstracted. Then, just when she least expected it, he addressed her with feverish intensity:

"Did you know, madame, that Egypt now has thirteen million inhabitants? Four times as many as there were in the time of Bonaparte! Alarming, isn't it?"

Edmond Touta mopped his brow with his napkin as if personally stifled by this mass of humanity. Then, with a faraway look in his eye, he reimmersed himself in his thoughts. Françoise came to the conclusion that all these orientals were cracked.

Between *kubeiba* and *kunafa* conversation turned to tarbooshes. The factory was still losing money after three years in operation, having failed to wrest a substantial share of the market from the Italian and Czechoslovak manufacturers who had gained a decisive lead just after the war. Georges, who was barely managing to sell seven thousand tarbooshes a year, realized that it was not enough to drop his prices and charm the buyers of big stores like Cicurel, Orosdi-Back, or Sednaoui. The quality of his products was at fault: Batrakani tarbooshes were not colour-fast and the felt tended to fray. Several retailers in Cairo and Alexandria had complained of this, obliging him to replace their defective batches free of charge.

"I told you Egypt was no place for industry," my grandfather would tell Édouard Dhellemmes during his spells of discouragement, but that did not prevent him from agitating for protectionist measures in company with a small association of industrialists that had recently been formed in Cairo.

Mademoiselle Guyomard discreetly left the dining room when the *kunafa* was served, to reappear a few minutes later with a coffee-coloured doll in her arms. There was a chorus of admiring cries. Even Françoise Dhellemmes broke her silence and emitted a series of appropriate miaows. Viviane had green eyes . . .

Madame Rathl had been summoned twelve days earlier by Maggi, who had just witnessed her sister's first labour pains. It was eight o'clock at night, and the *daaya*, who was just going out, arrived in an evening gown. She removed her bracelets, donned an apron, asked for some hot water, and set to work at once.

Madame Rathl had played midwife to the whole of Shubra for years. A veritable walking newspaper, she brought tidings of births in other families, of pregnancies gone wrong, of those that could lactate and those that couldn't. She also purveyed a certain amount of non-gynecological tittle-tattle, but no one disputed her competence as a midwife. This she had acquired while working with her aunt, the celebrated Om Yousef, whom she had succeeded in 1912.

The child was presenting well. While disengaging its head the *daaya* directed a continuous flow of Arabic at Yolande, whose groans were growing steadily louder: "Go on, my dear . . . And again, my pet . . . Yes, that's it, that's it!"

Madame Rathl extricated the baby at last. Maggi, who saw her face fall abruptly because it was a girl, congratulated her sister in a falsely exuberant tone.

"*Mabrouk*, my dear," she said, "you've got a regular princess there!"

With a grimace, Madame Rathl removed her apron and washed her hands. For a girl parents paid her the standard fee; for a boy they showered her with gifts.

"Poor Georges," Yolande said at length, with tears in her eyes.

She had given her husband three boys without drawing breath, then a fourth, Charles, who had been carried off in infancy by pleurisy. Alex had arrived after a long interval. Lola, who turned up several years later, Georges had regarded as a pleasant quirk of nature. But to present him with another daughter when the Jesuits had just robbed him of his eldest son . . .

Maggi bravely left the room and went off to acquaint her brother-in-law with the sad news. She knew him too well to beat about the bush.

"It's a girl, Georges. Yola is doing fine."

He turned pale and walked off without a word.

Another hour went by before my grandfather visited his wife. He handed her a jewel case containing a cameo ring purchased two days earlier from the jeweller in Opera Square. Then, with only a vague glance and a wry smile at the baby, he went off and closeted himself in his study until dinner time.

Georges Batrakani did not set foot in his office or the factory for three days. Maggi expressed surprise at this.

"Another girl!" he snapped. "What does that make me look like in front of my staff?"

Françoise Dhellemmes redoubled her miaows. Mademoiselle Guyomard had just made a third circuit of the table with Viviane in her arms.

"Yes, yes, that'll do, you can put her back in her cot," Georges said irritably. "No need to make an exhibition of her."

That Sunday lunch with the Dhellemmes is described in some detail in Michel's diary. We learn, among other things, that Maggi Touta laughed uproariously at all Édouard's jokes, which must have added to his wife's annoyance.

Michel had just started his first year at university, where he was reading literature and history. Gaunt, semi-vegetarian, and engrossed in his books, he was the despair of his uncle Nando. He could occasionally be seen at his father's office in Opera Square, but only on sentimental visits unconnected with the activities that went on there. My godfather spent most of his time on the balcony, daydreaming. On returning home he would dabble at poetry or fill a page of his diary.

The following few lines, dated 1 March 1922, are reproduced from the second volume:

Egypt has been independent since this morning. Sultan Fouad has assumed the title king and the British have formally guaranteed that his son Farouq will succeed him in due course. There is talk of replacing the red flag with a green one, which will likewise bear three white stars and a white crescent.

Papa, who has been in a rather better mood for some time, comments sarcastically on the changes that have taken place. At table yesterday he said, "Over the past century Egypt has had viceroys, then khedives, then a sultan, then a sultan transformed into a king. All we need now, while waiting for a pharaoh, is an emperor. Nothing changes, though: it's still the British who rule the country."

PART THREE

The Basilica at Heliopolis

I

I have said nothing so far about my father's family, doubtless because there's less to tell. The Yareds have never produced a Michel whose historian's temperament might have prompted him to take an interest in our genealogy. In any case, would he have gleaned anything?

Mima, my paternal grandmother, was an orphan whom the Dames du Bon Pasteur at Shubra took in at the age of eight. The French nuns did their best to teach her good manners and devout habits, but the pretty little savage – she was said, even then, to be "lovely as the moon" – seemed unmanageable. Her wild dashes along the convent corridors and her crystalline laugh were at odds with that world of wax polish, veils, and whispers.

She did at least learn good French. At sixteen, her superb figure and quick wit turned the heads of the few men who happened to cross her path in Shubra.

Mima fell – literally – into Khalid Yared's arms on Palm Sunday 1914. Having tripped over a step in the porch of St Mark's church, she was caught by an athletic young man in a white suit. He smiled; she blushed and apologized. According to family legend, Khalil gazed at her for three long seconds. Then:

"How about getting married on the sixth of September? It's a Sunday."

Mima was still madly in love with her hurricane of a husband ten years later, and he returned her love in full. In public they devoured each other with their eyes, surreptitiously held hands, and brushed against each other with mysterious little laughs. Whenever Khalil came back from a trip to the country they would lock their bedroom door and not emerge until two days later, worn out with lovemaking but blissfully happy. The two maidservants looked after their children in the interim.

Twenty-six at the time of his marriage, my paternal grandfather was the son of a humble cloth merchant who went from door to door with his bundle on his shoulder. He had been launched into existence without money or education, but with a fierce appetite for life.

A small-time builder, Khalil Yared nearly lost his shirt during the slump of 1907. He doubtless owed his recovery to providence. Or to his resilience. Or to his remarkable ability to get on with people and charm them on the spot with his good humour and aura of unfailing good health.

This was what had endeared Khalil to Habib Ayrout, a Greek Catholic civil engineer who was Baron Édouard Empain's favourite building contractor. In 1912, thanks to Ayrout, he landed a contract for the construction of eight small apartments in Heliopolis. Other projects followed, because the new town continued to rise from the sand.

In the early years of the century Baron Empain had invited a celebrated architect to ride out into the desert with him. Not far from the old road to Suez they ascended a small plateau with a dry wind blowing across it.

"I plan to build a town here," the Belgian industrialist announced with an air of determination that impressed his companion. "It will be called Heliopolis, or City of the Sun. I shall begin by erecting a palace – an enormous palace . . . "

In 1905 Baron Empain purchased six thousand feddans of desert on the arid plateau. Everyone called him insane. How many people would want to exile themselves ten kilometres north-east of Cairo for the sake of clean air and low rents? Would an electric train linking Heliopolis with the capital be sufficient to attract the crowds?

Ignoring the shrugs and sneers, Empain invested on an immense scale. Building materials and topsoil were imported on donkey- or camelback. An army of European architects, town planners, civil engineers and inspectors quartered the desert, charged with creating a unique garden city and model town, a marriage between East and West.

The Heliopolis Oases Company functioned like a municipality. It provided policing and street-cleaning services, maintained brickworks of its own, and was itself responsible for supplying contractors with building materials. Contractors had to adhere strictly to plans worked out in every detail and were heavily penalized if they failed to meet a deadline.

Khalil had adapted himself perfectly to these constraints. He ruled his workforce — labourers recruited for a few piastres and subject to instant dismissal — with a rod of iron. His bank account looked more presentable year by year.

"You wait, my dove," he told Mima, holding her close. "I'm going to build you a splendid villa within a stone's throw of the basilica."

By 1912, when Khalil Yared appeared on the scene, the town already numbered a thousand inhabitants and the finishing touches were being put to a white basilica: a scaled-down replica of the Church of Hagia Sophia in Constantinople — a basilica in the heart of a Muslim city! No one seemed surprised.

The Heliopolis Palace was already the talk of the town, with its giant elevators, its billiard rooms and Turkish baths, and the panoramic terrace that afforded a distant view of the Pyramids. The racecourse attracted Cairene racegoers every Sunday, and the funfair could claim to be the biggest in the Middle East.

Everything was outsize, in fact, and this applied first and foremost to the width of the streets: over thirty metres in the case of 'Abbas Boulevard, which was flanked by arcades, and at least twice that for the Avenue of the Palaces, which was dominated by a startling edifice of Indian appearance. Seven arterial roads converged on Basilica Square. As for the surrounding desert, it was being eaten away on all sides by luxuriant vegetation: hibiscus, jacaranda and casarina bordering the streets and honeysuckle, nasturtiums and bougainvillea climbing the low walls.

Khalil had developed a passion for this pale yellow town (its colour was prescribed by the Company), which derived from no architectural textbook and adhered to no accepted style. European buildings were juxtaposed with all kinds of oriental features: minarets, domes, *mashrabiyas* incongruously located on balconies. The purists squawked, Khalil exulted.

Three or four times a week he would take the new electric train from Limoun Bridge and go to inspect his building site, but after an hour or so he would leave a foreman in charge and set off in a westerly direction. A small sand-dune served him as an observation post. There, with his shoes coated in dust and his head seething with innumerable plans, my grandfather would cast loving glances at the adolescent oasis where he would some day site his dream house.

Not for him one of the Company's standard models. He intended to build himself a villa to his own far superior design. The plans were almost complete.

"Just you wait, my lovely one," he told Mima. "We'll have a majestic bedroom fit to turn all the Sakakinis and Taklas green with envy!"

In August of every year Khalil took his family to Ras al-Barr, where he also had a building site. The idea of doing business on holiday appealed to him. As he saw it, work and leisure went together like marriage and pleasure.

"What I like about Ras al-Barr," he explained to Mima, "is the way we tear the whole place down and start again from scratch every year."

Sandwiched between the Nile and the Mediterranean, part of the peninsula was covered by the waves for several months each year, so the resort had to be dismantled in October and rebuilt the following May.

The huts were regular houses on piles, with floors, steps and balconies. Each was built to the tenant's requirements, and each had a bathing hut on the beach. For twenty pounds the season, one acquired comfortable accommodation complete with everything save linen and silver, which were brought from home.

The six rows of huts were separated by wide streets illuminated at night. The hotels, the casino, the sporting club and the government pharmacy were situated in Nile Street. The second row contained the cafés and the post and telegraph offices. Behind that came the market, and behind that again the residential quarter. Drinking water came by barge from Damietta, but from August onwards, when the barrage at Faraskour was opened, the sea retreated and the Nile regained its sweetness. Water was then drawn on the spot, filtered in *zirs*, and boiled as an additional precaution.

At Ras al-Barr the children frolicked all day long amid rocks, sand, and pebbles. Khalil went for walks barefoot in a striped *galabiya* and a broad-brimmed straw hat. Mima found this get-up amusing, but she preferred the black bathing costume that clung to his athletic torso.

At night he would don a white suit and take his wife and a whole party of friends to the Hôtel Marine, where the band played lively quadrilles. Several dozen couples would follow the various figures Khalil called out in a singsong voice:

"Four steps forward . . . Bow . . . Change partners . . . "

From the quadrille they proceeded to the Boston, and from the Boston to the Double Boston . . .

On 15 November 1924 Mima was in Cairo, waiting for her husband to return from setting up a new construction project at Ras al-Barr with one of his brothers. It would soon be midnight, and still he didn't come. Mima was growing impatient. Late that afternoon she had entrusted the children to their nurses and arranged some menus and outings for the next two days — days of lovemaking and laughter.

Fathiya would bring the couple their breakfast in bed after fetching the milk from downstairs. The goatherd used to emerge from the depths of Faggaala, carrying beneath his arm the little stuffed and mummified calf that accompanied him everywhere. His goats followed behind, filling the street with their bleating, and were milked in the middle of the roadway. The simpering maidservant would hold out her saucepan to be filled, then hurry upstairs to the apartment, where she boiled the milk on a hissing primus stove and carefully skimmed off the cream. Half of this *ishta* was destined for the children, the other half for the *khawaga* whose naked torso Fathiya hardly dared to look at when she entered the bedroom.

It was half-past midnight. Too sleepy to stay up any longer, Mima decided to wait for Khalil in bed. She was bound to doze off, but never mind. In any case, she loved being awakened by his caresses. He had been gone three days, and she was starting to miss him terribly.

She awoke with a start, roused by Fathiya's cries and the sound of her hammering on the door. The bedroom was already bathed in sunlight — it had to be eight a.m. at least.

The two maidservants, with contorted faces and bulging eyes, were symbolically tearing their hair. When Khalil's brother appeared in the doorway behind them, Mima realized that a calamity had occurred.

Khalil Yared had been returning to Cairo by rail with his brother. At Wasta they slowed abruptly with a screech of brakes before running full tilt into a misrouted freight train. The brother escaped with a few bruises; Khalil was hurled against a seat.

"He was killed outright – he didn't suffer," said the brother, hardly venturing to look at Mima.

Seated on the bed with one shoulder bare and tears streaming down her cheeks, she stared out of the window at a kite circling in the sky.

The maids continued to moan and wail. Four-year-old Selim, who had been roused by the noise, sidled into the bedroom. Instinctively, he ran towards his mother. Then, noticing her tears, he stopped short.

2

Édouard Dhellemmes returned to Cairo in October 1924, this time alone and firmly resolved to visit all the places his wife had prevented him from visiting two years before. He was eager to get to know the Egyptian countryside, so Georges Batrakani took him to his properties in the Delta to show him the cotton harvest.

The black, top-heavy Chevrolet lurched at every bump, leaving a cloud of dust in its wake. On either side of the road, fields dotted with little white specks and criss-crossed by narrow canals stretched away to the horizon. A handful of palm trees and some thin screens of poplars could be seen, but not a sign of a hill. "I've never seen flatter countryside," Édouard wrote to his chilly wife, who couldn't have cared less.

"You see, my dear friend," said Georges, chewing his cigar, "everyone here swears by cotton. It's their sole criterion, the measure of wealth and power. Prices may fall – they may even collapse – but it makes no difference: from the biggest landowner to the humblest peasant, everyone wants to plant cotton. They don't know what to do with it any more. This year the government will have to underpin the market yet again by buying hundreds of thousands of *qantars*. It's ridiculous . . . "

A treacherous pothole made him drop his cigar. While brushing away the sparks that had distributed themselves across the sleeve of his jacket, my grandfather curtly ordered the chauffeur to slow down. The car was new, he said, and there was no reason for it to end up in the canal.

"Personally," he went on, "I didn't wait for any government proclamation before sowing some cereals, and I congratulate myself every day. Any idea how much the price of wheat has risen in the last twenty years? Have a guess. Three hundred and fifty per cent! Very nice, no?"

Édouard now visited Cairo every two or three years to take stock of the situation with his partner. They jointly reviewed the market in tarbooshes, but also in lingerie, because Georges Batrakani had since become the Dhellemmes factories' agent for the Middle East.

"In short," Édouard said, chuckling, "you engage in farming, industry and commerce all at once. A perfect combination."

"You're forgetting the stock exchange, my friend!"

Georges did in fact share the predilection of many prosperous Syrians for speculation and gambling. On two occasions he had actually returned from Alexandria with a bagful of coins, his day's profit on several hundred shares — much to the disapproval of his wife, who thought him madly imprudent.

The chauffeur pulled up on the verge to give way to the *'umda*, who was riding towards them on his donkey with a bodyguard following on foot.

"*Salamaat ya hagg!*" Georges called loudly.

The local dignitary, whose obese form overflowed his blue velvet saddle, responded with a polite salutation and a little jerk of his parasol. The barefoot bodyguard, thin as the sycamore branch he was holding, bared all his teeth in a smile.

"The local mayor," Georges explained. "An absolute good-for-nothing. His office exempts him from taxes and military service and permits him to engage in a variety of profitable little deals. He's addressed as *hagg* because he made a pilgrimage to Mecca in 1912 or 1913 — the high-water mark of his existence. Since then he's had the front of his house painted white and adorned with stupid drawings: a boat, a train, some camels . . . "

Édouard Dhellemmes always took the keenest pleasure in his partner's descriptions of Egypt as a caricature of a country, a place where everything seemed tragic and, at the same time, laughable. Georges spoke of it with the experience of a native and the detachment of an outside observer with a foot in each camp. In the eight years since he had known him, Édouard had never really managed to place this Levantine who hovered between two cultures, juggled with three languages, and possessed no well-defined status of his own.

The Egyptians had still to pass their celebrated law on nationality. My grandfather seemed made for this ambiguous situation. Acquiring a nationality, whether Syrian or Lebanese, held no interest for him unless it enabled him to benefit from the Capitulations.

"I'd sooner be a semi-national than a semi-foreigner," he said.

Édouard looked puzzled. "Why a semi-national?"

"Because we'll never be regarded as a hundred per cent Egyptian."

"But that's unfair. When one thinks of all the Syrians have done for Egypt: the press, the theatre . . . "

"No, no, my friend, it's our only hope of survival."

Édouard gave him another look of incomprehension.

"It's like this," Georges explained, chewing his cigar. "We're a race of merchants and middlemen. We've always kept one buttock on each stool – an uncomfortable position at times, but I think we're made that way. All who plump for one stool or the other end by getting badly hurt."

They were nearing their destination at last. It was a vast field in which rows of peasants were working under the watchful gaze of overseers. With their *galabiyas* hitched up to form sacklike receptacles, the harvesters filled these with the balls of cotton they had picked, then regularly emptied them out on to a big mound of the white gold. Meantime, led by a peasant woman in black, they sang softly as they worked.

They fell silent and straightened up, all smiles, when the Chevrolet stopped on a level with them. Moments later, at an order from a *rayis*, the woman resumed her litany and the others went back to work. The overseers came over, one by one, to pay their respects to *Khawaga* Batrakani. His very first question elicited a chorus of eager replies accompanied by emphatic gestures.

"How touching," muttered Édouard.

"They hate us," was Georges's only response, uttered in a low growl.

My grandfather developed this theme in the car on the way home. "Ah no, my friend, they've no love for us. They fear us only because we're powerful. Mind you, I think they feel much the same about their Muslim bosses. They're all smiles and bustle when you're there, but as soon as you turn your back they lose all respect. They're lazy and lethargic and utterly devoid of initiative. It's a process of debasement that's been going on for centuries. With them, it's always *bukara*."

"Meaning?"

"My dear Édouard, there are two words you simply must know if you're to understand this country. The first is *bukara*, which means 'tomorrow'. If someone asks you to return something, you always answer, '*Bukara*'. The second word, which you must have heard a thousand times, is *ma'alish*. It means 'never mind, it doesn't matter'."

"But I'll never pronounce them properly."

"*Ma'alish.*"

"Even so, will you teach me some other words?"

"*Bukara.*"

3

My beloved parents,

I've hurried up to my room to write you these few lines, my heart trembling with joy. Yes, it's done: a few minutes ago I made my vows of poverty, chastity and obedience. Here I am, enlisted for ever in the army of Jesus Christ. Pray for me, dear parents, so that I may draw nearer to sanctity.

The ceremony, which was wonderfully fervent, took place under the gentle gaze of the Virgin Mary. I was given the biretta and square cap of the scholastics. After Mass everyone embraced, and I thought of you, Papa and Maman, who had surely accompanied me with your prayers.

I now begin a new life in which only Latin will be spoken. The language of Virgil has never been my strong point, as you know, but I must equip myself to enter the service of the Great Friend!

Revered parents, may Our Lord Jesus Christ reveal Himself to you in all His beauty and goodness. May you be blessed and happy, and may the poor around you sense it because of your charitable acts.

Your

André, S.J.

PS. Did Alex receive my card dated 25 March? I've had no word from him.

Georges Batrakani sometimes found it difficult to come to terms with his eldest son's tone. André's letters annoyed and disconcerted him with their outpourings of affection. For quite a while he hadn't even wanted to open them.

"Here, a letter from André," he would say, handing the envelope to Yolande unopened.

As if she were the sole addressee! As if André didn't mean his letters to be read by his father most of all . . .

After sulking for several months, Georges had finally deigned to utter his son's name. He did not, however, go so far as to communicate with him. It was Yolande who kept in touch.

André had forced my grandfather's hand two-and-a-half years earlier, a thing that very rarely happened to him in business. With characteristic realism Georges decided to admit defeat, at least for the moment, telling himself that there was still time to bring his misguided son down to earth. But the letter of 8 June 1924 made him fear that a point of no return had been passed. He would probably have to resign himself to seeing André – an intelligent youngster notwithstanding – progress from the noviciate to the juvenate and other absurdities. In other words, he would have to write him off.

For the two years following André's departure, Georges Batrakani concentrated his wrath on Alex, his youngest son. An artful and courageous boy, Alex seemed admirably equipped for a career in business, but first he would have to learn to do his sums. After several warnings the Jesuits sent him home for "disobedience, irreligion, and habitual laziness".

"They wash their hands of one boy after kidnapping the other!" was my grandfather's furious verdict.

Alex now collected his zeros from the Brothers of the Écoles Chrétiennes at Zaher.

"You've spoilt him," Georges kept telling his wife.

André's letters continued to ask news of Alex, whose state of mind worried him.

"You should write to your eldest brother," Yolande told her youngest son in a plaintive voice.

"You really think he needs my advice?" Alex retorted gaily, planting a kiss on her brow.

* * *

Georges Batrakani's consolation might possibly have been Michel, his second son, who had enrolled at Cairo's French law school in 1923. Within six months, however, Michel withdrew, confined to bed with violent headaches and a high temperature. Dr Dabbas, who was called in, sensibly opined that his course of study didn't suit him. Georges himself had already grasped that Michel, a sensitive young man with a penchant for poetry, would never make a lawyer or sell a single crate of patent medicines, so he didn't press the matter. My godfather recovered and was able to start studying for an arts degree the following year.

Happily, there was still Paul. Having passed his *baccalauréat* with flying colours, he likewise – but enthusiastically – entered the French law school, that ideal route to a business career on which his father would so much have liked to embark a quarter of a century earlier.

"Messieurs, you live in a legal Tower of Babel," they were told at the very outset by their lecturer in civil law, an elderly Toulousain with pince-nez and a goatee.

Paul, who was carefully taking notes, resolved to pass this dictum on to his father.

"Egypt has four judicial systems, not one," the lecturer went on. "There are the religious courts, the native courts, the consular courts . . . "

Paul scribbled away feverishly. A slim, elegant, ambitious young man, he would gladly have become an assize court barrister, but criminal cases – the only ones that attracted the limelight – came within the orbit either of the consular courts, which were closed to him, or of the native courts, in which he had no desire to set foot.

"As for the fourth category, gentlemen, you're all familiar with it: the mixed courts."

Like most of his fellow students, Paul was destined for the mixed courts, where hearings were conducted exclusively in French. Founded in 1875, this prestigious institution was competent to handle all civil or commercial litigation between foreigners of different nationalities, or between foreigners and Egyptians. But the latter were eager to have their disputes settled in the mixed courts, being convinced that they would be far better defended there than in the native courts.

"You will note, gentlemen, that a 'mixed interest' can be readily invented. Every limited company is already subject to this first-class judicial system by definition, because one of its shareholders may be a foreigner. As for creditors in possession of bills signed by natives, they contrive to endorse them in favour of an obliging European and thus escape local justice."

Georges Batrakani himself took advantage of this device.

"Egypt is indeed a legal Tower of Babel," he told his son. "However, I trust your teacher realizes the great merits of the present system. I won't give much for our chances the day some idiot takes it into his head to tinker with it."

4

My grandfather had entered the mixed courts by the tradesmen's entrance. Although unglamorous, his clerk's job had at least enabled him to observe, at close quarters, the workings of an amazing institution in which Europeans played the leading roles and senior Egyptian magistrates were merely extras.

At that time, Cairo's high court was still housed in one of the khedivial family's former palaces in 'Ataba al-Khadra Square. It was a positive ruin. Although the ceilings still bore traces of gilding, the tattered curtains harboured nests of vermin. Whole slabs of plaster kept falling off the walls of the barristers' changing room, and the records office was so cramped that its staff had had to annex a courtroom.

Georges and his youthful colleagues, all bachelors like himself, regularly frequented the Ezbekiyah Gardens. Enclosed by high railings, this thirty-acre paradise was inaccessible to the lower classes because it cost a piastre to get in. The justices' clerks knew every inch of its pathways, which were flanked by baobabs, papayas, and sycamores. At sunset they would often traverse the ornamental lake by canoe or pedalo, dodging the swans and ogling some beauty on the terrace at Santi's.

I hardly dare speak of the Ezbekiyah when I think of what remains of it today. The gardens still preserved some vestiges of their beauty during my childhood in the 1950s, but nothing compared to my grandfather's fantastic descriptions of them.

It was at the Ezbekiyah that Georges would meet his friend Makram, the Copt, to exchange barbed remarks. The dimly lit paths formed a perfect venue for their jousts, many of which related to the press.

"If it weren't for the Syrians," said Georges, "Egypt wouldn't have any newspapers worthy of the name."

Most of the leading dailies — *Al-Ahram, Al-Muqattam, Al-Muqtataf* — were owned by Syrians. Founded not long before, these papers had transformed the Arabic language in Egypt. Gone was the rhetoric, the aesthetic, exhilarating, complacent style of writing: Christian intellectuals from Beirut or Damascus had introduced a lively modern idiom that took the public by storm.

One evening in August 1901, as they were strolling down one of the Ezbekiyah's gloomy paths, Georges invited Makram to explain why he and some other militant nationalists had smashed *Al-Muqattam*'s windows.

The Copt puffed nervously at his cigarette. Thin as a rake, he seemed to live on tobacco smoke.

"*Al-Muqattam* is a traitors' newspaper financed by the British. We wanted to show that the Egyptian people are opposed to traitors, especially when they're outsiders."

"Outsiders? Don't tell me you're starting *that* again! Even your beloved Moustafa Kemal has contributed to *Al-Ahram*."

"I don't claim that all Syrians are traitors, but we refuse to tolerate the ones who spit on Egypt after making their fortunes here."

Makram's accusation was equivocal nonetheless. Even if not all Syrians were traitors, all were outsiders.

Their verbal duel was interrupted by the Belvedere's illuminations. They leant on the balustrade and looked down at the cascade breaking amid the papyrus below them. Two thousand five hundred gas jets — another of Khedive Isma'il's whims — formed a ring of fire around the lake.

Georges took good care not to tell Makram what Colonel Simpson had said to his father some weeks earlier: "In the final analysis, it's because of you Syrians that the British are so unpopular with certain Egyptians. We've appointed you to positions of responsibility, and they haven't forgiven us. Copts and Muslims will take orders from an Englishman, but they can't bear to be supplanted by Levantines . . . "

In the bandstand behind the baobab trees, a military band was bringing its evening programme to an end.

"Even the music is English!" grumbled Makram as they made

their way along the dark path that led to the photography pavilion.

Several members of his family had seen their careers blighted by the British occupation. Coptic accountants had passed on their know-how from generation to generation — esoteric bookkeeping methods that guaranteed them control of government accounts. By introducing more modern systems, the British had changed the rules of the game. A youth like Makram, who would normally have benefited from the expertise of his father and his uncles, was now obliged to sit for an accountant's diploma.

"You're right," said Georges, "English music is unbearable. I much prefer French."

"Very funny," growled Makram.

"Still, you've got to admit the British have restored order in this country."

"But at what a price! Egypt is steadily losing her soul and her sons at the same time. Did you know that three out of every five peasant children die before reaching adulthood?"

"I don't see the connection."

"You never see the connection!"

They were interrupted by some muffled detonations. Almost simultaneously, the sky became a mass of luminous trails: fireworks heralding the Nile festival scheduled for the next morning.

"Let's go home," said Makram. "I have to be up early for the ceremony."

Every year on the appointed day in August, a huge crowd gathered opposite Roda Island in the presence of the khedive. Before the waters were released, a block of clay representing a human figure was thrown into the river. This was the "Nile doll" that took the place of the young virgin sacrificed in bygone days as an aid to irrigation.

At a signal from the khedive, a breach was made in the barrier with mattocks, whereupon scores of men and children dived into the river, artillery fire rent the air, and the Citadel's cannon informed all Cairo that the Nile had attained its customary level.

The annual breaching of the barrier was carried out by Muslims, Copts and Jews in turn. It was the Copts' turn in 1901, but that wasn't Makram's reason for wanting to go to Roda: he was simply eager to see, in the midst of his people, the young Khedive 'Abbas whose hatred of the British he shared.

"I'm sorry I wasn't there the other day," he said. "Some youthful enthusiasts unhitched 'Abbas's horses and hauled his carriage to Sayidna-l-Hussein Mosque themselves."

Georges was staggered. "You, a Christian, would have escorted the khedive to a mosque?"

"Where Egypt is concerned," the Copt replied in a low voice, "I can be a Muslim."

5

To please André, who wanted a detailed account of it, I've had to type out a full description of the "Catholic Family Conference". What a shambles!

Over twelve thousand people gathered at the Collège des Frères in Zaher. I'm told it was the biggest meeting of its kind ever organized in Egypt — indeed, in the whole of the Middle East. The purpose, if I've understood it correctly, was to defend the family, but also to demonstrate the unity of the different rites and the power of the Catholic Church in Egypt.

Nearly five thousand pupils from various colleges and boarding schools turned up under the supervision of their teachers and religious instructors of both sexes. For once, all competition was abolished between Jesuits and Brothers, Sacré-Cœur and Mère de Dieu, Délivrande and Bon Pasteur . . . Passages from the Scriptures relating to the education of children were displayed on big notices nailed to posts or tree trunks. It brought tears to my eyes to hear that huge crowd intoning "We want God" to the accompaniment of the Brothers' brass band, but the conference itself, which went on for a week, was enough to dissuade one from getting married — and give Uncle Edmond apoplexy: Make children, make children . . .

Michel had sent André some extracts from the most notable address, which was delivered by a certain Counsellor Midan (probably a highly placed lawyer in the mixed courts):

"The perpetuation of the species," asserted this distinguished orator, "must not be meanly undertaken, but liberally and abundantly, because death can suddenly swoop on the best-tended cradles. And then, confronted by the sole cradle which the sinister visitor has just emptied, good will may be too slow to revive, and the organism, hitherto worn down by voluntary restraint and sterile pleasure, may no longer summon up the strength to repair the deficiency . . . " After condemning flirtation, "marriage for passion", modern female fashions, modern dances, the abolition of chaperonage, and heaven knows what else, Counsellor Midan wound up: "Under the satanic sign of debauchery glorified in its consummation and in all the incitements and laxities that conduce to it, the world of today resembles – alas! – a gigantic brothel."

I don't know if Counsellor Midan was acquainted with Maggi Touta, but he would certainly have deprecated the trip my great aunt made to Europe the following year – one that would live in her memory for ever.

Bare-breasted and lying on her back, Maggi laughed uproariously as Georges, suiting the action to the word, crooned a song that had just conquered France:

> "*Elle avait de tout petits tétons*
> "*que je tâtais à tâtons . . .*
> "*Valentine, Valentine . . .*"

Visible through the open window was a huge orange sun already half-immersed in the Bay of Cannes. The hotel terrace was a mass of flowers.

Maggi had dreamt for years of this trip to Europe with her brother-in-law, not that she had ever ventured to suggest it because Georges was so anxious to conceal their affair. One day, in spite of all his precautions, he had almost bumped into Michel outside her apartment building in Qasr al-Nil Street.

But now, in the spring of 1926, chance had come to their aid. Maggi had been invited to Lille by the Dhellemmes just when Georges happened to be making a business trip to Paris. Inventing an excuse, she had left her hosts a few days earlier than planned and joined him on the Côte d'Azur.

Georges brushed one of her breasts with his lips. No, hers were no "*petits tétons*" but two splendid, amaranthine areolae whose nipples stood erect at the least caress. At thirty-nine, Maggi Touta was still a superb animal made for love.

She now had her hair cut in the Lapplander style, with the nape of her neck shorn and a fringe in front. Her lips were sometimes red, sometimes violet, sometimes, even, green. This was more than just an adherence to fashion: ever since devouring Victor Margueritte's *La Garçonne*, Maggi had striven to resemble its heroine.

"Poor Édouard Dhellemmes," she said to Georges as she slipped into a daring dress that ended above the knee, "his wife gives him a really hard time."

"I know. The woman's a regular icebox."

"She made a terrible scene after his last trip to Cairo — as if he'd been unfaithful to her with Egypt . . ."

Maggi had treated herself to Édouard at her Qasr al-Nil apartment in May 1916. It was just a passing fancy, and the young man's clumsiness had dissuaded her from pursuing it further. Édouard himself had never sought another assignation with this insatiable tigress, but he was very fond of her and had welcomed her to his bleak abode in Boulevard Vauban with the greatest pleasure.

"Aren't you going to take the opportunity to go to Lyon and see André?" asked Maggi as she refreshed her violet lipstick in the mirror.

"No."

"I'm sure it would give him pleasure."

"No."

"You're wrong, Georges."

"Do you know what the time is? Eight already! We'll get no dinner if we don't hurry up. The French live with a clock in their heads."

As they went downstairs to the terrace, where each table was lit by a Chinese lantern, Georges was thinking not of André but of his wife. He would choose Yolande some jewellery in Place Vendôme. A bottle of perfume, too, and some silk scarves. He would go and buy them with Maggi, who was well acquainted with her sister's tastes.

Maggi herself had several purchases to make in Paris. Her brother Edmond, in particular, had asked her to buy him a special chronometer with a button-operated striking mechanism, for Edmond Touta distrusted Egyptian population statistics. Unable to check the accuracy of the official figures, he carried out some parallel experiments of his own. On the same date every year, the eccentric young man would station himself at one end of Qasr al-Nil Bridge and spend six hours counting the passers-by in each direction. The various calculations to be made during his next experiment called for a very exceptional chronometer sold only, it seemed, by a specialized shop in Boulevard de la Madeleine, Paris.

As for Michel, he had asked his aunt to buy him an illustrated book on pre-war Châtel-Guyon, the spa in which he had been greatly interested since learning that Sultan Hussein used to take the waters there every year.

"He was the opposite of his father," Maggi told me one day, referring to Michel at that period. "He lived with his head in the clouds, and I don't think he cared much for women."

This last assertion, albeit coming from an expert on the subject, should be qualified. The most that can be said is that the third volume of Michel's diary contains not a single reference to the opposite sex. That volume ends in the summer of 1926. Twenty-one at the time, Michel kept his eyes firmly focused on the past.

10 July 1926

I'm filing all I can glean about Hussein Kamil in some big folders. One day I may write a biography of that brilliant sultan whom everyone seems to have forgotten so soon.

Some months before his death the sultan had a presentiment that his son Kemal ed-Din would be unable to succeed him. Consequently, he feared that he would be the grave-digger of Muhammad Ali's dynasty, an idea with which he had become doubly obsessed since the Aga Khan's attempt to mount the throne of Egypt in 1914.

Dr Comanos Pasha assures us in his memoirs that the sultan sent for him discreetly, six months before his death, and asked to be examined. "Swear to me on your Gospel that you'll tell me the truth." Comanos did so. He was then compelled to inform Hussein that his illness was incurable.

Two days later Comanos was summoned by the British high commissioner, Lord Wingate, who requested information about the sovereign's state of health. The good doctor feigned shock, but his protests were swept aside: "You know perfectly well that medical confidentiality doesn't exist in this country." So Comanos divulged all he knew. According to him, the high commissioner buried his head in his hands and began to weep, saying, "What a calamity! In Hussein Kamil, Britain will be losing one of her most loyal and devoted friends. I myself love him like a brother, believe me."

The high commissioner must have been something of an actor — unless Comanos was deliberately embroidering. At all events, the Greek physician was not the only person privy to the sultan's state of health. In 1917 Hussein Kamil employed six other medical consultants including Dr Brossard, whom Papa claims to have been regularly in touch with the French agency.

PART FOUR

The Bey First Class

I

"Sémoditchek" first appeared on the scene in the early 1930s. Georges, who had only just begun to overcome the felting and dyeing problems that had afflicted his tarbooshes, was coming up against some very tough foreign competition. The pre-war market had been monopolized by the Austrians, but it was Czechoslovak firms that were now grabbing most of the cake.

"*Ces maudits Tchèques!*" was my grandfather's invariable exclamation as soon as tarbooshes were mentioned, directly or indirectly, at Sunday lunch. The "confounded Czechs" were much on his mind.

Rashid, the *sufragi*, ended by asking Yolande discreetly, "The *khawaga* often speaks of 'Sémoditchek'. Who is the gentleman in question?"

The word amused the family for weeks. Then it entered the Batrakani vocabulary – in fact Georges ended by adopting it himself. "Sémoditchek has landed another big order at Alexandria," he would say, or, "According to my information, Sémoditchek is launching a new model this autumn."

So as not to be put out of business by this formidable competitor, the house of Batrakani had to keep its prices very low. At the same time, Georges changed tack to take account of the powerful upsurge in nationalism. Early in 1923 his tarbooshes were abruptly Egyptianized. "*Fabrication à la française*" was out from now on; his new models bore the words "Made in Egypt". Their names, too, had changed: the *Versailles* was replaced by the *Malaki*, the *Marseille* by the *Damanhour*, and the *Clemenceau* by the *Biladi*.

But this policy yielded meagre results. The ten thousand tarbooshes Georges just managed to sell in 1925 were barely enough to cover his costs.

Fortunately, he no longer relied on the Shubra factory for his livelihood.

In Turkey that year, Moustafa Kemal embarked on a merciless war against the fez. He began by adding a small peak to his soldiers' headgear, then set off on a tour of the provinces to persuade the population to adopt hats in the Western style. He himself appeared bareheaded, panama hat in hand. "We need to dress in a civilized, cosmopolitan manner," he declared. "The fez has been with us for only a century. It originated in Greece, not Turkey, and has no religious significance."

The peasants nodded politely but didn't believe a word of it. Their religious leaders told them the diametrical opposite: the peak or brim on Western headgear was a sign of Christian impurity, of reluctance to meet the eye of God. Besides, hats with peaks or brims prevented the believer from touching the ground with his forehead, and there was, of course, no question of praying bareheaded.

Unable to convince, Atatürk proceeded to coerce. He decreed that wearing a fez was an attack on the security of the state, and woe betide any citizens who broke the law. The police swooped on them, tore off their felt caps, and trampled them underfoot. Recalcitrant individuals were manhandled and imprisoned. Some actually wound up in front of a firing squad or on the end of a rope.

Georges Batrakani had observed these developments from afar. The fez wasn't his concern. He was having enough trouble manufacturing a tarboosh in the Egyptian style, but still . . . The way in which Atatürk had bloodied its close cousin struck him as a bad omen.

Reactions in the countries of the former Ottoman Empire were mixed. In February 1926, a French-language weekly published in Cairo, *L'Illustration égyptienne*, launched "a sensational inquiry into the tarboosh" and sent out questionnaires to a number of prominent figures. Its theme: "For or against? Which of the two camps will win the battle? That of the moderns, with their mania for hygiene and symbolic gestures, or that of the traditionalists and poets, who are only half willing to sacrifice a secular and more elementary costume?"

"I don't understand a word of this gibberish," was my grandfather's comment when Michel showed him the periodical. "What are they meddling in, the damned nuisances?"

L'Illustration égyptienne proceeded to publish a number of replies, some opposed to the tarboosh, others favourable. Georges pronounced the former outrageous and the latter pathetically feeble.

"I'm going to write to the editors of that rag myself," he fumed. "Not that they'll print my letter."

"Why not meet with them in person?" suggested Michel, who knew one of the amateur journalists concerned.

"They need only knock on my door," Georges retorted grandly, and left his son to set up the interview.

The editors of *L'Illustration égyptienne* were delighted with the idea and kicked themselves for not having thought of it in the first place. My grandfather was called on by the entire editorial board, more precisely, a foursome including the editor-in-chief and the general manager. He received them at his office in Opera Square.

"Monsieur Batrakani, we don't propose to ask if you're for or against the tarboosh — "

"Quite right too," Georges said curtly. "There are no two ways about it."

He paused for effect. Having slowly lit a cigar, he directed three smoke-rings at the ceiling.

"There are no two ways about it, gentlemen, because the the tarboosh is more than a form of headgear. It's an emblem, a symbol. Does anyone dispute the colour of the national flag? There are things one has no right to tamper with."

Georges put on a wonderful act. He set himself up as guardian of the Temple and keeper of its sacred objects. He realized, he said, that there were some in Cairo who thought it bizarre, if not shocking, that the national headdress should be manufactured by a Syrian, and a Christian to boot.

"But the tarboosh isn't our national headdress," one of the journalists objected. "Foreigners wear it too."

"That's stupid! The foreigners you speak of don't wear the tarboosh when they're in London or Paris. They wear it in Egypt because they grasp and appreciate its significance. The tarboosh enables a European to integrate himself in the Orient. Conversely, the European suit can be adopted by an oriental without sacrificing his specific character."

The visitors felt they were becoming bogged down in profundities. They gave up and tried another tack.

"The tarboosh isn't suited to the Egyptian climate," one of them said with a certain touch of spirit. "It makes one perspire, brings on headaches, encourages baldness — "

" – and gives you piles, don't tell me!" Georges cut in.

"Monsieur Batrakani, even you must admit that the tarboosh is torture in summer. People spend the whole time taking it off and mopping their brow."

"So what? If you only knew what it was like in the last century! The old tarboosh was lower and softer than today's, nor did it have a lining. You had to wear a little white skullcap beneath it to prevent the red dye from running and staining your hair and forehead. For another thing, were you aware that the old tarboosh had to be pressed every day? It was the British who introduced the modern tarboosh: being straw-lined, it retains its shape and needs pressing only once a week. *There's* some interesting historical information for you! *There's* the kind of information a leading periodical like yours should publish instead of stirring up bogus controversies."

One of the young men refused to be squashed. He returned to the attack.

"But hasn't the tarboosh become completely unpractical? It used to be enclosed by a turban, which rendered it more stable and lent it a more harmonious appearance. One little jolt, and the modern flowerpot goes rolling along the ground."

"I forbid you to call it a flowerpot — or, for that matter, to distort historical fact. The tarboosh was introduced into Egypt by Ibrahim Pasha early in the last century to replace the turban, which was too heavy and bulky. It was an aid to modernity, my dear sir — mark that word: modernity. At the same time, Ibrahim decreed that the divans in court-rooms should be replaced by chairs and the streets be swept twice a day."

"To return to the subject, Monsieur Batrakani, allow me to ask you a simple question: isn't the European hat more becoming and more practical than the tarboosh?"

Georges looked distressed and shook his head several times.

"If you placed a European hat and a tarboosh on a table side by side, the former might possibly win the day. But put them on your head and you'll notice the difference. The tarboosh is a living thing, gentlemen, an eloquent thing. See how straight it sits on the heads of serious-minded men — the kind that dislike drawing attention to themselves. Stylish people, on the other hand, nearly always wear it at an angle — to right or left, depending on their taste and temperament. But if the tarboosh is tilted backwards, its owner is usually a *bon viveur*."

"What about forwards, Monsieur Batrakani?" one of the young men inquired sarcastically.

"When the tarboosh is tilted forwards," Georges replied, giving him a piercing look, "you can bet you're dealing with a fool or a boor."

The others burst out laughing.

"But you mustn't print that," Georges added. "I've no wish to lose some of my customers."

"And you yourself, Monsieur Batrakani?" said the editor-in-chief. "How do you wear the tarboosh?"

Alive to the journalists' growing interest, Georges came out with his *tour de force*:

"Ah, but I don't wear it; I let myself be worn *by* it — or, rather, by them. Why 'them'? Because, like any self-respecting person, I have at home a whole assortment of tarbooshes in different shades appropriate to every situation — every mood, I should say."

He was still holding forth ten minutes later, wreathed in cigar smoke, while his interviewers feverishly took notes.

"The tarboosh, gentlemen, is as much a part of the Egyptian landscape as the Sphinx or the Pyramids. Have you never seen a beggar, when he runs out of arguments, touch the other man's tarboosh to symbolize that he's brushing off the dust? If I were you, I would write that the tarboosh is a prime necessity. It ought to be subsidized, not taxed."

The interview with Georges Batrakani appeared under a banner headline the following week, as a tailpiece to the inquiry. The same night, each journalist had a *Malaki* of the finest quality delivered to his home, together with instructions on how to keep it in good condition.

2

Among my grandfather's Syrian friends was a senior palace official whom he had known since childhood. The said friend never omitted to lower the window of his car and give him a little wave when the king's cortège drove through Opera Square. On such occasions Georges would stand on the office balcony and respond with a sweeping gesture.

The senior official was kind enough to show the king the interview in *L'Illustration égyptienne*. Fouad, who detested Atatürk's republican whims, approved of Georges Batrakani's reply and decided to reward him: the very next day he made him a bey, first class, "for outstanding services to local industry" and invited him and his wife to a reception at 'Abdin Palace.

The news went round the family like wildfire. The telephone never stopped ringing and congratulatory telegrams poured in. Georges was in the seventh heaven. He revelled in the *"sa'at-al-bey"* with which his chauffeur, servants and employees now addressed him at every opportunity. He had his visiting cards reprinted and the copper plate beside his front door re-engraved. He wrote to various year-books and associations to announce the event. He was a completely different man: henceforward, his name was Georges Bey Batrakani.

"Before, my dear," he told Yolande, "you were only the sister of a Count-my-backside. Now you're the wife of a genuine bey, a bey first class!"

If Henri Touta was jealous of his brother-in-law, he didn't show it. "My dear Georges," he told him amiably at the dinner given in his honour the following Sunday, "*Audaces fortuna juvat!* You're on the right track. How soon do we call you pasha?"

My grandfather thoroughly appreciated this remark. To cover his embarrassment, he recounted one of the stories that had delighted him as a child.

"In January 1863, Saʿid Pasha was sinking fast and would not, according to his doctors, last the winter. His nephew Ismaʿil was awaiting the end with mounting impatience. For fear the throne would elude him, he had promised preferment to the person who first informed him of the viceroy's death: the bearer of the news would be made a bey, or, if he already held that rank, a pasha.

"After being operated on for a tumour, Saʿid had been taken to the pavilion of one of his palaces at Alexandria, where he was surrounded by the incessant comings and goings of doctors, relatives, and courtiers. Back in Cairo, the crown prince had instructed the director of communications, Bessy Bey, to remain beside the telegraph day and night so as to be able to bring him the telegram announcing his uncle's death without delay.

"After forty-eight hours, when nothing had happened and he was utterly exhausted, Bessy Bey asked one of his clerks to take over from him. He left the clerk his carriage with instructions to inform him at once of any news, promising him a reward of a hundred talaris.

"The telegram arrived. The clerk grabbed it, jumped into Bessy's carriage, and ordered the coachman to drive to the crown prince's palace. On arrival he threw himself at Ismaʿil's feet and acquainted him with the glad tidings. Overjoyed, Ismaʿil promised to make him a bey.

"Taking advantage of the commotion prevailing in the room, the clerk retrieved the telegram and hurried off to rouse Bessy Bey, who gave him the promised hundred talaris. With promotion to pasha already his, or so he thought, Bessy hurried to the palace in his turn. Once there, he discovered that he had been duped and flew into a fury. He sought out his clerk and demanded an explanation. The clerk received him very coldly: 'A trifle more respect, if you please. I'm a bey myself, or didn't you know?'"

It was the first time my grandparents had entered ʿAbdin Palace. In order to erect this sumptuous palace in the heart of Cairo during the 1860s, Khedive Ismaʿil had expropriated several hundred dwellings and employed Turkish, French and Italian decorators to do up the interior.

The Batrakanis were overcome with emotion as they ascended the vast, alabaster staircase in evening dress. Flanking them were lancers of the royal guard, giants in blue and scarlet uniforms, their images reflected *ad infinitum* in a battery of mirrors. As custom demanded, Yolande had removed her right glove in readiness to pay her respects to the king.

The Suez Canal Drawing Room was brilliantly illuminated. There they were welcomed with the utmost courtesy by Sa'id Zul-Fiqar Pasha, who looked extremely elegant in his *stambouline* with green silk lapels.

"His Majesty is eager to make your acquaintance, Monsieur Batrakani. The introductions will follow in a few minutes."

Georges shook hands warmly with the Syrian official to whom he owed his appointment. The latter gave the Batrakanis a guided tour of the massive paintings that adorned the room, all of which depicted ships negotiating the Canal. Meanwhile, servants in red *sirwaals* embroidered with gold thread passed among the guests bearing silver salvers laden with glasses of orangeade and *petits fours*.

The king did not make his entrance for another half-hour, only to offer his arm to the French minister's wife and head at once for the dining room. The whole company trailed after them. Yolande, feeling somewhat disappointed, almost donned her glove again.

Dinner was served at the double. Innumerable *sufragis* hovered behind the guests and changed their plates as though under orders to accelerate the passage of time. Less than an hour later the king was back in the drawing room, having certain selected guests presented to him.

Fouad was a short, potbellied man with a square face. He kept his left hand buried in the pocket of his *stambouline* with a walking stick of some precious wood hooked over his arm. When my grandparents approached, conducted by Zul-Fiqar, he was talking to Betsy Takla, one of the most prominent members of the Syrian Greek Catholic community. Daughter-in-law of the founder of *Al-Ahram*, she was regarded in Cairo as a repository of political power. She had run the prestigious newspaper after her husband's death with great skill while waiting for her son Gabriel to take over from her. The latter, with a faint smile on his lips, was listening as the king told his mother exactly what he thought of the leaders of the Wafd – a dig at Gabriel himself, who had been elected to the Chamber of Deputies on a Wafdist ticket.

The king detested Sa'ad Zaghloul's party, which had just won a majority in the Chamber. His one consolation was that he had removed this nationalist leader from the government in November 1924, after the British sirdar, Sir Lee Stack, had been assassinated in Cairo.

Catching sight of the Batrakanis, Gabriel Takla gratified my grandfather immensely by greeting him with a familiar *"Mabrouk ya bey!"*

Since the Taklas had taken charge of the introductions, Zul-Fiqar seized the opportunity to go to greet an old, half-blind pasha wearing a black-and-gold uniform and a ceremonial sword, who seemed to have lost his way.

Fouad spoke French with a slight Italian accent acquired at the military academy in Turin, where he had been a student. He addressed a few trivial remarks to the Batrakanis but made no mention of tarbooshes. Georges ended by wondering if the king really knew of his activities. Then, all of a sudden, Fouad emitted a sort of hoarse cry that made Yolande jump.

She was standing back a little, fortunately, so her start of alarm passed unnoticed. Besides, Fouad had already resumed his conversation with Betsy Takla as if nothing had happened and Zul-Fiqar was approaching with the ancient pasha on his arm.

Georges shot his wife a withering glance. She was unforgivable! Hadn't he warned her more than once against that predictable phenomenon? Everyone in Cairo was aware of the king's infirmity. His visits to schools were always preceded by an injunction to pupils not to flinch in the event of a royal yelp.

It dated back to the spring of 1898, when Fouad was married to Princess Shivekiar. The princess, who accused him of being autocratic and violent, took refuge in her parents' palace at Qasr al-'Aali. Fouad promptly went to fetch her back with a squad of policemen.

Shivekiar was virtually imprisoned in the marital home from then on. She eventually sent a despairing letter to her brother Saif ad-Din, who read it and went berserk. He raced to the Muhammad Ali Club, where Prince Fouad was playing billiards, and burst in on him with a pistol in his hand. There followed a wild race around the billiard table accompanied by gunfire. One shot hit Fouad in the lung, another in the buttock, and a third in the throat. It was the last bullet, which could not be extracted, that caused the king to utter the strange cry that was to give Georges Batrakani's wife nightmares for a whole week.

Zul-Fiqar's aides discreetly shepherded the guests in the direction of the theatre, where a French company was to perform Labiche's *La Cagnotte*. Several hundred gilded chairs were arrayed in the imposing auditorium, which was flanked by columns and chandeliers with crystal pendants. Queen Nazli, Fouad's second wife, who had presented him with an heir in 1920, attended the performance in a screened box.

Georges, comfortably seated with a beaming smile on his face, didn't follow a word of the play. He was a bey. That appointment had altogether changed his view of Egypt. At forty-six he now felt completely at home here, integrated and respected. Was he Egyptian? The question didn't even arise. Who, among this audience, was truly Egyptian? The king, Albanian by descent and brought up in Italy, spoke Arabic badly. The queen was the great granddaughter of a Frenchman . . .

Georges had intended to raise a little dust by giving an interview to *L'Illustration égyptienne*. Now, thinking back on his remarks with due gravity, he found them largely justified. The tarboosh was indeed the common denominator of this cosmopolitan country in which each had his place. What was there to prevent the bey of today from becoming a pasha tomorrow?

Maggi never missed a trick. "Your husband is a changed man, my dear," she mischievously remarked to her sister the following week. "He's an altogether different person since his beytification."

My father's family was far removed from the world of beys and pashas.

"What's the northernmost department of France?" called a stern voice from inside the lavatory.

Selim Yared, perched on a stool with his legs dangling, cudgelled his brain to no avail.

A violent blow with a ruler on the inside of the door made him jump.

"Nord, of course, *ya fellah!*"

Selim heaved a deep sigh. He hated his elder brother's habit of catechizing him while engaged on his number twos. Nothing could be worse than these interrogations by an unseen inquisitor. In school, at least, you had time to see the ruler come down on the desk or your hand. Here, it came as a complete surprise — accompanied, what was more, by a nasty smell.

He was finally delivered from his ordeal by the explosive sound of the lavatory being flushed. All that remained was to fake a studious expression and stoically await the ritual tongue-lashing that accompanied the opening of the door.

"Believe me, if you haven't done your homework you won't go to the cinema on Sunday!"

On certain Sunday afternoons the maidservant would take Selim and his brother Jean, aged eight and six respectively, to the cinema in Zaher. The third-class seats at the foot of the screen cost only a piastre. An attendant armed with a stick prevented the occupants of these cheap seats from climbing the barrier into the second-class section. When the film didn't meet with the audience's approval they would stamp their bare feet and chant "*Cinema awanta, haatu filusna*", or, freely translated, "What a rotten film, give us our money back!" On such occasions the attendant would brandish his stick in vain. The lights went up, went out again, and the film recommenced to the cracking of dried watermelon seeds whose husks the cinemagoers spat out at the necks of those in front of them.

"Did you hear, you dunce? You won't go to the cinema on Sunday!"

Roger Yared was only thirteen, but he had moulded himself into the head of the family since his father's death. Mima gave him a free hand, half admiring, half frightened of his fits of temper, not that it prevented her from sometimes coming to the defence of the younger ones.

"You'll give him pneumonia!" she would protest when her elder son compelled Jean or Selim to remain outside on the landing in midwinter because of a bad school report.

"Put something on his head, then," Roger would yell from the other end of the corridor. "The dunce's cap is in the cupboard."

A brilliant pupil himself, Roger had inherited his father's iron determination, but not the perpetual gaiety and serenity under pressure that had constituted Khalil's charm.

Mima's life had been utterly disrupted by her husband's death. She remained prostrated, almost stupefied, for three whole days. The doctor having prescribed a change of scene, she went to recover with the Dames du Bon Pasteur, who waited on her hand and foot. It was Mima this, Mima that, though heaven alone knew how greatly she had shocked the good nuns since her marriage, what with her daring outfits, her freedom of expression, and her disconcerting way of seeming thoroughly at ease with herself.

Her brother-in-law Na'aman was chosen to be the children's guardian. On his advice, Mima got rid of the second maidservant and limited herself to Fathiya. With five children to bring up and Khalil's modest bank account in danger of being nibbled away, she had to draw in her horns.

Selim had completed his first year's schooling at the patriarchal college. Most of the pupils, who came from humble backgrounds, had a poor knowledge of French. It was forbidden to speak Arabic in the playground, and the priests set an example — even those who, like Father 'Akaawi, were far from proficient in the language of Bossuet. That voluminous ecclesiastic thought he was doing the right thing by systematically translating Arabic idioms into French. In his parlance the tap of the drinking fountain was "the mother of the fountain", and he could be heard calling from one end of the playground to the other, "Hey, you, turn off the mother!"

One of Father 'Akaawi's duties was to chase up pupils whose school fees had not been paid. To do this he would go over to the boy concerned during break and tap him on the shoulder with his little bell. Selim had more than once been subjected to this resonant rebuke, which made him blush to the roots of his hair. He didn't dare tell Mima, knowing the financial difficulties she had to contend with, but addressed himself to his elder brother. Roger inveighed against "those thieving priests" but went at once to see Uncle Na'aman and ask him to banish the threat of Father 'Akaawi's little bell.

Selim was now at the Collège de la Salle in Zaher, which was run by the Frères des Écoles Chrétiennes. The Brothers did not teach Latin, but their pupils had beautiful handwriting – as the Jesuits used charitably to say – and, above all, they knew their arithmetic thanks to a little gem devised by "a teachers' symposium": the celebrated *Problems Involving Four Basic Mathematical Operations*. "Two twos are four, three twos are six . . ." All day long, Selim and his classmates recited their tables in time to a wooden clapper whose rhythmical beat governed their entire school existence. They learned about France, the putative land of their fathers, and in the evenings, to let off steam a little, they would march in step along the alleyways of Zaher, chanting, "We want God, He's our Father . . ."

The Brothers, whose pupils in Egypt were over eight thousand strong, had a liking for large-scale demonstrations complete with flags and parades. The Collège de la Salle, which had revived its fine old pre-war traditions, held an annual sports day attended by numerous dignitaries. Little ones like Selim and Jean wore white sweaters, blue belts, and berets pulled down to their ears. Wide-eyed, they witnessed gladiatorial contests, games of skill on stilts, and exhibitions of French boxing.

The Très Chers Frères bore names that might have come from another planet: Néarque, Solaire, Gervais-Marie, Gordien-Désiré. Unlike Father 'Akaawi, they did not venture to employ Arabic idioms. They were French from cowl to sandal. One of them was forever pinching Selim's ear and scolding him as follows:

"Get a move on, you little Oriental!"

The object of his animosity wound up rather confused by all these contradictions. It wasn't easy to reconcile the land of his fathers with the disapproving gaze of the Très Cher Frère or his Gallic ancestors with the orientality that adhered to his person.

Every morning when he awoke, Georges Batrakani reminded himself that he was a bey. He derived intense pleasure from the thought. His one regret was that his parents hadn't lived long enough to witness his elevation – not only his father Élias, but, more especially, his mother Linda, who had died in 1894, when he was only fourteen. Hers was a death of which my grandfather could not refrain from thinking regularly – a death that had, beyond all doubt, been the most distressing and traumatic event in his life.

Linda had held her peace for thirty-four years, either out of delicacy, or so as not to distress her children, or simply from a desire to keep her memories at bay. When she was dying, however, her defences crumbled one after another and she let herself go at last. It was as if a suppurating wound, unable to retain its contents any longer, were overflowing in all directions.

Sitting up in bed with the tears streaming down her cheeks, the dying woman told and retold her story for six long days and nights. As though ridding herself of a burden before going to heaven, she repeated it in the same words to each of her anguished offspring.

"It was shortly after noon," she said in a quavering voice. "The muezzins had just called the faithful to prayer from their minarets. We heard two cannon shots, followed by a great commotion. Then hundreds of soldiers burst into the Christian quarter followed by Muslim civilians brandishing scimitars, brand-new axes, and huge blunderbusses. Behind them came looters and women of easy virtue, who loudly egged them on. Coming to one of our houses, they broke down the door. Some of the people inside had their throats cut, others were dragged away. Anything that took the rioters' fancy they bundled up and carried off. Having set fire to one house, they would move on to the next, and woe betide any Christians who tried to escape from their blazing homes! Some had all their limbs broken, others were cut to ribbons with knives, others suspended by their feet above the flames . . . "

"That's enough, Maman," said Georges. "What's the use? You'll only make yourself worse."

But Linda wouldn't listen.

"And woe betide the pregnant women!" she went on. "Those brutes slit open their bellies and hurled their unborn children to the ground, then stamped them to death. Sometimes — Holy Mary, Mother of God! — sometimes they even roasted them over the flames on the point of a bayonet . . . "

"What's the use, *ya Mama*?" Georges implored with tears in his eyes. "What's the use?"

But Linda Batrakani had gone back in time and was describing how the Christians of Damascus lived before the events of 1860. She conjured up a captivating picture of a city within a city, more prosperous and far cleaner than the Muslim quarter.

"There were three thousand eight hundred houses in Haret al-Nassarah. Merchants, craftsmen, architects, physicians . . . Well educated and well brought up, the Christians had gentle, refined manners. Some, my father among them, were employed by the local court: no legal document or judgement could have been drafted without them. Others, like my uncle Hanna, handled millions of piastres and were moneylenders to the pasha. Christians were not entitled to own land, so they spent all their income on beautifying their homes and smothering their wives and daughters in jewels."

With a bloodless, trembling hand, Linda Batrakani took hold of the slender chain she wore round her neck and showed off her only relic of those days, a small cross set with turquoises.

"Our houses were nothing much to look at on the outside — it wasn't wise to be conspicuous — but inside they were delightful. Our courtyard was paved with marble and had an ornamental fountain surrounded by orange and lemon trees. All the doors were carved, all the ceilings panelled. Our terrace overlooked the city's gardens. It also afforded a distant view of the mountains in which flowed the multitude of streams that made Damascus the best irrigated, most enchanting city in Syria."

Linda asked for a glass of water. Georges hurried off to get one, hoping that this time her story would end there.

"The Christians of Damascus were sweet as honey, peaceful as lambs," Linda went on. "None of our houses had ever harboured a single gun, a single yataghan. Why did those people act as they did? Why? Why?"

She started to cry, upsetting the glass over her bedclothes. Georges handed her a big white handkerchief.

"Rest, *ya Mami*. Try to get a little sleep . . . "

"My two older brothers had ridden off that morning, accompanied by some other young men of the quarter, to warn Emir 'Abdel-Qader. They had been alerted to the danger by the sight of some signs scrawled in charcoal on the doors of Christian houses during the night. My poor father decided to stay with us. The brutes dragged him off after looting our house and setting fire to it. I never saw him again.

"My mother and I, together with my other three brothers and my older sisters, knocked on the door of a Muslim neighbour of ours. She agreed to shelter us in return for ten pieces of gold, but early the next morning she took fright and sent us packing. We had no choice but to leave, hugging the walls.

"We hadn't gone far when three armed men emerged from a side street. Two of them seized my sisters, who started screaming. Heedless of my mother's entreaties, they threw them roughly over their shoulders and carried them into a nearby house. There, only a few feet away, they subjected them to the ultimate outrage while the third man held us at bay with an enormous pistol. We could hear them screaming, screaming . . . "

Linda herself started screaming. Georges tried to calm his mother by dabbing her face with rose water, but the wound continued to suppurate.

"'Get out, you dogs!' called the man with the pistol, then fired a shot in our direction. My brother Kemal fell to the ground, his face a mass of blood. At a run, my mother led us back to the house we'd just left.

She hammered on the door and shouted at the top of her voice, then thrust the Muslim woman aside to let us pass. Utterly exhausted, we remained in that house for several days and nights."

Georges was appalled by his mother's story, but even more so by the thought that she had remained silent for so long. All she had ever revealed of her childhood in Damascus was the sunny side. And now, quite suddenly, she had opened a Pandora's box filled with images of death and destruction. Georges had often heard grown-ups talking about the massacres at Damascus, to be sure, but to hear them described at first hand, and by someone so close to him, was like a blow in the face. Everything took on shape and everything made sense at last.

Linda did something rather strange before continuing her account: she unfolded the moist handkerchief and draped it over her face.

"Some young Christians had been shut up in a big shop guarded by men brandishing axes. The youths were led out, one by one, to be questioned. 'Are you willing to become a Muslim?' Those who answered 'no' had their skulls split open on the spot; those who answered 'yes' were taken away to be circumcised. And woe betide those who hesitated! They were bombarded with questions, taunted and abused before being felled with a blow from an axe."

Crossing herself once more, Linda told how Emir 'Abdel-Qader, to whom she vowed eternal gratitude, had sheltered them and another three thousand Christians in his palace in Damascus — not that the massacres ceased. She described in a wealth of horrific detail how Christians were crucified and children beheaded on their mothers' knees.

Georges made no attempt to interrupt her when she came to the best part of the story: the exodus to Beirut, their welcome by the religious community there, the French soldiers whom they smothered with kisses — and, the following year, their departure for Alexandria. The heavy seas, the storm, the barrels of olives snapping their chains and rolling around the deck. And then, at dawn, an oily sea and a sky like satin. Egypt!

"We all went up on deck. Leaning on the rail, we watched a collection of white cubes, sand dunes and palm trees grow bigger on the horizon. Some sailing boats approached our ship at the harbour mouth. Their occupants greeted us in Egyptian, and we answered them in our

Syrian-accented Arabic. We were so wild with joy, we should have liked to give them some money, some gold pieces. But we had nothing, of course, so I untied the scarf that hid my hair and threw it over the side."

Linda's face lit up.

"A young man beside me was roaring with laughter. He came from Aleppo, and he was as handsome as the angel Gabriel. His name was Élias Batrakani."

5

I have in front of me a charming booklet produced in 1929 to mark the fiftieth anniversary of the Collège de la Sainte-Famille. In particular, it features an account of an old boys' reunion held the previous year in honour of Mahmoud Fakhry Pasha, the king's son-in-law. Paul attended it, as did Michel, who devotes considerable space to the occasion in the fourth volume of his diary. This musical afternoon, which he mentioned to me more than once, seemed to him to epitomize the good old days.

Sa'id Zul-Fiqar Pasha had devised this charming idea, and Michel was not the last to go and congratulate him on it. The old boys' tea was a pleasant revival of its kind. My godfather introduced himself to the grand chamberlain, who, although he didn't know Michel, shook hands with him as warmly as he was obliged to, day after day, with the many and various visitors to 'Abdin Palace.

Eternal Zul-Fiqar! It was twelve years since the sultan's visit to the school, which he himself had been largely responsible for organizing. Twelve years of crises and innovations, bereavements and births. But the grand chamberlain continued to wear the same smile and fulfil the same function – a function which, to judge by his array of twenty-seven orders and decorations, had earned him the gratitude of the entire world: Knight Commander of the British Empire, Grand Officier de la Légion d'Honneur, Grand Officer of the Crown of Siam and the Royal Crown of Prussia, Grand Cordon of the Order of Isma'il, Grand Cordon of the Order of the Nile, Grand Cordon of the Nahda of Hejaz, Grand Cordon of the Order of the Holy Trinity of Ethiopia . . .

Twelve years passed in review before Michel's inner eye: the death of Sultan Hussein; crowds thronging Opera Square; Zaki the coachman's bleeding face; the Wafd; Sa'ad Zaghloul, national hero; his wife on the balcony, waving the green flag; independent Egypt; Fouad I, a swaggering figure with upswept mustachios; the Wafd's resounding victory in the 1924 elections; Zaghloul's premiership; a Copt at the foreign ministry; the assassination of Sir Lee Stack; Zaghloul's enforced resignation; Fouad's visit to Europe; his audience with the Pope; Sa'ad Zaghloul's death; women tearing their veils and wailing; the Wafd, always the Wafd . . .

And here was Zul-Fiqar, still faithfully at his post. He had succeeded Mahmoud Fakhry as president of the old boys' association only when the latter became Egypt's minister plenipotentiary in Paris. And it was to coincide with Fakhry Pasha's presence in Cairo on 5 February 1928 that Zul-Fiqar had arranged this gathering with tea to follow.

The school's assembly hall was decked out in the colours of Egypt, France and the Vatican. No fewer than four pashas could be seen at the Father Rector's table, and the body of the hall bristled with royal councillors, senior civil servants and magistrates, all of them united in an atmosphere of joyful camaraderie.

Michel sighted his brother Paul chatting with a Swiss surgeon at the other end of the hall. Now twenty-two, Paul was as smartly dressed and snobbish as ever. His legal career was shaping brilliantly, and he always sought the company of Europeans.

Zul-Fiqar had arranged things well. The afternoon's programme was musically inaugurated by Dr Édouard Shuqair, who conjured some agreeably plaintive notes from his violin. Another doctor, Oscar Chidiac, followed up with a felicitous rendering of a song with words by Théodore Botrel. Both performers were loudly applauded.

Michel beamed with delight. He felt he was in good company, in a delicious cocoon – in the bosom of a privileged club in which the barriers of religion counted for nothing. Well, almost nothing . . . Here at the school, roles were reversed as they had been in class in the old days: the Muslims, being in a minority, were like guests. Egypt was on French soil and thought in French.

Not even the presence of Victor Lévy at a nearby table could blight my godfather's pleasure. Estranged by one of La Fontaine's fables, the two former classmates hadn't exchanged a word since leaving school five years earlier. Whenever their paths happened to cross in the street, at the cinema, or at the Café Groppi, they pretended not to see each other.

Victor Lévy was attending the École des Beaux-Arts, whereas Michel, having obtained his degree in history, was debating the subject of his future doctoral thesis. Should it cover the entire lifetime of Sultan Hussein, or only his thirty-three months in power? Each formula had its disadvantages . . .

There was a chorus of "Ssh!" from the body of the hall. Joseph Bey Cassis, deputy head of the state legal department, was about to recite a poem he had composed for the occasion:

> "*Honneur et vertu, telle est la devise insigne*
> "*Qui nous vient d'un pasha bien-aimé, bien connu.*
> "*Saluons, tout joyeux, ce président si digne,*
> "*Et le remercions d'être aujourd'hui venu!*"

[Honour and virtue, such is the motto
that comes to us from a well-liked, well-known pasha.
Let us joyfully hail our worthy president
and thank him for having come today.]

All present smiled delightedly. No doubt about it: Joseph Cassis was in excellent form.

> "*Le roi Fouad premier, notre auguste monarque,*
> "*Vous nommant à Paris ministre, ambassadeur,*
> "*Donne de son estime une royale marque,*
> "*Et le pape à son tour vous nomme commandeur.*"

[King Fouad the First, our august monarch,
by appointing you minister, ambassador in Paris,
confers a royal mark of esteem,
and the Pope, in his turn, appoints you a commander.]

Applause rang out. Mahmoud Fakhry rose and gave a little bow.

"L'Égypte est mieux connue: en chaque capitale,
"On fit à notre roi le plus cordial accueil.
"Partout le faste et la splendeur orientale:
"C'est pour nous, ses sujets, un vrai sujet d'orgeuil."

[Egypt is better known: in every capital
our king receives the warmest of welcomes.
Pomp and oriental splendour are everywhere,
to us, his subjects, a true source of pride.]

At that point, if the fiftieth anniversary booklet is to be believed, Joseph
Cassis had to break off for a good minute to allow the clapping and
cheering to run its course. But he hadn't omitted anyone:

"Sujet d'orgeuil aussi pour la chère Amicale
"Qui fut avec le roi partout présente, car
"Toujours au premier rang de l'escorte royale
"Était le distingué président Zul-Fiqar!"

[A source of pride, too, to our beloved Old Boys'
    Association,
which accompanied the king everywhere, for
always in the front rank of the royal escort
was our distinguished president, Zul-Fiqar!]

The Father Rector turned to the grand chamberlain and gave an
approving nod, thereby unleashing another ovation.

The alumni were enjoying each other's company too much to go their
separate ways. Even Fakhry Pasha seemed to have all the time in the world.
When everyone rose from the tea table, a small group gathered round
him. Michel joined them just as a Belgian banker was questioning the
guest of honour about the future of the Capitulations. Had Egypt really
decided, as the rumour ran, to revoke the privileges accorded for so long
to the nationals of certain foreign powers?

"The system makes no sense any more," Fakhry Pasha replied firmly.
"Egypt is almost the only country to have retained it. In the old days,
those privileges and immunities were intended to enable foreigners resident

in the Ottoman Empire to regulate their mutual relations in conformity with their own laws and without the sultan's intervention. But, as the empire grew weaker, those guarantees developed into straightforward extraterritorial rights."

"Isn't that a trifle overstated, Minister?"

"Not at all. In Egypt today, as you're well aware, foreigners of various nationalities implicated in the same crime are tried by mixed courts, each by his own consular court and according to the law of his native land. It's a preposterous state of affairs."

"So you intend to abolish the mixed courts?" asked the Belgian.

"Who said anything about abolishing them?" said Fakhry Pasha, looking slightly nettled. "Believe it or not, it was my father who presided over their establishment in 1875, when he was minister of justice. I've no wish to abolish them, my dear sir. On the contrary, I want to increase their powers. It is they, and not the consular courts, that ought to deal with penal offences involving foreigners, but Egyptian magistrates should be rather better represented on them."

"Would you concede, Minister, that the Capitulations aren't the greatest injustice to which Egypt is currently subjected?"

"Perhaps not, my dear sir, perhaps not, but the disadvantage of this particular injustice is that it paralyses the country. The judicial system isn't the only issue, you know that perfectly well. Don't forget that no direct tax may be levied on foreigners resident in Egypt without the consent of all the capitular powers. Well, the Egyptian government needs new sources of revenue."

"There's nothing to prevent it from raising new taxes."

"It would still have to get foreigners to pay them and subject them to the appropriate penalties if they failed to do so. On a number of occasions, the mixed courts have actually forbidden the government to tax foreigners."

The Belgian refused to climb down.

"Why attach so much importance to foreigners? To the best of my knowledge, there are only a hundred and sixty thousand Europeans in Egypt."

"*Only* a hundred and sixty thousand?" a Coptic lawyer cut in rather sharply. "But my friend, those hundred and sixty thousand own a large proportion of this country's wealth. Did you know that one-seventh of our agricultural land belongs to foreigners?"

Perturbed by the conversation's mounting vehemence, the Father Rector deemed this an opportune moment to rescue Fakhry Pasha. All smiles, the minister allowed himself to be escorted back to his car amid general applause.

"What has he got against foreigners, that peasant of a Copt?" grumbled Paul Batrakani, who was standing behind Michel.

6

Her big brothers belonged to a different world. Aged six, Viviane didn't know where she stood in relation to Michel and Paul, who talked, dressed and behaved like grown-ups. As for André, whom she had never even seen, she pictured him sometimes as Lucifer and sometimes as a white-bearded St Peter.

The little girl was sitting in the drawing room with Georges Batrakani beside her and a big album open on her lap. She pointed to a rather faded photograph.

"Who's that?"

"My poor mother, of course. In Shubra Street – look, you can make out the Pyramids in the distance."

Viviane looked in vain for something that resembled the Pyramids, but the photo was very fuzzy. Either that, or the photographer's aim was poor.

"And that fat boy on the donkey?"

"Hush, that's your uncle Nando."

She burst out laughing. Her father laughed too, and, for a long moment, hugged her tight.

Viviane had almost died of meningitis at the age of five. That was when Georges became aware of his youngest child's existence and developed a sudden passion for her. He remained at her bedside for hours on end, called the doctor in the middle of the night, and commanded him to save her life. On his way to the factory next morning he told the chauffeur to make a detour so that he could light some candles in Radwaniya church – something he had never done before. That afternoon he cancelled all his appointments and dashed back home.

Days went by, and Viviane's life continued to hang by a thread.

"Where's that ass of a doctor?" Georges would call whenever he came home, removing his tarboosh.

One Wednesday he was greeted by an impression of a donkey braying. Dr Dabbas, who had a sense of humour, had just satisfied himself that Viviane was on the road to recovery . . .

The little girl pointed to another photograph. Its subject, a European army officer, seemed to be presenting his best profile to the camera.

"Is that General Simpson?"

"Colonel Simpson. And the horse beside him is Mrs Simpson."

Viviane couldn't see any horse . . .

Élias Batrakani's three children had no difficulty in dividing up his meagre estate when he died in 1920. Nando had his eye on three feddans of land near al-Mansoura, which he himself had persuaded his father to buy. Nini wanted the table silver. As for Georges, he was only interested in the dusty camera, complete with bulb, bellows and tripod.

"Mind if I have the photographs too?" he asked.

"You're welcome to them," replied Nando, whose sole preoccupation was printed paper.

Georges's chauffeur had to make two trips to transport all the hatboxes in which Élias Batrakani had kept his work. Many of the photographs were not worth keeping, but enough remained to fill nine large albums. The camera itself, repaired and regularly dusted by a servant, stood proudly in the corner of Georges's office.

On Sunday afternoons Viviane would often get out one of the brown leather albums and ask her father to comment on its contents. Among other things, there was a whole series of shots of the terrace of Shepheard's taken from the street. One showed Georges as a child, sitting astride one of the two little sphinxes. He had never forgotten that day. It was the only occasion on which, thanks to an obliging dragoman who was probably interested in examining Élias's camera, he had been lifted over the balustrade into the magical world that lay beyond it.

One afternoon, having replaced the album on its shelf, Viviane sneaked off to the pantry to get a biscuit without being spotted by Mademoiselle

Guyomard. She knew she could count on the discretion of Rashid, the scar-faced *sufragi*. On entering the pantry, however, she found herself face to face with a boy in a blue *galabiya*. He must have been a little older than herself, eight or possibly nine.

"Who are you?" she asked in Arabic, looking defiant.

Rashid answered for him. "This is Hassan, the son of my brother Sabri, who died in the riots of 1919, poor man."

Viviane and Hassan continued to eye each other in silence while the *sufragi* busied himself at the big icebox.

Then, through the open window, they heard a distant cry like a litany. It drew nearer.

"*Sundouq ad-dunya, sundouq ad-dunya . . .* "

Viviane's heart began to pound. It was Abu Simsim the showman. Instinctively, the two children hurried to the window. A man in a turban was just emerging from a side street laden with a bench, a big box, and a trestle.

"I'm going out there," Hassan told his uncle, and set off without waiting for a reply.

Viviane, knowing that she couldn't follow him, was incensed. Her mother had forbidden her a hundred times to look into Abu Simsim's magic box.

"It's dirty – it's teeming with germs. You see? They're all Arabs."

She leant on the windowsill, angrily watching Hassan walk over to the bench. Some other local children had come running up. In return for a small coin, five of them were permitted to approach the five magic lenses. Abu Simsim draped a black cloth over their heads, then operated a lever, chanting as he did so:

> "*Ya salaam, ya salaam,*
> "*shouf al-forga di keman!*"

The children saw, in succession, a big sailing ship, Satan and the angel Gabriel, a man with a woman's gory head in his hand, Yousef and 'Aziza, a locomotive, Samson toppling the columns of the temple, and numerous other marvels. When the cloth was removed from their heads, they all laughed and chattered at the same time. Hassan, who had no money, stood there while five more customers came up.

Abruptly, Viviane shut the window and stalked out of the pantry while Abu Simsim's muffled voice resumed its monotonous refrain:

"*Ya salaam, ya salaam,*
"*shouf al-forga di keman!*"

7

André Batrakani's first few years of religious instruction at Lyon passed like a dream. Blissfully happy, he allowed himself to become gently impregnated by his social environment. Many of his fellow students belonged to the French nobility or upper middle class. He had taken to addressing his parents in the formal second person plural as they did. A letter dating from the summer of 1924 perfectly illustrates this cultural integration: "I would have you know, dearest Maman, that we spent a good part of this 14th of July praying in chapel, far from the horrible festivities in town . . . "

By 1926 André was once more addressing his parents in the second person singular. He no longer dreamed of crossing swords with the French Revolution. His feet were back on the ground – Egyptian ground. His perception of the world had been transformed by an incident that occurred one winter Sunday.

The Father Superior had summoned him to his study after the communal walk.

"Next week we're to receive a visit from the Maronite bishop of Beirut, who's spending a few days in France. I'd like to give him a nice surprise. Could you compose an address in Arabic describing the content and spirit of the training we give here?"

Sheepishly, André had to confess that he was quite incapable of doing so. He spoke and read Arabic fairly well and could write it a little, but not well enough to draft an address. The Father Superior was astonished.

"I don't understand. Many French Jesuits from the Levant make strenuous efforts to learn Arabic, but you, who have studied it since childhood, who are Egyptian and destined to fulfil your ministry in the Middle East – you see fit to lack an appropriate knowledge of the language!"

My uncle blushed, blurted out some response, and retired to his room in deep dismay. No such consideration had ever crossed his mind. At school in Cairo he had been taught Arabic by some excellent Syrian teachers, but their pupils looked upon it as a foreign language and took as little interest in it as possible. Even those who were preparing for the Egyptian *baccalauréat* chose to sit the examinations in French, as the law permitted. To be honest, they were only following an example set at the very top: King Fouad's knowledge of Arabic was poor and the members of his cabinet generally conferred in French.

But André made no excuses for himself. He wrote to his parents the very same night, urgently requesting an Arabic grammar, a dictionary, a subscription to two Cairo magazines, and a batch of square-nibbed pens.

"Unless I'm much mistaken, my dear," Maggi remarked to her sister, "your son has gone all the way to Lyon to learn Arabic."

A rapprochement between Georges Batrakani and his eldest son began at the end of 1926 – thanks partly to Egypt, because both regarded themselves as semi-nationals from then on. The new bey and the new Arabist labelled themselves Egyptians, even though the celebrated law on nationality was still shelved. It had become a new bone of contention between King Fouad and the Wafd, so the vote had been postponed indefinitely.

André's letters betrayed growing conviction and self-assurance as the years went by. The future priest wrote voluminously to all the members of his family, giving them frank advice, if not straightforward injunctions, on how to run their lives. A long-range preceptor who tackled the most diverse subjects head-on, André kept an eagle eye on Lola's religious instruction, Viviane's school reports, his father's business ventures, his mother's good works.

Highly impressed by her son's refinement and religious faith, Yolande used to preserve some of his letters and read them aloud to her women friends on Tuesdays, when she held her at-homes.

"'Smallah, 'smallah!" the ladies would exclaim admiringly. "You've got a budding bishop there, Yola, no doubt about it!"

My grandmother would touch the wooden arm of her chair or make a covert gesture to ward off the evil eye.

As for Alex, he was treated to regular epistles from his eldest brother. Some of them enraged him, others he found hugely amusing.

Lyon, 15 June 1930
Trinity Sunday

My dear Alex,

You will soon be nineteen. It's a difficult age, waiting for the woman who will one day be united with you for better or worse.

As you may possibly know, early marriage is extremely inadvisable. Statistics demonstrate that the death rate among young men who marry under twenty-five — and young women under eighteen — is higher than among the celibate of the same age. According to some leading experts, in fact, the reproductive function entails a certain organic depletion that takes place at the expense of the organism itself.

I have no need to remind you, however, that chastity is mandatory prior to marriage. Young men who fail to remain continent expose themselves not only to a state of mortal sin, but also to grave physical hazards. Continence has never harmed anyone's constitution or claimed a victim, but it calls for a temperate life from which food and drink of an unduly stimulating nature must be excluded. Continence enables you to preserve your natural energies intact so that, when the day comes, they may be used to found a family of your own.

I should very much like, my dear Alex, to hear your views on all these matters. Do write to me from time to time.

Your brother, who never forgets you in his prayers,

André, S.J.

Alex had inherited a certain cunning and an avid love of life from his father. However, whereas Georges's energies were entirely devoted to social advancement, Alex dissipated his in random acts of self-indulgence and fits of short-lived enthusiasm.

My youngest uncle's sojourn with the Brothers had been as disastrous as his performance with the Jesuits: after being relegated twice more, he was politely asked to leave. No other seat of learning felt equal to the task of coaching him for the *baccalauréat*. It should be added that he himself had no desire to stay on at school, being, as he put it, "eager to embark on a business career". His mother was much impressed by this show of determination.

Alex had several fantastic jobs in view. Meantime, he played billiards at the Club Risotto, took driving lessons from his father's chauffeur, and spent the money lavished on him by his doting mother.

Not long before twelve one night he called Georges from a friend's house.

"Papa, I must see you urgently. It's about tarbooshes."

"Can't it wait till tomorrow?" asked Georges, who was already in his pyjamas.

My grandfather slept badly that night, plagued by thoughts of his tarboosh factory. Sales, which were stagnating, had barely exceeded twelve thousand units in 1929. The diabolical Sémoditchek seemed invincible . . .

In Opera Square the next morning, Alex unveiled a sensational plan.

"These tarbooshes of yours, Papa – how many colours do you make them in?"

"Five or six, like everyone else," replied Georges, raising his eyebrows.

"No, you don't! Like everyone else, you only make them in shades of red."

"Very well. What of it?"

"You must manufacture them in blue, white, black, yellow . . . "

"*What?*"

"But of course! That way, you'll drive your competitors out of business. It'll be a stunning sartorial revolution – every young man will sport a tarboosh!"

My grandfather stared at him. "Why not striped tarbooshes – why not floral tarbooshes, while you're about it? You really think you can tamper with traditions like that?"

"But Papa, the descendants of the Prophet happily wear green turbans — "

"Precisely, you fool: the descendants of the Prophet! You want to ruin us, or what?" Georges' voice rose steadily. "Last year you wanted me to produce a perforated tarboosh to keep people's heads cool. A perforated tarboosh! God knows what you'll be suggesting next. A tarboosh for ladies, a sprung tarboosh, a tarboosh with pedals . . . I'm sick of your puerile ideas! When are you going to grow up? When? Tell me when!"

Alex deplored his father's conservatism. Adroitly changing the subject, he asked him about his next car, a Dodge sedan, which was scheduled to arrive in Cairo the following month.

"They say it's very quiet . . . "

Georges gradually simmered down.

"Yes," he said, "and there's a new steering system specially designed for pneumatic tyres."

"I've also heard it's got an angled drive shaft with five bearings."

"You certainly know a bit about it, *ya ibni!*"

"How much is Marcarian charging you?"

"Two hundred and eighty pounds, including courtesy light, rear-view mirror, door pockets, and a silk curtain for the rear windscreen."

"What about the Ford you've got now?"

"What about it?"

"If you kept it, maybe I could — "

"Oh, yes?" snapped Georges. "Maybe you'd like the chauffeur as well, so he could wait at your beck and call outside the Club Risotto? D'you think I'm blind? I'm not your mother. You think I don't know about your racketing around?"

The telephone bell cut him short. Alex gave him a little wave and beat a retreat without waiting for any more.

8

The fourth volume of my godfather's diary covers the period 1926 to 1930. From now on Michel's tone is adult, even though he remains very dependent on his parents. His long accounts of Sunday lunches contain a mass of information of varying interest: the sale of a batch of tarbooshes to Cicurel, a new dress of Maggi's, a visit by Rashid to his native village . . . As time goes by there are more and more allusions to the disappearance of Shubra's trees and its growing population. My grandparents decided to leave there and buy a house in Garden City. The dinner described below must have taken place shortly before their move.

25 June 1930

Strangely enough, it was the very first time my parents had invited Makram and his wife to dinner. Seeing them turn up last night, arm in arm, one might have been watching a play by Naguib ar-Rihani: he, as emaciated as ever in his eternal black suit dusted with cigarette ash; she, a fleshy figure in a sugar-pink gown and far too much make-up.

Half the meal was devoted to an exchange of courtesies between the wife, a Copt who doesn't know a word of French, and Maman, whose Arabic is appalling. Papa and Makram, each with his nose buried in his plate, didn't seem to have much to say to each other. It was intensely boring.

The end of dinner was enlivened by a power cut. Everyone went out on the terrace to take advantage of the full moon while Rashid lit some candles. Papa and Makram started arguing about the Sidqi government. "We're living under a semi-dictatorship," said Makram, who's more Wafdist than ever. "It's an outrageous attack on the parliamentary system. Riots are breaking out all over the place."

Papa, by contrast, greatly admires the firm-handed approach adopted by Sidqi Pasha, who, it appears, obtained his baccalauréat *with the Brothers in 1889, some ten years before himself.*

When the lights came back on, the argument subsided and the ladies resumed their exchange of courtesies. I seized the opportunity to steer conversation towards Sultan Hussein.

The scope of Makram's knowledge surprised me. He claims that Hussein Kamil, who was Khedive Isma'il's favourite son, had wanted to succeed him in 1879, and that he was bitterly resentful of Tewfiq's accession. This is at odds with the image of a man devoid of personal ambition — one who sacrificed himself in 1914 to preserve the dynasty of Muhammad Ali and prevent Egypt from being simply annexed by the British.

One should doubtless be wary of Makram's interpretations, which are those of a political militant, not an historian. But none of this is helping me to settle on a subject for my thesis. "Why not 'Sultan Hussein and La Fontaine the Moralist'?", André suggested in his most recent letter. Well, why not?

9

Somewhat dazed by the midday sun, Lola was daydreaming on her tummy on the moist sand. The dying waves that lapped at her feet and calves would sometimes creep up her thighs, making her shiver all over with pleasure. She was pretty as a picture and starting to become aware of the fact.

"You're thirteen now. You're too old to expose yourself like that in front of the opposite sex."

Thus her mother, to whom Mademoiselle Guyomard had made representations, but Lola was undeterred. The governess had long since given her up as a bad job.

Her midriff was suddenly immersed by a somewhat livelier wave. She uttered a little shriek that attracted the gaze of a thin youth with tousled hair, whom she had seen in the baker's shop at San Stefano the day before.

It would soon be time for lunch. Servants laden with steaming dishes would emerge from the house behind the dunes and set them out on some upturned canoes near the bathing huts. Today as every day, it would be a big family meal shared by uncles, aunts, and cousins.

Everyone knew each other on Glymenopoulo Beach, which the Syrians colonized in the same way that the Jews monopolized Stanley Beach near by. They felt at home and among their own kind — so much so that they would express loud surprise if a Coptic or Muslim family had the bad form to plant its sun umbrella there.

Lola adored the long summer holidays at Alexandria. She dreamed for weeks in advance of pulling into Sidi Gaber station, and of the enormous black taxi that transported them to the villa in a cloud of steam. In her room she found her old toys safely *in situ*. She would finger them, sniff them, and sometimes apply her tongue to them to make sure they still tasted of salt. Then, with Viviane at her heels, she would run to the neighbouring houses to link up with their cousins and friends.

A small group of bathers tended to gather round Nando Batrakani and Count Henri Touta whenever the pair embarked on a game of backgammon, each having first placed fifty piastres on the table.

Nando's mountainous body overflowed a canvas armchair of appropriate size, which had been specially transported to the beach for his benefit. My grandfather's eldest brother was steadily putting on weight. Rumour had it that he was worth eight hundred thousand Egyptian pounds and weighed over two hundred and fifty avoirdupois pounds in the buff. People wondered how on earth *la* Doumaar, his slim and gentle wife of thirty years' standing, had survived the onslaughts of such a monster for so long.

Count Henri, already the recipient of Liechtenstein's gratitude, had since become the Peruvian consul but was still based at the same address. Attired in a striped green bathrobe, he shook the dice in his hand for an eternity before tossing them on to the wooden board with its mother-of-pearl inlays.

"Yesterday, *ya Comte*," said his opponent, "you had the luck of the devil, but today, I swear by all that's holy —"

"Don't swear, you wretched man! You don't know what you're in for. *Abyssus abyssum invocat.*"

Tension mounted. Nando's pudgy fingers slammed the pieces down more and more violently. Plenty of double threes, double fives and double sixes were thrown, and each throw was greeted by its nickname.

"*Dosh!*"

"*Dabash!*"

Yolande, standing beside the huts, rang a little bell: the stuffed vine leaves would get cold. Nando, who was starving, promptly abandoned the game in spite of Henri Touta's protests.

Lola slipped into the place beside her aunt Maggi. She was fascinated by this enchantress who, at forty-four, looked fifteen years younger and continued to break men's hearts. Her most recent lovers included a big Jewish merchant, an Italian basketball player with the Pro Patria team, and a scion of the royal family.

"But where's Edmond?" asked Yolande, surprised to find her brother missing.

Ensconced in a deck chair facing the sea, Edmond Touta was doing his sums. The last census, which put the population of Egypt at over fourteen million, had upset him terribly. He had decided to write to King Fouad and propose a drastic remedy: a ban on marriage for men under twenty-eight and women under twenty-five.

"My measure will cut the birth rate by fifty per cent," he announced in a feverish voice.

Laughing up their sleeves, his nephews concocted all kinds of stories to get him going.

"Did you see that report in *La Réforme*, Uncle Edmond — the one about the woman from Port Sa'id who's had eighteen children?"

"My God! Eighteen children?"

"Yes, and she's expecting her nineteenth any day."

Appalled, Edmond revised his calculations, raising the bar to twenty-nine for men and twenty-six for women.

The servants were not allowed to bathe until the end of the afternoon, when washing-up and housework had been completed. That was when the children went off to buy doughnuts at the baker's in San Stefano, having travelled there by tram.

On some afternoons they played at Mass. The Greek Catholic liturgy, which was far more colourful than the Latin, enabled them to communicate in two kinds — bread and blackberry cordial — but the crux of the ceremony was a sermon in French. Several budding barristers among the cousins vied for the preacher's role. Another function much in demand was that of cantor. As for the girls, they could only serve in a subordinate capacity as altar boys or members of the congregation. Lola avenged herself by sowing confusion in her cousins' minds:

"Don't you think André would be angry if he knew we were playing games with the Almighty?"

On the first Sunday in August the childen paid a traditional visit to their Touta cousins at Sidi Bishr. This was the Alexandria branch of the family – "the dotty branch", as Georges used to call it, to underline the fact that Edmond's eccentricity ran in the family.

There were eleven brothers and sisters, all of whom had been given pharaonic names by their parents. Sesostris, the eldest, who had attained the rank of bey before he was forty, had taken it into his head to live "afloat". He had built himself a seaside house in the form of a ship. A hundred feet long, it was complete with decks and a gangway, accommodation ladders and companionways.

Sesostris Bey, wearing an admiral's cap, welcomed his guests on the poop deck. His sisters Isis and Nephtys handed round cakes and lemonade, and the master of the house allowed the delighted children to scan the sea through his outsize binoculars.

All the cabbies in Ramleh knew the address. One had only to say, "We're going to Sesostris Bey's."

The cab traversed peaceful streets flanked by magnolias and tamarisks beyond which slumbered mansions buried in vegetation and screened by *mashrabiyas*. The cab's bell punctured the silence, seeming sometimes to echo the plaintive tolling of the bells in a nearby church tower. The children shut their eyes, the better to savour the scent of seaweed. Alexandria at this time of year was redolent of jasmine and the sea.

PART FIVE

The Ankara Incident

I

A vile stench seized Rashid by the throat as soon as he entered. My grandparents' manservant lifted the hem of his *galabiya* and picked his way carefully between the pools of blood and knots of entrails on the floor.

The slaughterhouse was in constant commotion. Men bustled to and fro, cursing each other and brandishing knives. Rashid looked for his nephew, but how was he to make out a face in this dim light and in the midst of such a milling crowd?

He had been infuriated to learn, two days ago, that Hassan had given up school and was now working in the camel slaughterhouse at Giza — doubtless at the instigation of his mother's new husband, who must have thought it a good way of exploiting the thirteen-year-old.

The *sufragi* could neither read nor write, but he was sure that his brother Sabri, the cigarette factory worker who had been killed during a demonstration in 1919, would have wanted his son to go to school. Sabri himself had said innumerable times how much he regretted being illiterate.

"You'll be a *muwazzaf* one day," Rashid used to tell his nephew when the latter paid his annual visit to the Batrakani residence. A *muwazzaf* was an official or functionary, and wasn't that the most prestigious of jobs?

Urged on by a "*Kss, kss!*" from its master, a camel made its way to the centre of the room, where it knelt in response to a curt command. Instantly, a huge knife slit its throat. Blood spurted for at least six feet and the beast rolled and struggled frantically, legs in the air, while a muscular, half-naked Sai'idi pinned its head to the ground. Its convulsions went on for a good minute.

When the animal lay still at last, Rashid saw a boy advance on it carrying a big pair of bellows. He thought for a moment that it was Hassan, but his nephew did not, thank God, have a limp like the young apprentice, who proceeded to inflate the animal's cadaver.

A second camel, terrified by the scent of blood, reared. Several butchers closed in on the slavering beast. One threw sand in its eyes to blind it while another ducked beneath it and drove his knife into its belly. The camel emitted a long groan and collapsed.

Rashid caught sight of his nephew among some boys converging with clubs in their hands. He hurried over to him.

"Come along!"

"But uncle — "

"Come along, I said." Grabbing Hassan by the sleeve, Rashid hauled him outside. "You're going back to school, you hear?"

A gaggle of black-veiled women outside the slaughterhouse drew nearer to eavesdrop on this altercation. They were waiting there, as they did every evening, for the butchers to stop work so that they could gather up the camel dung they used as fuel or manure.

"You're going back to school," Rashid repeated as they headed for the tram stop. "If your mother needs the money, she can get it from me."

In *An Officer's Career* Hassan says he saw his uncle enter the slaughterhouse.

> I hid behind a column in my bloodstained *galabiya*, not daring to show my face. I felt like a culprit caught in the act, but my uncle had only come to save me.
>
> I returned to school the next morning. My uncle, who couldn't read or write, insisted on seeing my reports at the end of every term. I took them to a big house in Garden City, where a wealthy family employed him as a *sufragi*. 'Have you been working hard?' he would ask without looking at the sheet of paper, which was unintelligible to him in any case. 'Yes, uncle,' I would reply, where- upon he would pinch my ear and say, 'You must work even harder if you're to become a *muwazzaf* one day.' When I left, he handed me two pathetic piastres wrapped up in a piece of paper . . .

2

Georges Batrakani took little initial interest in the Piastre Association, which was founded under a pasha's chairmanship in 1931. Street collections for the benefit of Egyptian industry struck him as futile and absurd. What of the students who accosted passers-by and asked them to buy one-piastre tickets? Did they themselves know exactly where all the money went?

At breakfast one Thursday morning, my grandfather was staggered to read in *La Bourse égyptienne* that the proceeds of the collection were to be used to launch a national tarboosh industry.

"A tarboosh industry?" he cried, upsetting the *ishta* bowl over the table. "But there is one already! What do I manufacture, pray? Chamber pots? Flush lavatories?"

Yolande, looking worried, silently draped a napkin over the spilt cream. It was better to say nothing on such occasions. Her husband could seize on the faintest hint of a sigh to make a terrible scene.

Ten minutes later, while Georges was angrily nicking himself with his razor, the telephone rang. It was Édouard Dhellemmes, calling from Shepheard's.

"Have you seen it?"

"I have indeed. It's outrageous. Call in at the office this morning."

An hour later Édouard was face to face with his partner in Opera Square. Still fuming, Georges Bey castigated the entire world with a dead cigar between his teeth.

"Till now we've had those confounded Czechs on our backs. If we have to fight off genuine local competition as well . . . This national factory will have access to better raw material than ours, and it'll certainly be able to undercut us. When I think of all the cretins who gave a piastre to those licensed beggars!"

Having examined the problem from every angle, the partners concluded that they would definitely have to close their factory. At the same time, any such decision seemed premature in default of adequate information about the government scheme.

Édouard returned to France. Some months later a terse telegram from Georges Batrakani informed him that the foundation stone of the national tarboosh factory would be laid on 14 October 1932.

Then came the Ankara incident. In high dudgeon, some Cairo newspapers reported that Moustafa Kemal had rebuked the Egyptian minister, 'Abdel-Malik Hamza Bey, for wearing his tarboosh at a gala dinner attended by members of the opposite sex, whereupon the Egyptian envoy had walked out in a huff. But there were rumours of an even more serious incident, namely, that Atatürk had knocked the diplomat's tarboosh off while he was bowing to him.

"Absolute nonsense!" declared Count Henri Touta, who knew the Turkish consul in Cairo. "It was a wholly innocuous incident. Moustafa Kemal went over to talk to the Egyptian minister. It was very hot in the room, so he kindly invited him to remove his tarboosh. *Non erat hic locus.* Taking courtesy to even greater lengths, Atatürk removed Hamza Bey's tarboosh with his own hands before kissing him on both cheeks."

"But that makes it even worse, *ya Comte!*" said Nando, roaring with laughter.

Some Egyptian newspapers demanded an official apology from Turkey, others bluntly called for diplomatic relations to be broken off. That was when Georges Batrakani had a brainwave.

The following week a full-page advertisement appeared in several Cairo and Alexandria dailies. It consisted of only two words in enormous letters — OUR PRIDE — and below them, on a more modest scale, "Batrakani Tarbooshes".

This form of words had the advantage of being thoroughly ambiguous. Some people took it at face value: the firm of Batrakani was proud of manufacturing tarbooshes of fine quality. Others construed it as a cry from the heart with a topical slant: the Egyptian nation was too proud to take Atatürk's insult lying down. But there was nothing to prevent one from favouring a more ambitious interpretation: Batrakani tarbooshes were as much the pride of Egypt as the Nile, the Pyramids, or stewed beans, and the best response to Atatürk's insult was to buy some.

Georges Bey detected a marked recovery in sales during the next few months. On making up his accounts he found that although the operation had not turned in a profit, allowing for the cost of the advertisements, it had brought him new customers and opened up new horizons.

Egypt and Europe had just been linked by a submarine telephone cable. Taking advantage of that innovation, Édouard Dhellemmes called my grandfather to ask how the liquidation of their business was going. He found his partner remarkably serene and cheerful in spite of the static on the line.

"Liquidation? Don't even dream of it, my dear Édouard! On the contrary, now's the time to strike."

"I can't hear you properly. Strike, did you say?"

"Yes, strike. Invest."

"But . . . This national factory they're building . . . "

"Exactly. Why not take advantage of it?"

The Frenchman cursed the hissing telephone. He could hear little and understand less.

"Think, Édouard," Georges said calmly. "The Piastre factory won't be in production for another eighteen months. There's nothing to prevent us from joining the movement, or even from stealing a march on it. The Egyptians want a national tarboosh? Very well, let's offer them one ourselves — before the others do. The cretins who contributed a piastre won't know the difference."

Édouard could hear better now. He reflected for a moment or two. It was worth a try, after all. The factory could struggle along for another couple of years as it had done hitherto. They wouldn't make any money, but they wouldn't lose any either. There would still be time to close the business down.

Georges Bey estimated that they would have to spend three thousand pounds on the advertising budget essential to the operation and twice that sum on improving their distribution network.

"Nine thousand pounds!" Édouard exclaimed. "That's crazy. Where are we going to find it?"

Édouard had no intention of ruining himself for the sake of tarboosh manufacture, an industrial activity that had never really interested him. He had redoubled his visits to Egypt, but only because the country fascinated him. Not that he knew it, Egypt would soon become inextricably associated in his dreams with the figure of a Syrian beauty encountered on a terrace in Heliopolis.

"I'm willing to put up the money myself," said Georges.

This implied a redistribution of their shares in the business, leaving Édouard with only twenty per cent. He agreed without hesitation.

Early in 1934, when the national factory had not yet started production, Batrakani tarbooshes became a talking point once more. This time the advertisements were smaller but far more numerous. They limited themselves to a very restrained slogan composed of well-weighed words: "Batrakani Tarbooshes. A National Product of High Quality." The key word was "national" . . .

This massive advertising campaign, coupled with the hiring of five salesmen, was quick to bear fruit. Sales rose sixty per cent within a few months, and they had more than doubled by the time the Piastre tarbooshes, which were far from perfect, made their first appearance on the market. As for the foreign makes, they began to suffer from the effects of a customs reform that taxed them more heavily.

At the end of 1935 Georges Bey calculated that he had sold forty-two thousand tarbooshes during the year, and the future looked brighter still. Atatürk could keep his peaked cap and "Sémoditchek" could get lost.

3

When I think of my paternal grandmother, it isn't the most dramatic images that spring to mind. I don't see the girl of sixteen falling into Khalil Yared's arms one Palm Sunday, nor the blissful wife who used to spend forty-eight hours closeted with him in the bedroom, nor even the weeping woman roused by a maidservant's cries after her husband's accidental death. Instead, I see a woman staring pensively out of the window of a suburban train.

The harem compartment was almost deserted that early Sunday evening. The only other passenger, a young Muslim woman with her face half exposed, lowered her veil abruptly whenever the conductor appeared.

Mima, seated on the other side of the narrow aisle, watched the houses on the outskirts of Heliopolis glide past. A dry breeze caressed her cheeks. She half closed her eyes, lulled by the rhythmical movements of the carriage.

That Frenchman had made her head spin.

The Ayrouts' house in Baron Empain Street was quite delightful. Tea was served on a handsome, shady terrace flanked by a broad stone parapet, while the youngsters batted balls to and fro on a tennis court at the bottom of the garden. Despite the warmth of her welcome, Mima always found these visits painful. To think that, only a week before his death, Khalil had been deciding on the location of the bathtubs in their future villa at Heliopolis. "Just you wait, my lovely one. We'll have a majestic bedroom fit to turn all the Sakakinis and Taklas green with envy . . . "

His name was Édouard Délenne or Délaime – she hadn't caught it precisely. Forty? Forty-two? Charming, anyway, with his blue eyes, thin moustache, and well-cut, cream alpaca suit.

Not for the first time, Mima had worn the green, beribboned organdie dress that emphasized her youthful appearance. At thirty-six she still resembled a half-grown, luxuriant plant that had not finished flowering.

"You look good in anything," people always told her.

It was true – the simplest scarf made her look like a queen – but since Khalil's death she had lived on her existing wardrobe, which was starting to display serious signs of fatigue. To prevent her dresses from becoming too unfashionable she had performed miracles with the help of a skilful neighbour: a pleat here, a snip of the scissors there. The threadbare coat metamorphosed itself into a jacket, the tired jacket became a bolero . . .

Despite her brother-in-law's very careful management and an occasional grant-in-aid from the Greek Catholic Benevolent Society, Mima had found it difficult to get by with five children to look after. It would be a long time before she could count on Roger, the eldest, who was still a second-year medical student at Qasr al-'Aini.

It was not the first time since Khalil's death that Mima had sensed a man's eyes upon her. She knew perfectly well how to neutralize this form of advance with a look of complete indifference or a brusque gesture – even a moue of distaste. But this time, when immersed in the blue-eyed gaze of the man Délaime, who was sitting across the terrace from her, she had been surprised by her failure to react. Indeed, she had felt more cheerful than usual, and had actually roared with laughter at Habib Ayrout's humorous account of the Heliopolis Company's latest architectural brainwave.

Several of the guests had gone for a stroll in the garden and were heading for the tennis court. Mima was just about to follow them when Édouard came over to her.

"A delightful place, Heliopolis," he said in his unaccented French. "Do you live in the neighbourhood?"

She made some halting reply, felt herself blush like a young girl, and rebuked herself for being silly. Promptly recovering her composure, she described how the garden city had grown up out of the desert. Her husband had often talked to her about Baron Empain's schemes, so she was well acquainted with the subject.

Although Édouard Dhellemmes was entranced by anything to do with Egypt, he was gazing at Mima too intently to take in what she was saying. As for Mima herself, she was too mesmerized by the sight of the Frenchman's shapely hands resting on the terrace wall to pay much attention to her words. Their trancelike state was eventually dispelled by the *sufragi*, who proffered a tray of *petits fours*.

"Since you're going back to town," said Édouard, "we could give you a lift. I came with some friends, the Boulads – perhaps you know them . . . "

Mima almost accepted, then changed her mind. She invented a rather complicated excuse and said she had to leave at once. Having bidden farewell to Édouard Dhellemmes with sudden, incomprehensible urgency, she went and took leave of her hosts.

The Muslim woman got out at 'Abassiya. Abruptly, Mima felt very much alone in the deserted compartment. For the second time in a few hours, she rebuked herself for being silly. After all, why shouldn't she – a woman of thirty-six! – accept a lift from some friends?

Her doorbell rang the next afternoon. Not expecting anyone, she half-opened the door to find that a rose bush had sprouted on the landing. The capacious basket concealed a barefoot errand boy wearing a *bakshish* smile. Mima told him to deposit his burden in the hallway, then quietly closed the door, so taken aback that she forgot to give him the tip he was expecting.

A Shepheard's card was pinned to the basket. It read: "Delighted to have made your acquaintance at Heliopolis yesterday, Édouard Dhellemmes takes the liberty of sending you these few roses before leaving for Marseille. He very much hopes to see you again on his next visit to Egypt."

The basket was too lavish, too beautifully arranged for words. It was a mercy the woman next door hadn't spotted the errand boy and broad-cast the news from her balcony: "Mima, my dear, some flowers for you!"

The children would be back any minute. Mima ran to fetch a pair of scissors and hacked away at the wrapping. She divided the roses into six separate bunches and spread them around the apartment. She would tell the children that she had suddenly succumbed to an urge to buy some flowers. Roger, who held the purse strings, would naturally scold her for squandering money, but what else could she do? That Frenchman was crazy.

Mima kept bumping into Édouard Dhellemmes for the next three days. She encountered his flowers in the hallway, the dining room, the kitchen — wherever she went. Finally, with a mixture of gaiety and melancholy that she herself would have found hard to explain, she threw the roses away even before they had wilted.

4

It was an eternity before André gave notice of his return to Egypt. He had completed two years' noviciate, two years' juvenate, three years of philosophy and four years of theology, interrupted by a year's teaching. Even then he was not finished, because he had to do a third year's noviciate before taking his four solemn vows.

"Ah," the Greek Catholic patriarchal vicar said spitefully, when he came to inquire after the future Jesuit's progress, "with us, things go faster."

A grand family lunch had been arranged to mark my uncle's return. Yolande Batrakani was as nervous as a débutante, and heaven alone knew how many parties she had organized since her marriage. All kinds of very important people had visited the Batrakanis' home in Shubra and, more especially, the new house in Garden City: consuls, beys, pashas, even a minister in office. But this family lunch in André's honour made her more agitated than any other. From the menu to the seating plan to the dress she would wear, everything preyed on her mind. "I'm growing old," she told herself without conviction.

Georges Bey himself was alert to every detail in spite of his lordly air. "Of course the boy must sit at the end of the table! Everyone will want to see him, and besides, he's the eldest . . . "

My grandfather had performed a U-turn. He was now extremely proud of having a Jesuit son, the more so since a European ambassador had publicly congratulated him on that account at an evening reception.

The entire family would be there for Sunday lunch. Paul, newly married, was coming with his Swiss wife Marie-Laure, whom everyone already referred to as the "Swissess". Even Alex had promised to grace the meal with his presence.

"And please be good," implored his mother.

There would be twenty-six at table, counting some hand-picked uncles, aunts and cousins, but arrangements had been made to meet beforehand at the chapel of the Jesuit school where André was to celebrate Mass. He had arrived in Cairo the night before. Not wanting the family to meet him at the station, he had omitted to mention the time of his train.

His friends and relations turned up at the school all of twenty minutes early. They waited in the porter's lodge, then entered the chapel without seeing André until the organ struck up and the young Jesuit, preceded by some altar boys, emerged from the sacristy in his liturgical vestments. Georges and Yolande were transfixed. They had attended their son's ordination in Lebanon the previous year, to be sure, but this was the first time he had officiated in their presence. His transition to the other side of the communion table was complete.

Mass over, the hero of the day was hugged by all and sundry. Georges Batrakani's brand-new black-and-white Chrysler, its carriagework gleaming, glided silently up to the school entrance in Bustan al-Muski Street. The chauffeur got out and opened the doors to reveal some superb brown leather seats the size of sofas.

"*Mabrouk*, Papa!" André strove to sound enthusiastic as he boarded the mobile drawing room with some embarrassment. He knew how greatly his father appreciated such compliments and how much store he set by owning ultra-modern cars, which he regularly traded in for even newer models.

"It's an Airflow," Georges Bey told him. "Notice the suspension? Like velvet. The tank holds seventeen gallons, and the windows are fully retractable . . . "

The Chrysler sped along the Cairo streets, passing yellow trams and green-and-white buses, cabs and carts of all kinds. With the window down and his beard fluttering in the breeze, André was touched to see so many familiar landmarks almost unchanged. He had paid only two brief visits to Cairo in the past twelve years. Now that he had been appointed to teach the fourth form at the Collège de la Sainte-Famille, he would be settling down there.

He was struck by the maladroit way in which the *shawishes* endeavoured to direct the traffic at intersections with listless gestures and feeble blasts on their whistles. Never had those peasants in uniform seemed less robust or more incongruously attired. They conveyed all the wretchedness and gentleness of a country that failed to take itself seriously.

In Qasr al-Nil Street every building was in its due place: the former Suarès Bank, the Italian consulate, the French legation, Robert Hugues, Salon Vert. André fondly recalled accompanying his mother to the latter, a luxury establishment, to buy a dress length on Christmas Eve in 1915 or 1916.

Georges drew his son's attention to the imposing edifice that occupied the site of the former Savoy Hotel, but André only had eyes for his old acquaintances in Suleiman Pasha Square: the two ornamental turrets, Groppi's and its open-air cinema, the Club Risotto, where all the young people went dancing at weekends, Café Riche . . . He couldn't resist glancing up at the Pension Righi, which had harboured so many clandestine love affairs. It was rumoured that Aunt Maggi herself . . .

The Chrysler was briefly waved to a stop by a *shawish* pretending to control the traffic. A ragged little girl, her face devoured by flies, seized the opportunity to come over and beg for money in a plaintive voice. The chauffeur told her to go away.

"Yallah ya bint!"

André felt uncomfortable but had no time to react. The car was already speeding down tree-lined Qasr al-'Aini Street. He recognized the terrace of the Muhammad Ali Club, where governments were formed and dismantled, as well as the Green brothers' villa, which was always shuttered and said to be haunted.

The chauffeur drove even faster after emerging from Qasr al-'Aini Street. They passed a succession of big private houses, so swiftly that Georges barely had time to list their occupants: the Hararis, the Adèses, the Toledanos, Alexandre Shadid Bey, Fakhry Pasha. André spotted some beautiful white palm trees as they skirted the palace of the dowager khediva. They were nearly home.

"I hope you'll enjoy my *molokhiya*," said Yolande.

André leant over and kissed her. She was quite overcome to feel his prickly beard against her cheek.

Drinks before lunch proved a rather stiff affair in spite of Nando's belly-laughs and banter from Maggi, who was sporting a magnificent pyjama suit in green crêpe satin. The Swissess failed to thaw and said nothing. Lola and Viviane were very intimidated by the soutane-clad big brother of whom they had heard so much, and Georges himself found it hard to get used to his son's way of speaking. Without having acquired a genuine French accent, André tended not to drawl so much. He pronounced certain words differently and used a lot of new ones.

Rashid the *sufragi* hovered in the background. Although he had welcomed the Batrakanis' eldest child with tears in his eyes when opening the door to him, he hardly dared to look at him. André had, however, kissed his scarred cheek before giving him a little present.

Edmond Touta, indifferent to all this embarrassment, questioned the Jesuit about the latest disturbing news on the demographic front.

"Did you know that the population of Egypt is not far short of fifteen million? Alarming, isn't it?"

Edmond had written some thirty letters to King Fouad. On the first occasion a palace pen-pusher had churned out a letter of acknowledgement assuring him that His Majesty had "taken careful note" of his remarks. Although the other twenty-nine letters remained unanswered, Edmond felt convinced that the sovereign was devouring his missives as an aid to perfecting a plan of campaign against overpopulation.

They went in to lunch. André made the sign of the cross and shut his eyes for a few moments, gathering his thoughts. Nobody dared to sit down, but it was he who broke the ice as he took his place at the end of the long table.

"Guess who I went to see before I left France?"

"The Dhellemmes."

"No."

"Alice Touta."

"No."

"Yvonne Printemps."

"Alex! You promised . . . "

"Mademoiselle Guyomard."

"Yes indeed! Sweet Henriette!"

A delighted hubbub arose. The name of the former governess, who had retired to France in 1931, was always greeted with the utmost hilarity.

Alex rose to his feet. "It's absurd, quite absurd," he said in a shrill voice. "You can't let that child loose in the midst of a filthy, hysterical mob. He'll get lost. He'll hurt himself or catch heaven knows what disease!"

General laughter.

"When I think," said Yolande, "that Micho nearly missed the sultan at school because the good Henriette failed to wake him punctually."

"Is that true?" Viviane asked, looking ingenuous. She knew the story by heart but never tired of hearing it.

So out it came once more: Michel's late call, his hurried departure with bootlaces trailing, the tram, the brother porter . . . From the far end of the table, Maggi intervened with a question that had bothered her for years.

"But how did the sultan come to know his La Fontaine, *ya Micho?*"

Michel's face lit up. "Hussein Kamil had received a first-class education in Paris. He had even become a playmate and fellow pupil of the Prince Imperial."

Michel now passed for a genuine expert on Sultan Hussein. He spoke of him with the assurance of an authorized biographer, even though his doctoral thesis was still bogged down for want of a well-defined subject. The more research he did, the harder he found it to make up his mind. There was another delicate matter, or possibly a pretext: could he write about Sultan Hussein without drawing invidious comparisons with King Fouad? So Michel's thesis was still unwritten. Meanwhile, he held down a part-time assistant lecturer's post at the university, frequented Amy Kheir's literary salon, and contributed an occasional article to the *Revue du Caire.*

"Yes indeed, Aunt Maggi, Khedive Isma'il sent his son to Paris. He even entrusted his education to General Fleury, aide-de-camp to Napoleon III."

"*Erudimini, qui judicatis terram!*" exclaimed Count Henri Touta.

"Educate yourselves, you that sit in judgement on the world," André translated with a smile. Then, turning to his mother, "Maman, I know I shouldn't put it like this, but your *molokhiya* is divine!"

Everyone applauded. Yolande was in the seventh heaven.

Later, when his son expressed a wish to return to the school, Georges Bey rang for the chauffeur. André firmly refused the offer, nor would he accept a lift from Nando or Henri Touta.

"As you wish, *ya ibni*, as you wish," Georges said sadly.

One had to face facts: the first Jesuit to have been spawned by the Batrakani family preferred to travel by tram.

5

June 1934. My father Selim was fourteen, and the shabby apartment in Faggaala was beginning to give him claustrophobia.

"Thirty piastres!" Roger shouted in Arabic. "You're mad! You want to ruin your mother?"

Selim gave his elder brother a look of fury before striding out of the room and slamming the door behind him. A minute later he was back again, hands on hips and trembling with rage.

"Yes, thirty piastres, that's the absolute minimum. We're not going to our cousins looking like beggars. We've got to be able to buy an ice-cream cornet now and then."

"The boy's mad! His mother deprives herself of everything, and all this *magnoun* can talk about is ice-cream cornets . . . "

The door slammed again.

Selim and Jean were to spend a fortnight of the holidays with some well-heeled cousins who rented a beach hut at Ras al-Barr. Mima would willingly have found them the requisite pocket money by pruning her household expenses a little more drastically, but her eldest son was making a song and dance about it. Roger, who led a spartan exis-tence, couldn't understand why anyone needed to go away on holiday at all. He himself would be swotting throughout the summer in order to do as brilliantly in his fifth year at medical college as he had in the previous four.

"Instead of spending money at Ras al-Barr," he told Selim, "you'd do better to start revising for next term."

The windows rattled to a gunshot from Muqattam. It was midday.

"In this heat," Mima put in, "I can understand why the boys want to go and cool off by the sea."

"What about me?" protested Solange, the youngest.

"That's enough!"

"It isn't fair . . . "

"That's enough, I said!" snapped Mima.

The little girl barely had time to open her mouth again. There was a resounding slap, followed at once by sobs and whimpers. Mima, at the end of her tether, started to weep herself, whereupon Solange fell into her arms. This, as usual, was the prelude to a shower of kisses, an ocean of tears, and a gale of irrepressible laughter.

Mima was like that. Forever on edge and brimming with vitality, she created a permanent field of tension around her. Every six months she would make a scene with Fathiya and fire her, accusing her of ruining the *kufta*, dawdling at the market, or giving her the evil eye. A replacement would be engaged, but a few days later, unable to dispense with her scapegoat any longer, Mima would take the tram to Sayida Zeinab and retrieve Fathiya from her hovel at the end of a squalid alleyway.

Roger left the room, shaking his head. He had decided to give his brothers twenty-five piastres — twenty-five only.

"You hear, Selim? Twenty-five piastres. You're not getting a millieme more!"

My father was disgusted by this penny-pinching attitude. He was sick of patched trousers, darned socks and endlessly resoled shoes. One day he would be rich, if only to impress this irreproachable, intolerable elder brother who had made him recite his lessons while enthroned, ruler in hand, on the lavatory.

6

All the balmy sweetness of the Heliopolis night came flooding in through
the big window, which was wide open. Michel Batrakani felt exultant.
Comfortably seated in an armchair with his eyes half-closed, he savoured
every note of the Chopin waltz that Lidy was playing so admirably.
From time to time the curtains stirred in a gentle breeze that seemed to
conjure up visions of a night without end.

Lectures formed the centrepiece of the Essayists' monthly meetings
at Heliopolis. This Friday in October 1934, a member of the literature
faculty had delivered a brilliant dissertation on "Boileau and the classicist-
modernist controversy tested by time". This sparked off a lively debate,
all memories of which had, as ever, been effaced by Lidy's piano-playing.

Michel's connection with the Essayists dated from the previous
February. It was the unexpected outcome of a year of Sunday squabbles
en famille about Nazi Germany.

"I met you thanks to that *bahlawan* Hitler," my godfather had told Lidy.

But Lidy did not consider Hitler a buffoon. Like all Cairo's middle-
class Jews, her family was filled with mounting anger and alarm by the
Nazis' anti-Semitic measures. In March 1933, under the leadership of
Joseph Cattaoui Pasha and Grand Rabbi Haïm Na'oum Effendi,
representatives of Jewish organizations had met and resolved to boycott
German products in Egypt. Because this ban extended to medicines,
the Jewish Hospitals Committee had requested French pharmaceutical
importers to supply substitutes. Among its other requirements was a
remedy for bilharzia to replace Fouadine, a celebrated product specially
developed for Egypt by the firm of Bayer–Meister.

Georges Batrakani was beside himself with indignation. "Who do they think they are, these Jews?" he protested. "They want us to starve, believe me!"

Being the agent for a pharmaceutical company based in Hamburg, Georges Bey posed as a direct victim of the boycott. Everyone knew, however, that German products accounted for only a very modest part of his turnover. He also represented four French laboratories, so the Jewish hospitals' new policy might well be to his advantage.

"What more do they want, these confounded Jews? They already own all the big stores in Egypt. Cicurel, that's theirs. Chemla, that's theirs. Gattegno, that's theirs. What about Orosdi-Back? Could that be theirs too, by any chance? At least we've got Sednaoui!"

"But Papa," Michel put in, "most of the agents for German pharmaceutical companies are Jews, you know that perfectly well. In a way, they're penalizing themselves."

"What an innocent you are! I've seen the way they operate. Either they remove the brand names from their merchandise and sell it anyway, or they stockpile it with an eye to the future and send prices rocketing."

Michel tried to steer conversation back to Hitler's anti-Semitic measures, only to clash with Paul. His brother had just returned, full of enthusiasm, from a visit to Berlin.

"Don't turn your nose up at the Germans. We could do with some of their discipline over here."

"But that's not the point, *ya akhi*. We weren't talking about discipline."

"Exactly. So let's talk about it!"

To smooth things over and repeat a story she never tired of telling, Yolande tried to introduce the subject of her ancestor the customs officer.

"Did you know that at the beginning of the eighteenth century Egypt's customs houses were controlled by Jews? It was all the Greek Catholics of Damietta could do to oust them and take over. My forebear the customs officer — "

"All I know," said Georges Bey, nipping this hoary old tale in the bud, "is that today the Jews rule the roost. The Suareses, the Cattaouis, the Rolos, the Mosseris — they taunt and humiliate us with all their factories, their banks, their palatial mansions . . . "

Sunday lunches became even more strained when Germany decided, by way of reprisal, to purchase no more Egyptian cotton. Georges Bey took this as personally as if the whole of his crop were destined for the land of Hitler.

"What have I done to them, to be penalized twice over? Not only can I not sell the cotton here, but I'm forbidden to send it over there. Just you wait, the Jews will soon ban the tarboosh. We'll all be going around in skullcaps, you mark my words!"

Michel fidgeted with his knife-rest, exasperated by all this animosity. "Sémoditchek", at least, had been a family joke.

Early in January 1934 the Jabès trial succeeded in rendering family lunches unbearable. The affair had begun several months earlier, when the German Club in Cairo published a violently anti-Semitic pamphlet. It accused "world Jewry" of being, among other things, "perniciously prolific" and "predisposed to certain crimes". Taking this as a personal insult, an Italian Jew named Umberto Jabès sued Count van Meeteren, chairman of the German Club, for libel.

"At least he's a genuine count," Georges said to Yolande, " – unlike your brother."

Michel had been outraged by the pamphlet. On 22 January 1934, he and another fifteen hundred protesters queued up outside the first chamber of the mixed court. Their purpose in being there was to boo Herr Grimm, who had been imported from Münster to lead the defence.

"The pamphlet at issue was referring to the status of Jews in Germany," Grimm contended. "It did not relate to Monsieur Jabès nor to any of the persons associated with his complaint. The charge is inadmissible."

Michel, egged on by the anger of those around him, protested loudly. The presiding judge threatened to clear the courtroom, then called upon Maître Léon Castro, counsel for the plaintiff, to speak. He rose to the occasion brilliantly.

"It is for the judge to show whether the injury was sustained by a collectivity or an individual. No Jewish collectivity exists, however. It is merely the sum of the individuals that comprise it."

In accordance with custom, Maître Castro replaced his tarboosh before bringing his speech to a spirited conclusion:

"An Egyptian mixed court composed of magistrates of all races, nationalities and religious denominations – a court that has for fifty years, and without fear or favour, accorded equal respect to all faiths, all races, and the laws of all nations – is no place in which to endeavour to show that one particular people, race or religion is undeserving of equal respect for its faith, its dignity, and its rights."

Michel applauded frantically. Just then he felt a hand on his shoulder and swung round. It was Victor Lévy.

The two former classmates exchanged a long look, incapable of uttering a word. Each was as moved as the other.

To a chorus of boos, the court dismissed Umberto Jabès's plea. Michel rose, torn between indignation and absolute delight. He had lost a case but gained a friend.

"Are you free for dinner?" Victor Lévy asked him when they met up at the entrance.

They were still at Groppi's at one o'clock in the morning, gaily trying to make up for a silence lasting eighteen years. The whole class of 1921 filed past to the accompaniment of bottles of Stella beer. They drank to the health of Father Korner, Sultan Hussein, the "*Laboureur*" and every one of his "*enfants*".

The same night, Victor Lévy invited Michel to join the Essayists, of which he was a leading light. A meeting of special interest was to be held in ten days' time. Its theme: "The topicality of *L'Esprit des lois*. A rereading of Montesquieu."

"And, if you're fond of the piano, you'll hear my cousin Lidy play. She always treats us to a short recital."

Michel detested the piano. Lidy he adored.

7

It was eleven o'clock when the telephone rang in the house at Garden City.

"Something's happened, Georges. Your brother Nando . . . "

Although he had a detailed report in front of him, the journalist cousin who worked for *La Bourse égyptienne* proved extremely vague about the circumstances surrounding the tragedy. His news was greeted with a long silence.

"Can you hear me, Georges? Did you get that?"

"I hear you," my grandfather said at length in a muffled voice. "If I ever lay hands on those swine . . . "

"The door was shut, but blood was oozing from under it – a little pool had formed outside. I couldn't see anything at first. Someone must have blown out the lamp."

The silent policeman kept dipping his pen in the inkwell. Some witnesses had to be bullied into giving evidence. Not so the 'umda, who never stopped talking and answered questions before they were asked.

"We'd arranged to meet to settle the sale of some land. The *khawaga* had told me to call on him after sunset. A dog was howling on the doorstep."

Ferdinand Batrakani was lying on his back with his throat cut, like a slaughtered sheep.

"I don't understand," said the 'umda. "Cutting his throat was enough. Why did they have to slit his belly open as well? His guts were hanging out, already thick with flies . . . "

* * *

Next morning Georges Batrakani went to visit Nando's widow. Then he drove to his brother's farm a few miles from al-Mansoura. His sons had offered to accompany him, but they met with a flat refusal.

"I'll take Makram. An accountant is all I need."

Twenty years after the event they were still wondering what he had meant by this. Makram himself, discreetly questioned in turn by Michel and Paul, was unable to provide a satisfactory explanation. According to him, Georges hadn't opened his mouth all the way to al-Mansoura.

To Makram the Copt, Ferdinand Batrakani was the archetypal parasite and exploiter. He had always regarded the gluttonous landowner and unscrupulous accumulator of feddans as an enemy of the people.

"Sooner or later your brother will get his just deserts," he used to say.

Could it have been simply that phrase which prompted Georges to take him to al-Mansoura? At all events, Makram's dark suit was appropriate for once.

It was clear that Nando had not been the chance victim of a lone bandit. Everything pointed to a local, communal conspiracy: the absence of servants, the worthless testimony of neighbours who knew nothing, had seen and heard nothing.

"If I had the murderer here I'd throttle him with my bare hands," Georges told the 'umda. "But the whole village colluded in this killing. His debtors are much mistaken if they think their crime has let them off the hook. My brother's financial records are in Cairo under lock and key. I shall personally uphold the interests of his widow and children, and woe betide those who can't pay!"

While driving back that evening he asked Makram to help him settle Nando's affairs. The Copt could hardly refuse.

Next day, Georges Bey called at the ministry of the interior and raised a rumpus, though only for form's and honour's sake. He had no illusions. Some months later the case was closed for want of sufficient evidence.

My grandfather was one of the few who knew how much effort, imagination and courage it had cost Nando to become a wealthy man. His fortune had been amassed from scratch, piastre by piastre, feddan by feddan. He had been bold enough to leave the city lights behind and venture out into the Egyptian countryside, that scorned and unfamiliar territory which he eventually came to know – and love – exceedingly well.

In 1890, at the age of eighteen, Georges's elder brother had entered the employ of one Xenakis, a Greek moneylender who, being laid up in Cairo with gout, needed a representative to go the rounds of his clients in the Delta.

At dawn four times a week, fat Nando would board the train to Benha with his provisions wrapped up in a double-page spread of *Le Bosphore égyptien*: two or three *fuul* sandwiches, a tomato or two, and a hunk of Constantinople cheese. The rest of his equipment was limited to a pencil and a little notebook. As for money, he concealed it in a special pocket stitched to the inside of his trousers by his sister Eugénie.

Nando used to open his package as soon as the train set off – travelling at that hour always gave him an appetite. The third-class compartment, which resembled a farmyard, made him feel he was already in the country. Hens and ducks roamed free, leaving excrement all over the yellow leather mules removed by passengers desirous of greater comfort and an opportunity to twiddle their toes.

At Benha, Nando hired a donkey with a glossy coat and a lively eye – always the same one. His job was to go from village to village, collecting interest and offering new loans. Each completed transaction earned him a commission of one per cent.

The Greek's clients, who could neither read nor write, signed their promissory notes with a thumbprint. One pound sterling was generally lent for one hundred and twenty-five piastres, which meant that it yielded interest at twenty-seven and a half per cent. The civil code did not authorize rates of interest exceeding twelve per cent, but how could farmers who were already in debt and saw agricultural prices falling year after year be prevented from becoming ensnared by moneylenders? They had to pay back the loans they'd taken out to buy seed or fertilizer. Family functions of any kind – weddings, circumcisions, funerals – upset their frail budget and compelled them to borrow still more, whatever the rate of interest.

These smallholders could have approached the banks like the pashas who owned vast estates, but banks insisted on their taking out a mortgage, and, in any case, they seldom lent such modest sums. What was more, it was the tax inspectors, execrated by country folk, who undertook to recover outstanding debts. No one had forgotten their activities prior to the British occupation: they were forever exacting crushing taxes with the aid of the *kurbag*, the sinister hippopotamus-hide whip whose use had been technically – but only technically – prohibited since 1883. An insolvent debtor who dealt with a bank risked having his land distrained, whereas he could always come to some arrangement with a moneylender.

Nando took his time and kept his ears open. He familiarized himself with village customs and agricultural methods. Before long he could, at a glance, assess the quality of a sugar-cane crop, the price of a draught water buffalo, or the output of a waterwheel. By observing the original way of measuring the volume of grain, which allowed for the greater density of the lowest layers, he also learnt that two and two do not necessarily make four – a lesson that was to stand him in good stead later on.

Once a week Nando brought the Greek his little notebook containing the names of borrowers and the date and extent of their loans. This did not prevent him from engaging in small-scale transactions on his own behalf. Sometimes, for instance, he would lend a farmer twenty piastres in return for a repayment of thirty on market day the following week.

After some years Nando gave the Greek the slip. Having learnt the ropes, he now knew how to exploit bankruptcies and cotton prices.

Although interest was calculated on a yearly basis, repayment was always demanded in October, at harvest time. This was the so-called "month of the moneylenders", to whom insolvent farmers were then compelled to sell their crops. But cotton prices fluctuated constantly. Well-organized moneylenders like Nando got their correspondents to wire them the latest prices and acted accordingly. Altogether, their profits could amount to as much as sixty per cent of their original outlay.

The growth of Nando's paunch matched that of his secret trouser pocket. When war broke out in 1914, this prince among moneylenders transformed himself into a property speculator. He bought up all the land that was on offer. By the time of his death twenty years later, he owned assets worth a million Egyptian pounds.

* * *

Georges had always maintained a complex attitude towards this elder brother who resembled him so little. He appeared to defend and find excuses for Nando without necessarily approving of him. He himself was the *de facto* elder brother, and his elevation to bey only accentuated this reversal of roles.

In the years that followed Nando's death my grandfather seemed, in a sense, to be canonizing the deceased. A frequent preamble of his, uttered in solemn tones, was: "As my brother Nando used to say . . . "

In fact, all everyone remembered of Ferdinand Batrakani was his healthy fortune, his prodigious appetite, and a huge, hoarse laugh that burst upon the ear like an old-fashioned lavatory being flushed.

PART SIX

The "*Quartiers Réservés*"

I

Father André Batrakani gritted his teeth and prayed to the Virgin Mary. Accompanied by worthy Ebeid, the school's oldest driver, he'd been traversing this loathsome district for a good five minutes. They'd had to park the Citroën quite some distance away before setting off down the narrow passage that marked the entrance to the Fish Market.

Not a fish in sight, of course. It soon dawned on any tourists who were conducted there by guides of mysterious mien that the Fish Market was Cairo's *"quartier réservé"*, or red-light district.

"Reserved for whom? For the British, like the Sporting Club?" Thus André himself, aged ten, at a family gathering. Everyone had roared with laughter.

He felt sorry for the child whom he still resembled so closely in certain respects. Reserved for whom? Why "reserved"? His questions had remained unanswered. That was in the days of the Sunday lunches at which his uncles used to tell him, with a knowing air, "You'll join the mixed courts when you grow up."

Mixed courts? The term had made him blush. What were these mysterious places? Courtyards where the sexes mingled — where men engaged in forbidden acts with girls of easy virtue?

Late that afternoon the school had received a phone call from a woman with a hoarse voice. "There's a boy here who isn't at all well," she croaked. "His friends tell me he's from your school. If you don't come soon I'm going to call the police."

The headmaster had promptly sent for André.

"Only someone with a good knowledge of Arabic can go and collect this boy. Can you leave at once? Ebeid will accompany you."

The district was a maze of narrow alleys and squat, grimy houses. Women of every description — black, Arab, Greek, Maltese, Jewish — hailed passers-by in a variety of languages. Notices on their doors gave their names and nationalities. They supplemented this information in person and supplied details of their amatory expertise, wiggling their hips and making suggestive movements.

Looking neither to right nor left, André mechanically followed Ebeid, who paused from time to time to ask the way. A dyed blonde with coal-black eyebrows and grotesquely rouged cheeks tugged at the sleeve of André's cassock.

"This way, you handsome boy! I know what you're after!"

He brusquely disengaged himself, white with anger, and Ebeid thrust the girl aside. She promptly showered them both with insults, some of which related to André's mother. Poor Ebeid walked on faster, shaking his head.

The houses in the next alleyway had grilles over their windows. Passers-by would take a run at the wall and cling to the bars for a few moments, the better to gauge the quality of the services on sale inside.

If André had been on his own he might well have turned back at this stage, but Ebeid, satisfied that they were heading in the right direction, was now striding along briskly.

"There it is," he said, pointing to a little knot of people clustered round an open doorway.

André saw two figures detach themselves from the group and slink off down a nearby alleyway: two boys from the senior school notorious for their idleness and indiscipline. They would be for it when he caught up with them . . .

"So you're here at last!" exclaimed a fleshy matron in down-at-heel slippers. "About time too! You're in luck, the boy's better. He passed out — we thought he was dead. *Yallah, yallah*, take him and go. I don't want any more children in my place."

The big cast-iron bed was half-obscured by some grimy muslin curtains, and stretched out on it was a boy with flushed cheeks: a fifth-former named Raouf B. He raised his head on seeing Father Batrakani.

"Will I be expelled, Father?" he asked anxiously.

André didn't answer. With a glance, he summoned Ebeid to help the boy to his feet. Then he set off, this time in the lead.

"*Yallah, yallah!*" the matron cried hoarsely, shooing away the onlookers. "There's nothing to see!"

2

Yolande Batrakani used to give a tea party at her home every Tuesday. As a rule Viviane avoided these gossipy social gatherings like the plague and contrived never to "come and pay your respects". This time she had not only turned up early but invited her girlfriend Salwah as well. The two teenagers were itching to meet the celebrated guest of honour, Huda Sha'arawi, leading light of the Egyptian feminist movement.

The previous month they had attended the wedding of a Muslim schoolmate who had only just turned sixteen, and whose family had arranged the marriage without even consulting her. Viviane had been shocked when she saw the bridegroom, a swarthy, potbellied, balding man in his forties. The bride changed her clothes several times during the festivities, according to custom, but her powdered face made her look like a corpse. She burst out sobbing when she saw her friends.

"Personally, I'd sooner have killed myself," Salwah told Viviane during break the next day. "I would – I'd have slit my wrists. Either that, or gone to see Huda Sha'arawi."

The teacher on duty was approaching. Seeing her, they made a great show of going their separate ways. "When two are together, the Devil is in the middle," the nuns used to say.

What exactly could the Devil mean to a Muslim like Salwah? She remained standing during prayers in class, silent and seemingly detached. Viviane used to watch her out of the corner of her eye. It was rumoured that one Muslim student of rhetoric had become converted without her parents' knowledge, and that the nuns made her communicate in private after Mass. True or false? In any case, that wasn't Salwah's style at all. Viviane knew her friend too well to be able to picture her on her knees in the sacristy.

The first time Salwah had invited her home, a big black limousine was waiting for them outside school. Viviane was astonished to see Salwah kiss her father's hand. Feeling very intimidated, she joined her friend on the back seat. The father, who was sitting beside the chauffeur, didn't favour them with a single word or glance all the way there.

Huda Sha'arawi's most recent provocation concerned marriage. She had just jolted Muslim tradition by arranging the wedding of her goddaughter, the lovely Huriya Idris. The bridegroom, a young diplomat, wore a dark suit and white gloves in the Western manner, while Huriya, resplendent in a white gown and a long veil, was attended by bridesmaids and a page. But it was the marriage contract that had really set tongues wagging. In return for her goddaughter's hand, Huda Sha'arawi had asked the bridegroom for the derisory sum of twenty-five piastres on signature and three hundred pounds payable in due course. Scandalized commentators accused her of "devaluing our girls".

Huda Sha'arawi smiled when a friend of Yolande's questioned her about this over the tinkle of silver teaspoons in teacups. "No, of course I'm not devaluing our girls, I'm simply making marriages easier. Under the present ludicrous system, a young man is expected to pay a *mahr* of exorbitant size. Either he abandons the idea of marriage altogether, or he incurs a substantial debt. Wouldn't the money be better spent on acquiring a comfortable home?"

"You're also accused of making divorce easier."

"What hypocrisy! I'm proud of having voted for a law that permits a woman to get divorced if she's subjected to physical violence. I also hope to be able to prohibit the marriage of girls under sixteen."

Salwah, sitting in the background with Viviane, drank in the words of this pasha's widow and supporter of Sa'ad Zaghloul.

"They married me off at thirteen," Huda Sha'arawi went on. "I was a total ignoramus. I asked my husband to allow me to spend some time on our family estate in Upper Egypt. Being a cultured and intelligent man, he agreed. When writing to me at that time he had to enclose his letters in an envelope addressed to the eunuch. Why? Because a woman's name was so secret that it couldn't even pass the postman's lips! While in Upper Egypt I devoured my father's European library. Later on I sent for more books from abroad – France, England, America. I spent years studying, pondering, comparing. Finally, when I was eighteen, I wrote and told the pasha that I felt worthy of him, and we resumed married life in the Muslim fashion."

During the disturbances of 1919 Huda Sha'arawi had demonstrated in the streets of Cairo with other women veiled like herself. Four years later, having founded the Egyptian Feminist Union, she represented Egypt at the Feminist Congress in Rome.

"Thousands of people had gathered at the station when our delegation returned to Cairo. I got out of the train dressed in black from head to foot. Then I threw back my veil. They could have spat in my face, but they remained calm. I made my way slowly through the crowd with tears streaming down my cheeks. The next day some old ulemas came and implored me to resume the veil. I replied that my conscience wouldn't permit it."

"Did the king support you?" asked Yolande.

Huda Sha'arawi wagged her head in an equivocal manner. Fouad had been unwilling to commit himself.

"In 1932, when Queen Sureya of Afghanistan visited Cairo, Fouad was afraid she would expose her face. He sent her a thick chiffon shawl with a jewelled clasp. Sureya arrived muffled up in this shawl. We members of the Feminist Union, who had gone to the station to welcome her, were also veiled by royal command. When Fouad's car passed us, however, we all threw back our veils at once. And then, to atone for our symbolic rebellion, we threw roses at him."

"How wonderful!" exclaimed Salwah, immediately turning puce as every eye swivelled in her direction.

Huda Sha'arawi gave her a friendly gesture of acknowledgement before continuing.

"Things are changing, it's true. Last year a female student applied to read for a degree in law. Two hundred thousand girls in Egypt now attend school, twice as many as in the early nineteen-twenties. Still, they represent fewer than ten per cent of girls of school age – and

I'm including young urban Christians like you, all of whom go to school."

Viviane was about to point out that her friend was a Muslim when Huda Sha'arawi went on:

"It's true that the harem compartments in trams are becoming less and less exclusive. Men can be found in them, and women don't hesitate to sit in the others. But mark my words, there's still a long way to go. Look at the fuss those two girl students caused by wearing swimsuits at the university water sports. I would also remind you that the sheikhs of Alexandria are proposing to divide the beaches into single-sex areas. They're going to open a seaside bathing-place at Sidi Bishr reserved for women alone. I know more than one dignitary who means to compel his wife to bathe in that seaside prison."

She turned to Salwah.

"The struggle to emancipate the women of Egypt is going to take a long, long time. There'll be setbacks and reverses, but we'll win in the end, I'm sure, especially if girls like you come and join us . . . "

Huda Sha'arawi broke off. The *sufragi* had burst into the drawing room with a look of feverish agitation on his face.

Yolande stared at him in surprise. "What is it, Rashid?"

"Excuse me, madame. His Majesty the King is dead."

3

Chairs were being rented in 'Abdin Street for thirty piastres the morning. People were even paying to perch on a big step-ladder that had been set up on the pavement by an astute grocer. But the truly privileged were awaiting the royal procession at the Continental Hotel, which had installed tiers of seats for the occasion.

Hassan, who had come to watch, felt trapped, as he later described in *An Officer's Career*. After all, he was helping to swell an immense crowd whose very presence would be construed as a blank cheque tendered to the new king.

Fouad had taken several days to die — days punctuated by falsely reassuring medical bulletins. None of the prayers offered up by ulemas, bishops of various denominations, or the grand rabbi had succeeded in keeping him here on earth.

Prince Farouq had had to wait for his father to give up the ghost completely before quitting his school at Woolwich, near London, and heading for Egypt. He arrived there five days after the funeral.

"The British offered to rush him here in a warship," said a tramway clerk behind Hassan.

"He refused, and quite right too," said someone else. "What would it have made us look like? No king of Egypt could come and take possession of his throne aboard a British gunboat!"

Farouq, who had just turned sixteen, was entitled to the full treatment. Received at Buckingham Palace by Edward VIII, he had left for Dover by special train. Two destroyers escorted his ship to Calais. From there he travelled on to Marseille, where an entire section of the *Viceroy of India* had been made ready for him.

But that was nothing to what awaited him in Egypt: the British fleet dressed overall, aircraft in the sky, and big crowds massed at every station to see his white train pass by. In Cairo, all along the route to be followed by his cortège, loudspeakers broadcast announcements, songs, and addresses of welcome.

"He's young, he's good-looking, and he'll kick the British out," said the tramway clerk.

"He certainly won't be short of pocket money," observed one of his colleagues. "They say Fouad left him several million pounds, not to mention his palaces and his stamp collection."

Hassan, who was the same age as Farouq, thought of the one-pound note Uncle Rashid had just sent him. A very handsome gift – his annual gift. He also thought of Viviane Batrakani, whose green eyes had haunted him ever since this morning. What had she been doing in the kitchen when he rang the tradesmen's bell? He very seldom came across any member of that family of *khawagas* on his rare visits to his uncle.

Hassan and Viviane had recognized each other at once, recalling their first encounter in the old house at Shubra six years earlier. Neither of them had forgotten Abu Simsim, the showman with his magic box and his cry of "*Ya salaam, ya salaam, shouf al-forga di keman . . .*"

"I've come to see my uncle Rashid," Hassan said haltingly, bedazzled by the green-eyed teenager Viviane had become.

Hassan's diffident voice contrasted with his handsome, hawklike face. What flustered Viviane most about Rashid's nephew, however, was the muscular chest that bulged beneath his white, sweat-stained shirt.

"Come in," she said, doing her best to sound thoroughly aloof. "I'll call Rashid."

The simple fact of having uttered those few words in Arabic helped to restore her composure and erect an invisible barrier between them, for each language had its proper function. No Batrakani would have dreamt of saying "*ça ne fait rien*" instead of "*ma'alish*" or of substituting "*félicitations*" for "*mabrouk*". Expressions of love, on the other hand, were inconceivable in any language but French – or English, at a pinch, on the cinema screen. To say "I love you" in Arabic would have sounded ludicrous, if not obscene.

Hassan had been subjugated by that self-assured, cosmopolitan, middle-class voice. He'd felt a fierce urge to take her in his arms and kiss her full on the lips.

The crowds near Opera Square began to shout and jostle. Hassan craned his neck. Escorted by several other vehicles, a big red motor car was slowly approaching to the accompaniment of steadily swelling cheers. The queen mother and her daughters were preceding Farouq to 'Abdin Palace so that they would be there to welcome him.

Rashid had been delighted by his nephew's visit. Having more or less acted as Hassan's guardian ever since rescuing him from the camel abattoir at Giza, he still dreamed of seeing him become a public servant of some kind.

"Why not put in for a job with the railways?" Rashid had suggested for the umpteenth time. "I could ask the *khawaga* to recommend you. He knows many people – he has a great deal of influence . . . "

"I'm going to apply to the Military Academy," said Hassan.

"The Military Academy? To become an officer? They'll never take you, *ya ibni*. They only take rich people or officers' sons."

Hassan realized that his acceptance by the Academy was anything but a foregone conclusion. "Although I could pass the physical aptitude test on my head," he writes in *An Officer's Career*, "I was as much in danger of failing the interview as most of my friends. The admissions board would certainly have asked if I'd had any political affiliations or taken part in the previous year's protests. What could I have said? Those haughty, arrogant senior officers were bound to have access to police files."

Hassan reflected that his father, too, must have acquired a police record before being gunned down in the street like a stray dog. He didn't even know what the man had looked like. No one possessed a photograph of him, neither Hassan's mother, who had become the village 'umda's third wife on her remarriage in 1920, nor Uncle Rashid, to whom he owed the information that his father the cigarette-factory worker had been a hot-blooded agitator and enemy of injustice.

Hassan's own blood boiled in his veins, but he couldn't claim to be an agitator. He was simply an agitated youth trying feverishly to decide between the Blueshirts of the Wafd — too pale for his taste — and the Greenshirts whose members concocted bombs in the desert at Helwan. The student demonstrations of November 1935 had been a blend of all colours.

On 13 November I went out into the streets, in company with many other secondary school pupils, to demand that the British clear out and the Constitution of 1923 be restored. We made for Rodah Bridge to link up with university students coming from the other side of the Nile. I was halfway across the bridge when I heard a bullet whistle past my ears. I promptly turned and took to my heels.

Two dead, dozens of wounded, numerous arrests. Schools were closed for a month by government decree. A few weeks later, however, King Fouad restored the 1923 Constitution. We had won. (*An Officer's Career*, p. 40.)

The hubbub coming from Opera Square increased in volume. The loudspeakers, which had been blaring nasal music, abruptly fell silent. All that heralded the procession's approach was a growing clatter of hoofs.

Hassan was transfixed by the sight of the royal bodyguard, a troop of mounted lancers. The officers rejoiced in white tunics, blue breeches with red stripes, and gilded breastplates. He was filled with an insane desire to look like them. For some moments he pictured himself in their midst, a mounted figure in uniform, riding past the home of that girl, Viviane Batrakani, who was leaning on the windowsill on the lookout for Abu Simsim . . .

Farouq was seated in an open carriage beside the prime minister, Ali Maher Pasha. Young and handsome, he was wearing a tarboosh and a black frock coat.

"Long live the king!" yelled the tramway clerk.

"Out with the British!" cried one of his neighbours.

Hassan felt his chest swell with emotion. This young, handsome king was going to drive the British out. Jumping up and down on the spot and waving his arms, the future officer proceeded to shout at the top of his voice, "*Ya'aish Farouq!*"

4

Farouq might be going to drive the British out, but for the moment they were very much still there, firmly installed in the heart of his capital. Although the British Residency remained Egypt's control-room, so to speak, the occupying power was additionally symbolized by other, more frivolous places: the Turf Club, for example, exclusively frequented by subjects of His Majesty who perused *The Times* in capacious leather armchairs amid clouds of Virginia tobacco smoke; or, nestling between two branches of the Nile, the Gezira Sporting Club whose acres of turf, close-shaven every morning, welcomed players of tennis, cricket, croquet, and polo.

My uncle Paul and his wife ardently desired to become members of the Sporting Club. The Swissess had her eye on the swimming pool, whereas Paul, who was not in the least athletic, merely aspired to enter the holy of holies.

The British, who had occupied the Sporting Club ever since its establishment, ran it by themselves. They had only just half-opened the door to some other foreign residents and a few handpicked Egyptians.

Paul Batrakani's application was submitted in June 1937 and rejected the same month. No reason was given, but the unsuccessful candidate did get to hear of a kindly remark voiced by one of the committee members:

"Tarboosh manufacturers don't belong in this club."

Paul was terribly upset by the whole business. It could have made him anti-British; instead, he became anti-tarboosh.

"You ought to consider producing something else," he told his father. "Tarbooshes are ridiculous. People look as if they're wearing flowerpots on their heads."

Georges Bey stared at him in amazement.

"Is that meant to be a joke?"

Paul launched into a long tirade on the unhygienic nature of the tarboosh in a country as hot as Egypt.

"You're crazy!" my grandfather cut in. "You're simply trotting out the same old hackneyed arguments I've heard a hundred times before. I'm neither a hygienist nor a creator of high fashion. Those flowerpots, as you call them, are selling better than ever."

Thanks to government measures for the protection of local industry, and doubtless because some members of the public preferred to buy Egyptian, imports of foreign tarbooshes had been dwindling year by year. Where national production was concerned, the house of Batrakani was starting to sweep the board. This rising curve was accompanied by several nice publicity coups. The wall above Georges Bey's desk bore a large photograph of the Egyptian Olympic team departing for the Berlin Games of 1936. It showed the smiling athletes clustered at the windows of the train that was taking them to Alexandria to sail for Europe, and all wore Batrakani tarbooshes graciously presented to them by the firm of origin.

But Paul persisted. He put forward a commercial argument – the only kind capable of impressing his father:

"I'm thinking of future sales, Papa. The tarboosh is bound to disappear sooner or later. Even today, young men wear them only when obliged to – when sitting government examinations, for instance. It's time you adapted yourself to changing attitudes."

"Changing attitudes be damned! And I'll thank you never to visit the factory again with a hat on your head, the way you did the other day. It's outrageous! You wouldn't see Henry Ford's son rolling up in a Pontiac or a Chrysler."

Paul shrugged his shoulders and changed the subject. He could have said so much more, tarbooshes apart. A brilliant lawyer, he was displaying an ever-increasing contempt for Egypt and an inordinate interest in everything European. He subscribed to *Le Temps* of Paris and never failed to comment at table on some manœuvre by Action Française, some project of Blum's, or some speech by Briand. This greatly tickled Alex, who made a point of addressing him by the Arabic version of his first name. At the risk of offending his Gallic ancestors, Paul had become "Boulos".

The following rather wry passage appears in the sixth volume of Michel's diary:

9 October 1937

Twenty years ago, the worthiest sovereign Egypt ever had lay dying. One cannot, alas, publicize that fact in writing. Everyone is overcome with blissful admiration for the boy Farouq, and Fouad's ghost still looms in our midst. A reign of nineteen years is not so easily effaced from the memory.

Honour is saved, so to speak, by the carpet seller in Isma'iliya Square, who keeps a big portrait of Sultan Hussein in the doorway of his shop. I go there occasionally, just for pleasure's sake, and seldom leave without buying something. I don't know where to put all the rugs I've acquired.

Poor Sultan Hussein! He died too soon and came to power too late. Farouq cannot say the same. This youth on whom fortune seems to smile in every way has inaugurated his reign with two historic agreements. They weren't his doing, but he takes the credit for them. The British military occupation of Egypt is more or less at an end, and the Capitulations have been done away with.

Paul can't get over this. With his habitual pessimism, he says the Montreux agreement spells "the end of the Syrians of Egypt". It's true that the abolition of the mixed courts, which is scheduled for 1949, will sooner or later compel him to change jobs. "Wouldn't it appeal to you, being a tarboosh manufacturer?" Alex asked him at lunch yesterday. They almost came to blows.

5

At Epiphany every year the Greek Catholic bishop went the rounds, blessing his flock and collecting money. He made another appearance in October or November to inquire how the faithful were faring and garner a more substantial sum. On the occasion of this second visit, which was known as the *nouriya*, most families donated one Egyptian pound. For his part, Georges Batrakani gave fifteen. The "king of the tarboosh", as the magazine *Images* was soon to christen him, had no wish to seem less munificent than a Kahil or a Sednaoui.

The duration of the bishop's visit was often proportional to the sum in the envelope. In the case of certain middle-class families with whom he was well acquainted, he would even stay to lunch. For the *nouriya* of 1938 my grandmother had ordered stuffed vine leaves.

The bishop took a second helping, then a third. He inquired after various members of the family, punctuating the information he received with admiring exclamations of "'*Smallah! 'Smallah!*" Over coffee he turned to Michel.

"What about you, *habibi*?" he said without warning. "Still unmarried?"

Taken aback, my godfather grunted an affirmative and nervously lit a cigarette.

"You know what they say," the bishop went on. "The '*arousa* or the *kallousa* . . . "

"A bride or the priest's hat," Yolande translated mechanically. She, too, considered that a bachelor of thirty-three ought to be starting a family instead of burying himself in his books.

Michel felt offended. There had never been any question of the *kallousa*, but the '*arousa*?

Favouring the bishop with a pinched smile, he lingered in the drawing room for another few minutes, just for courtesy's sake, and then slipped away.

At the Essayists' meeting three months earlier he had given a talk on "Rhythmical effects in the poetry of La Fontaine". It was warmly applauded, but the look Lidy gave him from her place at the piano outweighed all the compliments in the world.

Michel spent the rest of the evening in the clouds. Never since reciting for the sultan at school had he felt so exhilarated, so utterly fulfilled.

When the party began to break up he went over to the piano, where Lidy was tidying away her scores. She looked a trifle unreal, what with her white muslin dress, her diaphanous skin, and the limpid gaze that had so often set his pulses racing. Michel felt he was growing wings.

"Lidy," he said without preamble, stammering a little, "will you marry me?"

She stared at him wide-eyed.

"But Michel . . . "

It wasn't a premeditated proposal. Only yesterday, on hearing from brother Paul that the Swissess was expecting their second child, he had thanked his lucky stars he was a bachelor, free from cares and constraints.

"I'm a Jew, Michel."

That didn't matter in the least, he told her fervently. Love was all-powerful. Others in Egypt had ignored that form of barrier, and they were far from being the unhappiest couples around.

"But Michel, there's something else: I'm ill."

He smiled.

"I'll cure you."

"I'm very ill indeed. The doctor is afraid it's my lungs."

He continued to smile, but his ardour subsided a little. This unexpected ailment had brought him down to earth, so to speak. He realized now that he didn't want to get married at all.

His embarrassment must have been perceptible, because Lidy gently but firmly seized the initiative.

"No, Michel, really. You're a very dear friend. Let's stay that way, please."

He questioned her about her illness and clumsily tried to reassure her. Then, injecting as much sincerity into his voice as he could manage, he repeated his proposal of marriage.

"No, Michel, please don't go on."

He lowered his eyes with an air of resignation, simultaneously aware that the girl's refusal was an immense relief to him . . .

Any doubts about Lidy's condition were dispelled as the months went by and her cough grew worse. But the news from Europe had much to do with the often melancholy look in her eyes. She followed Hitler's provocative progress with close attention. Saddened by the fate of Austria, she spent hours discussing it with some Jewish musicians who had fled from Vienna and settled in Cairo.

At the Essayists' soirées Lidy would sometimes pause in the middle of a piece and turn towards the window as if listening for the tramp of jackboots. Then, with half-closed eyes, she would improvise some chords, wringing notes from her piano that were strange, subdued, and infinitely disturbing.

PART SEVEN

Sidi Bishr No. 2

I

The Metro Cinema was heavily patronized during the summer of 1941. Confined to the capital by the war, many Cairenes took advantage of the auditorium's revolutionary equipment – air-conditioning! – to escape from the sweltering heat. Selim Yared's motive in going there with his friend René 'Abdel-Messih was simply to have a Sunday afternoon siesta.

This Sunday they were showing an American B-feature subtitled, as usual, in three languages: French on the film itself and Greek and Arabic on a small screen alongside. Selim and René were half-asleep when the words THE END appeared. The Egyptian national anthem, broadcast at deafening volume and interspersed with static, reminded them that Great Britain was at war with Germany.

In one corner of the auditorium, six or seven rather tipsy British soldiers belted out a barrack-room ditty whose protagonists were King Farouq and his wife Farida. Some members of the audience shook their heads in consternation and a woman in the balcony cursed the sons of Albion in Arabic, screeching like a banshee, but everyone was already shuffling towards the exit.

Selim usually found the outside temperature a shock on emerging, but this time he didn't even notice it. His eye had at once been caught by a group of young people entering the foyer – more precisely, by a slender, laughing girl in a yellow dress.

René 'Abdel-Messih, who was acquainted with the new arrivals, introduced him.

"How was the film?" they asked.

"Trash," Selim replied on impulse. "But in that temperature, who cares?"

The girl laughed some more. She had green eyes. Selim would gladly have sat the picture round again for a chance to remain with her, but René was already making his adieus.

"Who was that girl in the yellow dress?" Selim asked a few minutes later, when they were installed at a table at Groppi's.

"Yellow? Oh yes, Viviane Batrakani. You know, tarbooshes . . . "

Prudence and common sense urged Selim to leave it at that. He'd been warned a hundred times about the frog that aspired to be the size of a bull. A Batrakani girl wasn't for him, who had had to discontinue his education after the *baccalauréat* and earned eleven pounds a month as a humble bookkeeper at Matossian's. He spent the rest of the evening at the Young Catholics' club in 'Emad ed-Din Street, trying to clear his head by dancing and playing poker.

Towards midnight René offered to take him home to Faggaala by taxi.

"Taxis are my life insurance," he said. "I don't propose to be beaten up by some tipsy Britisher or Australian. The other morning we found one dead drunk in the gutter only a few yards from our door."

The cabbies of Cairo did not share his apprehension. Like their horse-drawn predecessors during the First World War, they lay in wait for foreign soldiers who paid whatever they were asked — to the chagrin of prospective Egyptian customers, who found it hard to get a taxi at all.

But René employed his usual strategy. Concealed behind a lamppost, he shouted, "Hey, taxi!" in a stentorian voice and an accent that would have deceived a cockney. As soon as a cab pulled up on a level with them, he and Selim jumped in, one on either side, without giving the cabby time to object.

On reaching home Selim turned the key in the lock very quietly so as not to wake anyone — and promptly blundered into a chest of drawers he wasn't used to. Now that several of her children were working, Mima occasionally made up for fifteen lean years by treating herself to a small piece of furniture or a new dress. Or one of those big bunches of roses she was so fond of . . .

Not feeling sleepy, Selim went out on the balcony and leant on the balustrade. In the distance, fingers of light were traversing the sky above the Nile – a futile exercise, for no German aircraft would disturb the anti-aircraft defences tonight or any night. In Cairo the war meant chiefly blue paper on windowpanes, paper decorations stuck to mirrors to reduce the risk of flying glass – Mima had chosen a Pyramids pattern – and, of course, Anglo-Saxon drunks. Things were quite different in Alexandria, where a heavy air raid had recently devastated Geneina, the notorious red-light district, and claimed many lives.

Viviane Batrakani . . . She had green eyes and a musical laugh. Her father was reputed to supply tarbooshes to everyone in the ministry of foreign affairs. Egyptian ambassadors had them delivered to Europe by diplomatic bag . . .

Selim found it hard to sleep that night. His dreams were haunted by a strange creature wearing a green tarboosh and a rifle slung across its shoulders. It shouted, "Hey, taxi!" and roared with laughter.

2

The school chapel cannot have been much different from the way I knew it years later. The same wax-polished pews, the same fluted columns, the same atmosphere of calm, and the same scent of ashes at the close of day . . .

Father André Batrakani had been hearing confession there in French or Arabic one afternoon a week since the beginning of the war. There were regulars — elderly women as a rule — but also some unfamiliar first-timers whose faces he couldn't even make out.

This afternoon a woman was kneeling in the confessional. She didn't speak at first. Applying his ear to the grille, the Jesuit eventually heard a familiar voice.

"André, it's Maggi. Can you hear my confession?"

"Yes, of course, but it might be easier and more customary — "

"No, no, André, it's you I want, no one else."

Maggi Touta, her head draped in a black mantilla, emerged from the confessional half an hour later. She swiftly crossed herself and left the chapel at once.

"She didn't do her penance," grumbled one of the regulars. "She didn't even genuflect!"

André had confined himself to giving his aunt absolution, so overcome that he forgot to tell her what prayers to say. But in any case, how many Our Fathers and Hail Marys would it have taken to atone for what he had just been told?

He was bound by the secrecy of the confessional, and Maggi knew it. "Don't misunderstand me, André. I need to ask God's forgiveness even though I'm not entirely sure of having done wrong with your father. If I have done wrong, it's with other men, not with him. Anyway, it's over now – we're not of an age any longer, but I had to tell someone in the family. Not Yola, of course – she'd be cut to the quick. This secret can't remain between Georges and me. You're the only one . . . Your father has also done a lot of heart-searching over the years, but he'd never talk to you about it – he couldn't. You can pray for him . . . "

When describing this scene to me some twenty years later, Maggi told me that André had hardly uttered a word. I can well believe her. Hadn't everything been said, with overwhelming logic and sincerity, on the other side of the grille? The penitent hadn't come to ask for condemnation or advice, simply for a hearing and absolution. Her nephew had listened but asked no questions. When she left him, she felt as if a great weight had been lifted from her shoulders.

Maggi had never mentioned her initiative to Georges, and it was probably better that way.

"You see," she said to me, "if I'd told him about it, even after the event, it would have blighted his relationship with André. Georges himself would never have broached the subject to his son, even if his son already knew about it. And nothing is worse, *habibi*, than a secret shared but unspoken."

3

After two unsuccessful attempts, Hassan was finally admitted to the Military Academy in October 1938. He owed his acceptance to the Anglo-Egyptian treaty concluded twenty-six months earlier, under which Egypt was obliged to develop her army. Officers were needed even though the British occupation had not really ended, so the Academy had half opened its doors to sons of the people who would never have gained admission in former times.

Not that this prevented the new officer cadet from fiercely denouncing the Anglo-Egyptian treaty and calling for full independence. Only prudence deterred him from joining the students who had demonstrated in the streets of Cairo on 2 February 1942, crying, "We are Rommel's soldiers!"

German forces massed on the Libyan frontier were threatening to invade Egypt. On the principle that my enemy's enemy is my friend, Hassan was steadfastly pro-German. After all, it was rumoured in barracks that Hitler's emissaries had promised the Egyptian nationalists full and immediate independence.

"I had lost all respect for Farouq," Hassan wrote later in his book. "The king's escapades were becoming common knowledge. He was known to frequent the nightclubs of Cairo accompanied by his Italian clique, which was led by Antonio Pulli, the former palace electrician promoted bey. For all that, if Farouq had summoned us to help him fight the British in 1942, we should all have gone over to his side."

The palace Italians were a particular source of annoyance to the British ambassador, Sir Miles Lampson.

"After all," he once complained to some prominent Egyptians, "we're at war with Italy."

Farouq's retort went the rounds of Cairo's drawing rooms:

"If he wants me to give up my *Italiens*, let him start by giving up his *Italienne!*"

Lady Lampson was the daughter of Dr Aldo Castellani, formerly surgeon-general to Mussolini's troops in Ethiopia. But the British Residency's main worry was the pro-German tendencies of many members of the Egyptian government. To remove them from power, it urged that Nahas Pasha, leader of the Wafd, be reinstated as premier. The king stood firm in the face of repeated requests. There followed a *coup de force* – almost a *coup d'état* – to which Hassan devotes the two most virulent pages in his book:

> On 5 February 1942, Sir Miles went to 'Abdin Palace escorted by soldiers and armoured cars. The gates were shut. A revolver shot smashed the lock, and the other doors opened of their own accord. The ambassador presented Farouq with a document announcing his abdication and asked him to sign it. Having recovered from his surprise, Farouq took out a pen and was preparing to comply when his chief adviser spoke to him in Arabic. "Give me another chance," Farouq told the British ambassador. A few hours later Nahas Pasha was summoned to the palace and reappointed prime minister.
>
> Back at our barracks the effect of this news was positively explosive. I was the most infuriated of all. In Farouq's place, I said, I would have produced a revolver from my pocket, not a pen. From then on my determination was total: I would fight with all my might, and by all available means, to rid Egypt of the infamous occupying power. (*An Officer's Career*, pp. 78–9.)

4

Four months later Hassan hailed the Germans' advance from Libya with delight and high excitement. On 30 June 1942, after polishing off Sulloum and Marsa Matrouh in short order, the Afrikakorps crossed the frontier and reached El-Alamein.

The shopkeepers of Alexandria were already decorating their premises in readiness to welcome Rommel. Most Jews had left the city, and in Cairo many of them were queueing up in front of bank cashiers' windows to withdraw all their money, determined to get to Palestine or South Africa as soon as possible.

The British plastered the walls of the capital with posters urging the population to KEEP SMILING! Sir Miles Lampson did his best to reassure the Cairenes, but he was running out of ideas. He ostentatiously went shopping with his wife in the Muski and had the embassy railings repainted, but that didn't prevent his office staff from burning all their records on 1 July, and the cloud of smoke that rose above the Nile created a thoroughly bad impression.

Being unable to spend the summer at Alexandria, wealthy Cairenes fell back on Ras al-Barr, which they had hitherto regarded with disdain. The best beach houses had been rented by pashas resigned to rubbing shoulders for once with the common herd. Part of the Hôtel Cristal had even been reserved for the queen mother and her daughters.

Ras al-Barr was better than nothing. Pestered by the Swissess, who insisted that the children needed some sea air, Paul Batrakani had reluctantly rented a beach house there. The *sufragi* and the maidservant went on ahead to reconnoitre the place, satisfy themselves that it was habitable, and lend it a touch of class. One room was reserved for Viviane, who was to meet some friends there, and Michel had promised to pay a brief visit. Even André would be coming spend a few days at Ras al-Barr, where the Jesuits maintained a holiday camp complete with a thatched chapel built on piles.

Several times a day, little knots of people gathered outside the Hôtel Cristal. Queen Nazli issued appeals to them by loudspeaker to leave her in peace on the grounds that she wanted to be free to spend the holidays with her daughters like anyone else.

"She's right," said Viviane to a girlfriend with chestnut hair. "It's ridiculous. Let's go."

Turning, she found herself face to face with Selim Yared. Selim couldn't get a word out, he was so overcome, yet heaven alone knew how often he had gone looking for her in the year since their first encounter. He had remained a regular patron of the Metro Cinema throughout the rest of the previous summer. The merest glimpse of a yellow dress sent him into an emotional tailspin. He had naturally found out where the Batrakanis lived. On three occasions he walked along the shady street on the off chance that a door would open. Once, with a pounding heart, he saw a car pull up outside the imposing wrought-iron gate. The stranger who alighted, a tall, slim, extremely elegant man, had signalled to his chauffeur to wait, then disappeared into the house.

"Hello," Viviane said politely. "We've seen each other before somewhere, haven't we? Groppi's, wasn't it?"

"The Metro, I think . . . "

This scintillating conversation, which couldn't in any case have proceeded much further, was conveniently cut short by the girl with the chestnut hair.

"We're going to be late, *chérie*. Perhaps your friend would care to join us later on . . . "

"There's a party of us going down to the beach," was all Viviane could find to say. "If you'd like to . . . We've arranged to meet outside the Hôtel Courteille at ten."

Rather haltingly, Selim accepted. As soon as the girls had gone, he dashed off to get changed at the beach house rented by the cousins who were putting him up for the weekend.

Forty-five minutes later they were all lolling on the sand. Selim hardly dared to glance at Viviane, who was idly dabbling her toes in the dying waves. She looked quite stunning in a tangerine-coloured bathing costume.

"Have you just come from Cairo?" asked a tall, thin young man with a moustache.

To general amusement, Selim revealed that the British embassy's records had not been entirely consumed by fire on 1 July. Numerous sheets of paper had escaped the flames and fluttered off into the streets near by.

"A few days later the ice-cream seller in Opera Square was making his cornets out of the British commercial attaché's letters, marked 'Top Secret'."

Still laughing, they all got up for a swim. Viviane was the first to dive in, her perfect crawl bearing witness to three years' regular use of the pool at the Gezira Sporting Club, of which Paul Batrakani had at last, in 1939, become a member. Her two sisters dived in after her.

Viviane and her girlfriend had taken to going to the Sporting Club very early in the morning, when the pool was deserted save for a few British officers turned lobster-pink by the Egyptian sun. The two girls, who did not find the sight of their bare torsos distasteful, would swim a few lengths and then stretch out in deck chairs. This was the hour at which General Sir Archibald Wavell, the British commander-in-chief, would practise his diving. Sir Archibald's squint inspired great anxiety in the few people present, and everyone shut their eyes when he hit the water with an enormous splash.

Selim sprinted into the sea and dived in too. No one had taught him how to flap his legs and work his arms. He had learnt the crawl on his own, by watching other people at Ras al-Barr.

He joined Viviane beside the white buoy to which she was clinging to regain her breath. He saw the sunlight glisten on her streaming face, on the bosom that rose and fell as the foam alternately immersed and exposed it, and he felt perturbed. Some instinct warned him of imminent danger. He'd always been told that, in matters of the heart as in everything else, a man should never live above his means. But Selim didn't feel like a prudent, frugal pen-pusher. He had no desire to let go of this buoy that rocked them to the same rhythm on the foam-flecked sea. It wasn't until the other members of the party joined them that he slid beneath the surface and swam ashore at a leisurely breaststroke.

Stretched out on the hot sand a little while later, he saw Viviane Batrakani wade ashore in her turn. Pausing halfway, she bent to cup some water in her hands and sluice herself down. Then she walked on with the inimitable, swaying gait of a woman surfeited with swimming.

She came over and sat down beside him – quite naturally, as if proof against any man's gaze. Selim told himself that any girl as thoroughly at ease with herself must have a regular, universally acknowledged boyfriend, possibly a member of the present party.

"Have you been to Ras al-Barr before?" she asked, looking out to sea.

"Yes, we used to come here every year as children. In memory of my father, who was very fond of the place."

Viviane's brown skin was beaded with moisture. She was making little dents in the sand with her toes. Selim adored every one of those toes.

"My father liked to stroll along the beach in a *galabiya* and a big straw hat," he went on. "In the evenings he used to take a whole bunch of friends to the Hôtel Marine, where he led them in lively quadrilles . . . "

Several hours later, aboard the train that was taking him back to Cairo, Selim relived every moment of that God-given day. His departure from Ras al-Barr had not, for once, depressed him. He was brimming with *joie de vivre*.

"That friend of yours has plenty of charm," the girl with the chestnut hair said to Viviane. "But don't you find him a trifle *baladi*?"

No real compliment, that. *Baladi* implied local colour and a lack of sophistication verging on vulgarity.

It was true that Selim had used a lot of Arabic phrases – in fact his French sounded at times like a translation – and one particular remark of his had grated on their ears:

"I'm a bookkeeper at Matossian's."

But there were other little things that tended to brand him as dangerously *baladi* in the eyes of two young ladies from the Collège de la Mère de Dieu: the way he neatly refolded his handkerchief after blowing his nose, for instance, or his fancy black-and-white shoes, which looked as if he'd bought them in a sale at 'Ataba al-Khadra.

The girl with the chestnut hair went on to remark that "the bumpkin" didn't know a thing about Paris, the city of which both girls dreamed, and which Viviane had actually visited with her parents in 1937, during the World Exhibition.

At the same time, Selim had undermined his status still further by displaying a close acquaintanceship with Ras al-Barr. Everyone had sensed that, far from being a place of wartime exile, it was a regular haunt of his and the repository of childhood memories which he made no attempt to conceal.

"Yes, I suppose he is a bit *baladi*," Viviane replied, feeling rather embarrassed. She wondered what had possessed her to go and sit beside that forthright young man, with his sturdy body and infectious good humour.

Then, in the same tone, she semi-excused herself by adding, "But I don't really know him. I'd only seen him once before — at Groppi's or the Metro, I've forgotten which . . . "

5

19 September 1942

A little surprise party at home to celebrate the millionth Batrakani tarboosh. Papa, who hadn't suspected a thing, was very touched.

Each of us gave him an original present associated with the event. André had obtained (heaven knows how!) a Coptic Catholic seminarist's tarboosh dating from 1880 with the owner's name embroidered inside. Aunt Maggi had ordered her present from Eliakim, the jeweller's: a thimble-sized tarboosh in gold bearing the initials G.B.

The other gifts included a encyclopedia of headgear down the ages (Paul), an old copper tarboosh press (Lola), a French translation of one of Ataturk's speeches denouncing the fez (Uncle Henri), and a straw boater (Alex).

For my part, I gave Papa the only existing photograph of Sultan Hussein with his tarboosh tilted to the right, not the left. However, I fear he didn't really appreciate its documentary value.

Maman had got Usta Ali to make some nut ka'ak in the shape of tarbooshes with black sugar tassels. She was sick with worry all yesterday: "What a stupid idea of mine — Georges will think it's ridiculous!", etc. As if sensing her agony of mind, Papa — to loud applause — gave her a lingering kiss.

20 October 1942

Splendid news!!! Rommel's Afrikakorps has been smashed at El-Alamein.

I told Victor that I would take care of the champagne. We're going to share it with Lidy at the hospital tomorrow.

Michel was so elated, he adorned this page with a garland of flowers — the only drawing in any of his eleven notebooks!

My godfather also wrote a letter of thanks to General Montgomery and handed it in at the British embassy the same evening. To him, El-Alamein would always symbolize barbarism halted in its tracks.

In 1946, four years later, when Michel had forgotten all about his letter, the postman delivered a handwritten reply signed "Montgomery of Alamein". One can only assume that Rommel's adversary had a backlog of correspondence to deal with, and that he had been particularly touched by the enthusiastic comments of a Cairo Syrian less at home in the language of Shakespeare than in that of La Fontaine.

6

Alex Batrakani was running-in a green Morris convertible, which had just been delivered to him, and a Maltese call-girl, whom he had picked up at the Perroquet the night before. Eager to try out the former and impress the latter, my uncle was racing along the desert road from Almaza with the hood down.

Intrigued to see some headlights flash in his rear-view mirror, he slowed to let the other car pass. A sports convertible with two men on board, it drew level, then ostentatiously accelerated away. Alex, who took this as a challenge, stepped on the gas himself.

Thrust back into her seat, the Maltese girl shut her eyes, half scared, half revelling in the gusts of warm desert air that buffeted her face. Alex slowed abruptly when he sighted the other car parked beside the road. The driver was still behind the wheel, but his companion, who was standing beside the car, signalled to Alex to stop. Alex backed up and got out.

"Are you Egyptian?" the man asked. Without really waiting for an answer, he went on, "His Majesty would like a word with you."

Flabbergasted, Alex walked over to the sports car. Farouq was at the wheel. He smiled.

"How many cylinders?" he asked in French, indicating the Morris.

"Six, Your Majesty," Alex said nervously.

"Servo-assisted brakes?"

Everyone knew of the king's passion for fast cars. Alex, who was on familiar territory, slowly relaxed.

"Yes, but they're a bit harsh. They aren't the car's strongest point, but it does have excellent road-holding qualities."

"I'm going on to the Auberge des Pyramides. Like to follow me?"

Alex ran back to his Morris. The other car drove off, tyres squealing.

"Who was that windbag?" asked the Maltese girl.

"The king."

She burst out laughing. "Oh, sure, and the fellow beside him was the pope, right?"

Alex didn't reply. He grasped the wheel with both hands and kept his eyes fixed on the rear lights of the other car as it sped through Heliopolis, most of whose inhabitants were already asleep.

The king owned several dozen cars including the Mercedes with which Hitler had presented him in 1938, on the occasion of his marriage to Farida. All kinds of stories were told about these red projectiles that hurtled along the thoroughfares of Cairo and its environs after nightfall, sometimes passing the Pyramids and racing across the desert on the new highway to Alexandria. One night, a car driven by Farouq had grazed the central reservation in a Cairo street. The very next morning saw an army of workmen busy removing that presumptuous obstacle . . .

Less than ten minutes after leaving Heliopolis the two sports cars were racing down Malika Nazli Avenue. On the left, opposite the railway station, Alex could just make out the grey bulk of the Jesuit school, the unloved institution from which he had twice been expelled. It occurred to him that his brother André must be asleep inside there at that moment, his soul at peace. He pictured himself recounting his adventure at the next family lunch.

The Pyramids were beginning to show up in the distance when the king's passenger put out his arm and signalled that they were stopping. The Maltese girl swore as André screeched to a halt.

Farouq got out and transferred to a Cadillac, which must have been following them for some time. He gave Alex a friendly little wave. Alex swelled with pride; the girl said nothing, but her eyes popped.

When they reached the Auberge, the proprietor of that well-known establishment, a Syrian by the name of Albert Bey Soussa, hurried on ahead of them. The king had a table permanently reserved for him, as he did in another half-dozen Cairo nightclubs. Glasses of fruit juice and platefuls of *mezze* were served at once.

Farouq was also brought a bowl containing little balls of coloured paper with which he amused himself by pelting the dancers. Every time a missile found its mark he gave a roar of laughter which was instantly echoed by his entourage.

That night Alex Batrakani made the acquaintance of Farouq's two closest cronies: Antonio Pulli, the Italian palace electrician who had become the King's private secretary; and Karim Sabet, son of the Syrian founder of *Al-Muqattam*, who was said to be his *éminence grise*.

Alex led the Maltese girl on to the dance floor. The band was playing a tango, a dance at which she excelled, and he felt he had never held a more erotic creature in his arms. No doubt about it: tonight marked a milestone in his existence!

In the small hours one of the king's companions took him aside. "Would it be too much, my dear sir, to ask you to refrain from escorting your lady-friend home? His Majesty has invited her back to the palace, an honour of which she is deeply sensible . . . "

Alex gave a resigned nod. What else could he do? Ten minutes later he was in his green Morris, this time with the hood up, driving slowly in the direction of Garden City and wondering how he was going to round off the story to his family and friends.

7

Georges Batrakani couldn't believe his ears. It was Édouard Dhellemmes, calling from Shepheard's.

"You here? It's incredible, the way you contrive to be in Egypt whenever there's a war on."

The Frenchman laughed. "Yes, thanks to a little wire-pulling."

"All the better, all the better. I can't wait to see you. How long are you staying?"

"I'm not leaving."

"Not leaving? What do you mean?"

"I plan to settle here permanently, Georges."

My grandfather was speechless with surprise. He knew, of course, that many foreigners had transferred their assets to Cairo when the war broke out. He also knew that there was nothing to keep Édouard Dhellemmes in Lille since his divorce, and that Egypt acted on him like a lodestone, but to settle here in the middle of the war . . .

"Any chance of our seeing each other this evening?" Édouard asked gaily.

"But of course! We'll expect you to dinner. I'll pick you up at Shepheard's on my way back from the palace. It's my signature day."

Every three months or so, Georges Bey wrote off an entire afternoon. After taking a siesta he donned one of his smartest suits, broke out a brand-new tarboosh, and summoned his chauffeur.

At 'Abdin Palace he was greeted by a master of ceremonies who steered each visitor, according to his importance, towards such and such a senior official in charge of protocol. Georges Bey was first entertained to a glass of cordial or a coffee in the chamberlains' office. One of the chamberlains would then conduct him to the signing room, where some big red leather books lay open on tables made of precious woods. He signed his name as legibly as possible, knowing that a palace official was instructed to compile a list of visitors after every reception. It was possible that the king himself glanced through the said list.

Another master of ceremonies would then escort my grandfather along interminable passages to the queen's wing, where the same ritual was repeated. But there had been a third port of call ever since Farouq's marriage, because the queen mother refused to withdraw from public life and kept a visitors' book of her own . . .

These signing sessions, which were held on public holidays or special occasions, resembled social functions. *Sufragis* threaded their way through the visitors, bearing sumptuous trays of cakes and drinks. All the main political leaders were present, surrounded by their supporters, and life-long enemies conversed for once in a civilized manner. The "truce of the signature" prevailed.

Georges took advantage of such occasions to cultivate his business connections – sometimes, even, to close a deal between one *petit four* and another – so he preserved memories of some very good signings. The one in Ramadan 1937, for example, had secured him the agency of a Swiss pharmaceutical firm, and the one held to mark the marriage of Farouq and Farida in January of the previous year had enabled him to dispose of a batch of four thousand tarbooshes.

Knowing that Georges was a regular visitor to the palace, Edmond Touta had entrusted his brother-in-law with an important mission: to ascertain the king's reaction to his numerous letters about the population explosion, for Farouq was proving as poor a correspondent as his father Fouad.

"Well," said Edmond at lunch the following Sunday, "did you see the king?"

"I saw him," Georges replied gravely. "Your file is shaping well."

Edmond's face lit up.

"How do you find your beloved Shepheard's?" my grandfather asked Édouard Dhellemmes when they met early that evening.

"Ugh, it's packed with British officers. You can hardly get near the bar."

"Don't complain, at least they've declared it off-limits to other ranks. They're regular thugs, those fellows. Do you know one of their favourite pastimes? It's called 'the tarboosh game'."

"Good publicity for you, no?"

"Some publicity! Their stupid game consists in driving past pedestrians in cars or taxis and knocking off their tarbooshes. The winner is the one who knocks off the most. I've complained in writing to the chief of police, needless to say."

Édouard looked thoughtful. "The British are so polite back home. I can't understand why they become such boors when they're in Egypt. But talking of tarbooshes, Georges, I was going to tell you something: I'd like to sell my shares in the firm."

"Sell them? You're crazy! Business is booming. Imports of foreign tarbooshes have ceased altogether. We control a large sector of the market. Our sales topped a hundred and sixty thousand units last year, and they're still rising. Don't be foolish, Édouard. Never jump off a horse when it's winning, as my brother Ferdinand used to say. Think it over."

"I already have, Georges. I plan to open a shop specializing in Egyptian antiquities. You're aware of my passion for that sort of thing."

"I am, and it defeats me."

"I'll help you to find a buyer if necessary."

"No need, I'm afraid. My idiot of a brother-in-law, Count-my-backside Henri Touta, doesn't know what to do with his money. He's always asking to come in with us. I won't be able to turn him down, not now, but I'll say it again: you're making a big mistake."

8

If Ras al-Barr had been the holidaymakers' rendezvous in 1942, it was Alexandria for which *le tout* Cairo made a beeline during the summer of 1943. Now that the Germans had been defeated at El-Alamein there was nothing more to fear in Egypt's "second capital".

"The war's over," Georges Batrakani decreed.

Over or not, he was doing well out of it. The huge stockpiles he had built up before the war — notably several thousand tyres which he sold in dribs and drabs to the British army or to dealers — were making him a fortune. Unlike many Cairo entrepreneurs younger than himself, Georges Bey could remember 1914–18. He knew how to exploit a world war and even to prepare for one. His system had been put in place immediately after Munich. He bought up everything he could lay hands on and carefully stockpiled it in two big purpose-built warehouses, one situated behind the tarboosh factory at Shubra, the other on his estate at Damanhour.

The sale of a batch of sanitary equipment was enough by itself to enable him to purchase a handsome seaside villa at Sidi Bishr for nine thousand pounds. It was arranged that Yolande would spend most of the summer there with Viviane and the servants, and other members of the family took it in turns to stay whenever their business commitments permitted.

Selim Yared, too, was to spend a few days with some cousins at Alexandria. Viviane, whom he bumped into on the terrace at Groppi's one afternoon in May, had issued an invitation that did not fall on deaf ears:

"If you're going to Alexandria, why not join us? My family has a beach house at Sidi Bishr. I'll be there with some friends."

"Which beach at Sidi Bishr?" Selim asked innocently.

"Number 2," she replied as if that went without saying – as if No. 2 were the only socially acceptable beach on the entire coast.

At Sidi Bishr Selim was reunited with the Ras al-Barr set, among them the girl with the chestnut hair, but he only had eyes for Viviane, who, vivacious as ever, played hostess with remarkable aplomb.

Visible at a distance of some thirty yards from the Batrakanis' beach hut was the gleaming, pointed bald pate of the prime minister, Nahas Pasha. Ensconced in his deck chair in a pistachio-green burnous, he gazed out to sea – or was it the sea that gazed in fascination at the most idolized, most hated man in the country?

One sensed that Nahas was the centre of much covert activity. He was there with his court – Egypt's second court. From time to time a friend, relation or courtier would approach the deck chair and whisper something in the great man's ear or show him a newspaper article. The Wafdist leader's sole response would be to gesture evasively.

Selim couldn't take his eyes off those famous hands on which so many good folk had swooped for the past fifteen years in their eagerness to kiss them. Did Nahas owe his popularity to his oratorical skill? To his struggles in the old days, when he would bed down in railway stations with other Wafdist leaders because he was forbidden to tour the provinces? Or simply to the fact that millions of people could readily identify with this bucolic, portly figure with the pronounced squint?

King Fouad had hated Nahas. He had done his best to prevent the Wafd from coming to power throughout his nineteen years on the throne, but the crowds could never have been weaned away from Nahas by such an unpopular king. Farouq, on the other hand, had genuinely worried Nahas when he came to the throne. The young king was a redoutable competitor. Whenever Farouq made a trip to the provinces, the Wafd leader followed hard on his heels, choosing the same route and attracting the same ovations.

At half-past twelve a black Packard pulled up behind the Batrakanis' beach hut, from which the strains of a record-player were issuing. The chauffeur and a *sufragi* got out, laden with steaming dishes.

"Lunchtime!" called Viviane. "Quick, before the *kubeiba* gets cold!"

Lunch was dominated by male voices. Selim was surprised to note that these Syrian residents of Egypt were divided into Gaullists and Pétainists. The two groups argued quite heatedly.

"How about you?" asked the girl next to him. "You don't say much."

"All that interests me," he couldn't help saying, "is Egypt."

His remark cast a chill. To dispel the tension Viviane put on a record of Tino Rossi's *Marinella*, and everyone sang along with it. Then she suggested going off to the tea dance at the Monseigneur.

Ten minutes after they got to that fashionable establishment, Viviane was led on to the floor by a scrawny beanpole named Raoul. He took hold of his partner and clasped her to him, gazing over her shoulder with an air of proprietorial self-assurance that left no room for doubt.

Selim sat down, weak at the knees. He had a whisky to buck himself up, then another to wash down the first. The end of the evening found him still in his chair, half stunned and incapable of reacting. It was clear as daylight now: Viviane Batrakani would never be his.

For the whole of the following week Selim feigned gaiety and allowed himself to be drawn into a maelstrom of social activities. These children of wealthy families were good at filling their days and varying their amusements. Between two sessions at the beach he accompanied them to Athinéos and the Grand Trianon, where groups of dancers performed. With them he gorged himself on cakes at Délices and on fish at Xénophon's. Rather worried about his budget, he took in the latest American fims at the Strand and the Alhambra and patronized the Muhammad Ali Theatre, where Taha Hussein's son was presenting Molière plays performed by local actors. He even yawned his way through a lecture on the Impressionists at the Amitiés Françaises and spent an evening on a sumptuous yacht at the Sailing Club.

They were forever boarding the Packard and two convertibles for trips along the coast to Montaza, the Mex, or even 'Agami. Once a day they looked in at the Hôtel Métropole, where a telex spat out the latest news from the Russian front and a large wall map studded with little flags indicated the positions of the opposing armies – occasion enough for a clash between the Gaullists and Pétainists. Selim had christened them the Ahlawi and the Zamalkawi, after the supporters of Cairo's two leading football teams.

On the eve of his departure they hired a boat for a nocturnal tour of the harbour. The balmy night was illumined by a lovely crescent moon. The lapping of the water against the hull was drowned from time to time by laughter or a chorus of the *Marseillaise*.

Raoul had decided to do some fishing and was by himself in the stern. Selim, who had contrived to sit beside Viviane, thrilled to the pressure of her thigh against his.

"With all this noise going on," he said, "your fiancé will be lucky to catch anything."

"Who told you he was my fiancé?" she replied.

Instantly, hope surged through him. "Who told you?" sounded very much like a denial. Gradually, however, the probable truth dawned on him: "Who told you?" must mean "How did you guess?" In any case, Viviane had left him and gone to join the idiot who was trailing his line over the stern . . .

That night, as he tossed and turned between his overly coarse sheets, Selim wept with rage. He called down the foulest Arabic curses on the Batrakanis, the Raouls, and all their kind, whether Gaullist or Pétainist, Ahlawi or Zamalkawi. Those people had a surprise in store. One day he would return to Sidi Bishr No. 2 a rich and powerful man. He would buy Nahas Pasha's beach hut. He would have a whole army of courtiers . . .

9

Georges and Makram were dining together at Groppi's. They had been given their usual corner table, far from the lights and the noise.

"Well," said my grandfather, "how much longer do you think Nahas is going to keep the premiership? I hear the king is determined to kick him out this time."

It gave Georges Bey malicious pleasure to twist the knife in the wound. He was well aware that Makram had been torn for some months between the prime minister and another Wafdist leader who had made serious accusations against him.

"Nahas will stand firm," the Copt replied. "In any case, no one knows what Farouq's true intentions are. He seems to be toying with another scheme – one that transcends local politics. He's after the caliphate. Why else would he be growing a beard?"

"A caliph is all we need!"

"Anyway, he's being pampered in a British military hospital at present. It's disgraceful!"

Farouq, who had been involved in a car crash, was in hospital outside town. Food from the palace kitchens was delivered daily, and numerous visitors came to pay their respects. He seemed reluctant to leave.

"Meanwhile," said Georges Bey, "your Nahas has a free hand."

"He isn't 'my' Nahas. Besides, the British call the tune, you know that perfectly well."

"Talking of the British, yesterday, in Garden City, I passed Russell Pasha out riding on his white horse. What style! The tarboosh suits them to a tee, no two ways about it. And that horse! Its hoofs were polished like dancing pumps . . . As long as there's an Englishman in charge of the police force I sleep soundly at night."

"You're in for a rude awakening, Georges."

"Oh really? You mean it's a foregone conclusion?"

"We'll talk about it again when the war's over."

"That's just what you told me in 'fourteen-'eighteen, Makram Effendi."

"Well? I wasn't so wide of the mark. In 'nineteen we had Sa'ad Zaghloul."

"Yes, and today, twenty-four years later, Russell Pasha is patrolling the streets on his white horse and you're still wearing black."

18 October 1943

Lidy died at ten o'clock this morning, without a word of complaint. Victor sobbed on the phone, trying to find words of consolation for us both. "She won't suffer any more . . . "

The day after the victory at El-Alamein, when we entered her hospital room with the bottle of champagne, she looked radiant in spite of her emaciation. "But a nurse told me they'd reserved a room for Rommel at Shepheard's," she said. "I was getting ready to wear a yellow star like our cousins in France — and you, you turn up with champagne. You might have brought me a piano as well. I haven't touched a piano for two whole years, did you know that, Michel?"

Ah, Lidy! One night at Heliopolis, with an irresponsibility that shames me still, I asked you to marry me. You wisely refused, knowing how sick you were and how ill-equipped I was for marriage — knowing that we belonged to two different worlds. "Let's stay friends," you told me.

Lidy, dainty little creature astray in a violent world, frail little creature borne away by the wind . . .

IO

Selim Yared, who was a hopeless dancer, had come to his friend René 'Abdel-Messih's New Year's Eve party without much enthusiasm. He was trying hard to match his steps to those of a female Charleston fanatic when Viviane Batrakani turned up with some friends.

The sight of her took his breath away. To think he'd erased her from his life . . . Her unexpected arrival made him abandon all his good resolutions at a stroke, left him completely at sea. It took him back six months to Alexandria and that boat ride in the moonlight.

Skimping the end of the Charleston, he deserted his energetic partner and went over to Viviane.

"Hello, I didn't know you were coming."

"I wasn't. I was going to another party, but René insisted."

"Are you on your own? Isn't Raoul with you?"

Viviane's expression was tinged with mischief.

"No, Raoul isn't with me any more."

Selim's spirits rose abruptly.

"Would you like to dance?"

It was a slow foxtrot, fortunately for him. He put his arm round her waist, felt her face close to his, inhaled the scent of her hair, and, drunk with emotion, abandoned himself to the music. She smiled. His self-confidence fully restored, he asked what she'd been doing with herself.

"I'm leaving for al-Minya the day after tomorrow."

"Al-Minya? What on earth for?"

"I'm taking part in a hygiene mission to the schools of Upper Egypt. Haven't you heard of Father Ayrout's charity?"

He confessed his ignorance, but with the air of one who burned to know more.

"Let's sit down," said Viviane. "I'm dying of thirst."

He hurried off to the buffet to fetch some iced drinks.

Like André Batrakani, Henry Ayrout belonged to the Society of Jesus. He was the son of Habib Ayrout, Baron Empain's favourite building contractor, who had introduced Selim's father to Heliopolis in the old days. The young Jesuit had just published his thesis, *Fellahs d'Égypte*, a brilliant and authoritative work that had opened the eyes of Cairo's middle-class Christians to a world of which they knew absolutely nothing. Their first encounter with the author was another surprise: beneath the black cassock, the beard and round spectacles, smouldered a volcano.

"In December 1940," Viviane explained, "Father Ayrout invited a group of women and girls to a meeting at his parents' house in Heliopolis. I went reluctantly, and only because my Jesuit brother urged me to. 'You'll see,' he told me, 'he's a remarkable fellow.'"

"And you weren't disappointed, I gather."

"The young women who attended that meeting in Heliopolis came from all the communities: Greek Catholic, Maronite, Latin, Coptic. There were even some Orthodox. 'There's only one Christianity in Egypt,' Father Ayrout told us at the very outset. 'I don't want to hear any talk of different denominations in the charity we'll be setting up. Anyone who makes futile claims about her own rite will pay a fine of five piastres.'"

"You must have ruined yourselves!"

"We started to laugh – he'd won us over. But when he said there was only one Christianity he was thinking of the gulf between the towns and the countryside. His charity is devoted to the children of Upper Egypt. The free schools can't count on any financial support from Europe because of the war, so we have to collect money here. Together with other members of the organization, I collect outside churches, in clubs, banks, offices, and so on."

"*Ya salaam!*"

"The first collection brought in a thousand pounds, but we're aiming to double that next time. Just you wait, I'm going to put you down on my list!"

"All right, I'll *bakshish* you," Selim told her with a broad smile.

He wondered if he shouldn't urgently light a candle at Radwaniya, not only for the children of Upper Egypt but, more especially, for humble wage-earners like himself, who deserved a rise in order to be able to help them.

Viviane had come to this New Year's Eve party because Selim Yared's name was on the guest list René had shown her. She hadn't stopped thinking about him ever since the summer, though with mixed feelings. There was something about him that put her off – his *baladi* side, no doubt. At the same time, she found him absolutely charming. No male had ever attracted her as much, save possibly the youth she'd briefly encountered in 1936, when he came to see his uncle Rashid: Hassan of the sweat-stained shirt . . .

The coquetries and inanities of the Alexandria set had been shattered by Selim Yared's remarks – indeed, by his very presence. Having wallowed in this world since her adolescence, Viviane was only half aware of this, but she choked with laughter whenever Selim referred to the Gaullists and Pétainists as the Ahlawi and Zamalkawi.

Raoul, who subscribed to a prickly brand of Gaullism, didn't appreciate the joke at all. He would look askance at "that peasant", then launch into a scintillating account of the social repercussions of the Popular Front or Allied naval supremacy before excelling on the dance floor, performing an immaculate dive at San Stefano, or impressing female passengers in his Juvaquatre convertible.

Raoul used to ask Viviane to marry him roughly once a week. She hadn't said either yes or no. Born into a prosperous family, educated by the Jesuits, and holder of an engineering degree from Lyon University, Raoul was just the kind of son-in-law the Batrakanis wanted. By becoming his wife Viviane would be making as good a marriage as her sister Lola, who had recently, for better or worse, married the nephew of a big Cairo jeweller.

She had made a point of sitting beside Selim in the boat the night before he left. Lulled by the lapping of the water, Viviane would have liked nothing better than to rest her head on that muscular shoulder.

Then some fool had started to sing the *Marseillaise*. The others joined in and the spell was broken.

She had then joined Raoul, who was fishing from the stern, firmly resolved to tell him that no, having thought things over carefully, she didn't want to marry him. But Raoul proceeded to lecture her on the reasons why his inadequate fishing tackle had prevented him from catching any fish. She was obliged to wait until his next proposal of marriage, some days later, before putting an end to their semi-engagement.

"No, Raoul isn't with me any more."

Selim's face had lit up. And, during the slow foxtrot that followed, Viviane had felt carried away — overcome by sensations new in her experience.

But for all that, panic seized her at the thought of Selim attending a Sunday lunch at home. She pictured the faces of the others, especially her brother Paul, who was such a stickler for good manners and French grammar. "I'll *bakshish* you . . ." Really!

Two days later Selim rang the Batrakanis' doorbell on the stroke of eight. Viviane answered it herself. She had accepted his offer to collect her by taxi and accompany her to the station. There was a big suitcase in the hallway. He picked it up.

"*Ya satir*, this must weigh a good twenty kilos! You'll never be able to lift it when you get off the train. Are you taking the peasants some food as well?"

Viviane flushed a little. Not really knowing what conditions would be like down there, she had put in dresses of various kinds, sweaters of varying weight, a dozen blouses, and five pairs of shoes — not to mention the equipment every volunteer was expected to bring: a sewing box, a first-aid kit, books, notebooks, a water-bottle, some blankets, a whistle, a harmonica . . .

The mission to al-Minya, "supervised by Mademoiselle de Montvallon, qualified nurse", was scheduled to last a month. It would be based at the old Jesuit monastery, but the good works were to be performed in a number of villages round about.

"We've been strongly urged not to shock the peasants or arouse any feelings of envy," Viviane said as the taxi drove off. "Father Ayrout has laid down ten commandments for our benefit: Don't wear make-up, don't cross your legs, don't wear slacks or sleeveless blouses, don't laugh — "

"Sounds like fun!"

"Don't smoke, don't argue, don't speak a foreign language in front of them . . . "

"*Ya Allah!*"

With a deafening hiss, the locomotive alongside the platform at Bab al-Hadid station emitted a plume of white steam. A small group of women stood clustered round a black-bearded priest. Selim decided to slip away rather than embarrass Viviane. She rewarded him with a grateful smile.

II

Two months later René 'Abdel-Messih threw another party at his home. The furniture had been pushed back and the carpets rolled up, and several couples were dancing with abandon to a blaring gramophone.

Selim, who was sitting in a corner, watched them all the more enviously because Viviane was circling the floor in the arms of a young French officer. Damned Frenchmen! They'd been turning the heads of all the Syrian girls in Cairo ever since the outbreak of war.

Gloomily, Selim left the room and went out on the terrace to smoke a cigarette. He was tormented by the memory of his father. Khalil had taken three seconds to ask Mima to marry him. Selim calculated that he himself would soon have been hanging round Viviane for three years without daring to avow his love. He was paralysed by fear of a refusal. What did he, a humble bookkeeper, have to offer a Batrakani girl? Mima herself might have been an alarming proposition in her day, what with all the heads she turned, but she was a penniless orphan.

He reproved himself for thinking of that. His mother had amazed him one day, when describing the scene:

"It seems I smiled when your father said, 'How about getting married on the sixth of September? It's a Sunday.' I might have taken his proposal as a joke, but I didn't take it like that at all . . . "

Selim sensed a presence beside him. He didn't even have time to turn round.

"What are you thinking about?" Viviane asked softly.

"I was thinking of my father," he replied, and continued on impulse, "and the way he asked my mother to marry him within seconds of their very first meeting."

"Why should he have waited?"

Selim turned to face her. Then, without thinking, he took her hands in his. Viviane lowered her eyes. She seemed on the verge of tears.

An hour later, when they were sitting in the corner of the terrace and gazing into each other's eyes, heedless of the other guests' comings and goings, Viviane murmured, "A funny thing happened to me during the trip to al-Minya . . . "

Villagers greeted the volunteers like divine beings and mistook them for great doctors, when they hardly knew how to apply a compress, make boric water, or tell blue eye lotion from argyric. One day in the dispensary to which she had been assigned, Viviane saw a peasant enter with a bundle in his arms. He handed the baby to her without a word. Its face was deathly pale. The nun beside her whispered in French, "It's dying. Quick, think of a name and baptize it discreetly."

Mechanically, recalling her catechism classes at boarding school, Viviane laid her hand on the baby's forehead and muttered, "Selim, I baptize you in the name of the Father, the Son, and the Holy Spirit."

The baby died in her arms a few moments later. The father nodded without any particular display of emotion. It was his eighth child, and there would undoubtedly be more to come . . .

That night, when they were seated round the camp fire, Viviane kept herself to herself. She slept badly, too.

"I was feeling uneasy, in the first place because I'd baptized the child when there mightn't have been any real need to do so. Secondly, because I'd given it that name without thinking. And thirdly . . . "

She began to laugh with tears in her eyes.

"And thirdly because I wondered how valid the baptism was. I mean, is Selim really a saint's name?"

12

Mima Yared entered the Batrakanis' portals feeling rather tense. She dreaded any contact with these wealthy families whom Khalil had so often vowed to surpass and impress — not that he'd had the time, poor man. Besides, she felt uneasy in her mother-in-law's role despite the feathered hat which her neighbour had more or less forced on her, swearing that it perfectly complemented her brown suit with the white revers.

The only Batrakani she knew was Viviane, whom Selim had brought to see her three weeks ago. She had also heard Yolande's voice on the phone, inviting her to this engagement party.

Viviane had seemed rather stiff — she obviously wasn't expecting such a shabby, simply furnished apartment — and Selim hadn't really managed to thaw her out. He'd left quite soon, accompanied by that elegant young woman who looked like a being from another world.

"You might at least have waited for Roger!" Mima complained the next day.

Roger, with his doctor's title, was her pride and joy. No girl would ever be good enough for him. Mima had the knack of introducing "my son the doctor" into any conversation, whether devoted to stuffed vine leaves or the repair of laddered stockings.

Fathiya, who echoed her mistress, referred to the *duktour* at every opportunity. This misplaced publicity exasperated the person concerned, especially when the maidservant stationed herself at the kitchen window and hailed the launderer whose shop was two doors away.

"*Ya* Maurice!" Fathiya would call at the top of her voice. "The *duktour* is waiting for his shirt. He's in a hurry — it's the only one he's got!"

Mima turned up at the Batrakanis' on Roger's arm. With its surrounding trees, heavy wrought-iron gate, and liveried *sufragi* in white gloves, the fine house was all that she had hoped and feared: Selim was making a good marriage, but hadn't he set his sights too high? As for herself, what would she find to say to these people who couldn't fail to regard her with disdain?

A momentary silence fell when Mima entered the drawing room.

"Who's that lovely creature?" muttered Alex Batrakani.

Selim, who was standing just behind him, felt his eyes grow moist. Yes, at forty-six his mother was still beautiful. Abruptly aware of this, he was almost resentful when the others started chatting again.

Georges Batrakani managed to put Mima at her ease immediately by paying her a little compliment that came from the heart:

"Meningitis almost robbed us of Viviane at the age of five, *chère madame* — she only just survived it. Ever since then, I've sworn to make her happy and marry her well. As you see, I've kept my promise."

Georges Bey had been alarmed the previous year to see his daughter still unmarried. "How much longer, *ya binti*?"

Viviane had shrugged her shoulders. Then, just to annoy him:

"You know what Father Ayrout tells us at our meetings? 'Seek the Kingdom of God and you'll get your Prince Charming as a bonus.'"

"Ayrout's crazy!" snapped Georges Bey. "Swallow nonsense like that and you'll end up on the shelf!"

But Georges Batrakani was not the kind to marry off his daughter to the first man who came along. Viviane, who was dreading Selim's interview with her father, had already corrected his French on more than one occasion — a process of which he smilingly took note.

Viviane reflected that Georges Batrakani himself must have had a few such problems when marrying into the Toutas, whom he still occasionally referred to as "snobs and Latinists".

She introduced Selim to her father one afternoon on the terrace at Groppi's, firmly resolved to wage a stubborn battle for his consent. To her great surprise, Georges Bey was sweet as pie. Far from interrogating Selim about his financial or professional status, he seemed interested only in his opinion of Groppi's *millefeuilles à la crème*.

His own opinion of Selim he conveyed to his daughter at home that evening. "I don't know whether or not I should congratulate Father Ayrout," he quipped, "but your prince seems charming."

She flung her arms round his neck, unaware that he had made inquiries about Selim at Matossian's and had even sounded out the Très Chers Frères of Zaher.

Yolande Batrakani had told Mima on the phone that the party would be a simple, intimate, family occasion — and indeed, there were only sixty people present.

"Come and meet Viviane's godfather," said Yolande, taking her guest's arm.

Mima was deceived by the greying hair. She failed to recognize Édouard Dhellemmes until he turned and lingeringly kissed her hand.

"I had no idea . . . " she said. Her voice trailed away.

Yolande didn't notice a thing. "Ah yes," she went on, "Édouard is French. He's one of our dearest friends. He was passing through Cairo in 1922, just when Viviane was born . . . Please excuse me, I'll leave you two together, someone's signalling to me."

"You haven't changed," Édouard told Mima when they were alone.

Her only response was a vague smile and a shrug. She had never consented to see him again since their meeting on the Ayrouts' terrace at Heliopolis ten years earlier.

"I've been living in Egypt for nearly two years now, did you know? I've opened an antique shop at the end of Suleiman Pasha Street. Do you like antiques?"

Mima smiled. "I can hardly afford to buy new things, let alone antiques."

"Why not do me the pleasure of visiting my shop? I could show you some wonderful things, just for interest's sake. I'm there every afternoon. May I count on you?"

He put it so nicely that Mima promised to visit him the following Wednesday.

Something of a commotion was in progress at the far end of the first drawing room: Father André Batrakani had just arrived, and several of the guests were eagerly greeting him. Having shaken a hand or two, the Jesuit went over to Viviane. He kissed her, took her paternally by the shoulder, and whispered in her ear, "I wish you a demanding husband!"

Édouard Dhellemmes offered to introduce the man who would solemnize the marriage in a few weeks' time.

"He's a splendid fellow, you'll see," he told Mima. "I knew him when he was still a child, but I must admit he overawes me a little today with his beard, his soutane, and that piercing gaze."

Viviane and Selim would, of course, be getting married at Sainte Marie de la Paix. Consecrated only very recently, this church in Garden City was already regarded as *the* Sunday rendezvous for members of good Greek Catholic society. They owed its acquisition to Mary Kahil, a wealthy unmarried heiress with a Syrian father and a German mother. A fanatical believer, she had been profoundly influenced by her contacts with the islamologist Louis Massignon.

"Massignon got himself ordained a Greek Catholic priest," Viviane explained to Selim. "He involved Mary in some mystical experience which no one understands. I only know that the church used to belong to the Anglicans, and that Mary set her heart on it. She enlisted the hosts of heaven in her attempts to acquire the building. One day she even sneaked up to the churchyard wall and tossed a medal of St Theresa over it."

"And St Theresa got the message, naturally."

"Mary managed to buy the church for ten thousand pounds in December 1941. It being wartime, they naturally called it Sainte Marie de la Paix. The maintenance costs are borne by Papa and several other subscribers."

Salwah, Viviane's Muslim friend, was in the second drawing room with Roger Yared, who had just been introduced to her. They were arguing.

"Wouldn't you agree, doctor, that female circumcision is an outrageous form of mutilation?"

"All the more outrageous, mademoiselle, because it's performed with unsterilized razor blades."

"The medical profession ought to mobilize. There should be a law against it."

"You really think a law can induce country folk to change their ways?"

One of Huda Sha'arawi's most ardent disciples, Salwah was now a very active militant feminist. She had held out against her parents, who wanted to marry her off at eighteen, and was reading for a law degree.

"Speaking for myself," she told Viviane, whom she reproached for only sitting the first part of her *baccalauréat*, "I don't intend to marry until I've graduated."

Lola's arrival in the first drawing room was greeted with loud applause. Although four months pregnant, she had poured herself into a scarlet dress that accentuated her vamp's figure and the sensuality of her features. Her slim, elegant husband Roland followed her in, flashing Hollywood smiles in all directions. Everyone remembered the honeymoon photograph of them in *Images* three years earlier. It showed them outside the Mena House Hotel in their Bugatti convertible: a wealthy young couple who seemed to symbolize all the blessings of heaven – and all the injustice in the world.

"You're an accountant, I gather." The speaker was an odd-looking man in a floppy mauve bow tie. "In that case, you must know the precise population of Egypt."

Selim didn't know, nor, to be honest, had he ever given the matter any thought.

"You're keeping something from me," whispered the man in the bow tie.

Selim cast a worried glance at Viviane, who was watching them out of the corner of her eye. She had forgotten to warn him about her maternal uncle's obsession.

"Fifteen million, perhaps," he said, picking a figure at random.

"You're joking!" cried Edmond Touta.

Viviane's shoulders were shaking with suppressed mirth. Selim saw this and relaxed.

"Fifteen million seven hundred and fifty thousand, according to our latest calculations," he tried again in a more peremptory tone.

His companion was bathed in perspiration. He mopped his brow with one end of his immense bow tie.

"But that's impossible, young man! There were seventeen million of them at the beginning of the year. Seventeen million! Alarming, isn't it?"

PART EIGHT

The Antique Shop

I

30 September 1945

So here I am, a godfather! I could hardly have turned Viviane down.

My godson was to be called Rafiq, but Papa, who got to the maternity wing before everyone else, insisted on his being christened Charles.

Selim is rather annoyed, and I sympathize with him. Poor fellow, he still hasn't grasped what it means to have a father-in-law like Georges Batrakani!

Papa's methods apart, I don't really know what to make of this new vogue for saddling new-born babies with Arab names like the Rizqallahs, Habibs and Khalils of old. It's true that the present upsurge of nationalist sentiment is an incentive to err on the side of caution. "Wars are the midwives of revolutions," Makram said the other day. But the man in the dark suit often mistakes his wishes for their fulfilment. That's why Papa wanted to contradict him by transforming Rafiq into Charles.

As for my young sister, she doesn't seem dismayed by the change in her son's name, especially as I'm told that Professor Martin-Bérard thinks it a very judicious choice. Ah, these Frenchmen!

In the old days our mothers used to give birth at home. It was Om Yousef, and later her niece Madame Rathl, who used to welcome us into this world. But the Jesuits or the Brothers were never far off, ready to take delivery of us . . .

Needless to say, Michel almost missed my christening. He'd gone to Sainte Marie de la Paix, forgetting that my parents lived in Heliopolis. His taxi got to Korba church thirty-five minutes late.

"You can't blame it on Mademoiselle Guyomard, not this time!" said André, who'd been about to baptize me with the aid of a proxy.

Ever cheerful, René 'Abdel-Messih told my father, "Your son has already changed names — now he's going to change godfathers. Never mind, *ya sidi*. Just as long as he doesn't change his sex . . . "

The photographs show André in his finest liturgical vestments. Selim, standing slightly to the rear, is wearing a white tie and jacket. Viviane has still to regain her girlish figure, but her radiant expression suits her wonderfully well. Michel, looking rather on edge, seems hampered by my lace christening robe. He'd never held a baby in his arms before.

2

"It'll be your honeymoon proper," Georges Bey had said.

Selim wasn't immediately thrilled by his father-in-law's proposal that they should visit Europe *en famille*, but Viviane's cries of enthusiasm – and his brothers' admiring whistles – quickly changed his mind.

The fact was, Georges Batrakani had bought the air tickets without consulting anyone. He was anxious not to miss Air France's first scheduled flight from Cairo to Paris. It was the same with cars: you didn't wait for everyone in town to try out a new model before ordering one.

My grandmother was scared stiff by the thought of soaring above the clouds, but Georges Bey brushed her objections aside with an impatient shrug. Paul and the Swissess would be in the party, Michel too. As for Lola, who was stuck in Cairo, she had offered to give me a home while my parents were away, together with my nurse. I was just over ten months old.

Before they went through customs at Almaza Airport, Selim saw Georges Batrakani remove his purple tarboosh with both hands and substitute a magnificent straw hat. He adjusted the boater on his head with a facility that left my father open-mouthed. They were exchanging one world for another.

The flight lasted thirteen hours, including a stop at Tunis. Yolande crossed herself three times when the DC4's propellers started to turn. Selim himself, whose heart was thumping, prayed to the Virgin Mary and pretended to look out of the window. It defeated him how Viviane could be so casual. She was leaning across the aisle, telling the Swissess about her first visit to Paris in 1937.

"Our parents took us, Lola and me, to the World Exhibition. In the

[265]

middle of the Mediterranean, which was like glass, they announced that our liner, which was flying the Egyptian flag, was going to pass the king's yacht, the *Fakhr al-Bahar*. All the passengers assembled on deck. We waited until the two ships were on a level before shouting, all together: '*Ta'ish bilaadi wa yahi-al-malik!*' – which means 'Long live my country and long live the king!' Farouq raised his hand in acknowledgement. He was eighteen, and very good-looking."

"You haven't done up your seat belt tight enough," Selim said nervously.

Four rooms had been reserved at the Scribe, one of the few decent hotels in Paris unoccupied by Allied troops. The proprietor greeted the Batrakanis, bowing low, and showed them round the dining room in person.

"From tomorrow," he whispered in my grandfather's ear, "you can have your meals served in your rooms. They'll be a little more expensive but far less rationed."

Egyptian pounds were like gold dust in a Europe that had still to recover from the war. Selim inferred this from the bellboy's dumbfounded expression when he slipped the equivalent of two piastres into his hand. Passports inscribed "Kingdom of Egypt" had earned the party deferential smiles as soon as they presented them at the reception desk.

My parents' room had a rather acrid smell, like that of a stuffy old library. To Selim, that would always be the odour of Paris, France, and Europe in general.

While Viviane set the taps hissing in the bathroom, my father drew aside the floral cretonne curtain and looked out of the window. Never had he imagined that buildings could be so neatly aligned – the streets might have been drawn with a straight-edge! Despite the scars of war and food rationing, Paris seemed to exude an air of vast wealth amassed in the course of centuries. Selim thought he knew France from books, films, and descriptions given by the Très Chers Frères, but his very first glimpse of the country had transfixed him with amazement. He could still hear Roger sternly catechizing him from inside the lavatory:

"What's the northernmost department of France?"

Silence.

"Nord, *ya fellah!*"

[266]

He glued his nose to the windowpane like the child who used to watch kites circling over Faggaala. There it was before his very eyes, the putative land of his forefathers, and there were its inhabitants, those little figures hurrying along without a glance to left or right.

The bathroom door opened. Viviane, smilingly attired in a pink costume, was ready to go down to dinner. Selim's heart leapt as it had the very first time he saw her. He went over and took her in his arms. And, as their lips met, he told himself that he was in Paris, that it wasn't a dream, and that this woman nestling against him was indeed Viviane Batrakani . . .

The staff of the Scribe lavished attention on Georges Bey and his clan. As for the cabbies stationed outside the hotel, they competed for the privilege of driving them all over the city.

"We can congratulate ourselves on being Egyptians," Michel remarked during a visit to the Café de la Paix.

"We aren't Egyptians," Paul said curtly.

The waiter came up to take their order.

"*Moi, je prendrai une gazeuse avec un chalumeau*," said my father.

The waiter looked puzzled.

"*Monsieur voudrait un citron pressé avec une paille*," Paul explained in a starchy voice.

Under other circumstances Selim would have burst out laughing, but his brother-in-law's tone annoyed him. In Paul Batrakani's eyes he was a peasant seeing Paris for the first time.

Selim had in fact been wide-eyed with wonder for the previous two days. To one who had never visited Upper Egypt, or even the Cairo Museum, even the Pharaonic treasures in the Louvre were a source of amazement. He knew nothing of ancient Egypt save the Pyramids and the Sphinx, whereas the Swissess commented blithely on hieroglyphs and juggled with dynasties.

After a week they left Paris for St Moritz, where Georges Bey had booked rooms. My grandfather wanted to take the mountain air and pay a visit to the Swissess's parents, who owned a chalet not far away.

There was something unreal about the picture postcard scenery. At every bend in the switchback road Selim sighted overly green pastures, overly plump cows. He felt he was in Shangri La.

"Ah, so you're Egyptians too!" the hotel receptionist exclaimed with a broad smile.

Hamdi Pasha, the senator for Alexandria, was also holidaying at the hotel with his family. At dinner my grandfather sent a waiter over with his card, then rose and introduced himself. Every meal thereafter was accompanied by *salamaats* and distant smiles. It was an encounter between two Egypts unacquainted with each other but far from hostile.

Selim found this little game a bore. Everything in St Moritz bored him, to be honest. Apart from daily snacks in the village and walks along mountain paths that ruined his town shoes, the days were utterly uneventful. He hung round Viviane, who showed little enthusiasm for amatory siestas, which were too much like a means of killing time.

"What if we go back to Paris ahead of the others?" she suggested point-blank one afternoon while my father, slumped in an armchair, was sullenly glancing through *La Tribune de Genève*.

"But . . . What about your parents?"

"Leave them to me."

He hurried to the reception desk to inquire the time of the next train. *That* was their honeymoon proper.

By the time the others joined them at the Hôtel Scribe ten days later, Selim was in high spirits and knew Paris like the back of his hand. They had strolled tirelessly along the *quais*, traversed Montmartre in all directions, travelled hundreds of kilometres by Métro. Flitting from one diversion to the next, they had rocked with laughter at *Blum! Blum! Tra-la-la*, listened to a recital by André Claveau, and attended the final of the 1946 bathing beauty contest at the Piscine Molitor.

The end of their stay in Paris was devoted to shopping. The women tore themselves away from the big department stores to go and choose some hats at a famous milliner's in rue Royale. Georges Bey picked up some rare tapestries in the Cour de Rohan, while Michel scoured the shelves for antique books. My father spent most of his time trying to find a present for Mima. He went from shop to shop, retraced his steps, became more and more agitated. Viviane, who had had enough of this, ended by choosing a lizard-skin bag at Lancel in his place, although she knew that what her mother-in-law would appreciate most of all were some kitchen utensils she'd bought for a few francs in the big boulevards.

Georges Bey had been observing his new son-in-law throughout the trip. On their last day he took him aside in the hotel foyer.

"Are you happy at Matossian's? I only ask because you might care to come and work with us. Think it over, you don't have to give me an answer right away."

They were booked on the Air France flight on 6 September. Three days earlier the Copenhagen–Paris plane crashed on take-off and caught fire. Yolande Batrakani was in a terrible state about this. The others did their best to reassure her in a jocular way. On 4 September the Paris–London plane crashed too, reducing all its passengers to ashes.

"Not a word to Yola!" Georges commanded his children.

They all felt weak at the knees as they boarded the Air France DC4 two days later. Selim and his mother-in-law were not alone in praying to the Virgin Mary.

When the aircraft finally touched down at Almaza the passengers broke into deafening applause and Yolande crossed herself one last time. The various families had turned out *en masse* and were waiting on the airport's little terrace. Selim, with one arm round Viviane's waist and the other waving vigorously, felt a regular hero. It was as if he had returned from the ends of the earth after an eternity away. He saw Egypt with new eyes, surprised to find it so arid, so yellow.

Ten minutes later he was hugging a tearful Mima while the Batrakanis' chauffeur berated the porters for getting all the baggage mixed up. The new arrivals laughed and chattered, fanned themselves and boasted of their experiences. They were home again.

3

"While you were trailing round Europe, *mes chéris*, the king treated himself to a romantic cruise in the Mediterranean," Alex said casually, picking at the stuffed vine leaf on his plate. He was certain of his effect.

"A romantic cruise?"

"Go on, *ya Alex!*"

André's absence from this Sunday's lunch was an invitation to frivolity. My uncle Alex had been an expert on Farouq's philanderings ever since their famous encounter on the road. He had kept in touch with some of the palace night owls, who treated him as a playmate and didn't hesitate to mention the king's exploits or *bons mots* in his presence.

"Early this summer Farouq fell in love with a young Alexandrian Jewess – you know, the celebrated Camélia, who used to sing at the Auberge des Pyramides. The king made up his mind to take her with him on his first Mediterranean cruise since the war. Camélia left for Cyprus. Without telling the government, Farouq had his yacht fitted out for a pleasure trip with her and some friends."

"But they say he's impotent."

"Paul, please! There are children present."

"Let's say there are occasions when he finds it difficult to finish the job," Alex said gaily. "It's different with Camélia, though. She's a miracle-worker."

"Nobody's said a word about my vine leaves," Yolande put in firmly. "Don't you like them? Perhaps you'd have preferred some *molokhiya* . . . "

Compliments were showered on her from all directions.

"Talking of Farouq," said Georges Bey, "I frankly think he's becoming obese."

"You should see what he puts away for breakfast!" Alex said with the air of a permanent denizen of 'Abdin Palace. "A dozen eggs, lobster, stuffed quail, ice cream. And before every official palace dinner he raids the kitchens for whipped cream."

"It isn't just that he's deformed. He looks ridiculous in those dark glasses he wears all the time. Fouad had style, at least."

"Style? What style, pray?" exclaimed Michel, for whom things had gone steadily downhill since Sultan Hussein's death in 1917.

"Farouq may be an oaf, but he certainly doesn't lack cheek or a sense of humour. You know the story of the poker game?"

Everyone knew it, but one of the children always asked to hear it again, and Georges Bey complied with pleasure.

"Farouq had called four kings, but he only put down three. The other players stared at each other in embarrassment. At length, rather timidly, one of them inquired where the fourth king was. '*I'm* the fourth!' cried Farouq, bellowing with laughter as he scooped the kitty."

"Farouq sometimes calls his card-playing cronies in the middle of the night and asks them to join him at the club in Qasr al-Nil Street. You can hear his belly-laugh through the open window."

"They say nobody dares to leave the neighbouring tables until the king has finished playing – which may not be before dawn."

"Did you know he sometimes invites himself to private parties? When he saw some lights on at the Taklas' a few nights ago, he simply rang the bell and walked in."

"Farouq isn't just content to steal other men's wives," said Paul. "He's a genuine kleptomaniac. A diplomat told me the other day that he pinched Churchill's watch in 'forty-two."

"You're joking!"

"No, it's true."

"Well, go on."

"You recall how Churchill came here to tour the battlefield during the war? Well, Farouq insisted on inviting him to dinner at the Mena House, so they arranged to meet there. Churchill was very pressed for time and wanted to make this clear – he was due to leave for Gibraltar the same night – so he put his hand in his pocket and felt for his gold watch. It was gone. Having heard of Farouq's little foibles, Churchill intimated as calmly and courteously as possible that his watch had disappeared, that he was very attached to it, and that he wouldn't sit down to dinner before he found it. Farouq inveighed against the thieves but promised to put things right. He left the table, to return in triumph ten minutes later with the watch in his hand. Beat that, anyone."

"I can," said Alex, "but it's a story I'm not allowed to tell . . . "

"Stop playing hard to get."

"No, honestly, I promised."

"Get on with it, *ya Alex!*"

"Very well. It was during the war. The British reproved Farouq for surrounding himself with Italians — they'd counted seventeen at the palace. 'After all,' the British ambassador protested, 'we're at war with Italy. Other Italians in Egypt are detained in camps, whereas yours, Your Majesty, hold key posts.' The Egyptian government also begged Farouq to get rid of Pulli and company, pointing out that all these foreigners were very unpopular with parliament. Foreigners? No problem! Farouq decided to grant them Egyptian nationality on the spot."

"And to think we've been waiting for decades!"

"A little while later, being anxious to do things properly, Farouq sent for some of his Italians. 'Muslims are always circumcised, as you know,' he told them. 'To help you become genuine Egyptians, I've asked my surgeon to perform a minor operation on you.'"

"Alex, the children are listening . . . "

"None of the Italians displayed much enthusiasm, as you can imagine, so Farouq told them it was a royal command. One of them refused despite this. The next day he woke up in the palace hospital. The king and his barber were beside his bed, doubled up with laughter. Thanks to some knockout drops slipped into his drink the night before, he'd become a genuine Egyptian!"

"And the *kunafa*? How do you find my *kunafa*?" implored Yolande, telling herself that the children must eat on their own in future.

One afternoon in August, while the family were away in Paris, Alex was summoned to the Jesuit school by his brother André. It was the first time the unruliest of my uncles had revisited that unloved institution since his boyhood.

Pupils very seldom ascended to the Fathers' quarters on the third floor. Alex felt almost as nervous, while making his way along the silent corridor, as he had in the days of his zeros and relegations. He checked the name on the door twice before knocking.

André's big, bare room was lit by a large window. There was a prie-dieu beside the bed, and above it a rather faded Byzantine icon. Bookshelves sagged under the weight of the volumes arrayed on them. The Risotto Club was a million miles away.

The Jesuit promptly got down to brass tacks:

"You're thirty-five, Alex. Many men of your age have already founded a family."

So that was it. Alex started to smile. When he was nineteen his elder brother had warned him against marrying too soon; now he was reproaching him for having waited too long.

"I must be abnormal," he said, chuckling.

"On the contrary, you're typical of your generation. That's just what saddens me. Young Syrians of today tend to put off marrying from year to year. One suspects either that they're shirking their responsibilities or that they've lost faith in the future."

"I shall definitely marry a foreigner."

"You all want to marry foreigners!"

"Syrian girls are uninteresting."

"Nonsense! They're different from you, that's all. They're romantic, you're worldly. They look younger than their years, whereas you've grown old before your time."

Alex still felt very young. His only worry was an incipient bald patch inherited from the Toutas. However, his cronies at the billiards club held that men suffering from hair loss were attractive to women and sexually more potent than the hirsute.

"Don't worry, André. I get at least one proposal a month, not to mention all the splendid matches Maman insists on finding for me. I'll marry in the end, never fear."

4

Father André sometimes dined at our house in Heliopolis when I was nine or ten years old. While the grown-ups were having their pre-dinner drinks he would leave them in the drawing room and come to say evening prayers with us children. But before lights-out my brothers and I were entitled to an edifying story – always the same one – whose hero was Maximos Mazloum, our Church's most illustrious patriarch.

Father André wore a black cassock in winter and a white one in summer. Seated on the edge of one of our beds, he always began by asking a question:

"Do you know what year Mazloum was elected patriarch?"

We hazarded a guess.

"It was 1833," he amended. "And in 1833 our Church was not universally recognized in the Ottoman Empire. Every time our ancestors wanted to register a birth or a marriage, and every time they wanted to confirm a new appointment, they had to apply to the Orthodox Church. The latter made life difficult for them because they had sided with the Pope. The Orthodox patriarchate of Constantinople even went so far as to forbid our priests to wear the *kallousa*. Which of you can describe the *kallousa* for me?"

We all answered at once, having often seen our Greek Catholic priest wearing the cylindrical black headgear typical of Byzantine clergy.

"Well, the *kallousa* became a political matter. At Constantinople the Russian ambassador backed the Orthodox Church, whereas we were supported by France. Torn between the great powers, the sultan kept issuing contradictory edicts. On one occasion our Greek Catholic clergy had to change their headgear altogether; on another they were merely invited to adopt a violet *kallousa* or one with four corners."

Father André skated over the details of this diplomatic battle, which were too complicated for us, and confined himself to a few vivid images.

"One day, wanting to humiliate us at all costs, the Orthodox proposed to make our priests wear a new form of headgear in the shape of a cone or pyramid."

"A pyramid!"

"Yes indeed! Just imagine our bishops with pyramids on their heads . . . But Patriarch Mazloum was not a man to be trifled with. Thoroughly infuriated, he went off to Constantinople to obtain satisfaction. For that he needed to see the sultan, but the grand vizier, who had been bribed by the Orthodox, denied him an audience. Accordingly, Mazloum resorted to extreme measures. One Friday, accompanied by two priests wearing the *kallousa* like himself, he stationed himself on the sultan's route brandishing a poster attached to the end of a pole. The sultan stopped his cortège to question them. Mazloum handed him a letter explaining his request. On returning to the palace, the sultan commanded the grand vizier to admit our patriarch. When he arrived at the palace the grand vizier pointed to a little six-sided table encrusted with mother-of-pearl. 'Would you accept a hat of that shape?' he asked. Mazloum agreed. And that was how, for quite some time, our priests came to wear a violet *kallousa* with a six-sided brim instead of a round one like that of the Orthodox."

There the story ended, but we asked sundry questions to postpone lights-out. Father André would look worried and pretend to consult his wristwatch, but he ended by sitting down again.

"In 1848 – remember that date – the sultan finally granted our Roman Catholic nation the same privileges as the Orthodox. Our patriarch was able to govern his community, set up courts and levy taxes throughout the Ottoman Empire. Mazloum had won. He returned to Aleppo in triumph, but that displeased the Muslims of the city, and one night they sacked the Christian houses of an entire district. To escape unrecognized, our patriarch had to dress up as a woman with a veil on his head."

"A veil? Like our maidservant?"

"Yes indeed! But then, to get to Antioch, he had to disguise himself as a European general in a cocked hat!"

"It was worth it, though, wasn't it, Uncle André, fighting for the *kallousa* all those years?"

Sometimes we managed to persuade the storyteller to recount a final episode: great Maximos's death at Alexandria — an epic death that released him from terrible sufferings which all the barber's leeches had failed to alleviate.

"Our patriarch prayed courageously until the Lord recalled him to Himself. His body was lightly embalmed, attired in his vestments, and seated on a throne so that for four days, despite the heat, people could file past him and pay their last respects. The Greek Catholic church at Alexandria was too small, so the funeral service was held in the Latin church. But the body was then transported by train to Cairo — the railway line had only just been laid — where Maximos was given another funeral. He was buried behind the altar of the church at Darb al-Geneina, one of the twenty-four churches erected at the bidding of this great man, this giant among men, our first 'Patriarch of Alexandria, Antioch, Jerusalem, and all the East'."

"Alexandria, Antioch, Jerusalem, and all the East," we murmured in unison. Father André kissed us on the forehead, tickling us with his beard. Then he turned out the light and quietly closed the door. We heard the squeak of his crêpe soles in the passage as he made his way back to the drawing room.

5

"Do me the pleasure of accepting this little lamp. It's an old mosque lamp . . . "

Édouard Dhellemmes was so gently insistent that Mima Yared ended by saying yes.

Her visit to the shop in Suleiman Pasha Street had left her feeling quite dazed. Édouard abandoned some customers to the care of an assistant and devoted two whole hours to her. His shop was a regular little museum divided into various sections: ancient Egypt, the Islamic period, Coptic art. He had acquired his treasures piecemeal from shops in the old quarter of Cairo, during his peregrinations in Upper Egypt, and in the monasteries of Wadi Natroun.

"Now I'm going to take you to tea at Groppi's," he said when the two hours were up. "Don't say no, I must have tired you out."

Édouard ordered a mountain of cakes. At forty-six, my grandmother had the air of a girl being taken out for the very first time. They talked of Viviane and Selim, of Roger — needless to say — and of the Batrakanis.

"Georges took it into his head to teach me Arabic, can you imagine?"

Mima rocked with laughter when he told her that Edmond Touta, who was a lone cinemagoer, always reserved four extra seats — one on either side, one in front, and one behind — so as not to be asphyxiated by the audience.

The following week they were back at Groppi's, lunching together.

"You've been in my thoughts for ten long years," Édouard said softly.

"Don't be silly."

"Ten years is plenty of time for reflection. My dearest wish, Mima, is that you should become my wife."

She looked panic-stricken.

"Perhaps you think me too old. I'm fifty-three, it's true, but — "

"Don't be silly! I'm a widow. I've got children."

"I've been married too. As for your being a widow, why remain one for ever?"

She shut up like a clam and begged him to change the subject.

They saw each other several times for Sunday lunch at the Batrakanis' and on other occasions for tea at Groppi's, but she never consented to come back to his Zamalek apartment, just as he never dared to mention marriage again. Fearful of spoiling everything, he carefully concealed his love and limited himself to being her friend, a role he found terribly frustrating.

6

I was two years old in 1947, when the cholera epidemic broke out. Everyone in the family was vaccinated, fruit and vegetables were disinfected, and Yolande went so far as to instruct the chef to wash our meat with soap and water.

Edmond Touta was in a fever of excitement. Good news at last on the demographic front! With nearly nineteen million inhabitants, Egypt had doubled her population in fifty years, yet she'd stubbornly avoided involvement in both world wars. A few measly train crashes or sinkings on the Nile were quite insufficient to solve her problem. Only a good epidemic could inflict the necessary fatalities.

"Did you know that cholera wiped out a third of the population of Cairo in 1834?" Edmond kept saying with an avid look on his face.

Georges Bey listened to his brother-in-law's ravings with only half an ear. He told himself that heaven, wishing to punish him for having taken two Touta girls, had saddled him with the boys as well: Edmond the crackpot and Henri the good-for-nothing, a shareholder in his firm since the withdrawal of Édouard Dhellemmes – Henri, who had been thanked for his services by Peru and now functioned as Costa Rican consul at the same address.

"Cholera occurs in Egypt every thirty years or so," Michel observed. "After the epidemic of 1834 came the one of 1865, which was followed by another in 1883 . . . "

"That one I can remember," Georges Bey said thoughtfully. "Or, rather, I often heard people speak of it, but my brother Ferdinand could remember it very well."

Fat Nando was then a pupil at Khurunfish. He had every reason to hate Fridays, a meatless day with a double helping of prayers: in addition to morning Mass, an afternoon salute to the Blessed Sacrament in the school chapel. This was the Brothers' way of commemorating the cholera epidemic of 1865, during which they had displayed remarkable zeal, nursing and baptizing the sick with all their might. Miraculously, every last one of them escaped infection that year. This wondrous immunity they attributed to the Sacred Heart of Jesus. A medal of honour sent them by Napoleon III was placed in the chapel as an ex-voto, and a salute to the Blessed Sacrament had been held there every Friday thereafter.

Nando Batrakani ended by taking a certain relish in these pious excursions, which enabled him to dream of the exploits of the Très Chers Frères and identify himself with those oddly named heroes: Idelfonsus, Cyprien-Pierre, Baptistin-Honorat . . .

Nando, who was thirteen when cholera broke out at Damietta in June 1883, jumped for joy at the news. His rendezvous with history seemed to have come. He already had visions of himself as a first-aid worker braving death, miraculously immune and soon to be decorated, but he found his father's brusque assertions worrying.

"There won't be any cholera in Cairo," Élias said firmly. "In 1865 the flies, mosquitoes and nightingales sensed the approach of the epidemic and made themselves scarce. The sky was filled with a kind of greyish mist that made it hard to breathe at times, whereas today, look: you've never seen so many flies and mosquitoes. The nightingales are singing and the sky is blue."

He repeated his categorical prediction on 14 July. On 15 July Cairo recorded its first three fatal cases of cholera. There were another three the next day, the day after that forty-six, the day after that sixty-nine. The death rate continued to climb, yet the sky was still blue and the *bulbuls* still sang.

Élias issued a general alert. His delighted son's hopes rose once more. From Giza and Bulaq the epidemic spread to other districts. Even the Batrakanis' small apartment building seemed to be affected: according to a rumour current in the stairwell, the Armenian tenant on the mezzanine was suffering from diarrhoea.

"If it's only diarrhoea, I wouldn't commit myself," Élias said gravely. "But if he's vomiting, it's cholera."

They all listened for suspicious sounds. Someone was dispatched to put his ear to the Armenian's door. The Armenian didn't have diarrhoea and he wasn't vomiting, but his voice was faint and his skin discoloured. Before Nando could spring into action, so-called "dry" cholera carried him off within forty-eight hours.

The same day two sinister-looking cleaners turned up with big buckets of disinfectant. They sluiced the corpse and bore it off in a tarred coffin. Nando, stationed at the window, saw the hearse, which was drawn by a black horse, disappear round the corner. His first prospective patient had given him the slip.

The British closed Cairo's big tannery and disinfected the mosques' public latrines. Fires were lit at night to purify the air. To preclude panic, the numerous funeral processions were restricted to special routes. One night, in an excess of zeal, some Egyptian officials set fire to several hundred hovels in Bulaq after evicting their inhabitants. Men, women and children, donkeys, goats and poultry set off under guard and were escorted out of the city, but many of them escaped and were not recaptured.

Chaos reigned in the Delta. The Batrakanis received alarming news from Damietta, whose thirty-five thousand inhabitants included a thousand or more Syrians. One of Élias's cousins managed to cross the cordon sanitaire and catch a train to Cairo, where he turned up unexpectedly on the first Sunday in August.

"I don't want him in here!" cried Linda Batrakani, who had shut herself up in the kitchen.

Élias parleyed with his cousin through the front door. The cousin swore on his wife's head that a doctor had examined him that morning and pronounced him free from infection. Knowing the man's wife, Élias was mistrustful.

"Swear on the heads of your children."

The door finally opened, and the Batrakani's self-invited guest was favoured with all the traditional words of welcome:

"*Ahlan wa sahlan!* We've missed you. Where have you been, *ya akhi*? We never see you these days . . ."

At table conversation naturally turned to the epidemic.

"Good for the English!" the cousin said sardonically. "They introduced the disease into this country by doing away with quarantine for their ships from India."

"That," retorted Élias, automatically springing to the defence of perfidious Albion, "is an unfounded allegation. This country had already been infected for months. The cholera spread slowly, without being recognized."

"Well, conditions at Damietta certainly provided all the makings of an epidemic. Near the Jews' *wekaala* there's a big well full of fecal matter which they clean out with the aid of a mechanical pump. The excrement flows along open sewers into the outlet from the public baths and from there into the river. And where, pray, do the inhabitants draw their water?"

Linda couldn't wait to interrupt this nauseating recital. "Right," she said, "I'll serve the *molokhiya* now."

"Contaminated water is one thing," the cousin pursued with his mouth full and his napkin knotted around his neck, "but there's also the question of infected meat. In one village near Damietta people have been feeding on the meat of water buffalo that have died of typhus. It's almost black, and sells for two piastres an *oke* instead of twelve." He broke off. "Incidentally, Linda, your *molokhiya* is quite delicious. On the head of my wife, I've never eaten better."

Élias smothered a guffaw.

"At Damietta," the cousin went on, "the Muslims continue to bury their next of kin in the middle of residential districts. Nobody dares to sprinkle their corpses with chloride of lime because it'll deprive them of the hair they need to be hoisted into paradise. The workmen in charge of sealing the vaults don't do so; they sell the plaster instead. Why bother, they say, when the vaults will have to be reopened the same day for another burial? Access to the Arab cemetery has been prohibited, but the soldiers will admit people who want to pray for their dead in return for a half-piastre or a sesame-seed cake."

The cousin refilled his plate with rice, chicken, onions and gravy, periodically washing them down with generous swigs of 'araqi. Nando, feeling sick, abruptly left the table and hurried off to bring up his lunch. On that August day in 1883 he gave up cholera for good: he would find some other means of going down in history.

7

It had just been announced that the plane would be an hour late. The Syrian and Lebanese premiers returned to the VIP lounge while the Greek Catholic dignitaries continue to chat on the terrace of the little airport at Almaza, facing the desert.

Georges Batrakani was already cursing to himself at the thought of the business appointment he'd had to cancel to join this reception committee. But the new patriarch's arrival in Egypt had at least afforded him an opportunity to collect André from the school and spend forty-five minutes with him *en route* – a rare occurrence. His eldest son had thus been able to gauge the qualities of his wonderful new fifteen-horsepower, front-wheel drive Citroën . . .

Their wait on the terrace was enlivened by a jovial, garrulous priest from Alexandria.

"Did you know that our great patriarch Maximos Mazloum – may his soul rest in peace! – made his entry into Egypt a century ago? Imagine, he arrived here on horseback after stopping off at Acre and Jaffa. It was the middle of Ramadan, so he could only enter Cairo at night. This was in 1836, mark you, when our Church had still to be officially recognized."

Chairs were brought and a servant came to take orders for drinks. With a resigned shrug, Georges Bey sat down beside the speaker.

"Mazloum spent three years in Cairo, time enough to instil a little order into the Egyptian community and get a number of churches built. He was preparing to return to Damascus when Egyptian troops in Syria came under attack from insurgents. The patriarch was very embarrassed by this. Put yourself in his place, Monsieur Batrakani. He couldn't dissociate himself from Muhammad Ali, who had done a great deal for the Greek Catholics and, in any case, had the Egyptian community at his mercy. On the other hand, to have sided with Muhammad Ali against the sultan would have been to expose all the other Melchites in the Ottoman Empire to grave reprisals."

"True . . . "

"Wisely, our patriarch decided to retire from the fray. He went off to live for varying periods in Rome, Paris, and Marseille."

"You've forgotten to mention, Father, that he'd settled the headgear question in the interim," said an ex-president of the mixed courts bar association.

"No, no, the battle of the *kallousa* wasn't won until years later. That's another story . . . Incidentally, Monsieur Batrakani, don't you manufacture *kallousas* as well?"

My grandfather burst out laughing. "No, Abuna. The *kallousa* has nothing in common with the tarboosh despite its cylindrical shape. Besides, we wouldn't find enough customers."

"Sadly, Monsieur Batrakani, sadly! It can't be said that Greek Catholic families compete to supply our Church with priests. That doesn't apply to you, of course . . . "

Georges Bey was beginning to find this ecclesiastic a trifle importunate. Any minute now he would be soliciting money for his good works or cadging a lift back to Cairo. He excused himself, pleading a call of nature.

"Go whither duty calls you!" boomed the priest, who was fond of uttering orotundities.

My grandfather went off to shake a few hands in the VIP lounge. When he returned to the terrace half an hour later, the crowd was stirring. Fingers were pointing to a minuscule speck in the sky. The plane touched down at last to a chorus of welcoming cheers.

The new patriarch was not by any means a young man, having just celebrated his seventieth birthday. André thought highly of Maximos Sayigh, as he had told his father in the car.

"He's an exceptional person – a man of Mazloum's calibre. He's already demonstrated that as metropolitan of Tyre and later of Beirut. His great merit is always to have lived in poverty."

"Poverty, poverty!" Georges Bey exclaimed. "You're always harping on it."

"But Papa, the Church *must* be poor in the image of Christ."

"But not *too* poor, *ya ibni*."

"I've never understood why there's so much gold and marble in our churches," André went on. "Especially as we're such a small community."

"You're being obtuse, *ya ibni*," Georges Bey told him. "It's precisely because we're small that we have to seem big." And he translated one of his favourite Arabic proverbs into French: "When a dog is wealthy he's addressed as *Monsieur le Chien*."

André cast his eyes up to heaven.

Having greeted the reception committee and permitted the Greek Catholic dignitaries to kiss his patriarchal ring, Maximos IV set off for Cairo followed by a cortège of several dozen cars. My grandfather took André and the priest from Alexandria in his Citroën.

"May we drop you somewhere, Abuna?"

"No, no, I don't want to be any trouble. I'll go to the cathedral with you."

"But the patriarch is calling at the palace first."

"Never mind, I'll accompany you to the palace."

Maximos IV was welcomed by 'Abdel-Latif Tala'at Pasha, who had succeeded Zul-Fiqar as grand chamberlain. He was solemnly handed two decrees signed by King Farouq, one appointing him patriarch of the Greek Catholics in Egypt, the other granting him Egyptian nationality.

The bells were ringing when Maximos's car arrived at the cathedral, where he was awaited by the governor of Cairo and numerous members of the diplomatic corps. White doves were released from the top of the stands by the little girls of the École de Saint-Thècle at Heliopolis, and the choir launched into the *Theos Kyrios*.

"The East is menaced by atheistic materialism," the new patriarch declared. "Our primary task is to ward off that danger. We must act not in an aggressive, combative spirit, as our enemy does, but in a spirit of peace, unity, and love."

"I told you he was a great man," André whispered to his father.

Continuing his address, the patriarch paid tribute to "our beloved sovereign Farouq I, whose wise counsels point the way ahead".

"What wise counsels does he mean?" Georges Bey whispered back. "Tips on driving cars and playing poker dice?"

8

For me, 1949 seems to mark the end of an era. The eighth volume of Michel's diary, which covers the relevant period, is strewn with wry remarks and disquieting little facts. I do, however, possess a nice snapshot dating from March 1949, when I was four-and-a-half. It shows me perched on the bonnet of my father's first car, a Topolino, with Rashid standing alongside. His white hair makes his skin look even darker, and his scar is masked by a rather weary smile. It's one of the few photographs on which my grandparents' *sufragi* appears, and certainly the last to be taken of him. I've inserted it between the following two pages in Michel's diary:

10 April 1949

Rashid died during the night of Friday—Saturday, as unobtrusively as he had lived. We were all very distressed.

I can still see him in Opera Square in 1917, the day of the sultan's funeral. He had one eye on me and the other on Zaki the coachman, who was too overwrought for his taste. Rashid said nothing when Papa fired Zaki next day. I think he was relieved.

Would he have reacted the same way two years later? His brother's death had made him hate the British. The circumstances of Sabri's death were never very clear, however, and Papa thought him a dangerous agitator.

We were all in the drawing room after lunch on Sunday when the doorbell rang. Being still unacquainted with the ways of the household, the new sufragi admitted the visitor without more ado. He was probably overawed by his officer's uniform, too. And that was how Rashid's nephew found himself in the presence of the entire family. He looked stern, as if rebuking us for chatting in the middle of a funeral service.

While Papa was getting up to conduct him to the study, Hassan turned and looked at Viviane in a peculiar way. Selim must have felt as uneasy as I did.

After ten minutes or so, Papa returned to the drawing room in a rather bad temper. "That ill-mannered lout began by asking me for all his uncle's personal effects," he said. "I mean, as if I were going to keep Rashid's galabiyas! He obviously detests us. Yet another one who resents the outcome of the Palestine War! When I think I put in a good word for him at Rashid's request, to help him get into the Military Academy . . ."

Papa gradually simmered down. He recalled how he'd employed Rashid in 1906, after he'd had his cheek laid open by a cabby's whip on account of some candles. The wound suppurated for a week, and the maidservant put vine leaves on it. Paul's children never tire of listening to that story, which they've heard a hundred times. Poor Rashid!

23 April 1949

The confounded war in Palestine has had some disastrous consequences. Cairo's Jewish shopkeepers haven't slept a wink since those bombs went off at Gattegno, Benzion and David Adès.

Victor Lévy tells me that some families in his neighbourhood are thinking of leaving the country. But this feeling of uneasiness isn't confined to the Jewish community. The other day Nino arrived home trembling with rage — fear too, no doubt. Someone in the street had just yelled "Zionist!" at him because of his chestnut hair. Nino is seriously talking of moving to Europe. Everyone says he's mad. Paul is the only person who agrees with him.

The Nino to whom Michel refers was none other than Antoine Touta, the family's celebrated "cousin from America". The freckles that covered his face are said to have set tongues wagging as soon as he was born. Nino may well have been thinking of leaving for Europe at the time when Michel wrote the above lines, but in June 1950 he emigrated to Brazil, where, twenty years later, he was elected governor of Mato Grosso.

As a child I pictured Antoine Touta with a gigantic nose smothered in freckles . . .

9

By the beginning of the 1950s the office in Opera Square bore absolutely no resemblance to the one that Édouard Dhellemmes had known during the First World War. Having progressively enlarged it, Georges Batrakani now occupied the entire building. He also maintained a branch office in Alexandria and the tarboosh factory in Shubra.

Although pharmaceutical products remained the linchpin of his business, my grandfather also represented several foreign manufacturers of machine tools and watches, not to mention perfumes, lingerie, and lace. When the bosses of those European firms visited Cairo he entertained them royally, organizing big dinners and excursions to the Pyramids. A box was permanently reserved for them at the Opera.

The business employed sixty staff including four sales directors: two Syrians, one Jew, and one Armenian. As for the bookkeepers, whom Makram supervised from outside, all were Copts with the exception of my father.

Paul had retained his law office in the building. Now that the mixed courts had been abolished, however, he worked almost exclusively for the family business, dealing with contractual matters and relations with foreign firms. Georges Bey had given up his visits to Europe, so it was Paul who went there two or three times a year. More elegant than ever, he bought his suits and shoes from the finest establishments in London or Milan.

Alex had been assigned to the tarboosh factory. No one apart from his father knew exactly what he did there. Although he didn't seem to do much, it was enough to enable Georges Bey to pay him a salary and get him out from under his feet. In 1948 the family good-for-nothing had surprised everyone by making a very good marriage to one of the Karam girls, who was pretty into the bargain.

The Shubra factory was doing extremely well. Foreign competition had been non-existent since the end of the war. The seven hundred and fifty-thousand tarbooshes sold in 1950 were all of local manufacture, and of those two-thirds came from Georges Bey's moulds. In many shops, customers now asked for "a Batrakani" instead of a tarboosh.

The army and the police had patronized Shubra for years. My grandfather never missed a military parade. A Batrakani tarboosh jutted from every gun turret until the military authorities banished such conspicuous objects from their tank commanders' heads. Georges Bey demonstrated his powers of imagination: he quickly stole a march on his competitors by sheathing his tarbooshes in khaki cloth and adding a peak and a neck protector.

In June 1951 the magazine *Rose al-Yousef* devoted two pages to the Shubra factory's success story. The article was prettily entitled "Tarboosh Bey". My grandfather was exultant.

But the following week another Arab-language periodical published a vitriolic piece in which the author expressed surprise that an article as important as the tarboosh should be manufactured by "a foreigner, not even a Muslim". Georges Batrakani was beside himself with rage. He sent the editor a furious five-page letter quoting the number of his Egyptian passport and King Fouad's citation appointing him a bey first class "for outstanding services to local industry". It was never published.

IO

A senior representative of the Egyptian section of the Louvre was passing through Cairo, and Édouard Dhellemmes had invited him to lunch at Shepheard's. Saturday was the day he reserved for such semi-professional engagements at a venue that never failed to delight him. Although he had a smart apartment overlooking the Nile in Zamalek, Édouard's heart belonged to the hotel where he had stayed so many times since 1916, and where the staff treated him with the deference due to a patron of long standing.

On arriving there at twelve-thirty he followed his usual practice and went to the manager's office to pass the time of day. The manager held out one of the hotel's two visitors' books, which he had been about to replace in the safe.

"Look who we've had this week!"

Édouard gave an admiring whistle, then leafed through the book at random. It held no secrets for him, but he preferred the first volume with its worn cover and array of signatures penned by legendary figures: Théophile Gautier, invited to Egypt for the opening of the Suez Canal and condemned to camp on the hotel terrace because of a broken leg; or Stanley, bound for his umpteenth expedition to Black Africa, who had taken advantage of his stay to edit his celebrated *Memories of Emin Pasha*.

Some minutes later Édouard was called to the phone. It was the assistant curator of the Louvre, regretting that he couldn't make lunch after all because of the tension in the city.

Édouard shrugged his shoulders. These Frenchmen from France were a stupid bunch. Too bad, he would lunch alone, even if it did mean brooding yet again on his solitary state.

Tension in the city? A little agitation was only to be expected after the events of the previous day, but he hadn't noticed anything out of the ordinary during the taxi ride from Zamalek.

Guerrillas had been harassing British forces in the Canal Zone for months, but their latest hit-and-run attack had been heavier than usual. Infuriated by the equivocal attitude of the Egyptian authorities, the British laid into the *buluknizaam*, or police auxiliaries. Their assault on two of their barracks at Isma'iliya had left several dozen dead.

Édouard slowly savoured his stuffed quail in aspic, congratulating himself on having chosen a Ksara wine to accompany it. Just as his gigot arrived, however, he became aware of an unwonted commotion in the restaurant. Guests were getting up, peering out of the french windows, summoning waiters, demanding explanations. Édouard eventually laid his napkin aside and went in search of news.

"They've burnt down the Rivoli Cinema," a *maître d'hôtel* told him. "The Metro is also on fire, they say . . . "

Before Édouard could reach the manager's office, pandemonium broke out in the lobby. People were running in panic from the fire that had just been lit there. He could see frenzied figures tugging at curtains and snatching up pieces of furniture with which to feed the flames.

Édouard, too, broke into a run. He found himself in the passage leading to the kitchens, where a *sufragi* was busy bundling up some silver cutlery in a tablecloth. Caught in the act, the man seized his loot and made swiftly for a service entrance.

"After him!" called a German hotel guest, who had also spotted the man.

The rioters outside were yelling anti-British slogans. They almost went berserk on seeing two foreigners emerge. The German hesitated for a moment, then walked towards them.

"*Ana Almani!*" he called. "*Ana Almani!*"

If he was *Almani* he could only be against the *Inglisi*. At once, the yells gave way to cheers. The German was borne away in triumph. As for Édouard, he seized the opportunity to melt into the crowd.

Flames were already issuing from several hotel rooms. Distraught and uncomprehending, a number of guests had assembled in the garden adjoining Alfi Street. One of them, a soprano from the Italian opera company, was barefoot and in her dressing gown, having been roused from her siesta.

Édouard was relieved to see firemen arrive, crank up their ladders, and proceed to douse the building with their hoses. But it wasn't long before the jets died away to a dribble: the hoses had been severed. The firemen gave up and climbed down, shaking their heads, amid cheers from the mob. Shepheard's was doomed.

Averting his eyes from this unbearable sight, Édouard headed for the city centre. In the distance he made out the building that housed the Diana Cinema. It had already been gutted by fire, and rioters were hurling chairs out of the upstairs windows, whence they landed with a crash in the roadway.

Other rioters armed with axes and crowbars were breaking down the door of Avierino's. One by one, they made their way into the big store carrying cans of petrol obtained from a tanker sedately parked on the street corner. The fire took hold at once, the crowd shrank back in alarm. Screams could be heard, but not for long: one of the arsonists had failed to get out in time and transformed himself into a human torch.

Shots rang out, probably fired by plain-clothes policemen. Édouard saw several demonstrators fall to the ground in a welter of blood. Their companions scattered hurriedly, only to reassemble outside Sednaoui's in Khazindar Square.

Concealed in a doorway and powerless to intervene, Édouard watched the looters at work. They levered the metal shutters open with crowbars, smashed the windows, and disappeared inside, to emerge laden with booty of all kinds. His thoughts turned abruptly to his own shop, which was always shut at weekends.

Heedless of the risk he was running, Édouard hurried the length of Qasr al-Nil Street. Robert Hugues had been burnt down, but Salon Vert just beside it was intact thanks to some shrewd employees who had hoisted the national flag and shouted "Egypt for the Egyptians!" Gattegno's had saved itself even more simply by handing out money to the rioters and sending them on their way.

Édouard reached the end of Suleiman Pasha Street and stopped dead. It was as if his entire body had been anaesthetized. He felt nothing, just stared straight ahead as though turned to stone: all that was left of his antique shop was a big black shell with a few tongues of flame dancing here and there.

Ten minutes went by, and still he didn't move, still he continued to lean against the same lamppost, gazing at the horrific sight with an air of stupefaction. At length he walked slowly towards what was left of his shop. Heedless of the smell of burning that issued from the blackened walls and the heaps of debris on the floor, Édouard looked desperately for the objects he had lovingly assembled for so many years. Not a stick of furniture was left. Not a footstool, not even a screen.

On the left-hand wall, known as the "Coptic" wall, nothing remained of the icons of St Theodore and St Basil. Gone, too, were the lectern inlaid with ebony, the cymanders from Wadi Natroun, the perfume burners in bronze, and a thousand other treasures.

The illuminated Koran must have been quickly consumed by the flames, but other less vulnerable objects had vanished too: copper trays inlaid with silver, pistols, muskets, daggers, camel saddles, mosque lamps . . .

Automatically, Édouard looked up at the gaping ceiling. No, no sign of the bronze chandelier – a magnificent hexagonal chandelier with forty-eight lights. Squatting down, he picked up pieces of debris and turned them over in his hands: the foot of a cane chair, an urn stand bereft of its purpose, half of a blue faience gazelle, a twisted altar candlestick, the remains of a canopic casket. One miraculous survivor of the conflagration was an ostrich-feather fan at least a hunded years old. Édouard picked it up, opened it, closed it, then put it in his pocket and strode off without a backward glance.

He walked aimlessly through the streets of Cairo, indifferent to wailing sirens and sporadic gunfire. Nothing held his gaze, neither the ruins of Groppi's in Suleiman Pasha Street, nor gutted Cicurel's in Fouad Street, nor the non-existent Turf Club, where six Britishers had been burnt to death.

From time to time he put his hand in his jacket pocket and gave the fan a squeeze. Another man might have lamented his failure to insure against rioters, but what insurance policy could have given him back his bronze chandelier, his nineteenth-century carpets, his crouching scribe in ebony? "I loved this country," he kept telling himself, "and it didn't want me."

He had a little money left in France, but the thought of resuming life in Boulevard Vauban filled him with dread.

Night had already fallen. A taxi stopped beside him. The cabby opened the door and almost commanded him to get in.

Twenty minutes later Édouard entered his apartment building like a sleepwalker, his suit black with soot. He didn't even acknowledge the *bawab*'s greeting. While the lift was taking him up to the fifth floor he felt for his key and came across the fan. He felt immeasurably sad.

Exhausted, he opened the lift gates and stepped out on to the landing without even bothering to switch on the light.

He stopped short, his heart in his mouth: a shadowy figure was seated on the stairs.

"Ah, there you are at last!" said Mima. She rose to her feet with a radiant smile. "I was getting worried . . . "

II

Thursday, 24 April 1952

*Alex swears that Farouq wept at the sight of Cairo burning on 26 January last.
Although they may not have been crocodile tears, no one has ever explained to me
why, on that particular day, the king should have chosen to keep his police chiefs
at 'Abdin Palace for an interminable lunch to mark the crown prince's birth. The
forces of law and order were waiting for instructions that never came. In any
case, the king benefited from the day's events, which enabled him to blame them
on Nahas Pasha and dismiss him on the spot.*

*According to the latest figures, over four hundred commercial establishments
were set on fire and looted in the course of Black Saturday, but the instigators
are still unidentified. The military court is taking it out on their underlings.*

*On Monday Édouard Dhellemmes went to the Governorate, where articles
recovered by the police are on display. There were dozens of rifles and revolvers, a
few sewing machines, an icebox, a hundred cans of sardines, and two photographs
of the king, but no sign of any icons or statuettes.*

*Édouard is taking it all far better than anyone would have expected. "He's
almost perky," says Papa. "He never ceases to surprise me. Well, I told him to stay
in tarbooshes and not to spend his money on old bric-à-brac."*

*Strangely enough, Édouard seems more affected by the destruction of
Shepheard's than by that of his shop. It seems that only one of the hotel's thirteen
safe-deposit boxes was destroyed by the flames, namely, the manager's. It contained
the two visitors' books.*

An Officer's Career, originally published in Arabic at Dar al-Ma'arif and
translated into English some years later, is not great literature. One could
also quarrel with some of Hassan's assertions, even if — fortunately — his

book omits all mention of our family's name. Certain passages do ring true, however, for instance his account of the night of 23 July 1952, during which Egypt lapsed into revolution with surprising ease.

"The motorized column advanced slowly, all lights extinguished," writes Hassan. "Seated beside the driver of the fourth armoured truck, I nervously consulted my watch: it was midnight plus thirty, and our orders were still as vague as ever. We were making for the headquarters of the armed forces at Kubbeh Bridge with no precise knowledge of what to do when we got there."

Captain Hassan Sabri was delighted to be doing something at last but annoyed at not being kept better informed by his superiors.

"'Ready your men, we're going into action tonight.' That was all I had been told by Lieutenant-Colonel Yousef Sadiq, who commanded the 1st Motorized Battalion.

"A conspiratorial atmosphere had prevailed in the barracks for several days. The name of the Free Officers' Committee was on everyone's lips, but no one seemed to know who belonged to that clandestine body. We knew only that it had managed to get a hero of the Palestine War, General Muhammad Naguib, elected chairman of the Officers' Club — an election promptly quashed by the king, who felt humiliated by the defeat of his own candidate."

The driver braked abruptly so as not to collide with the vehicle ahead of them.

"What is it?" asked Hassan, putting his head out of the window.

He got out of the truck, revolver in hand. Lieutenant-Colonel Yousef Sadiq's jeep drove to the head of the convoy in quest of news.

Officers from the leading armoured vehicle were surrounding a Morris saloon. The two civilians inside it had been ordered out with their hands up and told to freeze, but moments later, having been recognized by Sadiq, they were issuing orders in their turn:

"The operation has had to be brought forward. You must occupy GHQ at once."

Led by Sadiq's jeep, the convoy headed for its objective, this time at full speed. Hassan found it hard to contain his excitement: the long-awaited overthrow of the monarchy was imminent.

He had looked forward to it for ten years, ever since that dark day in February 1942, when the British ambassador had driven up to 'Abdin Palace with an armoured escort and compelled Farouq to change prime ministers.

Then there was the Palestine War. Hassan and a number of his brother officers had entered the fray with enthusiasm, only to discover, all too soon, that it was a lost cause: ill-coordinated Arab armies, operations launched without preparation, and defective weapons, which were later found to have derived from scandalous arms deals involving senior government officials, if not the king himself.

Hassan had returned to Cairo beside himself with rage and eager for a fight. He almost joined the Muslim Brotherhood, but the movement was too religious and rather too wait-and-see for his taste. Heated arguments raged in the barracks at night — sometimes all night long. Hassan advocated radical methods such as blowing up the British embassy or assassinating a dozen leading members of the regime. He was called an extremist, just as he angrily referred to those who counselled prudence as *mara'*, or women. Even at the Academy he used to seethe with impatience when cadets in his batch spent hours in the library reading Clausewitz or Elgood instead of learning to shoot, and it galled him to note that those intellectuals had climbed the military ladder more rapidly than himself.

For a year now, Hassan had readily assisted the guerrilla fighters who were harassing British troops in the Canal Zone. Some of his brother officers supplied them with arms and ammunition; he trained small groups in tactics.

The torching of Cairo had surprised but not really shocked him. He suddenly saw it as a good means of sweeping away all that had disgusted or humiliated him for so long. Those Batrakanis, for example, to whom Uncle Rashid had been so well-disposed during his lifetime. Hassan had found it intolerable to hear him say "the Bey did this" or "the Bey thinks that". Bey be damned! He was a filthy profiteer, not even a genuine Egyptian, who had the cheek to be king of the tarboosh . . .

Hassan had felt even more humiliated when Rashid died.

"Rashid was a very generous man," Georges Batrakani had told him.

"He gave away all he earned. I ended by putting aside some money every month, intending to give it to him one day. Here it is."

Throughout the afternoon, Hassan and his comrades in the officers' mess had received scraps of information from Alexandria, where the king and the entire political establishment were on holiday. Farouq had just formed a government in his own way and played a little trick on the premier designate. The latter, having been unable to placate the army by securing General Muhammad Naguib's appointment as minister of war, had resigned himself to entrusting that portfolio to the minister of the interior. Then, just as the members of the government were preparing to take the oath, Colonel Isma'il Sherine, the king's brother-in-law, entered the room.

"Meet the minister of war," Farouq told his thunderstruck cabinet, roaring with laughter.

"The armoured vehicles of the 1st Motorized Battalion quietly took up their positions around GHQ," Hassan writes. "A senior officer went from one vehicle to the next, issuing us with instructions. I felt exhilarated when the first shots rang out. 'Follow me!' called Yousef Sadiq. The chief of the general staff was hiding behind a screen when we burst into his office. He fired three shots for honour's sake, then surrendered. GHQ had fallen."

Hassan was shifting some vehicles parked in front of the central building when an officer rushed up to him in high delight.

"Hussein Shafe'i's tanks have seized the railway and radio stations!" he cried.

They embraced each other. Everyone exchanged hugs.

Jubilation reigned at headquarters, which was lit up as bright as day. Jeeps came and went with slim, mustachioed young officers on board. All smiles, they were awaiting the arrival of General Muhammad Naguib, leader-designate of a *coup d'état* about which he hadn't at first been informed.

"At three a.m. I went outside to stretch my legs. My thoughts turned to my father, Sabri, killed during the revolution of 1919, the year of my birth — a father whose face I had never seen, even in a photograph. As a child I knew him only through the medium of my Uncle Rashid, who described him as a passionate man in love with social justice. Later on, a former employee of the Sayida Zeinab cigarette factory gave me a detailed account of the exploits of my martyred father, who had been gunned down in the street like a dog for loving his country too dearly." (*An Officer's Career*, p. 135.)

Captain Hassan Sabri gazed at the brightly illuminated headquarters building with a thoughtful expression. Stroking the butt of his revolver, he saluted the memory of the martyr of 1919, killed by the bullet that had pierced his *galabiya*.

PART NINE

A Rather Likeable Fellow

I

My grandfather refused to be pacified.

"They're communists — communists and uneducated oafs. They'll send this country to the dogs."

The officers who overthrew Farouq on 23 July 1952 had been quick to abolish all local titles: Egypt had no more beys or pashas. That was a crime for which Georges Bey would never forgive them.

"And to think my idiot of a brother-in-law is still a count! Count my backside!"

Three months later the uneducated oafs added insult to injury by promulgating a new agrarian law. From now on, no one could own more than two hundred feddans of cultivated land.

"If that isn't communism, what is?" protested Georges Batrakani, who owned nearly four hundred.

"In communist countries assets are requisitioned without compensation," Makram retorted coolly. "You'll be indemnified."

"Come off it! Their indemnities are paid in treasury bonds redeemable in thirty years. I'll never see the colour of their money."

"You'll be indemnified, I tell you. In any case, before the requisition order comes into force you're entitled by law to sell a hundred feddans to your children and the balance to small farmers."

"Don't play the innocent! The fellahin don't have the wherewithal, you know that perfectly well. They'd sooner sit back and wait for the state to present them with what it has stolen from us. As my brother Ferdinand used to say . . . "

Makram, whose sight was deteriorating, couldn't roll himself a cigarette in the gloom. He went over to the window to take advantage of the flashing Coca-Cola sign.

"And *you* know perfectly well, Georges, that the ownership of land in this country is outrageously inequitable. Sixty-odd landowners own one-twentieth of all the cultivated land."

"I'm not one of the sixty."

"But you're one of the five hundred who own more than one-tenth of the land, and there are two million seven hundred landowners in all."

"So what? Are you a communist too?"

The man in black preferred to remain silent when their arguments took such a turn. He recalled the conversation they'd had in this very same office soon after 25 July.

"A fundamental change has set in, have you noticed?" Georges had asked.

"Of course, and I welcome it. For the first time in centuries, Egypt is being governed by Egyptians."

"Yes, yes, but I'm talking about something more profound, more serious. Haven't you seen Naguib's head?"

"What's the matter with his head?"

"He doesn't wear a tarboosh! No Egyptian head of government has ever appeared in public without a tarboosh."

"Naguib's a general. He wears a peaked cap, it's only natural."

"No, you don't understand. He doesn't have the head for a tarboosh, nor do the officers in his entourage. That's serious, Makram, very serious. You never know where you are with such people."

"We know where we've been, anyway, and that's reason enough to forge ahead," the Copt replied with a smile. "The main change *I've* noticed is that these *bikbashis* are slim and athletic. The reign of the obese is over."

"Never fear, they'll put on weight in just the same way as your beloved Wafd grew fat on power. The officers are calling for the party to be purged."

Dismissed from office after the burning of Cairo, Nahas Pasha had gone off to recuperate at Vichy with his wife, the celebrated Zouzou, who was suspected of selling favours and manipulating cotton prices. The military *putsch* had caught them in mid cure. Nahas boarded the first available plane to Cairo. Arriving there at one a.m., he knocked on General Naguib's door in the middle of the night, convinced that he and his officers were waiting to entrust him with power. Their only response was to invite the Wafd to purge itself thoroughly, like the other parties, and Nahas himself to abstain from all political activity in the future.

"You didn't take my worries about the tarboosh seriously," said Georges. "Those communists want to deprive the nation of its headgear, that's obvious."

People were, in fact, beginning to debate the merits of the tarboosh. "It's a relic of the past," declared certain members of the new regime. To ingratiate themselves, some Muslim scholars had unearthed ancient *fatwas* that permitted the faithful to wear hats or caps as long as they weren't designed to cast scorn on religion or patriotism.

"What cheek!" was my grandfather's comment. "When I think that the tarboosh used to be regarded as a symbol of nationalism and Islam! I used to be criticized for manufacturing them on the grounds that I was a *khawaga*; now we're told that the Arabs used to wear hats with brims in times gone by, and that the tarboosh originated in the West — that it's the ancestor of the Phrygian bonnet!"

To open his newspaper, with its bold red headlines, was a proceeding that made Georges quail every morning. One never knew what those trails of blood portended. One day it would be a fifteen per cent cut in rents; the next the abolition of the notorious *waqfs*, or inalienable private assets; the day after that a wave of arrests. The hangman of Alexandria, a patriotic soul, had telegraphed the new rulers as follows: "Am prepared to hang traitors free of charge."

My grandfather cursed himself for having publicly congratulated the king on his birthday the previous 11 February. Together with some thirty other companies (Gattegno, Air Mist, Hannaux, Savonneries Kahla, etc.), the firm of Batrakani & Sons had inserted a full-page advertisement in the *Progrès égyptien*. It conveyed a desire "to place at the foot of the throne the expression of their most respectful good wishes and their infinite gratitude".

"Gratitude for what?" Makram said sarcastically. "For having allowed four hundred businesses in Cairo to be burnt or looted on Black Saturday?"

The Coca-Cola sign was flooding the office with red-and-white light.

"It's a civilized revolution, you can't deny," the Copt went on. "Not a drop of blood has been spilt. They've allowed Farouq to sail for Capri in his yacht, complete with his family and his private fortune."

"Much good that does me! Farouq was a fool. He had all the makings of a big success. People admired and flattered him when he arrived here in 'thirty-six. They applauded him even during the war, in spite of his escapades, but he was a sick man. A glandular problem . . . "

"He was spoilt by his entourage."

"Not only by his entourage, Makram Effendi! I shall never forget that Nahas of yours, kowtowing to him as boy of seventeen. 'Your Majesty, I have a privilege to request of you: May I kiss your hand?' A fine crew, your Wafdists!"

"A new era has begun, Georges."

"Yes, no more Wafdists, just uneducated oafs in uniform munching *fuul* sandwiches in the palaces where they've installed themselves. They're going to send us all to the dogs. To the dogs, d'you hear?"

2

"What a lovely bag, *chérie*. I bet you got it at Cicurel's."

"Cicurel's nothing! At Orosdi's, that's all."

"Swear it."

"*Christos anesti!*"

"But Alex, I wasn't expecting you for lunch. They told me you were taking part in some rally on the Alexandria road."

"No, Easter Sunday is sacred. I never miss Maman's *ka'ak*."

"Thank you, *habibi*. But in a minute you simply must tell me, all of you, what you think of my *kubeiba*. I'm afraid Usta Ali has been too generous with the salt."

"What about this General Naguib, Georges? Don't you think he's a rather likeable fellow?"

"Selim won't quarrel with that. He adores him."

"*De gustibus et coloribus . . .*"

"Naguib makes a very British impression, what with his pipe and that walking stick tucked under his arm."

"What do you mean, British! On the contrary, he looks very fellahi with his broken nose and swarthy Sai'idi complexion."

"Personally, I think he looks a scream, driving around in that yellow Chevrolet convertible of his."

"At least it makes a change from the king's red cars."

"Seems they've found four hundred of them in the garages of the various palaces."

"I'd be interested to know what's become of the Mercedes Hitler gave him in 'thirty-eight."

"What a superb fan, Mima. Ostrich feathers, aren't they?"

"By the way, André, you know Monsignor Zughby, don't you? What's he up to, serenading Naguib like that? 'We love you as we've never loved anyone before . . . We're ready to make any sacrifice to please you . . . ' Is he mad, or what?"

"Why mad? Plenty of Christians think the same way."

"André's right, the worthy Naguib is making a lot of friendly gestures. He seems to spend his life in church. Midnight Mass at Christmas with the Orthodox Copts, Mass again at Easter, heaven knows what ceremony with the Maronites . . . "

"Papa, did you read about his interview with the student who was wounded at the university the other day? He presented him with a gilt-edged New Testament."

"I missed the bit about the gilt edges . . . You're young, *mes enfants*, you get carried away. Personally, I summed up our new, bareheaded, tarbooshless rulers at a glance. Naguib's churchgoing excursions are all very well, and so is the way he compares us minorities to precious stones, but it's *kalam*, the whole thing. A man must be judged by his deeds, not his words, as my brother Ferdinand used to say."

"Your father's right. Will the junta retain Islam as the official religion? Will it abolish our religious courts? Those are the key questions. All the news we've had so far has been bad."

"Precisely. They've passed an idiotic agrarian law that's already revealing its limitations. They've also passed an even more idiotic law governing industrial disputes, its sole aim being to do employers down . . . "

"I wrote Naguib a long letter."

"Did he reply, Uncle Edmond?"

"He must be still in shock, poor man, in view of the statistics I quoted."

"Did you read that report in *Le Journal d'Égypte*, Uncle Edmond? About the three sisters from al-Mansoura who all gave birth to quintuplets on the same day? Fifteen children at a stroke!"

"Fifteen? My God, alarming, isn't it?"

"Won't you come to table? The *kubeiba* will get cold. André, you sit opposite your father. You young marrieds can sit next to each other. Yes, yes, Mima next to Édouard, it's the tradition."

"Did you know that someone at the palace kept a file on all Farouq's girlfriends? Names, addresses, phone numbers, photos, CVs, the lot!"

"Alex, please! There are children present."

"Mind you, I'm not saying Farouq was a champion in that respect. He needed stimulation. A party of foreign journalists was taken round the king's secret collection at Kubbeh Palace the other day. You wouldn't believe what they — "

"Alex, *please!*"

"Quite apart from what Alex is talking about, Kubbeh and 'Abdin contain some genuine treasures. They're all to be auctioned, had you heard? They say it'll be the sale of the century."

"*Beati possidentes!*"

"It seems that Farouq didn't only collect stamps, coins and precious stones, but ties, pipes, opera glasses — even tarbooshes."

"Why 'even'?"

"Sorry, Georges . . . Anyway, our friend Édouard Dhellemmes will find plenty there to stock his new shop with."

"Oh sure, I'll go to the auction with Mima when we've won the lottery."

"Monsieur Dhellemmes, do you by any chance know if they've found a series of candelabra at Kubbeh representing the fables of La Fontaine?"

"No, Michel, but in view of all the things Farouq appropriated . . . I had to laugh when I heard the other day that one of the chests at the palace was found to contain the Shah of Iran's sword."

"Churchill recovered his property right away. You know the story of Churchill's watch?"

"No, do tell."

"Maman, your *kubeiba* is divine. My Samia could never cook like this!"

We talked and talked. We talked interminably, and in every conceivable key.

As children we would compete to describe the most trivial fall from a bicycle, the humblest incident. "I simply must tell you!" cried whichever of us had undergone some slightly odd or faintly amusing experience. I think, by the way, that we underwent certain experiences purely for the pleasure of recounting them later.

We invented and embroidered a little. In our mouths, insipid facts took on epic dimensions. The same sets of circumstances were recounted five, ten, twenty times, but they ceased to be identical. Thus our family histories are larded with anecdotes which, though only half true, have become established by virtue of frequent repetition and embellishment.

This verbal diarrhoea may have been attributable to our powerlessness. After all, weren't our garrulity and grandiloquence exactly proportional to our lack of control over events? Speech compensated us for inaction and was rendered easier by the use of two or three languages simultaneously. We could always, as we talked, insert an exclamation in English or conjugate an Arabic verb in the pluperfect. Not having a complete command of any of our languages, we needed all of them at once. We would nibble at two or three plates as the requirements of the moment prescribed. Instead of taking the trouble to find the right word in one language, we fell back on another that offered it to us on a platter. This automatism enabled us to talk and talk without encountering any obstacle other than our listeners, who were itching to hold forth themselves.

3

I was eight years old and in paradise. We'd been staying at Dakheila since the first heat and would not be leaving before the end of September. Ten or twelve other families were holidaying there, quite apart from friends of friends.

In front of us lay the sea, behind us the desert. Selim and Viviane had rented a yellow house a little way outside the village. Most of the other families inhabited the apartment house next door. We children lived in each other's pockets, without doorbells or fuss, like little savages. Holidays at Dakheila meant several months of bathing, fishing among the rocks, climbing fig trees, playing cops and robbers.

There were no huts or swimming instructors on the beach, just seaweed, little blobs of tar, and one or two bottles kindly jettisoned by distant ships, though none of them ever contained a message. We went around unwashed and unsupervised. Rough weather was hard luck on the soldiers in the nearby barracks, who were peasants unable to swim. But the very next day would bring a glassy sea that was perfect for canoeing and filled us with joy.

At four in the afternoon, after the obligatory siesta, the "ice-cream-gelati" vendor, a polyglot during the season, would turn up on his tricycle. His treasures cost a piastre apiece, added colouring guaranteed. Twenty children, all licking their ices and fingers, trailed after him while he made his rounds.

The rest of the time we played soldiers. All that was needed to make a bow and arrow was a palm frond stripped of its foliage. Horses could simply be imagined. Mine was pure white and called Tarboosh.

The environs of Dakheila still bore traces of the wartime courtesies exchanged by Rommel and Montgomery, a regular godsend to us cops and robbers and cowboys and Indians, who could use their concrete strongpoints. We would break off at the end of the afternoon to go and put old tin cans on the railway line. How flat they were after the train had gone by! It carried no passengers, that little train, and no one had ever known where it was going or why.

Viviane and Lola and their women friends were alone with the children from Monday to Friday. Anxious not to lose their figures, they used to preface each swim by playing beach tennis like mad things.

On Saturdays we would station ourselves beside the desert road to watch the arrival of our fathers and guests. The road was a wretched ribbon of asphalt half melted by the heat, and creeping along it now and then would come old Chevrolet trucks, sweating and sneezing in a pathetic way.

Alex, who used to spend weekends at Dakheila, scored a great success with us children. His jeep was surrounded, sniffed, stroked. We clambered aboard it ten at a time and went for rides, shaken like rag dolls and yelling with delight. What with his amazing cars, open-necked khaki shirts and very British-looking moustache, Alex at forty-two had the aura of a genuine adventurer.

"Is he really your uncle?"

"Yes, really, and he's done the Cairo—Alexandria Rally four times."

Another occasional visitor was Mima, whose floral dresses earned her numerous compliments. We would run to embrace her, our eyes fixed on Édouard Dhellemmes, a smiling figure in the background laden with treasures bought at Pastroudis: chocolate éclairs, *millefeuilles à la crème*, rum babas . . .

In Édouard Dhellemmes I had a French grandfather, which filled me with pride. We called him *Bon-papa* because the usual terms, *nonno* or *giddu*, could not be applied to a grandfather with such blue eyes and white skin — one, moreover, whose knowledge of Arabic was negligible.

Mima should traditionally have been called *teta*, but all her grand-children addressed her by the subtle Eurarabic name of Tita.

Bon-papa and Tita generally had to return to Alexandria the same day, but we sometimes managed to persuade them to stay overnight or even longer. I would proudly remind my playmates that I had a French grandfather and, exaggerating a trifle, credit him with wearing tricolour pyjamas designed to emphasize his prestigious nationality.

Needless to say, Paul and the Swissess never for a moment considered spending the summer at Dakheila, which they regarded as a godforsaken hole devoid of cachet and prestige. They holidayed in a big house at 'Agami overlooking a magnificent white beach lapped by turquoise waves. We visited them roughly once a month. Selim's 203 always got stuck in the sand *en route*, and I trembled with fear, convinced that it would never budge again.

Every Sunday an Italian Franciscan from Alexandria would open the little church that nestled beside the road at Dakheila. The Mass, of course, was said in Latin. This was the only occasion during the week when our shirts were white and our hair was combed.

In the middle of summer the whole family foregathered in Georges and Yolande Batrakanis' villa at Sidi Bishr, almost an hour away by car. Viviane would hold her nose as we drove past the tanneries after the Mex. In the back, we cheered, wound down the windows, and filled our lungs with the stench that was as much a part of the holidays as the scent of seaweed and jasmine. As for Selim, he hailed the event with a long blast on the horn.

At Sidi Bishr we passed Sesostris Bey's "houseboat". The owner, by then nearly ninety, still had his sea legs but saw no one except the man who delivered his groceries twice a week. He could be discerned on the bridge, a solitary figure scanning the sea through his outsize binoculars.

In the Batrakanis' garden we played "Sultan Hussein" with our cousins: his arrival at the school, the poem recited by Michel, the subsequent congratulations. All kinds of squabbles and arguments were provoked by the successive distortions to which this story had been subjected in the course of time.

My grandmother to her daughter Lola in the late 1920s:

"Micho recited his poem so beautifully that the sultan came over and embraced him. Then all the boys in the class broke into applause."

Lola twenty years later, describing the same scene to Paul's two sons:

"A big marquee had been erected in the courtyard. Your uncle Michel recited his poem so well that all the boys in the school applauded. The sultan rose from his chair and commanded the guards' band to play the *Marseillaise*."

During our games in 1953 or 1954 we generally took our cue from one of Paul's sons, who was older than us:

"Uncle Micho could recite '*Le Laboureur et ses enfants*' so well that he became the talk of Cairo. Sultan Hussein, who was fond of La Fontaine, wanted to hear this prodigy, so arrangements were made for him to visit the Jesuit school. After the recitation he embraced Uncle Micho and invited him to the palace. The musicians of the sultan's guard lined the route with their bows raised."

Our disputes were sometimes submitted for arbitration to the person concerned:

"The sultan turned up at the school on a big white horse and rode back to the palace with you behind him, isn't that right, Uncle Micho?"

My godfather would stare at us in perplexity, then offer some minor corrections. He didn't want to disappoint us too much, but I think he felt rather hijacked. These apocryphal, increasingly colourful accounts were eroding the official version and might some day replace it altogether.

Once, in the midst of an argument, I referred to Michel as "Uncle Sultan". I said it so spontaneously that the grown-ups present burst out laughing. The nickname was very soon adopted by all the other children in the family.

4

Whenever Georges Batrakani sighted a funeral procession in the distance, he would ask his chauffeur to pull over and wait for it to pass. It always moved him to see a tarboosh riding on the coffin in token that the deceased had been a man. Sadly, this tradition was dying. Attacks on the tarboosh were beginning to bear rotten fruit.

My grandfather had stopped taking *Le Journal d'Égypte*, whose Syrian owner was desperately anxious to obliterate his former links with the palace. His daily paper had been trumpeting the anthem of the decapitators of tradition ever since the summer of 1952. It denounced "fanaticism based on the tarboosh", called for the abolition of "a type of headgear which people persist in wearing to qualify as Egyptians", and issued the following appeal: "Let it be replaced by the Mexican sombrero or the boater. The essential thing is to decide to do away with it."

"The Mexican sombrero! You hear that, Yola? They want Mexican someros, the cretins!"

Le Journal d'Égypte was merely echoing the anti-tarboosh tirades printed by certain Arabic-language publications. "This headgear," declared *al-Akhbar*, "represents an obsolete, reactionary and outdated mentality: that of servitude. All the ills that afflict us, both in government and in our everyday lives, will disappear once we have deposed the tarboosh, that emblem of a bygone era."

The situation was deteriorating week by week. In September the minister of finance authorized his officials to work without wearing the tarboosh. It was then announced that the police would be adopting the *fouadiya* beret. Meanwhile, the committee appointed to study a new national costume had published a draft law aimed at replacing the tarboosh and *galabiya* with the European hat and suit. Certain tarboosh manufacturers had already ceased production and ordered new machinery with a view to changing horses.

Georges Bey — everyone continued to call him that despite the abolition of titles — refused to join this trend and pinned his remaining hopes on the Muslim rector of al-Azhar University, who was firmly opposed to the hat. For all that, he was agreeably surprised when, six months after the *coup d'état*, the newspapers published their first photograph of Naguib in civilian clothes: the general was wearing a tarboosh!

My grandfather got hold of this picture. He had it blown up, framed, and prominently displayed in his office.

"Naguib looks less stupid in a tarboosh," he remarked to his sons. "Don't you agree?"

None of my uncles was of much assistance to him in this campaign. Paul was a long-time opponent of his father's "flowerpots". Michel's approach to the problem was, as usual, purely sentimental and poetic: to him the tarboosh evoked Sultan Hussein, who had worn one at a stylish angle. As for André, he disliked seeing his father rant and rave, revile the whole world, and get into such a state over such a trivial matter.

"Tarboosh or no tarboosh," said the Jesuit, "Egypt needs to purge herself and tackle the problems that beset her. It isn't costumes or uniforms that matter, but the moral and spiritual health of those who wear them."

Alex, ever imaginative and constructive, advised his father to get ahead of the field.

"The Egyptians admire their officers. All they want is to look like them. Why not launch a fashion for military caps made of cloth or even light felt?"

That day, he almost got an ashtray hurled at his head.

Yolande trembled for her husband. She wasn't the only one to fear some skulduggery on the part of the anti-tarboosh brigade. The factory was guarded at night, but fires were so easily started.

* * *

To celebrate six months of revolution on 26 January 1953 the government proposed to stage a parade through the streets of Cairo in which major industrial and commercial enterprises would take part. To the surprise of the family circle, Georges Bey decided to join in.

Egypt witnessed an unprecedented spectacle on the appointed day. Gattegno, Benzion, Sednaoui and another score of firms sent flower-bedecked floats parading past the official stand. Laboratoire Doche had assembled forty thousand tulips, Groppi flaunted a gigantic pie, and Cicurel displayed a model of its new building, which had been opened two months earlier to replace the one burnt down in the course of Black Saturday.

The Batrakani float was almost the last in line. It evoked murmurs from the official stand and cheers from the crowd. On a low-loader entirely covered with roses Georges Bey had erected an enormous, outsize tarboosh all of ten metres high. When it reached the stand, the upper part of the tarboosh rose slowly into the air, drawn skyward by balloons of every colour, and five hundred pigeons were released. All the dignitaries applauded. General Naguib removed his cap and waved it several times at the workers seated on the low-loader, who were going through the motions of pressing tarbooshes into shape.

The next day's newspapers enthusiastically published photographs of the event, pointing out that every Batrakani pigeon had a voucher worth one Egyptian pound clipped to its leg. Édouard Dhellemmes, filled with admiration, hurried to the phone.

"Wonderful, Georges! What a stroke of genius! You've saved the tarboosh."

"I've saved nothing, Édouard. I simply wanted to raise a lot of eyebrows and go out with a bang. I've decided to close the factory."

Édouard's dumbstruck silence made my grandfather smile.

"One has to be realistic," he went on calmly, almost gaily. "The Egyptians won't wear the tarboosh any more. Nor, whatever those cretins say, will they adopt the hat, cap, or Mexican sombrero. They'll go around bareheaded — bareheaded for the first time in centuries. Well, on their own heads be it."

5

One afternoon in February 1954 Paul and the Swissess went to the Collège de la Sainte-Famille to attend a performance of *Le Cid*, in which one of their sons had a small part. The theatre was approached via a large hall once dominated by a portrait of King Farouq. The Jesuits had substituted a photograph of General Naguib after the revolution, but they had just undertaken yet another change because the Revolutionary Council had deposed the *liwa* some days earlier, accusing him of "autocracy and psychological instability". From now on the hall would be dominated by the predatory features of Lieutenant-Colonel Gamal 'Abdel-Nasser, the regime's strongman.

My uncle Paul had bumped into his sons' French literature teacher at the entrance to the theatre. He digested their encounter while waiting for the curtain to go up.

"We've two kinds of pupils here, *Maître* Batrakani," the teacher had told him fiercely. "The ones that study for the French *bachot* may be cultured but they're not Egyptian, and the ones that study for the Egyptian *bachot* may be Egyptian but they aren't cultured."

"Boulos" got terribly bored during the Cid's harangues. Only his son's brief appearance and his uncomfortable wooden seat prevented him from dozing off altogether. On leaving the theatre at seven that evening he almost fell over backwards: Nasser's photograph had disappeared, and the worthy Naguib, with his debonair mien and bushy eyebrows, was presiding over the hall once more.

"Wait for me, I won't be a minute," he told the Swissess, who had noticed nothing.

From the porter's lodge he telephoned his brother André, who was in the Fathers' common room with some other Jesuits.

"We're just listening to the radio," André said gaily. "Yes, Naguib is back. He's going to resume his duties."

Paul's car was halted several times on the way home by knots of demonstrators joyfully chanting the *liwa*'s name. The crowds were getting bigger by the minute. It was clear that the young turks of the Revolutionary Council had underestimated Naguib's popularity.

The crowds next day were such that the authorities had to open the gates of 'Abdin Palace, now the seat of the president of the republic. Everyone went wild. For the first time in their lives, my father, René 'Abdel-Messih and other Syrians of the same age left their balconies and mingled with the demonstrators.

The ensuing months were euphoric. Censorship and martial law were officially abolished, and plans were made to create a constituent assembly that would establish a genuine parliamentary republic. London and Cairo concluded an agreement under which British troops would evacuate the Canal Zone within twenty months. A start was made on the construction of a new, Nile-side Shepheard's designed by a Syrian architect. My grandmother organized a splendid party at Garden City in honour of Alex, who had come third in the Cairo—Luxor Rally.

The first clouds appeared on the horizon in October, when news of a Muslim Brotherhood conspiracy was followed by numerous arrests. Some weeks later Naguib was deposed once more and placed under house arrest. His photoportrait was removed from the school hall and replaced by that of Nasser. For good, this time.

6

It was an autumn of whispers. All the grown-ups spoke through their teeth, breaking off and pulling faces as soon as one of us came within earshot. As if Paul's sons hadn't told us everything — or as much as they knew or imagined.

"Roland was drunk. He phoned from the Auberge des Pyramides and threatened her . . ."

"She was scared. She packed her things in three big suitcases and called a taxi . . ."

My aunt Lola swore that she would "never again set foot in the same house as that swine". Her eyes flashed angrily, making her look more beautiful than ever.

And to think that her marriage to Roland in 1940 had aroused so much envy! A Don Juan and a vamp, both of them scions of wealthy families, they were two luxury articles that had seemed made to measure and perfectly suited to each other.

Cracks had appeared in their *grand amour* as soon as their first child, a girl, was born. Roland liked to gamble. He spent more and more time in smoke-filled rooms, losing fortunes at poker. The birth of the son he demanded changed nothing. He came home ever later, thoroughly drunk, and forced his wife to have sex with him. She either submitted with tears in her eyes or provoked intolerable scenes by locking her bedroom door.

Georges Batrakani would have given his son-in-law a good talking-to — Roland was very much in awe of him — but he didn't know exactly what was happening and wanted to avoid a clash with Lola. Being proud and jealous of her independence, she forbade anyone to meddle in her affairs until she'd had enough and phoned for a taxi in the small hours.

Heedless of her husband's protests, Lola instituted separation proceedings before the Greek Catholic *maglis milli*. The court delivered its verdict quite quickly, awarding custody of the two children to their mother and sentencing the father to pay her a monthly allowance of forty pounds.

At ten o'clock one night a month later Roland phoned the villa in Garden City and demanded to speak with his wife.

"For your information," he told her, "I've become a Muslim, and I intend to apply to the *Shari'a* court."

"Apply to anyone you like and go to hell!" Lola retorted, and hung up.

Michel, who was near by, asked if Roland had sounded drunk.

"No, far from it, quite calm," my aunt replied. "That's just what infuriated me."

Michel looked grave. "You'd better tell Papa," he said.

Inquiries established that Roland was indeed a convert to Islam and could therefore apply to the Muslim court, which would be bound to pronounce in his favour. In a similar case at Alexandria some months earlier the *Shari'a* judges had awarded the father custody of a girl of eight. "The child," they stated, "must go with whichever of her parents adheres to the better religion. If she remains with the mother, she will be in danger of learning *kufr* from her."

"What's *kufr*?" demanded Lola, who had been fuming ever since the previous night.

"Impiety, unbelief," Georges Bey explained.

"But that's outrageous!"

"You're right, *ya binti*, but we don't have time this afternoon to reform the Egyptian judicial system. Wait here, I've a little call to pay."

At sunset, accompanied by his chauffeur, the factory's lawyer, and Paul, my grandfather rang Roland's doorbell. He came straight to the point.

"How much do you want?"

His son-in-law feigned umbrage.

"How much?" persisted Georges Bey, indicating the bag in his lawyer's hand. "I pay cash."

Roland launched into a tearful account of his recent gambling losses and the poor state of his portfolio. Then, realizing that no one was taking him seriously, he blurted out, "Two thousand pounds, since you insist . . . "

"I'll give you six thousand and exempt you from paying her an allowance," said Georges Bey in a tone that brooked no refusal. "You may see the children regularly, of course, in accordance with the terms laid down by the *maglis milli*. It's all set out in this document. There are two other copies which I'll thank you to sign as well."

Another ten minutes, and the matter was settled. It only remained for Lola, with Father André's help, to apply to the Vatican and initiate the lengthy annulment procedure.

"You really think that swine was worth six thousand pounds?" Viviane asked her sister.

"You don't imagine Papa consulted me, do you?"

They were in my parents' bedroom, three-quarters naked. One foot propped on the edge of the bed, each was stripping off depilatory paste with a series of little groans. Samia, the maidservant, had spoilt the *helawa* twice by burning it, but the consistency of her third attempt at this mixture of sugar, water and lemon juice was just right.

"I don't understand how you put up with that crook for eleven years."

"It wasn't all bad, you know. Roland has his good sides. He was a wonderful lover when he hadn't been drinking. How is it with Selim, by the way?"

"All right."

"Does he make you happy?"

"I told you, it's all right."

"Answer me, it's important."

"Well . . . He's in a bit of a hurry, let's say."

"Practice makes perfect, *chérie*."

"I bought a copy of *Le Mariage parfait*. He hasn't even opened it. Selim only reads the newspapers and the files he brings home from the office."

"There are things books can't teach you, *chérie*, take it from me . . . "

A quarter of an hour later they were giggling like schoolgirls as they smeared their smarting legs with an ultra-soft, rose-scented cream.

7

Father André was not the type to keep an intimate diary, but he did carefully preserve the texts of his lectures. From time to time he would also sit down at his ancient Remington with its English keyboard and type out detailed accounts of the important meetings he attended. Most of these papers are now contained in three files labelled "André Batrakani, S.J., Texts and Notes". A mine of information for anyone with a mind to play the historian . . .

"Well?" asked Father Larivière, who was surrounded by most of the school's Jesuit staff.

But he had already inferred the answer from my uncle's sombre expression. André sat down and, even before filling his pipe, disclosed the extent of the damage in two short sentences.

"They wouldn't listen. This time they really mean to enforce the law."

The Catholic delegates had come up against a brick wall. In a curt, disagreeable voice, the under-secretary of state had proceeded – as if they didn't already know it by heart! – to read out Article 17 of the new law: "Free schools will give their Egyptian pupils religious instruction, each according to his religion, in conformity with the programmes laid down by the minister . . . " In other words, Catholic institutions had to instruct their Muslim pupils in the Koran.

"But you must see that's impossible," said the bishop who headed the delegation. "We're religious schools — "

"You aren't religious schools," the under-secretary of state retorted, "because you teach secular subjects." Then, chastened by their dumb-founded expressions and, no doubt, by the embarrassment of his own subordinates, he corrected his aim:

"Can you explain to me why religious institutions should *not* give their pupils religious instruction?"

"Of course we teach religion," Father André put in, trying his best to sound amiable, "but only to our Christian pupils. That has been our practice for over a hundred years."

But only to the Christians . . . My uncle's mind went back to his own days at the college. Not only had the Jewish and Muslim pupils attended morning and evening prayers, but they ended by knowing them backwards, if not actually reciting them with the rest of the class. Some of them had even attended catechism classes with their parents' consent. It was another age.

"If your Christian pupils are entitled to a religious education," the under-secretary of state said sarcastically, "I don't see why the Muslims should be deprived of one."

"You must be well aware," André rejoined, "that our schools are subject to Vatican rules. Those rules forbid them to teach any religion other than the Catholic."

"You're in Egypt," snapped the under-secretary. "You must observe Egyptian law, and if your far-off superiors fail to understand that, it's up to you to make it clear to them."

Father Larivière, who had listened in silence to André's account of the interview, wondered if there was any way of countering this move. The government had already introduced religious instruction in the free schools on two occasions, in 1948 and 1953, but the law had not been enforced. This time the situation was serious. It remained to be seen if a compromise was possible, as in Syria. There the Catholic schools had secured a *modus vivendi*: they formally proclaimed their inability to teach the Muslim religion but informed the ministry of their Muslim pupils' names and their free periods during the week. The government undertook their Koranic instruction on premises of its own.

"Did you quote the Syrian arrangement?" asked Father Larivière.

"Of course, but he wouldn't listen."

"So what's your conclusion?"

André Batrakani knocked out his pipe in one of the common room's unlovely ashtrays, taking his time about it. "I don't think we've any choice," he muttered. "If we don't comply, we risk being closed down or taken over."

"How can you be so defeatist?" a Swiss Jesuit protested fiercely. "Have you considered the consequences? Compliance would spell the progressive Islamization of this school. Having begun by giving the Muslims religious instruction, we'd have to offer them a place of prayer — yes, don't shake your head, a place of prayer! How could we teach them that the Prophet demands five daily prayers without granting them the means to fulfil that obligation? In the end the school would have to adapt its curriculum to the Muslim festivals. There would be no more Christmas holidays, no more Easter holidays . . . "

"You're going a little fast," André said with a smile.

"Not at all, my dear Father, not at all. And think of the disastrous effects on our Christian pupils. If all religions are taught here, they'll say to themselves, doesn't that prove they're all of equal merit?"

"May I point out that Coptic schools are already giving classes in the Koran?"

"Leave the Copts out of it, please! Don't compel me to be uncharitable. Anyway, why not talk about the Protestant schools? They're taking an exemplary stand in this matter. The American Mission is threatening to close its doors, you know that as well as I do. But we've no need to cite examples either way. The plain fact is, we're being asked to teach a religion we believe to be false, in other words, to collaborate in doing evil."

"It would be an enforced collaboration. It would take place subject to the law and to the threat of an even greater evil, because our Christian pupils might be deprived of an education altogether."

"Enforced collaboration, perhaps, but active, not just passive. We should have to arrange the timetables and select the premises — even the teachers."

"Yes, but we'd have made our views known. The mischief would be formal, not material."

Father Larivière put an end to this casuistry by brusquely asking a question to which he himself had no reply:

"Under our present system the Muslim boys grow up without any form of religious instruction. Isn't that an evil too? Which is it better for them to be, Muslim believers or Muslim unbelievers?"

There was a long silence.

"At all events, I share Father Batrakani's belief that we no longer have a choice. We must get used to the idea of teaching Islam in this school."

Over lunch one Sunday Father André told us of a minor incident that had occurred when the papal legate was visiting Egypt shortly after the Second World War. On that occasion a solemn Mass had been organized in the school chapel – ill-organized, because the celebrants kept scolding the altar boys and casting irate glances at the choir, which always came in too early or too late. My uncle was in the second row, behind a string of dignitaries. During communion a Muslim pasha who had played a leading role in Fouad's reign turned to his neighbour, Canon Drioton, Egypt's Director of Antiquities.

"I rather think, Father," he said in an undertone, "that we're the only ones here who could instil a little order into this ceremony."

The canon smiled. Later, during the small reception that followed Mass, he expressed surprise at the Muslim's excellent knowledge of the liturgy. The pasha laughingly stated his qualifications: as a pupil of the school in the 1890s he had been not only an altar boy but master of religious ceremonies.

8

Yesterday brought the unexpected announcement that religious courts have been abolished. André was appalled. "From one day to the next," he said, "the Christians of Egypt are witnessing the collapse of the foundation on which their status has rested for centuries."

Unless I'm much mistaken, a marriage solemnized in church will be able to be dissolved by civil authorities comprising former judges of the Muslim courts, which have only been abolished in theory. Furthermore, Muslim law will in some cases be applicable to Christian spouses — if they are of a different denomination, for example, or if one of them has converted to Islam. "And that," says André, "will legalize and encourage conversions of convenience like Roland's."

Lola only just made it!

How long ago it seems since the good Fathers branded the Orthodox as schismatics and urged them to renounce their faith! The heads of all the Christian communities in Egypt met at the Coptic Orthodox patriarchate to draft a joint telegram to Nasser affirming their categorical opposition to the new law and requesting an interview. According to André, the telegram has remained unanswered.

The solemn protest which the Catholic bishops caused to be read out in the churches of all rites has had an unprecedented result: Monsignor Zughby and the Latin vicar apostolic were arrested this evening and confined in the Citadel. This has caused a tremendous stir.

19 December 1955

The two bishops will undoubtedly be released, but their detention has prompted the Holy Synod of the Coptic Orthodox to announce some very grave measures decided upon several days ago but not made public until now: the proclamation of general mourning accompanied by the death knell, fasting, and closure of all churches on the night of 6 January, the Orthodox Christmas. If the new law remains in force notwithstanding, the Coptic bishops will leave their residences and take refuge in monasteries.

7 January 1956

There wasn't any "Christmas strike". On the strength of some vague government promises, the Coptic Orthodox backed down at the last minute. Oh, those Copts!

17 January 1956

André is very concerned about the new Constitution, published yesterday, which stipulates that Islam is the state religion. According to him, this pours scorn on all its fine words about the equality of citizens.

9

Georges Batrakani summoned Selim to his office.

"Sit down. Coffee?"

This was quite unlike him. My grandfather picked up the phone without waiting for an answer, asked his secretary to get two *mazbouts* sent up, and told her to hold all his calls.

"I want to ask you something, Selim."

"Of course, Papa."

"I like it when you call me that."

Selim felt embarrassed. The "Papa" had slipped out, probably because of his father-in-law's unaccustomed tone. He usually forgot about family ties at work, even in the case of his sons: he was simply the boss.

All Georges Bey's business activities were directed from this spacious office, which was furnished like a drawing room and boasted a painting by Manet. Visitors who sank into the soft leather armchairs were puzzled by the presence in one corner of an antiquated camera on a tripod, complete with bulb and bellows. Gone was the photograph of General Naguib in a tarboosh that had held centre stage after December 1952. My grandfather had regretfully removed it and substituted a small likeness of Gamal 'Abdel Nasser.

The closure of the factory had vacated two storeys including the ground floor. Rather than let this to a tenant, Georges Bey offered it to Édouard Dhellemmes as rent-free premises for his new antique business. Very touched by this gesture, Édouard happily set up shop in Opera Square despite its proximity to the former site of Shepheard's, whose disappearance wrung his heart.

The revolution had slightly modified the firm's activities. Until 1952 import licences had cost nothing. They were now hard to obtain, and the budget devoted to backhanders had doubled. The banks continued to lend, but in a more restrictive manner. My grandfather liked to know at any given time what they thought of his business. Thanks to some well-placed *bakshish*, he had access to his file and could act accordingly.

"Selim," he said confidentially, "I don't regret closing the tarboosh factory. Relations with the workers had become intolerable since this confounded revolution. They resorted to the courts at the drop of a hat, as if the new labour laws, which are absurd enough in themselves, weren't enough for them. No, I'm happy to have fallen back on the commercial side of the business. It's a return to normality. Fundamentally, we Syrians are merchants. We may play at being industrialists, doctors or journalists, but it's against our nature."

There was a knock at the door. A small boy of ten or twelve came in with two cups of steaming Turkish coffee and two glasses of water on a tray. Selim slipped him a small coin. Then, to cover his growing embarrassment, he carried the tray over to his father-in-law.

"As I'm sure you're aware," Georges Bey went on, "I shall be seventy-five in another few months. It's time I changed my rhythm and gave some thought to the question of a successor."

My father lit a cigarette, feeling more and more uncomfortable.

"André chose the priesthood. How could I have stood in his way? The boy has radiated happiness ever since he put on a cassock, strange as it may seem. Michel has a lot of good qualities, but he lives with his head in the clouds — maybe he needed a wife. At all events, I can't see him telling off a sales representative or haggling with those oafs in customs."

Selim drank his coffee, taking noisy little gulps and avoiding his father-in-law's eye.

"Paul probably has management potential, but he doesn't like this country — anyway, he's convinced himself that he hates it. He already left Egypt some time ago, in his head, and you don't run a business at long range. As for Alex, the less said the better. Who does that leave?"

"Lola, Viviane . . . "

"Don't talk nonsense! You and I, Selim, have something in common: we were both brought up by the Brothers. A less refined education than the Jesuits', no doubt, but better suited to this country, wouldn't you agree?"

His tone changed abruptly. He ground out his cigar in the cut glass ashtray in front of him.

"Selim, you're going to run this business."

"But Papa, I'm only a bookkeeper."

"So? What was I in 1902, when I rented a cubby hole in this building to sell patent medicines from? What was I in 1919, when I took the plunge and went into tarbooshes? This business calls for common sense, *ya ibni*, not university degrees. It needs someone with both feet on the ground, like you. Besides, I'll be there to advise you, if I'm spared."

"What about Paul? And Michel?"

"That's not your problem. I'll have a word with them."

10

For some years now, Maggi Touta had been living in seclusion like some ageing film star at pains to conceal the ravages of time. She had closed her Qasr al-Nil apartment and moved into the Helwan hotel of which I have already spoken. Her visits to Cairo were limited to family functions such as christenings, marriages and funerals.

Georges Batrakani told his chauffeur to stop at the entrance to the grounds so that he could walk the rest of the way to the hotel terrace. Doctor Yared had advised him to take as much exercise as possible.

Maggi was sitting under a eucalyptus tree, lulled by the song of the cicadas. She was wearing a trouser suit and had an angora cat on her lap. Her face was hidden behind a large pair of dark glasses.

"Georges! What a surprise!" She kissed him on both cheeks, then ordered tea. "What news?"

"I've followed your example and retired. Selim will be running the firm from now on."

"Bravo! You deserve a rest. I know you, though: you'll be bored stiff."

Georges made an evasive gesture.

"How's Yola? She worried me the other day, with that low blood pressure of hers, and you know how I hate telephoning."

"No, no, it was nothing serious. Doctor Yared reassured her. He's an excellent man, you know."

The whole of the Batrakani family was now attended by Selim's brother, who had become one of the leading lights at Dar ash-Shifa' Hospital.

They were interrupted by the hotel *sufragi* carrying a tea tray. The pot was swathed in a woollen cosy. My grandfather produced a pillbox containing some yellow and blue capsules prescribed by Roger Yared.

"Speaking of Yola," he muttered, "I wanted to tell you . . . She knows everything."

"Everything about what?"

"About us."

Maggi nearly dropped her cup.

"You're joking!"

"No, I promise you. I'd been struck by one or two things she'd said lately. I wanted to have it out, so I asked her."

"You're mad!"

"She already knew, I tell you. She'd known for ages."

"And she never said a word!"

"She kept it to herself. Very wise of her . . . "

After a few moments' silence Maggi removed the dark glasses and wiped her eyes, which were brimming with tears.

"Poor Yola! How she must have suffered, and how she must hold it against me!"

"You're wrong. She probably did, at first – against me as well – but it's years since she felt that way. 'I pulled myself together when Paul was born,' she told me. 'I told myself that it was God's will, and that, of us two sisters, I'd been the luckier.'"

Maggi, her face buried in the cat's fur, was weeping silently. Georges put out his hand – his slightly tremulous, freckled hand – and gently stroked her hair. The daylight was fading, and a faint breeze had sprung up. A pump could be heard squeaking at the bottom of the garden.

20 June 1956

Papa feels Makram's death far more deeply than he cares to show. I suspect that, in the last analysis, Makram may have been his best friend.

The last time they saw each other was at home on 18 June, a few hours before the last contingent of British troops moved out. Makram turned up looking very chipper in a splendid white suit with a carnation in his buttonhole. Papa couldn't refrain from opening a bottle of champagne. Not, of course, to celebrate the departure of the British, but because Makram had at last, after forty-two years, come out of mourning. "Mind you," Papa said, "white shows the dirt.

Personally, I'd have chosen khaki. It's just as smart and far more in tune with the times." He now reproaches himself for that last little dig.

Papa's still grumbling about yesterday's parade. The army marched past with its new equipment and new uniforms. Not a tarboosh in sight!

He clearly considers himself duty-bound to wear his own tarboosh at all times. On the terrace at Groppi's this afternoon he glared contemptuously at several men of his own age who had adopted the beret, loudly referring to them as "khawagas".

Poor old Makram wore a tarboosh to the very end. From habit, no doubt. Or possibly just to please Papa . . .

II

An owl-faced police officer rang the doorbell at ten o'clock that night.

"Edward Dilame? *Faransawi?*"

Mima, who was hovering behind her husband, had no need to translate. The man's tone was peculiarly unpleasant.

"You are forbidden to leave your home until further notice. Do you have a radio?"

His question was as superfluous as a reply would have been. The drawing-room door was ajar, and issuing from it was the monotone voice of a BBC newscaster reading the latest reports of the battle for the Canal. Neither Mima nor Édouard had had the presence of mind to turn off the set. It wasn't tuned to Radio Israel, fortunately!

While Édouard was unplugging the radio prior to handing it over, my grandmother tried to engage Owl-Face in conversation. Why confiscate their radio? Why forbid them to go out?

"Ask Ben Gurion!" was the policeman's insolent reply.

Édouard had seen the storm coming since early that summer. "The Americans are crazy," he'd told Mima the day the United States brusquely declined to finance the construction of the High Dam at Aswan. "They'll drive Nasser into the arms of the Russians."

Profoundly humiliated, the *Rayis* responded by taking a gamble. On 23 July, the fourth anniversary of the revolution, he proclaimed the nationalization of the Suez Canal Company. Egypt, he told an exultant crowd, would have no further need to beg for money from Washington or Moscow: she would finance the dam herself, using the revenues of the Canal.

Dakheila might have been a million miles from all this commotion. To us the summer of 1956 seemed even more intoxicatingly beautiful than its predecessors. Selim brought the news from Cairo on Saturday evening – news not only from another world but reserved for the grown-ups: the rector of al-Azhar University had called for a holy war, several cabinet ministers were undergoing military training, and two hundred and forty thousand workers were sending Nasser a message of support written in blood.

We had already returned to school when Israel sent her tanks into Sinai on 29 October. The next day France and Great Britain intervened in their turn, ostensibly "to separate the combatants". It was war.

Shopkeepers stuck blue paper over their windows. The headlights of Selim's new Fiat were daubed with paint. The long vacation resumed, this time with real soldiers on Egyptian soil and British aircraft overflying Cairo with impunity. The foreign troops landed at Port Sa'id could have reached the capital overnight.

Salwah, my mother's Muslim friend, was all for going off to the Canal to fight. She was furious with the French.

"What's got into you?" Viviane demanded. "You, an old girl of the Mère de Dieu and steeped in French culture. You speak only of the French. There are some British there too, you know."

"Britain has always been our enemy, but France ... France has betrayed us!"

To everyone's surprise, the "threefold and cowardly" attack was discontinued by order of the United States. Stopped in their tracks, British, French and Israeli troops had no choice but to pack up and leave.

"What fools! What utter fools!" my uncle Paul kept saying, beside himself with rage and frustration.

"There's no doubt the Americans have prevented us from slipping up for the third time," Michel said thoughtfully.

"What are you talking about?"

"Nothing, just something that occurred to me."

Michel reflected that in 1798, when Bonaparte landed in Egypt, the Syrians had welcomed the French troops with open arms, and that in 1882, in the wake of 'Arabi Pasha's rebellion, they had hailed the British as their saviours. This time, although they would certainly have been more restrained, could they really have concealed their relief if the Americans . . .

"The Americans are fools too!" Paul insisted.

The Egyptians were noisily celebrating their "victory". Carried away by the prevailing atmosphere of jubilation and revenge, they blew up Ferdinand de Lesseps' statue at the mouth of the Canal.

"When I think that my father was present at the unveiling of that statue in 1899," said Georges Bey.

Yolande had tears in her eyes. "I can still hear your poor papa at our wedding dinner," she said, "describing the ceremony in that lovely voice of his."

"A ball had been organized on board the *Indus*. Khedive 'Abbas walked up the gangway with Madame de Lesseps on his arm."

"No, not Ferdinand's wife, his daughter-in-law. She was wearing the Grand Cordon of the Order of Marie-Louise around her neck on a chain."

"Talking of the Canal," Yolande said to everyone at large, "did you know that Georges's father almost made a fortune out of some rats?"

On 23 November 1956, Édouard and Mima's doorbell was rung by an Owl-Face even more insolent than the first.

"You have ten days to pack up your belongings and join your pathetic soldiers in France."

They were authorized to sell their furniture. The next day one of Owl-Face's colleagues put in a bid for the contents of the entire apartment. In tears, my grandmother saw Édouard's treasures borne off one by one. When the officer came to pay, he handed over one-tenth of the agreed sum. Then, without giving them time to protest, he got into the laden truck and promptly drove off.

On the day of their departure Édouard tried to give the porter a generous tip. The man politely declined it. Being familiar with local etiquette, Édouard persisted. The *bawab* still refused to listen. Eventually he turned to Mima.

"No," he said softly, "this is too sad a day. You can give it me when you return."

PART TEN

Silence and Self-Effacement

I

The departure of the British, the French and many of Cairo's Jewish residents left a great void.

"One feels so lonely these days," said Viviane, who had lost a lot of friends.

Selim, who now headed the firm, had thrown himself headlong into the fight for foreign concessions. There were openings in every commercial sector now that Western firms were trying to replace the agents that had been expelled by the Egyptian authorities.

The transfer of power at the office eighteen months earlier had caused ructions. Having relinquished the business of his own free will, Georges Batrakani gave the impression of wanting to hang on to it – in fact he almost accused Selim of forcing him out.

Distressed by this situation, Viviane hurried from one to the other in an attempt to patch things up, but her father was a different man. He had aged suddenly, becoming cantankerous and – for the first time in his life – neglectful of his appearance. One couldn't talk to him any more.

In desperation, Viviane fell ill. She developed a high temperature accompanied by spells of dizziness. Her condition puzzled Roger Yared and alarmed Selim, who ended by enlisting his mother-in-law's help.

Yolande Batrakani knew what needed to be said. Within twenty-four hours Georges Bey was his old self again. He hurried to his daughter's bedside and commanded the doctor to cure her, as he had in 1927. A week later Viviane was back on her feet, ten pounds lighter but looking radiant.

When quitting the firm, my grandfather had taken the opportunity to settle the matter of his succession. He divided the shares in the company equally between his children, of whom Father André presented his tranche to the Mission to the Schools of Upper Egypt. But the most ticklish problem was Selim's appointment as head of the business.

The man in the tarboosh confronted his children with a *fait accompli*. Although neither Paul nor Alex dared to oppose their brother-in-law's appointment openly, it was clear that they found his lightning promotion hard to swallow. Selim could only count on Michel's discreet but ineffective support and on the neutrality of Lola, who was on the point of remarrying, this time to a doctor from the upper crust of the Coptic community.

Alex subjected my father to a daily bombardment of weird and wonderful ideas. Why not obtain the concession for a South African arms manufacturer, or replace his travelling salesmen with some alluring females? One night, when Alex had driven him to the verge of a nervous breakdown by phoning just before midnight to suggest installing a gymnasium at the office, Selim blew up.

"Why don't you give him a job?" Viviane suggested.

"What! Give that *bahlawan* a job?"

"Yes."

After sleeping on the idea, my father offered Alex the vague post of "project director", a title which carried a very respectable salary but entailed no commitments. The only stipulation was that Alex should not concern himself with sectors already covered by the business, in other words, pharmaceutical products, perfumes, lace, and machine tools. His task would be to open up new horizons.

Alex was delighted by this proposal. Before leaving for a motorized safari in East Africa, however, he treated himself to a six-week holiday. On his return he devoted another six weeks to describing life in the bush with the monkeys and elephants. As project director he would breeze into the office at the end of the afternoon and give some muddled instructions to his secretary, who promptly got Selim to cancel them.

Paul Batrakani was another matter. Having long seen himself as his father's natural successor, "Boulos" failed to understand why Georges Bey should have imported one. He had a thorough knowledge of the firm's workings, being its lawyer, and could therefore counter each of Selim's decisions with a relatively valid argument. While awaiting better times, my father had to resign himself to waging a war of attrition.

Makram's death in 1956 brought the first change in the scenery. Selim had never felt entirely at ease with the accountant, who persisted in regarding him as a greenhorn and clung to his traditional methods. It was hard to stand up to him, given his seniority and his long-standing friendship with my grandfather.

To replace Makram, Selim thought at once of René 'Abdel-Messih, who ran a small but reputable firm of accountants: René, the friend who had providentially introduced him to Viviane at the Metro Cinema one afternoon in July 1941; René, at whose New Year's Eve party he had been reunited with her two-and-a-half years later . . .

Paul opposed Selim's choice on principle, but since he couldn't immediately suggest another candidate, and since an ongoing tax inspection made it essential to engage an expert right away, René got the job.

From then on, most of the decisions affecting the business were taken jointly. Georges and Makram had argued in the gloom, whereas Selim and René chatted away in a brightly lit office filled with the hum of the air-conditioning. It was like the intervals at the Metro Cinema.

In March 1957 my father happened to hear that a major German manufacturer of office equipment was looking for an opening in Egypt. It was a big prospect. My father delegated all his other work and toiled away relentlessly, sometimes even sleeping at the office despite Viviane's protests. He deluged Édouard Dhellemmes with telegrams and persuaded him to visit Munich twice to plead his cause. Finally, thanks to an influential Egyptian customer, he managed to obtain an exit visa. He made a lightning trip to Bavaria and ended by clinching the deal.

Champagne was opened in Opera Square in the presence of Georges Batrakani, who had gone there for the occasion. Even Paul had to concede that the contract was a genuine coup, and it definitely strengthened my father's hand.

Not long afterwards a government decree made it compulsory for all business to be transacted in Arabic. Paul, who spoke French on principle and from habit, inveighed against this measure, whereas Selim used it as a pretext for changing office and boardroom procedures. The reins of power were his at last.

The new boss gradually modelled himself on the person of Georges Bey. He smoked Havanas, ordered his suits from the best tailor in Cairo, and changed his car every year. His waistline expanded slightly. One Saturday in 1957, as he was leaving to play bridge at the Heliopolis Sporting Club, Viviane laughingly tweaked out his first white hair.

Having multiplied his income by ten, Selim was able to realize a project of long standing: the villa in Heliopolis of which his father had dreamt on the eve of his death in 1924. The architect's plans, which Mima had preserved at the back of a cupboard, required very few modifications.

The city created by Baron Empain already numbered a hundred thousand inhabitants. The plots of land around the basilica had all been built on for years, but a few good sites remained vacant in the palace district.

In October 1957, three hundred metres from the small Jesuit school and almost at the desert's edge, work commenced on an elegant villa with a stone terrace of traditional design. One of the seven bedrooms was reserved for Mima, to await the day when she and Édouard Dhellemmes returned to Egypt.

2

Cairo was in the throes of spy mania. People thought they detected microphones everywhere and distrusted their own servants. During Sunday lunches at my grandparents' home conversation would cease abruptly when the *sufragi* entered the dining room. Everyone feared spies and eavesdroppers, and all felt guilty of some offence: an incomplete tax return, money transferred to Europe, an injudicious remark . . .

Victor Lévy, sadly compelled to leave Egypt after the "threefold and cowardly", had asked Michel not to accompany him to the airport.

"They'd accuse you of being a Zionist, and I'd never forgive myself if I got you into trouble."

Corresponding with friends abroad called for extreme cunning. Early in 1957 Georges Batrakani sent Édouard Dhellemmes a skilfully worded missive informing him that he had sold one or two things which the latter had discreetly entrusted to him before his expulsion. Although the letter hoodwinked the Cairo censors, it was returned to sender by the French postal authorities because it bore a stamp celebrating the Egyptian "victory" at Suez.

The day he got it back, Georges Bey ignored the possibility of microphones and eavesdroppers. Beside himself with rage, he made the walls — whether or not they had ears — ring with his vituperations against "those French idiots".

22 January 1957

All that fuss about a returned letter! After ranting and raving, Papa retreated into a kind of sullen silence which was quite unlike him. Age, no doubt . . . Yesterday he gave vent to a bitter remark: "In the past there used to be a future!"

15 February 1957

More and more Greeks are selling up and leaving. It's a regular exodus. Apparently, a new Alexandria is coming into being in the suburbs of Athens. There used to be 120,000 Greeks in Egypt before the war. I doubt if there are half that number left.

13 March 1957

The expulsion of Father Chidiac came as a shock. To think he lunched with us only last Sunday . . . The authorities were very displeased by his article in the "Rayon d'Égypte", in which he attacked the dismissal of Christian officials and government employees.

30 April 1957

The departure of the British and French has made stars of the Americans here. They're doing all they can to ingratiate themselves. Some of them even feel duty-bound to wear the tarboosh! Even Papa finds that ridiculous . . .

31 July 1957

A special ten-millieme stamp has been issued to mark the opening of the new Shepheard's near Qasr al-Nil Bridge. Nine floors, all equipped with air-conditioning. "I always make a detour so as not to see that monstrosity," says Papa. His feelings would certainly be shared by Édouard Dhellemmes, who's still hoping to obtain an entry visa that will enable him and Mima to return to Egypt.

Édouard paid a special visit to Zurich last month to look through the third visitors' book from the old Shepheard's. Apparently, it was the personal property of Freddy Elwert, who managed the hotel during the 1930s. He took it with him when he left Cairo just before the war.

22 February 1958

No more Egypt, no more Syria. The United Arab Republic is now in being, and all of us are Arabs by decree. "Mabrouk!" the carpet seller in Midan Isma'iliya said to me. "You Syrians of Egypt must be overjoyed by this union between our two countries." If only he knew . . . At any rate, I note that he has substituted a portrait of Nasser for the one of Sultan Hussein.

* * *

"If only he knew . . . " The rulers of Damascus, who lacked Nasser's disquieting charm, were anything but a source of reassurance to us. Egypt and Syria united were merely two threats rolled into one.

I should point out that Michel was being very unwise. If the police were planting microphones and opening letters, what was there to prevent them from examining a personal diary? My godfather must have had his head too firmly in the clouds to appreciate such a danger. Or he may perhaps have felt safe because he was writing in French, as if his secret garden were proof against invasion by people incapable of reciting La Fontaine. Last but not least, he seemed less afraid of Nasser's police than he had been of Mademoiselle Guyomard, whose prying hands might at any moment have unearthed the notebook concealed beneath his mattress.

3

Georges Batrakani was buried in old Cairo's Greek Catholic cemetery one fine afternoon in April 1958. The air was balmy and redolent of spring, as it might have been for a wedding. Bougainvilleas ran the length of the bowl-shaped garden with the massive railed-off vault of the Sednaouis at its heart.

My grandmother was flanked and supported – almost carried – by Alex and Michel, who topped her by a head. She was weeping bitterly. Her sons avoided looking at her, either for propriety's sake or for fear her grief might prove infectious. Michel, as thin as ever, was very pale. Alex looked serious for once, which didn't suit him and added years to his age.

I stood a short distance away on the edge of the dip, looking down at all the figures in mourning. It was my first visit to the cemetery.

Side by side and looking superb in black, Lola and Viviane presented the onlookers with a new and disturbing version of the Batrakani girls. They wore no make-up, but had concealed their faces behind big dark glasses that rendered them more desirable than ever.

Paul seemed to be gazing into the far distance, as if his future lay elsewhere. He had seriously considered leaving Egypt for some months now, and his father's death was a kind of licence to turn over a new leaf. "And I'll thank you never to visit the factory again with a hat on your head, the way you did the other day. It's outrageous! You wouldn't see Henry Ford's son rolling up in a Pontiac or a Chrysler . . . " While Paul was visiting Berlin in 1933, a photograph had fallen out of his wallet. It showed Georges Bey wearing a tarboosh. "Who's that?" asked a German acquaintance. "No one special, just our porter," replied Boulos, who thought the headgear grotesque.

Father André officiated in a troubled, rather abstracted voice. He may have been thinking of the famous day in 1921 when he announced his intention of becoming a Jesuit and drew a surprising response: "Families like ours don't exist to supply the Church with priests; they exist to *run* it." Nor could he have forgotten Georges Bey's subsequent *cri de cœur*, which typified whole generations of Syrians: "You're being obtuse, *ya ibni*. It's precisely because we're small that we have to seem big!" The first letter he received from his father at Lyon in 1926 was written in green ink. He'd almost swooned with happiness . . .

Michel regretted that Georges Batrakani hadn't summoned his six children on the eve of his death and addressed them like La Fontaine's "*Laboureur*". Unhappily, things didn't always happen in real life the way they did in fables.

Viviane had spent the whole of Wednesday afternoon at her father's bedside. He never stopped smiling at her, now and then muttering a few barely audible words. For the umpteenth time he recalled her birth in 1922 and reproached Maggi for having failed to announce the happy event in the proper way.

Sorrowfully, Viviane pictured him striding into her room in the maternity wing of the French hospital at 'Abassiya on the day of my birth, followed by the chauffeur bearing a huge basket of roses. "*Mabrouk, mille mabrouks* . . . " Initially furious when they called me Charles, Selim had calmed down a little when Professor Martin-Bérard congratulated him on his choice.

The tombstone bore four names. At the head came that of my great grandmother Linda (1847–1894), the first Batrakani of our line to be buried in Egypt; then Élias (1841–1920), who had erected the vast Sienna marble slab surmounted by a dove; then those of Charles (1909), who had died at birth and bequeathed me his name, and Nando (1870–1934), butchered like a sheep.

Édouard Dhellemmes, holding Mima's hand, was staring fixedly at the coffin, on which a tarboosh had been placed. He seemed to hear Georges Bey's voice: "What do you expect, my dear Édouard? This is a country whose inhabitants have always gone around with their feet bare and their heads covered. They adhere to the principle that you catch cold through your head. That entitles them to think with their feet, no?" A whole Egypt was vanishing in company with my grandfather, a gentle, tragic caricature of a country.

Édouard had returned there with Mima when the frontiers were reopened to French citizens. They'd found an apartment at their old address in Zamalek, and the porter was waiting at the door with tears in his eyes. Thanks to my father, Édouard had just reopened his antique shop in Opera Square, though on a smaller scale.

"My dear Édouard, there are two words you simply must know: one is *ma'alish*, which means 'it doesn't matter'; the other is *bukara*, meaning 'tomorrow' . . . " But who, confronted by that coffin striped with sunlight, could say *ma'alish*, and who could think of *bukara*?

Selim concealed his distress by looking at the bougainvilleas. Orphaned at the age of four, he had now been orphaned a second time. "What do you think of these *millefeuilles*?" Georges Bey had asked him during their first interview at Groppi's in 1944. And Viviane on the phone that night: "Papa thought you were charming."

The funeral cortège had attracted a shower of stones while passing through the old quarter of Cairo. The same thing had occurred on the way to a cousin's funeral the previous winter. This time a stone had damaged the side of my father's gleaming Oldsmobile. Should he have the wing replaced or take the opportunity to exchange the Oldsmobile for one of the new Buicks that had just been delivered to the General Motors agent? Selim thought his father-in-law would have opted for the second course of action. He would buy one in red, a permissible colour since the revolution. "Good news, *mes enfants*: having taken all we possess, your General Naguib has just restored an essential freedom . . . "

Maggi Touta, with her eyes half closed, almost smiled as she recalled the strains of *Valentine* and seemed to feel, hot on her cheeks, the breath of the man with whom she had been obsessed for half a century. For the first time, Maggi looked like an old lady, but a very dignified old lady who had sworn not to shed a single tear at the cemetery. In front of all these people it was Yolande's place, and hers alone, to weep for

Georges Batrakani. That morning the two sisters had fallen into each other's arms without a word. There was nothing to be said.

My grandmother wept twice as bitterly when the tarboosh was removed to enable the coffin to be slid into the vault. Her sons shepherded her gently towards the exit. Then Lola and Viviane took over from them, plying their mother with sensible, futile words of consolation.

The bougainvilleas were stirring in a faint breeze. The cemetery attendant made a show of declining the tips the mourners slipped him as they filed out. I stood beside him, watching this little charade. Life was resuming its course. For me it was only just beginning.

4

At school during those years I dreaded passing Father André in the corridors. I had no idea what manner to adopt. This problem didn't arise at home, where my uncle himself took the initiative and kissed us in turn, his pepper-and-salt beard pricking our cheeks. But in the school corridors? At the first squeak of his crêpe soles I would retreat into my shell and shun the other boys' gaze. As for Father André, he didn't seem at all embarrassed. He would raise his hand in a friendly gesture, smile faintly, and continue on his way.

But that Wednesday, for the first time, André Batrakani didn't smile. None of the teachers did, for that matter. The Collège de la Sainte-Famille, having been summarily taken over on 26 January 1959, had just reopened its doors under the direction of an Egyptian headmaster appointed by the government. That worthy had installed himself in the Father Principal's study, and the Jesuits had been far from reassured by his claim to be a lover of French culture who had studied at "*la Sorrbon*".

The school had been charged with dispensing "an education incompatible with Arab national sentiment". Symptomatic of that offence were several textbooks, published in Paris, which "glorified Israel and propagated the love of France". The informer must have accused the priests of being Israeli spies, because some plain-clothes policemen had raided the cellars in search of radio transmitters. Needless to say, they found nothing.

The Jesuits proceeded to make an inventory after the premises were sealed, going so far as to count the teaspoons. The Father Rector, a Frenchman, was served with a deportation order. The papal nuncio finally managed to get this order revoked and lift the sequestration order as well, but the wound took time to heal.

President Nasser turned up at the school in a black Cadillac preceded by six police outriders. Awaiting him on the steps were the French ambassador and the Father Rector, together with most of the teaching staff.

When the *Rayis* entered our classroom, accompanied by a bevy of dignitaries, we all jumped to our feet. Standing almost at attention, we hardly dared look at this impressive man whose familiar face did not, on that particular morning, wear its famous smile.

Father Korner left his rostrum to welcome the president and inform him that the subject of the French lesson in progress was La Fontaine. In a low voice, an unknown man in a dark suit translated the Jesuit's remarks for the president's benefit. Father Korner bowed slightly, then turned to address the class.

"Michel Batrakani," he said crisply, "can you . . . " He broke off, then continued in the same tone of voice. "Charles Yared, can you recite '*Le Laboureur et ses enfants*' for His Excellency the President of the Republic?"

I got ready to say my piece, but Nasser turned to the interpreter.

"I want to hear a poem in Arabic," he said curtly.

Standing there with my arms hanging limp at my sides, I cast panic-stricken glances at Father Korner, the president, the ambassador. Finally, I confessed in a timid voice that I didn't know any poem in Arabic.

Nasser gave me a withering look, then turned on his heel and strode from the classroom, followed by the dismayed Jesuits.

I woke up trembling, my face streaming with sweat.

"What an odd dream," Michel said, smiling, when I told him about it.

I was all the more dismayed because I did, in fact, know two or three Arabic poems, having learnt them during the school year.

"You don't really know them," said my godfather. "You can recite them, but that's different. It could be worse, though. When your aunt Lola was thirteen or fourteen, I remember, the only way she could memorize a couple of lines in Arabic was to get them translated into French."

Michel himself would have been quite incapable of reciting an entire poem in Arabic, I'm sure. On the other hand, I often heard him declaim whole verses by Egyptian poets who wrote in French — Muhammad Khayri, for instance, whom he'd met in the old days at Amy Kheir's or Ketty Limongelli's literary salons:

> Ton cœur tremblant, ô narguilé
> Quand je bois l'encens de ton âme
> Me semble un cœur, un cœur de femme
> Qu'un souffle épars aurait troublé.

Or again:

> Dans l'intense lumière, une ample vision
> De palmiers, de bocages, en sites pittoresques,
> S'érige au ciel où planent, immense sillon,
> Des oiseaux gigantesques.

Michel knew Arabic well enough to be able to read *Al-Ahram* every morning and deal with officials and shopkeepers, but not as well as my father, who had spoken it at home throughout his childhood, or André, who had immersed himself in the subtleties of the *hamza, madda* and *tanwiin* in the course of his endless Jesuit studies.

"The Syrians of Egypt are unforgivable," André used to say. "It's criminal, the way so many of them have neglected Arabic. I'm ashamed to hear my sisters jabbering away to the servants when I recall how the Syrians spearheaded Egypt's cultural renaissance at the end of the last century. Khalil Mutran was hailed as the undisputed master of contemporary Arabic poetry. The Takla brothers founded *Al-Ahram*. Georges Abyad created the local theatre. Even today, what would popular theatre be without a Syrian like Naguib ar-Rihani, and would there be any Egyptian cinema without Yousef Chahine?"

For some time, in response to requests from Syrian parents who realized that the language would be indispensable to their children from now on, the school had been placing greater emphasis on the teaching of Arabic. The Copts and Muslims, whose children already had a perfect command of it, had no such worries. They campaigned for more English lessons, whereas the Jesuits defended French.

"We don't defend it purely for its own sake," Father André explained. "We defend it because it's an aid to intellectual development and an introduction to other languages. I remember the head of the Arabic department going to the head of the French department and complaining, in jest, 'Really, Father, what are your French teachers up to? Our pupils don't know Arabic any more!'"

5

The Swissess left for St Moritz in March 1959. Paul, having acquired a tourist visa at vast expense, took the boys and joined her there the following month. He went with only two suitcases and the few Egyptian pounds allowed him by law. However, Boulos had amassed a certain amount of capital in Switzerland over the years. He had also been able to dispatch to Geneva an entire wardrobe and a number of valuable pieces of furniture by virtue of an export licence purchased from a forwarding agent who, for his part, had bought it from an Italian resident leaving Egypt.

Although Paul Batrakani's departure surprised no one, that of Jean Yared, my father's brother, caused a sensation.

"Where's he going?"

"Canada, *chérie*."

"Canada? He's crazy! He'll catch cold."

Jean had managed to obtain an immigration visa on the strength of his engineering degree, the Canadians being happy to accept men with qualifications.

Selim pronounced his brother an idiot.

"What are you going to do with yourself in a frozen country on the edge of nowhere? You won't stick it longer than a couple of months. I hope you've bought a return ticket, at least, it saves money."

My father, who felt like a king in Egypt, couldn't understand all these departures. He was a member of the Heliopolis Rotary Club and played bridge three times a week at the Sporting Club. Many familiar faces had disappeared, it was true. Foreign products were hard to find in the shops and certain foodstuffs were rationed, but life was still very sweet for those with money, and Selim had never had so much. Business was booming despite all the bureaucratic chicanery of which bribes alone could dispose.

The union of Egypt and Syria did at least have the merit of permitting free access to "the Northern Province". Alex Batrakani and his family left for Damascus. From there he had no difficulty in getting to Beirut, where he settled for good.

"It's the brain drain," was Selim's jocular comment.

Alex now swore by Lebanon, "the land of our fathers", whose atmosphere of freedom and jingling cash registers he found irresistible. Within six months he was speaking Arabic like a local and larding his sentences with *Shou?* and *Wa law?*, determined that he, at least, would not be recognizable by his accent at a hundred paces like so many other Egyptians.

Father André was in touch with numerous Cairo families through the medium of the school and various youth clubs. He disapproved of this wave of departures and didn't hesitate to say so, referring to it as abdication or even desertion. His presence at Sunday lunches created a great deal of tension.

"But André," Lola said to him, "Christians are finding it more and more difficult to work here, can't you see that? Even the Copts have had enough. In my husband's family — "

"We're spied on," one of Henri Touta's sons broke in. "We've been robbed of our freedom of speech. What's more, we don't dare display our wealth."

"Silence and self-effacement," Michel commented with a smile. "They're depriving the Syrians of their two greatest pleasures."

But André wasn't in a jocular mood. "Christianity is never in danger when Christians are deprived of privileges," he said. "On the contrary: the more deprivation, the stronger the Church."

"But André — "

"Christians in other countries are suffering far more than us. Why not accept our share of the world's tribulations? A century of easy living has made us soft. Our ancestors experienced far worse. When I think

[359]

of our grandmother Linda in 1860, fleeing for her life through the blood-spattered alleyways of Damascus . . . Today life seems unbearable as soon as the going gets a little harder. We give up and try to get out instead of persevering."

"It isn't easy, though, you've got to admit."

"Life has its seasons. We've had a long summer. Now it's winter. So what? Spring will come in the end."

Selim nodded. He approved of the Jesuit's attitude, even though he was far from subscribing to all that stuff about the Church, deprivation, seasons, and the rest. He sorely missed his late father-in-law.

6

Chained up in their kennel, the two Alsatians were barking furiously. Viviane went over to her bedroom window and parted the silk curtains. All she could see was a black Ramses parked outside with a driver at the wheel.

"It's an officer asking for the *khawaga*," whispered the *sufragi*. Clearly overawed by the visitor's uniform, he had asked him to wait in the hall.

The officer was wearing dark glasses. My mother took a few seconds to recognize him even when he removed them.

It was Hassan, but how he had changed! What a difference from the nervous *yusbashi*, humiliated by the Palestine War, who had presented himself in the drawing room at Garden City a dozen years before! His face had filled out and his chest was covered with medal ribbons. Rashid's nephew wore the self-assured and complacent smile of a grandee of the new regime.

"What a charming house," he said smoothly. "Not long built, I take it?"

"To what do we owe the pleasure — "

"I've come to see the *khawaga* about a matter concerning his business."

"My husband isn't here. He's at his office at this hour."

That was when she perceived the flaw in his last statement. What person wishing to see the head of a business would call at his home at ten-thirty on a Wednesday morning?

"What a pity," said Lieutenant-Colonel Hassan Sabri. "And I've come all the way from 'Abassiya . . . "

My mother had no choice but to invite him to sit down and ask the *sufragi* to bring some refreshments, firmly resolved not to miss her eleven o'clock tennis at the Heliopolis Sporting Club.

Made ill at ease by the dark glasses behind which Hassan had once more entrenched himself – these people had no idea how to behave – and by her lack of fluency in Arabic, Viviane embarked on a laborious exchange of banalities.

"My father died two years ago."

"May God be merciful to him."

"He was in his seventy-eighth year . . . "

She was rescued by the telephone bell.

How he had changed, and yet . . . She recalled the dark eyes and defiant expression of the boy in the blue *galabiya*, come to see his uncle Rashid at the house in Shubra. She heard again the voice of Abu Simsim with his magic box:

> *Ya salaam, ya salaam*
> *shouf al-forga di keman.*

She also recalled the youth of 1936, with his hawklike, well-chiselled features. He had rung the bell, she had opened the door. He was wearing a white shirt with a frayed collar. She had dreamt of him all that summer . . .

"What a really charming house," Hassan repeated when she returned to the drawing room.

She thought she detected a hint of sarcasm in his voice. To change the subject, she asked what he was doing these days.

Hassan pointed to his badges of rank. He was a *bikbashi*, he said, and currently engaged on "special assignments".

The latter statement threw my mother into a turmoil. She thought of Selim's recent problems with the tax authorities. Only last month he had been summoned to the ministry of the interior and questioned, in a rather unpleasant way, on suspicion of having sent money abroad illegally.

"Very well," said Hassan, "I won't detain you any longer." He took a visiting card from a lizard-skin wallet and held it out. "Ask the *khawaga* to call me at that number."

And he shook her hand in a way that left her feeling uneasy for the rest of the day.

7

The summer of 1960 was a television summer. To mark the eighth anniversary of the revolution, huge screens had been erected in public places. My father had naturally hastened to acquire one of the first television sets on sale in Cairo. He had bought the biggest, the most expensive, and the most lavishly equipped with buttons – not that these were much use, if the truth be told, because most of what one picked up consisted of atmospherics interspersed with speeches by Nasser. The *sufragi* and the maidservant were fascinated by the "picture-box" and transfixed by the gaze of the president, who seemed to be addressing each of them personally. Mumbling prayers, they crouched in front of the set for hours on end.

A meagre little French-language programme was broadcast for one or two hours a day, the signature tune being *Moustafa*, a song of which rival versions had been recorded by Bob Azzam and Orlando, Dalida's brother. Half French, half Arabic, the lyrics were tirelessly sung in an Egyptian accent by all the pupils of the Brothers, the Jesuits, the Sacré-Cœur, and the Mère de Dieu.

Friday had been a compulsory holiday since the beginning of the year, in private schools as elsewhere. We paraded in the playground every morning, saluted the flag, and – to the Jesuits' consternation – chanted *"Allahu-Akbar!"* The older ones among us, clad in grey-blue uniforms and white gaiters, received military training twice a week under the supervision of an army officer. We loaded and fired some oily, antiquated Italian rifles and learnt to throw dummy grenades at the far end of the playground, near the urinals.

Father André, leaning on his third-floor windowsill and sucking his pipe, used to watch us with a pensive expression. Some weeks earlier, Edmond Touta had nearly wrenched the buttons off his cassock in a kind of final convulsion. Grabbing his nephew by the sleeve, he'd sat up on his deathbed and addressed him in a choking voice:

"The population of Egypt has passed the twenty-three-million mark. Alarming, isn't it?"

The floppy mauve bow tie was draped over the arm of a chair. Poor Uncle Edmond! Eccentric and prone to exaggeration, yes, but not so crazy after all. His anxiety was beginning to be shared by the Egyptian authorities. As for our families, the steady diminution of their own ranks made them all the more conscious of population pressure.

We shunned the overcrowded beaches. Summer holidays at Alexandria were out of the question now. Yolande Batrakani had sold the villa at Sidi Bishr, and Sesostris Bey's "houseboat", which had fallen into decay since his death, was surrounded by buildings under construction. Even 'Agami was ceasing to be a paradise for the happy few. Those in search of peace had to go much further: to Marsa Matrouh, for example, where Selim and Viviane had taken rooms at the Lido Hotel.

In that idyllic spot we felt among our own kind once more. The Jesuits ran a holiday camp there, and the Wadi al-Nil troop of Catholic Boy Scouts, to which I belonged, used to bivouac in a neighbouring palm grove where we daily hoisted the flag with far more gusto than at school.

Enclosed by this bay, where Rommel had called a halt during the war, the turquoise sea was smooth as silk. Our sisters and girl cousins were enraptured by some athletic young Scandinavians belonging to the United Nations' "Blue Berets", who had been stationed in Egypt since the "threefold and cowardly". The pair of them had traversed five hundred kilometres of desert on a motor scooter for this chance to immerse their alabaster bodies in the lukewarm water.

At breakfast every morning, lounging like a pasha on the terrace of the Lido, Selim would noisily lament the absence of his brother Jean.

"To think that idiot has gone and shut himself up in a refrigerator at the back of beyond! He can have Canada, believe me. He's welcome to it!"

8

One Monday morning Viviane took her courage in both hands and drove to the Jesuit school. She was feeling nervous and apprehensive. Even though she had the words off pat, she repeated them to herself for the tenth time.

My mother was dreading the moment when she broke the news to André. Her eldest brother had always intimidated her. He not only belonged to another world; he was of another generation – "the Sultan Hussein generation", as Alex derisively put it.

She was shown into the parlour to wait. Father André turned up ten minutes later, the skirts of his cassock rustling. He pricked her cheeks – his beard smelt as usual of tobacco – and led her into a small adjoining office.

"André, I've come to tell you — "

He absolved her from saying the rest.

"So you're leaving?" he said in a weary voice. "You too?"

"Selim is convinced that Lebanon . . . " She paused, then went on. "You know how it is, André . . . "

"I know."

My mother was expecting an indictment. All she got was some advice.

"You see, Viviane," André said in a low voice, "the Syrians of Egypt were mistaken. They thought that social success exempted them from the need to integrate. Don't make the same mistake in Lebanon: become full-blown Lebanese."

He'd said much the same thing a month before, when René 'Abdel-Messih and his wife had come to tell him they were emigrating to Canada: "Become thoroughly Canadian, and do your best with the children.

Your roots are here but the tree will be growing over there, so take care: trees of that kind can develop in a strange way. They sometimes bear disconcerting fruit . . . "

Selim's decision to quit had been taken three months before. A second visit to the house by Hassan, once again in his absence, had convinced him that the man would never give up. He claimed to be investigating a bribery case, but that was just a smokescreen.

Besides, even though Selim had not been affected by them personally, he was very perturbed by the first nationalization measures. "There's no place in our Arab and socialist society for millionaires and feudal lords," Nasser declared. If Georges Batrakani hadn't been astute enough to share out his assets among his children and put aside a little money in Switzerland, where would they be today? The press — itself nationalized — published lists of "millionaires and feudal lords" such as Count Henri Touta, who had seen the police turn up at his home within minutes of the government measures' being announced.

Frightening stories were told of the treatment to which political prisoners were being subjected. One man sentenced to hard labour at the Tura penitentiary had had both legs broken but was forced to crawl to his place of work each morning; another had been tortured to death after suffering sexual abuse. It was reported of a doctor of our acquaintance, who had been arrested for communist sympathies, that the guards had inserted a hose in his rectum, filled his stomach with water, and then stamped on him.

My father deliberately ignored these stories until the autumn of 1960, when his perception of things changed. He took to buying *La Revue du Liban* every week and never tired of skimming the gossip columns for references to "President Chamoun" or "Sheikh Pierre". Lebanese Christians not only enjoyed total economic and political freedom but held the levers of power. There was no lack of work in Beirut, whence trade could be carried on with the Emirates. Even that jackass Alex had managed to open a garage in the suburbs of Beirut. His mother had gone to pay him a visit and not come back. To Selim, Lebanon seemed more and more like the promised land.

As for Viviane, she had been shaken by two departures in particular: Michel's for France and Salwah's for Germany, where her husband was on the staff of the Egyptian embassy in Bonn.

Michel had lost his bearings some time ago. For him, time had stopped in the good old days: the old boys' teas at the school, the Essayists' lectures and debates, the literary soirées at Amy Kheir's or Ketty Limongelli's. On learning in the autumn of 1961 that Suleiman Pasha's statue was to be removed from the square that bore his name, my godfather felt there was nothing more to keep him in Egypt.

Salwah had no intention of hurrying back. She shared her husband's loathing of the new military bourgeoisie that had taken over all the government posts. Having to consort too closely with these parvenus was more than she could stand; it reactivated her "old Turkish family" side. Even Nasser no longer found favour with this Muslim feminist. Her patriotism was still intact, but for the moment she preferred to practise it far from her native land.

My father knew that he would never obtain an exit visa without a green light from the dreaded Hassan. He became more and more desperate, fell prey to insomnia and stomach cramps. Viviane continually burst into tears, which achieved nothing. Late one night, unable to bear it any longer, she came to a decision.

"I'll go to see Hassan tomorrow," she said. "I shall ask him for a visa."

"You're mad! You want to finish us? He's plain perverse, that man!"

At ten the next morning, trembling with apprehension, my mother made her way into a barracks at 'Abassiya. She was eyed up and down before being shown into the *bikbashi*'s office.

Surprised by her unheralded arrival and anxious to show himself off to advantage, Hassan feigned hectic activity for a good fifteen minutes. He sent for subordinates, dressed them down, swore at his orderly, bellowed orders down the phone. At last he lit a cigarette and deigned to grant my mother a hearing.

"I've come to ask you a favour . . ."

Dismayed by the sound of her own voice, she felt she was prostituting herself.

"We'd like to visit our family in Lebanon this summer, and — "

"I don't issue visas," he snapped.

"I know, but I thought . . ."

She felt quite naked.

Slowly, Hassan rose to his feet and came round the desk towards her. Viviane jumped up in a panic. On the point of dashing to the door, she stopped herself just in time.

They were face to face, eye to eye. An almost imperceptible smile appeared on Hassan's face. At that moment Viviane broke the silence. Her voice rose almost to a shout.

"Your uncle Rashid was part of our family – he looked on me as his daughter!"

Hassan was too taken aback to speak. Viviane pressed home her advantage.

"About this visa," she said firmly, almost impatiently, "may I count on your help?"

She never knew why Rashid had materialized between them, and why *Bikbashi* Hassan Sabri had given in so easily.

9

The floor of the airport departures hall was littered with rubbish.

"Everything's topsy-turvy," said Édouard Dhellemmes, doing his best to sound bright and cheerful. "You're leaving Egypt, I'm staying."

Mima was at his side, pale as death. Coming so soon after Jean's departure, Selim's was a heavy blow. Her younger son was sneaking off like a thief in the night, relinquishing his business to a sales director who wouldn't wait two minutes before pocketing the ready cash or notifying the police. But it was her eldest son's plans that distressed my grandmother most of all. Roger was proposing to settle in the United States, even though he would have to duplicate his medical studies – at the age of forty-six! – before he could qualify to practise there.

The airport customs officers were not noted for their kind-heartedness. They systematically searched departing travellers and had no hesitation in emptying out their suitcases. Smugglers were liable to imprisonment. My parents, obsessed by the prospect of running this gauntlet, had spent a sleepless night.

Father André had come to bid us farewell accompanied by a driver from the school.

"There'll be hardly any Batrakanis left in Egypt," said Viviane, nervously fiddling with her dark glasses, "and most of the people we know have gone. You'll be all on your own."

"Yes," André replied with a smile, "all on my own with twenty-eight million people."

"Twenty-eight million!" said Édouard Dhellemmes, mopping his brow with a handkerchief. "Alarming, isn't it?"

André and Selim laughed loudly – a little too loudly. My mother dissolved into tears.

Epilogue

MICHEL'S DIARY

Châtel-Guyon, 6 May 1964

I find my visits here more and more agreeable. It pleases me to think that Sultan Hussein made a cure here every year before the First World War. I feel at home in Châtel-Guyon. We've all, in our own way, built ourselves new nests. What a strange road we've travelled, we who were known as Syrians in Egypt, are now called Egyptians in Lebanon, and call ourselves Lebanese in Europe.

Lola seems to have settled down in Beirut — if "settled down" is the right expression. I wonder how André took the announcement of her third marriage. "You'll end up like your Aunt Maggi," he used to tell her in the old days. But Maggi collected lovers, whereas Lola makes a habit of marrying her suitors.

Lunched with Paul and the Swissess in Geneva last Sunday. No molokhiya, of course. Boulos has written off Egypt for good — he won't even talk about it. If you ask him a question in Arabic he replies in French, with that local intonation I can't get used to. By contrast, the Swissess never tires of talking about Cairo, and the children never stop questioning me.

"When you come down to it, Uncle Sultan," said the younger boy, "no one forced us to leave Egypt."

I stared at him, rather taken aback, before answering. "You're right, habibi,*" I told him. "No one actually forced us to leave, whereas other people were expelled. The Egyptians simply acted in such a way that we expelled ourselves. And that's a lot more painful than a kick in the backside!"*

I'm not sure he really understood. Was I satisfied with my own reply? Pithy phrases are ill-suited to a history in half-tones like ours. We weren't expelled and we didn't expel ourselves. The truth lies somewhere in between. We've always been in between: between two languages, two cultures, two Churches, two stools . . .

"Keeping one buttock on each stool can be rather uncomfortable at times," Papa used to say, "but our backsides are made that way." And if, like me, you've been on the fringes of your own community . . .

Being middlemen, as it were, we ought to have acted as a link. If the truth be told, we haven't often played that role, preferring to remain above and apart from the hurly-burly.

We watched Sultan Hussein's funeral procession from the balcony. "You get the best view from here," Papa told me when I came upstairs and joined the party. The fact is, we've spent the majority of our existence on the balcony, watching other people go by . . . The balcony conferred height, but it also, and more especially, conferred distance. It exempted us from being jostled and soiling our hands. It was a certificate of residence, a sign that we had taken root: we were among our own kind, whereas the people down below, who hailed from elsewhere, were venturing across unknown territory. I think the balcony conferred the additional advantage of being wholly ambiguous: up there we could pass for admirers, indignant spectators, or straightforward voyeurs. Have we ever been more at ease than when wrapped in ambiguity?

No, habibi, no one compelled us to leave Egypt, but the air was becoming unbreathable. Egypt wasn't the same any more. We left of our own accord, on tiptoe, sans tarboosh or trumpet.

Who, in the old days, could have foreseen such an outcome? Nothing could happen to us. We were invulnerable because the sultan was fond of La Fontaine . . .

"We're nothing," Count Henri used to say between two Latin tags. It wasn't entirely clear whether this statement worried or relieved him. Papa summed up the situation in a more subtle way: "We aren't Syrians and we aren't Egyptians: we're Greek Catholics."

André thinks the Syrians never made an effort to integrate themselves in Egypt. That's only half true. Integration entails authorization, and we were never really regarded as Egyptians, just Egyptianized.

But André himself is a special case. He has always been uncompromising. Papa was very perplexed by him. Although he admired him, he never entirely succeeded in acknowledging him as flesh of his flesh.

I suspect that my godson is going to give Selim a similar surprise, albeit more profane. In Lebanon, so I'm told, Selim has become grander than ever. His *business is thriving, and they say he's on the point of landing the agency for a major German marque. Everyone is struck by his resemblance to Papa. In Beirut's Egyptian circles he's known simply as "Selim Bey". But he despairs of his first-born: Charles wants to read for a degree in philosophy and dreams of nothing but France. Next thing you know, I'll be accused of having put him off a career in business . . .*

On the day of Papa's funeral Charles remained standing beside the attendant at the cemetery gate. No tears. He just looked at each of us in turn. I didn't say anything. I put my hand on his shoulder and we walked back to the cars together.

"What's that dove doing on top of the family tombstone?" he asked as we went. I'd never asked myself that question, and I still don't know what possessed my grandfather to order that Sienna marble tombstone — a far bigger one than those of the families around. Old Élias overdid it: he must have been allowing for several generations of Batrakanis, oblivious of our nomadic tendencies.

"Perhaps it isn't a dove, habibi. *Perhaps it's just a bird of passage . . . "*

THE END

Please visit the Harvill Press website at

www.harvill.com